# Every Woman

... *Every Woman* ...
*The Potter's House*. She lives in north London, and when not writing fiction spends her time travelling and mountaineering. Her most recent novel is *If My Father Loved Me*.

## Acclaim for Rosie Thomas

'... territory at which Rosie Thomas excels and to which she brings compassion and emotional intelligence'
*Sunday Times*

'Another absorbing story from Rosie Thomas, confronting all the complexities of love, passion, pain and the rebuilding of fractured lives'
*Daily Mirror*

'Rosie Thomas writes with beautiful effortless prose, and shows a rare compassion and a real understanding of the nature of love'
*The Times*

'Thomas's novels are beautifully written. This one is a treat'
*Marie Claire*

'A story full of passion . . . will keep you reading long after bedtime'
*New Woman*

'Honest and absorbing, Rosie Thomas mixes the bitter and the hopeful with the knowledge that the human heart is far more complicated than any rule suggests'
*Mail on Sunday*

# Every Woman
# Knows a Secret

## Rosie Thomas

arrow books

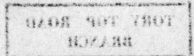

Published by Arrow Books in 2004

1 3 5 7 9 10 8 6 4 2

Copyright © Rosie Thomas 1996

First published in the United Kingdom in 1996 by William Heinemann
First published in paperback in 2002 by Arrow Books

Arrow Books
The Random House Group Limited
20 Vauxhall Bridge Road, London, SW1V 2SA

Random House Australia (Pty) Limited
20 Alfred Street, Milsons Point, Sydney,
New South Wales 2061, Australia

Random House New Zealand Limited
18 Poland Road, Glenfield,
Auckland 10, New Zealand

Random House (Pty) Limited
Endulini, 5a Jubilee Road, Parktown 2193, South Africa

The Random House Group Limited Reg. No. 954009

www.randomhouse.co.uk

A CIP catalogue record for this book
is available from the British Library

Papers used by Random House
are natural, recyclable products made from wood grown in
sustainable forests. The manufacturing processes conform to
the environmental regulations of the country of origin

ISBN 0 09 946484 5

Typeset by Palimpsest Book Production Limited,
Polmont, Stirlingshire
Printed and bound in Great Britain by
Bookmarque Ltd, Croydon, Surrey

For Lindsay

For their generous help and advice with aspects of this book I would like to thank Mr Peter Harvey and Dr Doreen Brown of the Royal Free Hospital, London, Inspector Paul Cox of the Metropolitan Police, Angelica Mitchell, Camilla Loewe and Nicholas Browne QC. Any errors or inconsistencies are the author's, not theirs. I am also grateful to Mark Lucas and Louise Moore for their unfailing support, and to my husband Caradoc King for his ideas and encouragement.

# One

Yesterday is gone for ever. And once each day is gone, it can only be seen through the one-way mirror of what has happened between then and now. In this way, every minute of every day that passes is a kind of bereavement.

Jess Arrowsmith was not thinking about any of this, not yet.

She was used to keeping her mind narrowly fixed on her work, and on this early winter's morning she was busy with plants and pots and compost. If her thinking strayed beyond them it was only to the comfortable prospect of hot coffee, and a fifteen-minute sit-down with the newspaper, the small rewards for one job properly completed before she had to begin the next.

It was a cold day but the big greenhouse was pleasantly warm; the ridges and valleys of glass overhead were faintly misted so the bone-whiteness of the sky above was softened. Jess worked steadily, without looking up, amongst scents that she loved but knew too well to distinguish separately: moist peat, washed gravel, the sharp tang of a crushed leaf. There was the steady drip of water, and the sound of another gardener tramping between the benches of a different aisle, hidden by a screen of leaves.

She took a new tray of plantlets from the waiting row and squared it in front of her. Tenderly she lifted a plantlet from the tray, holding one sturdy seed leaf and easing the stem and tiny root filaments free of the crumbs of earth. She tucked the little plant into a three-inch pot and firmed the fresh compost around the stem once more, then added a label. A new pelargonium, worth one pound twenty-five on the nursery by the end of May, although naturally not to Jess directly. She was only an employee. But she did not think of this either; the work was simply there, waiting to be done.

She moved steadily, smoothly lifting and settling plant after plant, until the seed trays were emptied. Then she straightened the rows of filled pots, checked the labels, and carried the trays to the trough at the end of the aisle. She scrubbed them out in freezing water and left them methodically stacked to dry.

At last she stood upright, easing her bent back with the heels of her hands. She wiped her palms on the backside of her dungarees and sighed in relief and satisfaction as she pushed a hank of hair out of her eyes.

The staff rest-room across the yard was empty. Jess left her boots outside the door and boiled water to make instant coffee, warming her icy fingers on the mug. She sat down in a sagging armchair and idly picked up a women's magazine that someone had left on the next chair. A beauty article was illustrated with photographs of hands, smooth and creamy and tipped with perfect scarlet and plum-red nails. On the glossy page Jess splayed her own hand, skin cracked and seamed with dirt, and laughed aloud.

'Someone's happy, then. Nice to hear, in this place.'

The woman who had come in was older than Jess, in her fifties. She was plump, dressed in a blue nylon overall.

Jess looked up at her. 'Am I? Is it? Joyce, you're late today.'

Joyce produced her own tea, sugar and powdered milk from her locker and locked it securely again.

'It's been bloody murder in the shop all morning. And that Tony's never there when you want him, for fetching and carrying. I can't lift no heavy stuff. I get enough of that at home.'

Joyce rattled with the kettle and her special cup and saucer, exuding weary displeasure. Jess had worked with her for three years. She knew why Joyce was tired and irritable.

'How's your mum?' she asked.

'About the same. No, not the same, she couldn't be, could she? Every day she gets a bit worse, loses a bit more of herself. Well, I lose a bit more of her really, because she doesn't know what's happening, does she? She can't feed herself any more. Has to have her mush spooned into her mouth.'

Jess listened, nodding, letting her talk because it was all she could offer. She couldn't relieve Joyce of the pity or the responsibility for her senile mother. When her fifteen-minute break was over she stood up and briefly put her arm round Joyce's shoulders, feeling the solid flesh insulated by woollens and the slither of nylon.

'I'd better get back to it.'

Joyce sniffed. 'You're a good girl. Really, you are. These things are sent to try us, aren't they?'

Outside, the cold air pinched Jess's face and fingers but she breathed it in, squaring herself to the weather as she pulled on her coat. She went to check stock plants on the open rows at the back of the nursery.

In Jess's home town of Ditchley, a dozen miles from the nursery, two boys arrived at a side-street gym. The road outside was busy with cars and delivery vans making their way around the pedestrianised main street, and the chain-stores in the precinct were busy with early lunch-time custom, but there was only a handful of people in the gym. The boys pushed their way into the locker room, confident to the point of arrogance, and changed into sweatpants with vests cut to bare their shoulders, and broad leather weight-lifters' belts. In the gym they stood in front of the mirrors waiting for a fresh loop of music to come pounding out of the overhead speakers, then began their workout. After a few minutes they were both slick with sweat and grinning with the high of their exertions.

The older one said, 'Right then, Dan. Alternate curls and kickbacks.'

Dan was nineteen, the younger by three years. He was dark

and good-looking, although thinner and less muscled than his friend. He rattled a pair of dumb-bells from the rack in front of the mirrors and weighed them in his hands. Then he began to work again, curling up and relaxing each arm in turn, fists clenched around the weights. The muscles of his upper arm tightened and the cords stood out in his neck. His lips pulled back in a painful grimace that bared his teeth and he began to grunt softly with the effort of hauling fist to shoulder.

His friend watched. 'Nine, ten, Danny boy. Eleven, twelve. Three more, go.' He was grinning again, circling him, taunting as well as encouraging. Danny finished the set with a gasp of triumph and let the weights drop.

'Shit, Rob.'

'Kickbacks now.' Rob would not let him rest between repetitions, and Danny did not want to seem to need a respite. He picked up another dumb-bell at once and bent from the waist. One-handed and with a stiff wrist he swung the weight up behind him and back like a piston. Down and up. His breath hissed as he counted the repetitions. At fifteen he changed hands and repeated the set. '*Yeah. Fuck,*' he groaned. He clanged the weight back on to the rack and dropped on to a bench, wiping his forehead with the inside of his wrist.

Rob picked a heavier pair of weights and squared himself to the mirror. His hair was long, shoulder length with a mass of coppery and bronze coils loosely tied with a piece of cord. He tossed it back with a jerk of his head as his arms curled taut, the triceps bulging. He made the weights look momentarily weightless.

Danny watched, openly admiring. At the changeover Rob smiled sidelong at him.

'See how it's done?'

'Yeah, right, Arnie.'

Rob mimed a punch and Danny parried it, snorting with laughter. They scuffled for a minute, with an edge of real threat between them only just submerged. The music pounded on

4

and one of the other men in the gym briefly glanced up from his exertions.

'C'mon. Bench press now,' Rob ordered.

Shoulder to shoulder Danny and Rob strode down the gym to where the big barbells were racked in sullen pyramids. Looking in the mirror behind Rob's back, Danny rotated each shoulder in turn, easing the protesting muscles.

When the boys emerged into the daylight after their workout, it was early in the afternoon. Young women were clicking back to work from their lunch-hour and the bins outside McDonald's were heaped with litter. Danny stood with his sports bag slung over one shoulder, challengingly watching a pair of girls go by. His black hair was wet, slicked flat from the shower. One of the pair glanced back at him over her shoulder, half smiling a sly invitation.

'Coming for a pint?' Rob asked. Danny nodded and turned his back on the girl.

Rob's hair took on a metallic glitter from the window lights of an electrical goods shop. His handsome face was sharpened by a thin nose and a long-lipped mouth curved like a woman's. He led the way through the bunches of shoppers, his shoulders broad in a scuffed leather jacket, his gym bag loosely held in one hand.

The pub was warm and steamy with the smell of beer and cigarette smoke. A television flickered over the bar and through an archway a man in overalls leaned on a snooker cue while his opponent lined up a shot. Rob flipped a coin on to the cushion and turned to the bar. With their full pints the boys sat at a table and stretched out their long legs, commandeering the space, pleased with the afterglow of exercise and the soft space of the afternoon ahead of them.

'You're doing well,' Rob said expansively. He folded his lower lip over the upper to erase the froth of beer. Danny checked his expression for mockery and decided that Rob was being straight.

'Yeah, thanks. I feel good.'

'You going to go on training?'

'Oh, yeah. I should think. You know?'

Sitting in the bleary comfort of the pub, with worked muscles and a thirst and an afternoon and an evening to enjoy, Dan had a precise awareness of the pleasures of life. He remembered the girl outside the gym. Nice legs. And then he forgot her again, because he never had any problems with getting girls. Rob's company was of a different order.

They had been at the same school, a tough, oversized comprehensive for boys, on the north side of the town, only a couple of miles from the pub where they were sitting. But the difference in their ages had meant that Rob had been too far ahead of Danny even to notice his existence. In those days, Rob had been a loner. He had been big and strong, but he had never bothered to involve himself with the football team or any other of the school sports that Danny hankered after. There was a self-containment and an aura of toughness about Rob Ellis that struck Danny as enviably cool.

And then, four months ago, after Danny had finished his A-levels and was idling away his time in a search for non-existent part-time work, he had seen Rob sitting in another pub. There was a toolbag at his feet and he was reading a paperback. Danny took the seat next to him, and when Rob failed to look up he asked him boldly if the book was good, since he seemed so absorbed in it. Rob glanced at him, without recognition, and flipped the book over so Danny could read the front cover. It was by Don DeLillo, a writer Danny had never heard of.

They had begun a desultory conversation and Rob agreed that he did remember Daniel Arrowsmith, just. After that they had met for a game of squash, then an evening's drinking. They had become friends, but even though the odd folding and eliding of adult time had made them more or less contemporaries, Danny had an uneasy sense that they were not equals. He needed to match Rob's achievements with his own. The murmured complaint of his shoulder and neck muscles was a reminder of it.

Dan took a long swallow of his beer. He was glad to be with Rob. The day was panning out fine.

The man in overalls passed in front of them.

'You're on.' He jerked his thumb at the table.

'Thanks, mate.'

Rob weighed a cue in his hand and massaged the tip of it with the chalk cube.

'Have a couple of quid on it?'

With a reflex motion Danny patted the back pocket of his jeans where his wallet sat.

'Sure.'

The pub emptied in the afternoon lull and there were no rival demands for the table. The racing flickered unwatched on the television while they played a competitive game, circling the table, standing with folded arms to watch one another's breaks, not talking much.

Danny won. 'Give you the best of three?' he offered, and bought another two pints.

Out of three games, Danny won two. Unable to stop himself smiling, he pocketed Rob's money.

'You've been getting some practice in,' Rob acknowledged. 'And I thought you students were supposed to go to lectures and study and worry about your loans and your CVs all the time.'

'It's not all beer and sex and snooker, mate.'

'Sounds like it is to me.'

This was not smooth ground. Rob had not achieved the necessary qualifications to go to university, even to the local polytechnic-turned-university where Danny was a student. He worked as a self-employed carpenter, building fitted kitchens if he was lucky and alcove shelves if he was not. It would not take much of a spark to fire an argument about the difference in their circumstances.

'You want another pint?' Danny asked, shrugging.

They had drunk three pints apiece and the afternoon had drifted away. Rob leaned against the wall with his arms stretched along the greasy dado rail. The bar was already filling again with little groups of day's-end people who put briefcases on the floor and draped mackintoshes over the chairs. The haven was being invaded and he was in any case bored with it.

'No. I could handle some food, though.'

Outside, the greenish remnants of daylight had been swallowed by the multicolours of shop windows and street lights. It was drizzling, and the black road was shining with wet and the red splinters of refracted tail-lights. The traffic had closed in and there was a thrum of idling engines at the traffic lights, and the compressed noise of lined-up in-car stereos. The boys hesitated, turning up the collars of their jackets and squinting in the rain. Most of the shops were closing but there was a café on the corner. Rob pointed and they ran to it.

At a table in a wood-partitioned booth they ordered a fry-up and chips. After a dozen mouthfuls Rob paused, his fork poised.

'What do you fancy doing tonight?' He looked sideways at Danny, across the narrow bridge of his nose. His eyes were elongated, greenish, expressing a challenge even when there was none.

Dan hesitated. 'I ought to go back.' He still lived at home. It was cheaper than digs and his grant didn't go far.

'Sure. Don't want to be late and get into trouble, do you?'

They both laughed at the idea. Again, Danny had an expansive sense of the pleasures of life, lent a hazy and seductive glow by the beer he had drunk. The door opened with a gust of cold and rain, and a gang of girls came in.

There were four of them. They wore little belted coats, shiny and crackling, that peeled off to reveal short skirts and fuzzy knitted tops. They crowded together into the booth opposite the boys, clattering and giggling and banging their handbags on the table. One of them had long thin legs in thick black tights, and buckled ankle boots with high heels. Her long dark hair was beaded with rain and as she flicked it back she stared boldly under her fringe at Danny.

Within a few minutes the boys were squeezing into the booth with them.

'D'you mind?' one of the girls pouted. 'This is a private celebration.'

'We don't object to a bit of privacy, Dan, do we?'

'Not at all. What are you celebrating? We'll help you out, if you want.'

The dark-haired one said, still looking at Dan, 'It's Zoe's birthday.'

Rob clicked his fingers. 'That's no problem. It so happens that birthdays are our real speciality, and Zoe's birthdays are what we do best of all. Waiter, bring flowers, ice, champagne.'

'You've got a bit of a cheek,' the plainest girl said, and one of the others laughed.

'Champagne? In this place? Two teas one teabag, more like.'

'We're going to a club later,' the dark one told Danny. The girls always gravitated towards him. He had an air of tender vulnerability, which Rob did not. Danny nodded seriously.

'What's your name?' he asked.

'Cat.'

'What sort of name's that?'

'Cat. For Catherine, you know.'

Jess was driving the twelve miles home from the nursery, along a route so familiar to her that all the features of it had been smoothed away. Ditchley was in the middle of England; it was neither southern nor northern, and whilst it was some distance from Birmingham or Sheffield or Nottingham, it was no longer just a country town. Jess had grown up there, and she had seen the surrounding countryside eaten up by new housing estates, and out-of-town shopping developments, and garden centres. The open fields had shrunk and had been hemmed in by roads, so it seemed now that she lived on an island triangle bounded by motorways. The town itself was prosaic and middling as it

9

had always been, but the last years had smeared it with tacky modernity. It now appeared brave but increasingly discomfited under its pedestrian centre and multi-storey car-park, like a middle-aged matron making an effort in an outfit too young for her.

Jess's face tipped into a sudden wry smile. It wasn't Ditchley that was middle-aged, but herself. *Am I so dull?* she wondered. *To have spent so much of my life in one place, and to have ended up disappointed in it, as well as in myself?*

Deliberately, to avoid the question, she turned her thoughts to Joyce. Joyce had gone home, as she did every night, to relieve her mother's day nurse and to look after the old woman until the nurse came back again in the morning, setting Joyce free once more for her work in the shop. Jess's sympathy for her colleague made her feel ashamed of her own trivial worries. She dismissed her anxiety about money, and the future, and the faint but persistent loneliness that lived inside her like a disease, and tried to be positive.

This was her good time of the day. For all its tedious familiarity the journey home was soothing. She liked the way the road unwound through a dark twist of fields towards the orange-rimmed straddle and loop of the motorway, and on to the choreographed knit and unravel of a pair of roundabouts and through tidy streets to the cul-de-sac where she lived.

Her house, when she reached it, was in darkness behind its unkempt hedge.

Jess let herself in, switching on the lights. She glanced at the brown envelopes thrown on the hallstand and passed on into the kitchen without picking them up. Automatically she brushed a scatter of crumbs off the table and dropped them in the sink, and put the butter dish back in the refrigerator. She opened the door of the freezer compartment and stared at the neat stack of ready-made meals, then slammed the door shut again so the rubber seal made its meaty reverse-kissing sound.

The living-room was tidy, and warm because the central heating had clicked on an hour before. The room was green with plants, weeping-leaved *Ficus* and palms and pink and purple-starred Saintpaulias. Jess moved from one pot to the next, touching the soil under the thick leaves with the tips of her fingers. The telephone rang.

'Darling, it's me. How's your day been?'

It was Jess's sister Lizzie. Jess smiled, looping the cord of the telephone away from the receiver and sitting down in the armchair, her feet tucked beneath her.

Lizzie was in her own home, twelve miles away. The sisters always tried to talk to each other every day, even when the differences in their lives kept them apart. Once it was Jess who had made the calls, mothering and reassuring her more exotic sister; now it was Lizzie's turn to ask the probing questions.

Lizzie slumped on her sofa, massaging her neck with her free hand and staring at the mess of toys on the carpet. There was a glob of baby food drying on her black jersey and she frowned, picking at it. She was the younger by four years. When Lizzie had been working as an actress, precariously balanced between waitressing jobs and the promise of making it big, Jess was already married and a mother. The home that Jess had made with Ian and their children had been a second home to Lizzie, whenever she had needed to crawl back to it after disappointment over a part or in love.

Now, their roles were reversed.

'My day was pretty ordinary. Not bad. It's rather nice in the greenhouses this time of year.'

Lizzie's frown darkened. Jess needed to get a hold on her life.

'All on your own, with soil and flowerpots and roots and muck?'

'Compost. And that's for outdoor work, you don't bring it in the greenhouse. I like peace and quiet.'

'Jess. I wish you'd get out of there.'

'I'm all right where I am.'

Lizzie tried to muster enough energy to renew her campaign for brightening Jess's life, but she felt too tired tonight. It had been a long day with a baby of twenty months. He was asleep now, pink and fragrant from his bath, and the delicious thought of him suddenly blotted out her concern for Jess.

As they talked, exchanging the small news of the day, Lizzie heard the sound of her husband's key in the lock. When James came in she looked up, beaming, and mimed a lingering kiss. She mouthed '*Jess*' in answer to his silent question, and James retreated. Lizzie knew that he was tiptoeing upstairs to lean over the cot and marvel at his baby son.

Lizzie was thinking, as she did a dozen times a day, that she couldn't quite believe in so much happiness. Now aged thirty-nine, within the last two and a half years, she had at last met the right man, married him, and had a baby. And just at the time when all this was happening, Jess's twenty-three-year-old marriage to Ian was acrimoniously ending.

'If you say so. I can't help thinking, you know.'

'Liz. I know what you want. You want me to be happy and with someone and doing and feeling the same things as you. But our lives have always been completely different, why should they start to be the same now?'

'I don't want you to be alone.'

This was the dark spot in Lizzie's brand-new, pin-bright happiness. If only Jess were not lonely. If only something would happen to her that would comfortably reflect Lizzie's own good fortune. A spring of maternal tenderness had been tapped in Liz by the birth of her child, and the overflow of it washed around Jess.

'Well, I'm not alone, am I? I'm lucky.'

Lizzie gathered her hair in one hand and artfully twisted it off her face, stretching her neck and posing as if for the camera.

'Darling, you can't live your life through him, it's not healthy for either of you.'

Jess said evenly, so that they both recognised it as a warning-off, 'I don't live through him, or anyone else. I've been a wife and a mother for twenty-three years. Now I want to be just what I am.'

There was a moment's awkward silence.

'I'm sorry,' Lizzie said.

Jess smiled into the mouthpiece. 'For what? For being yourself?' Briefly she became the comforter again; the balance between them tipped so easily. 'How's Sock? What's he doing?'

Christened Thomas Alexander, Lizzie's baby had been referred to in the womb as Socrates and was now invariably known as Sock.

Lizzie's voice lightened. 'Asleep at last, thank God. He's been tireless today, a chaos machine.'

Sock was a source of delight to everyone. For Jess the sight and smell and feel of him, the round head and peachy fuzz of skin, brought back piercingly sharp memories of her own babies. She turned her head to look at their photographs, framed on the shelf beside her chair. To see Sock was almost to have them back again.

'He's learnt so many new words.'

'What does he say?'

They could talk endlessly about his achievements. There were no complications in this.

'James is looking after him for the whole day tomorrow. I'm going to London to do the handcream voice-over. I'm swimming in free handouts of the stuff here, do you want some?'

'Handcream? Yes, can you take it intravenously?'

'Probably. I just hope they don't expect me to say so in thirty seconds. Darling, I've got to go.'

James reappeared, changed out of his business clothes into a sweater and corduroys. He made a little tilting movement with his fingers, asking if she wanted a drink. Lizzie mouthed, '*God, yes.*'

'Right. Hope the voice-over goes well. Call me soon.'

'Tomorrow night, or the day after. Promise you're all right?'

'Everything is fine here.'

'Good-night darling.'

James came to her as she put down the phone and slid his hands down to her hips, then kissed her thoroughly.

'Mmm. At last. How are you, my darling?'

She curled an arm around his neck. 'Feeling pretty fat and mumsy, actually.'

'You look wonderful. You feel wonderful.'

'Oh. Ah. Jim, what did my life consist of before there was you?'

Jess went slowly upstairs to the bathroom and tipped a heap of soiled clothes out of a basket. She stooped to sort them into differentiated piles and carried an armful down to the kitchen. She fed the bundle into the washing machine and slammed the round eye of the door, and while the clothes turned in the lace of suds she found a tin of soup in the cupboard and heated it up. She carried the bowl through into the living-room and watched the television news as she ate.

The club was packed. It was a popular DJ night and there were surges of dancers filling the floor. In the mass of people Rob could see Danny dancing with Cat. He was smiling broadly and bouncing on the spot, up and down fast from the knees, as if he was on springs. One hand held a bottle by the neck and the other waved in the air over his head. The four girls and Rob and Danny had all had a lot to drink, the celebration of Zoe's birthday moving on from the café to gather swift momentum in another pub and then the club. The beginning of the day seemed very long ago to Rob, at the far end of a multicoloured narrow tunnel. The music was loud, seeming to generate itself within his head. He followed the intricate cross-patterning of it in his mind, letting his eyes drift shut, then opening them again to see Cat standing in front of him. She was very pretty, he noticed for the first time. A little triangular face, just like a cat's, with a damp fringe of hair sticking to her forehead. Smoky eyes. He knew from dancing with her that she was thin and light-boned. Catty-like. He swayed towards her with music booming in his head. She was saying something to him.

'What?'

She repeated it, shouting with her mouth to his ear. Warm breath on his face. 'Where's *Rachel?*'

Rachel. Yes, the plain one of the foursome. She had been here a minute or perhaps an hour ago. He shrugged his shoulders against the waves of sound and Cat pushed away from him. Danny was at the bar now and Rob joined him. Another beer apiece, and when Danny tilted the bottle to his mouth a trail of silvery froth ran down his chin and glittered in the blue and purple lights. He wiped it away and moved his head to draw Rob closer. They stumbled together, Rob's arm round Dan's shoulders, a support for both of them.

'Not a bad night.' Dan was grinning, the angle of the lights making him seem cross-eyed.

'Yeah, pretty good.'

'Listen. I'm going back with her.'

'With who?'

'Cat.'

'Shit. I quite fancied her myself.'

Danny's grin widened. 'No chance, my son. I'm in there.'

'Who's driving, then?' Rob's old van was parked outside. After the pub they had all piled into it, the girls' legs and buttocks heaving and pressing in the passenger seat. Rob remembered laughing and gunning the clapped-out engine, and the traffic lights on sentry duty down a long stretch of wet road to the club warehouse.

'We'll get a cab or something,' Dan said vaguely, his smile beatific, irritating.

'Sod you then.' A prickle of antagonism renewed itself between them.

'What about what's-her-name, Zoe?'

'Thanks.'

Cat came back. She had pushed her hair off her face and her round forehead looked bare and vulnerable.

'Rachel's in the toilets. She's not very well.'

Danny took another pull on his beer.

'What's happening then?'

'We're going to take her home.'

'All of you? What is she, crippled?'

Cat hesitated. Her top lip crimped, making a new triangle in the inverted one of her face. 'Wait a minute, then.'

There was beer spilt on the bar, and a slick of it underfoot. The crowd standing three deep was now dotted with familiar faces, and the sweating barman in his soaked T-shirt was a regular at the gym. The gathering seemed suddenly tribal and this and the women's invisible crisis tipped the boys back into collusion. They turned their backs on the heaving dance floor and the barman saw them and sent two uncapped bottle slithering across. Dan clashed his against Rob's and they drank, leaning their heads back. The blue and purple lights recoloured Rob's sweat-darkened hair. Standing shoulder to shoulder while the surf of people and music crashed around them, they had almost forgotten Cat before she materialised again, with Zoe beside her.

'The other two have gone.'

Danny took hold of her wrist, his feral grin showing his teeth. 'C'mon then. We'll drive you girls home.'

The rain had thinned into drizzle once more. In the front of the van Cat sat across Danny's knees but her arm and shoulder and thigh were wedged against Rob. Zoe crouched in the space behind, her chin over Danny's shoulder. They were not singing or laughing any longer. Rob peered ahead, frowning through the hypnotising arcs of the wipers. The cab of the van vibrated with engine noise, but on a different frequency each of them plainly heard the ambiguous whisper of sex.

Jess washed up her soup pan and placed her bowl and spoon in the proper slots in the dishwasher. In the hallway she glanced at the security chain for the front door hanging loose from its bolts. She checked her watch and hesitated for a minute as a dark wing of anxiety shadowed her thoughts. Then she went slowly upstairs, leaving the door unsecured. Her bedroom and the inviting bed were as she had left them. She sat on the edge of the bed and wearily reached down to undo her shoes.

Cat's place was a rented room in a rambling mouldy-smelling house near the railway line. While Rob and Danny were waiting on the step for her to rummage for her keys they heard the muffled rumble of a goods train passing. Rob thought of heavy flasks of nuclear waste being transported from somewhere to somewhere in the midnight dark, and shivered as if a cold hand had been laid on him.

'There isn't much to drink. Some vodka I think, if you want that. Someone left it here.'

Cat produced a half-empty bottle from a partitioned sink cupboard.

'I'll have some,' Rob said. They had begun laughing again. The two boys stumbling in the cluttered room seemed incongruous, comically out of scale. Zoe peered at her pale reflection in her handbag mirror and stretched her mouth ready to coat it with lipstick. Her hand slipped with the cylinder and slashed scarlet across her teeth instead. Her helpless giggle turned into a hiccup.

Cat gave each of them a green glass with an inch of vodka in it. Danny took his and immediately put it aside, losing it. Cat slid a tape into a cassette player and music blurted out, much too loud. She laughed and prodded at the controls, then collapsed backwards on the bed beside her friend.

Danny mumbled, 'I'll roll a spliff.' He sat sideways at a tiny table and produced the pouch from his pocket, humming as he spread the papers.

Then they sat on the bed, one on either side of the girls, passing the clumsy roll-up between them. Cat's black legs sprawled impartially. Danny touched the curve of her thigh with the tips of his fingers and began to stroke, lightly, then more insistently.

He drew in a breath and held it. Then, abruptly, he lurched to his feet.

The room was spinning around him but he didn't care. There was a wash of light inside his head, golden light filled with stars that prickled within his brain in the way that not very long ago a certain type of sweets had been made to fizz on his tongue. It was impossible to contain this feeling of power, which was what the light was; he had to let it burst out. He could feel the wild breadth of his own smile. He was dry-mouthed and his gums squeaked against his teeth. He looked down at Cat to see her staring up at him, amazed. Zoe's eyes were closed, her head lolling on Rob's shoulder.

Danny flung out his arm. To his surprise, his fingers were still nipped on the roll-up. Tiny sparks smouldered for an instant in the air. He had been going to say something important but he had already forgotten it. No matter. He knelt down at Cat's feet instead. She leaned forward slowly until their foreheads were touching. Then she lightly kissed his mouth, but her fingers locked warningly in his black hair.

Danny breathed, 'I love you.'

Cat made a little bubble of a laugh. 'I know what that means; I've heard it all before.'

'No, no, it isn't that. I do. I really do.'

'Yeah, course you do.'

Her flippancy irritated him. He took her chin in his hand, twisting her head a little. The golden light in his head faded to dull, pounding redness.

'C'mon. Be nice.'

'You're hurting me.'

'You like it.'

'I don't. Stop.'

He pushed her backwards, reaching his hand up her skirt.

'Don't cocktease. Isn't this why we're here? Look, I love you. I mean it.'

'*I* mean it.' Cat was suddenly breathless. The changed note in her voice made Zoe's eyes snap open.

Rob was afraid of violence. The sight and most of all the

sounds of it set waves of panic and terror washing through him. The way that it could erupt out of nowhere as it did now, sudden and hideously defined from the muzzy bonhomie of drink, froze the breath in his lungs and stiffened his limbs into immobility. In the minutes that followed he wanted to shrink and hide, but he made himself act. He felt small and clumsy, but his reactions were quick, as he had learned to make them.

The cold air outside hit Rob in the face. He couldn't quite remember where he had left the van. Danny leaned dazedly against some railings next to the dustbins, rubbing his mouth.

Rob yelled at him. 'You fucking loser. Bloody come on, will you?'

Rob began to run and after a second Danny thumped in his wake. Far worse demons chased after Rob; images of violence gathered force behind him and loomed out of the blackness so that he ran faster, head bent and arms pumping like a little boy's, his breath coming in tearing gasps and the fear of a descending blow stiffening his shoulders in anticipation.

They reached the parked van by some stroke of good fortune and flung themselves into it. Rob started the clapped-out engine and reversed with a squeal of tyres, then accelerated hard away from Cat's street and the railway embankment. Rob tried to remember where he had been and where he should be going. The streets formed an intricate triangle, alternately dark and patched with lurid light. Danny sat slumped sideways in the passenger seat.

Rob muttered, 'Where the fuck are we?' The sideroads all looked the same. He jerked his head round furiously to Danny.

'I'm sorry,' Danny whined. 'I dunno what happened. I just lost it.'

Rob was afraid of the eruption of violence within himself, as well as in other people. As if he could smell his disgusted fear, Danny wheedled, 'You'll stick up for me? Our word against theirs, isn't it? If they catch us, that is.'

Rob only whispered on an exhaled breath, 'You little . . .'

But he didn't finish. Words that were too similar had been directed at him.

At last they reached the bypass, the open road that Rob had gunned the van down earlier on the way to the club. There was a bump and the tools in the back rattled a warning. He pulled the wheel and the van straightened again, then he blinked into the rear-view mirror and saw it. There was a flashing blue light behind them. He swore and Danny peered at him before looking behind.

'Shit. Drive,' Danny howled. 'Drive, will you?'

Instinctively Rob stamped his boot down hard. There was too much play in the accelerator. The van shuddered and whined and picked up speed. At half past one in the morning there was almost no traffic on the road. They hurtled forward, deafened by the racing engine, and for a minute or two it seemed that the police car was falling back.

'Yeah. *Go, man!*' Danny shouted, with sudden wild elation.

But the police siren was closing on them, audible even over the engine roar. The van juddered as if it would fall apart.

Rob stared ahead. There was a bridge. Concrete pillars daubed with graffiti.

Lights coming the other way. Fast, a dazzle in his eyes. The road vanishing.

Brakes, the brakes. A long squeal, shrieking in his head, echo of an echo. And then a smash. Explosion of glass and metal and pain.

Rob moved his head. There was cold air, and a bright light in his eyes. The light was his own headlamps shining on grass and concrete slewed at a terrible angle. He turned with cold precision and saw that the seat next to him was empty and the passenger door open. Had Danny undone his seat-belt? Or in their hurry to get away from Cat's had he never fastened it?

To undo his own caused him a breathtaking stab of pain. He swallowed it and pushed the driver's door open with his shoulder. He crawled out on to the grass and saw a car stopped behind him, someone running. Before anyone reached him he pulled himself around the back of the van because the front was all smashed in against the bridge.

Danny was lying on his side on the verge. Rob knelt down beside him. He saw that there was blood coming out of his ear and nose.

'Come on, mate.' He leaned over him. 'Get up now. Don't piss about. Just get up, will you?'

Hands grasped his arms and began to drag him backwards.

'He's my mate, he's all right,' Rob was shouting. 'What are you doing to him?'

A policeman knelt down in Rob's place beside Danny.

# Two

Cars slowed to a crawl as they approached the van smashed into the bridge and the police car with its revolving light and the starburst of broken glass glittering across the wet tarmac.

The headlights burned in Rob's eyes. As each car crept past he glimpsed white patches behind glass, staring faces. He wanted to shout at the people but he only blinked, and there was something sticky on his face. The policeman who was holding his arms made him sit down on the verge.

'You're hurt,' the man kept telling him. 'You've hurt yourself. Don't worry about your mate now.'

He couldn't see Danny. The other policeman was in the way, leaning over him and talking into his radio. Rob stared down the road at the cars and tried in the slippery daze of shock to connect up what had happened. It had been only a split second that had changed everything but he couldn't remember the instant itself; trying to focus on it was like staring at a brownish spot in a mirror where the silvering had worn away. The reflections around it were pin-sharp; here was the policeman and the shiny peak of his cap, and in his mind's eye Cat's room and the two girls and the green glass of vodka in his hand. But the spot in the middle from which his own eye should have gazed steadily back at him was a blank. He couldn't remember swerving or braking or hitting the bridge.

Rob put his hands up to his face. Blood was running from a cut on his forehead.

The other policeman stood up and Rob could see Danny

again. He was still curled on his side. As if he was asleep, only his white face was disfigured by the black trail coming out of his nose and another dribbling from his ear over his cheek and jaw. A sound rose in Rob's chest and burst out of him as a great roar.

'Danny, Dan. Open your eyes. Open them.'

Rob fought to get to his feet. A hand on his shoulder held him down.

'Can you hear me, Dan?'

'All right, lad. All right. We're waiting for the ambulance.'

As an answer, the wail of the sirens came first and then the blue lights, moving fast, up the road from the other direction. The first vehicle to pull up, at an angle across the road, was a white police Range Rover. Two more policemen in yellow-green fluorescent jackets leapt out of it. One stood in the road to slow the sparse traffic, the other ran to the van and Danny.

Yet more sirens and flashing lights were approaching. The police were waving the ambulance on. As soon as it crunched on to the hard shoulder the paramedics leapt out and ran to Danny.

A different policeman squatted on his haunches in front of Rob. Rob saw the tight rim of his shirt collar, even the prickle of stubble under his bottom lip.

'Are you hurt?'

'Not badly.' Feeling was beginning to return to his body. Pain everywhere in sullen pools and darting stabs.

'Were you the driver?'

Rob heard the stammer of two-way radios and the swish of tyres in the drizzle. He lifted his head.

'Yeah. I was driving.'

The policeman had a notebook.

'Tell us your name and address, son. And your friend's.'

There seemed to Rob to be a weightless and airless interval of infinite time that was without movement, even for all the rolling wheels and turning lights, and silent within the din of radio static and voices and hurrying feet. They were seeing to

Danny, crouching over him, shining a cruel light in his eyes.

Rob mumbled inaudibly through a mouth over which he had lost control, '*You be all right. You be. All right.*'

They were putting a tube down Danny's throat. There was a flurrying circle around him that Rob could not penetrate. Even the policeman who had been questioning him was looking at the ambulance crew.

One of the paramedics said, 'We need the air ambulance.'

When Rob heard it the realisation shot through him. *He might die.*

How fucking stupid. To be alive and having a drink and a smoke and the next minute to be lying by the roadside where you might be going to die. A huge anger swelled up in him. He wanted to roll up the realisation in his fist, crushing it into an atom that he could stuff through the blank mirror spot and obliterate.

'Have you been drinking?' the policeman was asking.

It was only now that the question dawned and the immediate certainty swam into his mind, an evil fish. *Did I do this to Danny?* And the answer. *Yes, I did it.*

'How much have you had to drink?' the policeman repeated.

The clarity of everything just before and after the moment of the smash was fading in Rob's mind. The empty blur at the centre of his field of vision bled outwards. The blue lights twinned and quadrupled and splintered into fragments and the looming faces split and swelled and he couldn't even properly distinguish the policeman's old-young eyes any longer in his young face.

Rob moved his lips. 'Not much. A couple. Just.' His voice croaked away, caught in his throat.

They were kneeling beside Danny. They were holding a bag up, tubes going into him.

They brought a small black box and a white tube to Rob and pressed the tube into his mouth.

He did what they told him. Blow.

People coming and going, voices over his head but he

24

couldn't hear any longer what they were saying. And the policeman again, asking questions, while one of the ambulance men looked at his head and tilted it on his neck and lifted his arms and shone a light in his streaming eyes.

'I don't know. He lives with his mother. I never went there, why would I? I don't know his address. *Please.*'

The lights shining in his eyes, showing up his tears. He hated crying, hated being seen to cry as much as he feared violence in himself and in others. They went together, the two things. Action and reaction, both fearsome.

The helicopter was coming.

After its lights appeared in the sky the noise grew suddenly loud, drowning out the police radios and the idling engines of cars, then became deafening. Rob crouched beneath the roaring, his head on his knees. The machine hovered over them and briefly stirred up a whirl of litter and wet leaves. Behind the verge was a field and a field gate. The paramedics lifted Danny on to a stretcher. A beam of hard light seeming as solid as a pillar shone from the helicopter and pinned them all to the earth. As if it was searching out him alone Rob stared straight up into the blinding nauseous eye of it. Then the helicopter sank to land in the field and the light abruptly snapped off and Danny, with the tubes and bags held over him, was spirited away to it.

Rob could see nothing now. They waited, separated by the hedge from Danny and the paramedics.

The noise swelled once more and the helicopter lifted, rocking over them as it rose, before it tilted and swung away over the wreck of the van and the stilled road. The busy rap of the engine changed in pitch, receded and was finally gone.

Rob leaned forward and retched into the grass between his feet.

'Come on, son,' one of the ambulancemen said. 'Your friend'll be in hospital in a minute or two. We'll get you in there as well.'

One of the policemen, bulky and creaking in his fluorescent coat, followed him into the back of the ambulance. Rob was under arrest. The doors slammed shut on them and the ambulance bumped away.

Alarm clock. Half six already.

Jess reached out from under the covers and felt for the button, but even when she found it and pressed it hard the ringing wouldn't stop. And as soon as she opened her eyes on the darkness Jess registered that it was the doorbell ringing, not her morning alarm. The time was almost three a.m. She groped for her dressing-gown, the old winter tartan one, and pushed her feet into her slippers. She lifted aside the window curtains and looked down into the road. There was a police car parked in front of the house. Its revolving light sent silent blue arcs sweeping over the street.

She ran down the stairs, a mumble of fear in her head. The door was still unchained, so he was not home yet. But that was not so unusual. Quite often he stayed out all night. He was an adult now; how could she stop him, even if it had seemed appropriate to try? Jess thought of these things as she unlocked the door, for a last instant keeping the smooth sequence of reason between her and the police and whatever they had brought to her house.

'Mrs Arrowsmith?'

'Yes.'

A woman police officer, round-faced and young, probably no older than Beth. If something had happened to Beth . . . Involuntarily Jess's hand came up to her mouth. The palm of it, pressed against her nostrils, still smelt cleanly of bed, warmth and safety.

The policewoman tilted her head to indicate the hallway.

'May I come in?' Holding up something, her warrant card, for Jess to see.

'Of course, come in. What's happened?'

They faced each other under the bright hall light.

'Is Daniel Arrowsmith your son?'

Jess almost laughed before the terror hit her. It couldn't be Dan because Dan was invulnerable. His happiness and ease protected him from injury. It was his older sister Beth who drew concern like a magnet.

A snapshot. Beth's small, furrowed face above a smocked frock and the wide gummy beam of her baby brother as she anxiously held him in her arms. Aged three and six months respectively. Ian had taken the picture with a new camera Jess had given him for his birthday. If only Ian were here now. She was afraid to hear this news on her own.

All these images flickered through Jess's mind faster than film through a projector.

'Yes. What's happened?'

Some escapade, perhaps that was it. Some explanation she was being hauled out to deliver on his behalf, as she had been in the past by teachers and other authority figures.

'I'm afraid he has been involved in a road traffic accident.'

The film slowed and stopped, frozen.

'Where? Is he hurt?'

'Yes, he is. I'm sorry. The accident happened out on the bypass.'

'How badly hurt?'

'I'm afraid I don't know exactly. He suffered head injuries and was airlifted to the Midland Hospital. We can take you there immediately, Mrs Arrowsmith. They will be able to tell you everything at the hospital.'

No use in asking anything more even though the clamour of questions piled up within her. But he would be all right. Dan would always be all right, that was how he was.

'Yes. I see. Can I . . . Will you just wait while I put my clothes on?'

'Of course.'

Half-way up the stairs, her hand gripping the banister rail to steady herself, Jess turned round.

'Whose car was he driving?' Dan did not own a car.

27

'He was a passenger in a vehicle driven by another young man.'

'What man?'

'His name is Robert Ellis.'

The name meant almost nothing. Dan might have mentioned it; she couldn't remember.

'Is he hurt?'

'Only slightly.'

'Was he drunk?' Jess asked. Her mouth was dry.

'The driver had been drinking, yes.'

'I see. Thank you.' She resumed the long journey up the stairs, past Danny's closed bedroom door, to her own room and the empty bed and the clothes hanging in her cupboard. Her hands shook as she searched through them. Numbed, she couldn't remember what she wore, or how to dress herself. On the way downstairs again she went into Danny's room and took clean jeans and a sweatshirt and underclothes out of his drawers and stuffed them into a holdall. He would be needing clothes to come home in.


'Mrs Arrowsmith? Come this way.'

Jess followed a nurse down a corridor. The bright lights and hurrying people made a weird daytime out of the depths of the night.

The nurse pushed through a set of doors and then another door. Jess wanted to run, to reach him quicker. But the nurse showed her into a small office, stuffy and overheated.

'He's in CT scanning. They are looking to see what is causing a build-up of pressure inside his skull. I'll be able to take you to see him as soon as the scan is done.'

Jess sat on a plastic chair, waiting. Danny had still been asleep when she left for work this morning. Yesterday morning now. The night before she had been reading in bed when he came home and tapped on her door. He had been himself, as always. He sat on the end of her bed for a minute and chatted. She couldn't remember now what it was they had talked about.

Jess thought, why didn't I tell him what I feel about him? I will now, she determined.

The nurse came back. 'This way,' she said. She put her hand to Jess's arm, steering her gently as if it were Jess who was hurt.

The room was full of people, doctors and a nurse, and a battery of machinery and equipment that frightened her.

Daniel was lying on a trolley. His eyes were closed and there were tubes coming out of his mouth and his arms. Jess darted to him and put her hand over his. She stood looking down at his face.

'I'm here, Dan,' she told him.

Then she bent forward and put her mouth to his cheek. She felt the shudder of an inward breath and the faint gasp of its expulsion. There were not, after all, any words that she could use belatedly to convey all the subterfuges and understatements of her love for him. *I'm here* was all that she could offer.

Imploringly Jess looked to the nearest face.

'How bad is it?' she demanded.

'Mrs Arrowsmith, I'm Dr Healey. What has happened is that your son hit his head when he was thrown out of the vehicle. We were afraid as soon as he came in that he had suffered a severe injury because his left pupil was dilating, indicating a build-up of pressure inside his head. We've just scanned him, and there is a mass of blood from the contusion building up between the lining of the brain, the *dura mater*, and the brain itself – an acute subdural haematoma – and it is pressing inwards on the brain tissue.'

Jess stared at his face. Dr Healey looked tired and one of his eyelids was twitching. She licked her dry lips and asked, 'What can you do?'

'We are preparing him for theatre now. The neurosurgical team will drill burr-holes in the skull through which the accumulated blood can be drained off to relieve the pressure on his brain.'

'Will that work?'

'Yes, in the immediate term.'

29

She didn't want to be angry but still anger twitched within her.

'What does that *mean*? Will he be all right?'

'It's too early to tell, Mrs Arrowsmith. He has a very serious head injury. The important thing is to operate as quickly as possible and to monitor him very carefully afterwards.'

Jess's eyes travelled from the doctor's face to Dan's. Extraordinarily, as she now realised, for the first time since the policewoman had broken the news she considered the possibility that her child might die.

Her dry lips moved again. 'He's a very determined person,' she said.

The doctor nodded. 'I'm sure he is.'

They wanted to take Dan away. Jess indicated her hand, still covering his.

'Can I . . . can I come up there with him?'

'Yes, of course. You can wait just outside theatre and see him as soon as he comes out.'


In the Accident and Emergency Department Rob waited in a cubicle. The policeman questioned him sharply.

'What were your movements this evening?'

Wearily Rob described them. He was only thinking of what might be happening to Danny.

He agreed that he had been at Catherine Watson's house, if that was what her name was, and if the address the policeman quoted was the bedsit house beside the railway line.

'And what happened there?'

Rob shrugged and then winced with pain. He described what had happened as faithfully as he could.

The policeman frowned. 'That's not quite how they reported it.'

'I don't give a bugger. That was how it was, see?' Rob began to shout, pointing at the curtains of the cubicle. 'Listen, he's lying there somewhere. Does this matter now?'

Rob loudly demanded news of Danny from everyone who

came within range, but no one would tell him anything.

'Your friend's being looked after. He's in the best hands,' a nurse tried to soothe him.

The policeman persisted. 'Let's talk about you, Robert. You were involved tonight as well, weren't you? You've got some form, son.'

'A fight. Three years ago.' Rob's mouth closed tight on the words.

'Common assault. A heavy fine and a caution, wasn't it?'

'That's all. Nothing else.'

'Until tonight, Robert.'

The cut over Rob's eye was stitched and his arm X-rayed. They told him that his elbow was fractured and needed to be put in plaster. There was also the possibility of concussion, and they would keep him for observation overnight if he calmed down enough to be admitted.

The divisional surgeon arrived to take a blood sample. He drew off the blood from Rob's uninjured arm and squirted it into two phials, neatly sealing them in front of him.

'Which one do you want sent for analysis?'

Rob shrugged. 'Does it matter?'

The man said coldly, 'Not really. But it's your right to choose.'

Rob pointed a finger and scrawled his name left-handed on the form that was pushed in front of him. He had no proper interest in this now. The policeman stood in the cubicle opening, cap under his arm. Rob was to present himself with his solicitor at the police station, the next day or as soon as he was discharged from hospital.

'I understand,' Rob said, although he did not, not fully. He was drunk and shocked, and he couldn't begin to follow the links of cause and effect connecting himself to tomorrow and the future. The focus of his fears was Danny.

Later, after his arm had been set in plaster, they put him to bed on a ward. The other beds were occupied by two old men who snored on their backs and a middle-aged man as thin as a skeleton who plucked at his sheets and glassily stared at the new arrival. Rob did not have to wait long for his chance. The lone nurse hurried away to some other section of the ward, and immediately he got out of bed. He put on the dressing-gown belonging to one of the old men on top of the hospital pyjamas and escaped.

The paper slippers they had given him impeded his steps. The right-angle of fresh plaster encasing his arm dragged him off balance, so sometimes his shoulder bumped against the shiny walls of the corridor.

At last he came to some heavy double doors marked *Theatres*. A nurse hurried round a corner with a box of sterile-wrapped dressings in her arms.

'What are you doing here?'

'I'm looking for Daniel Arrowsmith.'

'He's in there now. Are you a relative?'

'I was in the accident with him. I'm his brother. They said I could come up.'

'Your mother's waiting. Just along there, I'll come back and show you.'

Danny's mother. Of course she would be here.

'Don't worry. Tell me where, I'll find it.'

When he was almost at the door of the waiting room Rob stopped and leaned his head against the wall. He could hear his heart thumping and the sandpapery rasp of breath in his throat.

Danny had talked about his mother. Not that often; he wouldn't have gone on about her, not to Rob anyway, knowing what he and very few other people did know about him. He had just said something like, 'She's okay, my mum. She loves me.' And then he had grinned broadly. 'Worships the ground I tread on, in fact.'

Rob couldn't crash into the operating theatre and demand to be told what was happening. Nor could he hide himself from Dan's mother, although now he was here that was his impulse. The important thing was to find out how Dan was, and his mother would know. She would be able to tell him.

Before he opened the door he tried to think back. Driving, with Danny yelling him on. Rain on the windscreen. Then the brownish blur of oblivion.

The lights along the ceiling above him grew fuzzy outlines and danced into rainbows. He pushed the heel of his good hand into his eyes, then with a sudden roll he shoved his shoulder against the waiting-room door. It banged open.

She was alone, sitting in the corner by the wall. A white face, black eyebrows, hair the same colour as Dan's. She had been sitting with her head bent and her hands clasped in her lap. But she looked up at him at once, imploringly.

Jess saw a young man with a lacerated face and a white dressing over one eye. There was black blood still matted in his reddish hair and his arm bent in plaster was held across his chest like a shield.

She knew at once who he was.

He looked crazed. Like an Old Testament prophet, slippered, half wrapped in his robe, come to denounce or defy. He seemed taller and broader and more threatening than a mere man. And in his madness he blazed with the electricity of life. She had never seen anyone who looked so alive as Robert Ellis looked in this room bleached colourless with fear. He looked at her and Jess stared back, not knowing whether to attack him or to turn and run away.

He saw her face change as recognition flooded into it.

'How is he?' he asked.

She looked full at him for a minute, then the shock of her response faded. She bent her head again. Her fingers locked together, her fists rested on her knees. She had no energy to bring to bear on anything but the news she was waiting for.

'They're operating now. To drain off the blood that's pressing on his brain.'

'Is he going to live?' he brutally asked her.

'It's too soon to tell.'

Rob sat down on the farthest chair. As they waited in silence

33

he watched the second hand of the wall clock sweeping out its monotonous circuits.

Jess was lonelier than she had ever been in her life. She thought she had grown used to being divorced, but she had never reckoned how it would feel to be alone in a place like this. She could have telephoned her sister and her daughter, but she knew she would have to explain and try to reassure them when she longed to share her love and terror with an equal. So she sat motionless, waiting.

At last the door opened once more.

'Mrs Arrowsmith?' It was the surgeon.

Jess stumbled to her feet, almost falling over Dan's holdall. 'How is he?'

The surgeon glanced at Rob. 'This is Daniel's brother?'

Very clearly Jess explained, 'This is the young man who was driving the car. He is not my son, or Dan's brother. I don't know why you should think he is.'

'I told a nurse I was. She wouldn't have let me up here otherwise.'

Jess didn't look at Rob. She only had the sense that he was standing up, towering behind her, and she could feel the disturbing emanations of hope and fear coming off him, dry and burning like the heat from an electric fire. To the doctor she said, 'Could we speak in private?'

'Of course.' He held the door open for her. In the next room, a nursing office, she forgot the boy immediately. She listened to the surgeon's explanatory words as if the power of her concentration alone could influence their bearing.

The mass of blood had been sucked from beneath Danny's skull and the pressure on his brain relieved. That far, the operation had been successful. Still deeply unconscious, he had been taken to the IT unit.

'When will he . . . when will he come round?'

'That we don't know. The next twenty-four hours will tell us a lot more.'

'I see. Thank you. Can I go to him now?'

'Come this way.'

She had the impression of a large but busy and cluttered space. It was brightly lit, with people moving purposefully within it. There were several beds, widely separated by banks of shelves and machinery and white folding screens. In one of the beds lay Daniel. He was on his back, his head white-bandaged, covered to his shoulders with a light blanket.

She came closer and saw that there was a tube in his mouth, and another in his nose held in place with strips of tape that slashed his cheek like tribal markings. From under the blanket, wires and more tubes ran in every direction to the machines they had hooked him to. On the wall behind his bed was a screen across which red and blue and green traces steadily flickered. And his eyes were blind, covered by thick white cotton pads.

Jess leaned forward and tried to reach him by touching a strand of his hair that had escaped from the bandage.

Down in the scanning room she had felt Daniel's presence as if he had walked into the house and renewed a conversation with her. Now the bewildering complexity of machinery had interposed itself between them. She stared past it at the familiar tiny oval scar on Daniel's jaw, a relic of baby chickenpox. He was here; this was him.

At once a rush of tenderness and love surged up and blurred his face and the surroundings. The machinery seemed threatening because she could not understand or control it, that was all, and she was a mother who was used to tending to and understanding her children. The crash had robbed him of his independence; Dan had temporarily become a child again.

'I'm here,' she said again as she bent over him. 'Danny. I love you.'

She lifted the blanket an inch and found his hand lying palm upwards, the fingers loosely curled as if in sleep. A plastic tube was taped to the arm and she was afraid to dislodge it but she touched her fingertips to his and was reassured by their warmth.

She sank down on to the chair that they had placed for her at the bedside.

Jess watched and counted the breaths that the ventilator took for him and the oscillations of his heartbeat on the monitor screen. A nurse in a green overall and plastic apron appeared on the opposite side of the bed and smiled at her.

'How are you?' the nurse asked.

'I'm all right.' The question and answer seemed absurd.

The nurse folded back the blanket. The tube ran into a neat fresh wound beneath Dan's collarbone. There were white plastic circles and more tubes fastened to his chest. As Jess watched, one of the doctors came and pinched Danny's earlobe and beneath her own hand his fingers twitched a little.

'Look,' Jess almost shouted. 'He felt it. Is he coming round? Is that why you pinched him?'

'We want to check his responses,' the doctor said quietly.

The right response had not been there, Jess understood. But he had moved his fingers. She had felt and seen it for herself. The doctor took the white pads off his eyes and shone a torch into each in turn.

'Why do you have to cover his eyes like that?' Jess asked.

'To keep them moist for him.' He replaced the pads once more.

The extent of Jess's helplessness was becoming apparent to her.

'Is he in pain?' she asked.

'I think he's comfortable.'

'Is there something I can do for him? Anything?'

'Just what you are doing,' the doctor answered gently. He left her and the nurse turned to write on the charts clipped on the wall next to the bed.

While she sat and held his hand, Jess remembered versions of Danny that were remote from this white-lit room with its busy staff and supine bodies. She thought of holidays and Christmases and family celebrations, and tried to distil enough joy and warmth out of them to channel through her own fingers into Danny's, and so connect him to a happier version of the world he had grown into.

*I'm here.* The words ran round and round in her head. *Wake up. Come back. Wake up.*

After what seemed like a long time Jess laid her head down on the bed next to Danny's thigh and closed her eyes. For a few minutes she gratefully slept, and then when she woke up again she struggled to identify the place and the fear that had filled her brief doze with queasy vanished dreams. Then, remembering, she jerked up her head. Danny had not moved.

Later the surgeon came back again. He pressed the heel of his hand hard down against Danny's breastbone. And Danny stretched out his arms in response, fists clenched, as if he were troubled in his sleep. When she saw it a wide smile spread over Jess's face, cracking her dry lips. She pushed her hand through her hair, letting a warm current of hope and relief course through her.

Danny was there, he was only sleeping. He was responding to the doctor. He wouldn't die. The certainty of it flooded through her veins like a drug hit, dispelling her exhaustion. She stood up, easing the pain and stiffness out of her limbs. Her feet and her fingertips tingled with returning blood.

'It's wonderful to see him do that.' She smiled at the surgeon. 'It's good, isn't it? That he can feel and respond?'

'It's a positive response to stimulus, yes. But it's very early to tell.'

'I know. I understand that. But still, you know . . .'

Like a good girl, Jess did not want to press her need for hope and reassurance upon the surgeon. If she could be calm, if she met with everyone's approval in this test of her stoicism, it would be all the better for Dan.

'Thank you for everything you are doing for him,' she said meekly.

It was six o'clock in the morning.

Sock would be awake soon, if he was not already. Jess thought that she would telephone Lizzie and Beth and break the news now, now that there was this compensating fragment of brightness to offer them.

She must also speak to her ex-husband.

Ian had finally left Jess two years before, for a younger woman he had met through his work as a salesman. Ian had always been good at selling; he had a cheerful, dependable manner that masked his uncertain temper. Throughout their married life he had often been away travelling his territories, and the regular absences had helped them to ignore the truth that they had never made each other happy. Then Ian had met an Australian girl in her late twenties who had chosen to finance one leg of her European journey by working as a temporary administrator in the electrical goods company in which he was a sales manager. It was not the first affair he had had, but it was the first time Ian had fallen in love. He had been a conscientious if rather impatient father, but by this time Beth and Danny were both grown up. He had told Jess that he was leaving her; her response had been bitterness, followed by relief, and at last a kind of weary indifference.

Ian was married to Michelle now and they were living in Sydney, her home town. Jess had never been to Australia but she imagined a paved garden with tree ferns and hibiscus and a view of the blue bay, and heard the telephone ringing in a room barred with sun and shadow.

Jess lifted her head. She remembered that she had left Danny's holdall in the waiting room near the operating theatre. Glancing back down the night's tunnel it seemed a black joke that she had imagined Danny needing jeans and a sweatshirt to come home in this morning. She remembered seeing a telephone cubicle in the corridor outside. She would make the calls from there.

In the waiting room was an Indian family, elders and adults and small children crowded and perched on the plastic chairs.

Their faces turned up to her like so many thirsty plants, then drooped again. Robert Ellis was sitting in one corner on the chair he had originally occupied. Dan's holdall was gripped in his hands.

Jess stepped backwards into the hallway and he followed her out.

'Tell me how he is,' Rob demanded.

He no longer looked larger than life. His face was hollow and grey and his eyes were ringed with murky shadows.

Jess thought, with anger piercing her, *Good*. It's right that he should suffer too. Why should it all fall to Danny, and why should this young man only have bandages on his face and arms after drunkenly smashing her child into a bridge?

Her mouth tightened. Then she remembered that Danny had stirred in his coma and stretched out his arms, and that she had been sure that all would be well. That certainty was already draining away, water dripping into the dry sand of anxiety.

She told Robert Ellis what she knew and he listened silently with his eyes fixed on her face. At the end he nodded.

'Thank you.'

'You should go back to your ward. Go to bed.'

'I'm going home. I don't want to stay here.'

'You're lucky,' Jess said in a hard voice.

'If I could make it me, I would. And I'll be coming back. If you won't let me see him I'll wait outside.'

Jess shrugged. There was no space to admit anger for more than a passing instant. She held out her hand for Danny's bag, and after a second he handed it over. She was already turning away when he caught her arm.

'He moved, did he?'

He was searching at second hand for the reassurance she had sought from the surgeon.

'Yes.'

He was so close that she could smell his sweat and skin, a remembered and denied scent that caught in her throat and stirred the hair on the back of her neck. She withdrew her arm from his grasp.

'Yes,' she repeated softly. 'His surgeon said it was a response, but it's too early to tell anything yet.'

She walked away, to the telephone, and left him.

# Three

Lizzie and James sat down in their night-clothes on the end of their double bed. They held hands, shocked into immobility by the news that Jess had just telephoned from the hospital. The bedroom with its soft blue paint and heavy drawn curtains felt cold instead of cosy.

Lizzie said, 'You know, if it happens, if he does die, I'm afraid of what it'll mean for Jess. Danny's been her whole life. She always loved him best from the day he was born.'

'It might not happen. He might come round.'

James drew his wife's head down on to his shoulder and stroked her hair. He wanted to fuel her with enough love to carry her through the hours ahead. Even though concern for Danny and sympathy for Jess squeezed his lungs hard enough to make him breathless, most of his immediate concern was for Lizzie. He was afraid she would find the intensive care unit disturbing, and he would have gladly gone to the hospital if he had thought Jess would accept him in Lizzie's place. But he knew that it was not even worth suggesting it. Someone had to stay with Sock, and the sisters were too close for Jess to want anyone with her instead of Lizzie.

The telephone had woken the baby. Sock stirred in his cot beside the bed and then sleepily hoisted himself on all fours. He smiled at the sight of them, a radiant beam that revealed the tiny, perfectly white pegs of his teeth. James released Lizzie's hand and went to pick him up. He smelled of baby sleep and ammoniac nappy, and James squeezed him so tightly that Sock whimpered a little as they watched Lizzie stumble out of her nightdress. She had grown plump, and her stomach and thighs quivered with marble-white folds of flesh. As she bent over to step into her panties James felt himself stiffen and he crossed his legs, shamed by the inappositeness of his response. But yet, he acknowledged, sex was one of the many happy aspects of their partnership. He was still capable of being surprised by Lizzie's imaginative appetites.

After his first, childless marriage had ended when he was forty, James had existed through a series of more or less unsatisfactory but prolonged affairs that had left him feeling dried out and bored and sceptical of ever having a relationship in which mutual criticism was not the driving force. And then, at the age of fifty-one, he had met Lizzie Bowers at an unpromising cocktail party given by one of his clients. James was an accountant, the head of his own small practice. Very late that same night naked Lizzie had smiled up at him. 'As the actress said to the accountant,' she'd murmured busily.

Lizzie had pulled on a sweater and jeans. She ran unconsidering fingers through her hair.

'Let me make you some breakfast,' James offered, but she shook her head.

'I must go. Jess needs me.'

There was no argument. James followed her down the stairs still holding Sock in his arms.

'I don't know when I'll be able to get back. Oh God. The bloody handcream voice-over.'

'Don't worry. I'll speak to your agent. Go to the hospital now and stay with her. Call me as soon as you can.'

'Will you and Sock be safe?'

He knew what she was asking. If something so terrible could happen in a single instant to Danny, who had been so strong and carefree, what different nameless horrors might threaten their baby?

'We will,' James promised her as firmly as he could. 'We'll be here waiting for you.'

He watched her climb into her dented Golf and haphazardly reverse through the gate.

'Drive carefully,' he said inaudibly. He knew her faults and he still loved her, as she knew his and loved him in return. It seemed that that was the miracle.

Rob discharged himself from the hospital simply by walking out of the ward. From the depths of his being he hated institutions. All of them, of every variety, with their smells and sounds and associations. His mother had died when he was ten and his father had disappeared, and after that he had spent too much time in too many such places. He had made it one of his adult ambitions never to be trapped in one again. And yet now it seemed that the threat was closing in on him once more. He walked as fast as he could through the wet early-morning streets, ignoring the stares of the few passers-by.

His room, when he reached it, was exactly as he had left it only a day, only twenty-four hours ago, before meeting Danny at the gym. There was the double mattress on the floor in the corner, the quilt covered with a crumpled Indian-print cotton spread. A desk and shelves that he had built himself occupied the whole of the opposite wall, and the floor space in between bed and desk was scattered with discarded clothes and paperbacks and cassettes.

Rob stared at it all, then his mouth twisted as he pushed some of the mess aside with the toe of his boot. It was hard to comprehend how something so terrible could have intervened between yesterday and this moment and yet leave all these pieces of his existence the same, unmarked.

He crossed to the window and leaned his face against the murky glass. The view, a slice of garden matted with dripping evergreens and the backs of more houses, mocked him with its sameness. He screwed his eyes shut and rolled his forehead in the acrid condensation formed on the pane, but when he opened them and looked again there was still no change. He stumbled to his bed and sat down. He put his hand up to cover his face and waited in the silence for what would come next.

Jess sat in the long, narrow waiting room next to the IT unit. There was a row of dingy armchairs, a tray with a kettle and cups, a payphone and a contorted rubber plant on a corner shelf. The sister in charge of the unit had shown her the tiny bedroom provided for relatives and told her that she could buy breakfast down in the hospital cafeteria, but Jess could not imagine sleeping or eating. She sat with her fingers laced around a coffee mug, staring unseeingly at the curling posters on the wall. They were performing some procedure on Danny that they preferred her not to watch.

She heard a loud, strong voice asking questions outside in the corridor. A second later Lizzie appeared and Jess leaped up. Wordlessly the sisters clung to each other.

Lizzie had thrown a loose coat over her jeans. Her hair was tangled and her expressive actress's face was taut with anxiety and bare of any make-up. As they hugged, Jess noticed that Lizzie no longer smelled of cigarettes, although she always expected her to. Lizzie had stopped smoking when she was pregnant. Jess rarely smoked but she craved a cigarette now with an addict's longing.

'I'm so glad you're here,' she whispered.

'How is he? What's happening? Why can't we go in to him?' Lizzie's voice was husky, fully modulated. Her words and wide gestures seemed too pronounced for the cramped room.

'They're doing something in there now. We can go back when they've finished. You haven't got a cigarette, have you?'

Lizzie looked at her. All Lizzie's feelings were always clearly visible in her face. 'No. Do you want me to go down and get you some?'

Jess shook her head. 'Stay with me.'

After a few minutes Danny's nurse came to tell them they could come back to the ward again. Jess took Lizzie's hand and drew her through the double doors into the unit.

At the foot of Danny's bed Lizzie stopped. She drew in her breath with a sharp gasp, hand to her mouth, staring at the bandages and the tubes.

'Oh God, Jess. He looks so hurt.'

Jess tried to reassure her. For her own benefit as well as Lizzie's she said firmly, 'No. It's just all the technology; it looks worse than it is because we can't understand what it's for. He moved his hand in mine, and stretched out his arms. I told you.'

Apprehensively Lizzie tiptoed closer. She put her hand over Danny's, but he did not move. She sat down, and Jess drew up a stool next to her. The nurse circled around them to the other side of the bed, unclipped a bag filled with dark blood-stained urine and replaced it with an empty one. To Jess and Lizzie she was sympathetic, but Danny was her concern. Even his mother was irrelevant here.

On the train, Beth had been in a limbo. She had left London and Sam behind her, the monotony and the contradictory knife-sharp intervals of happiness that made up her everyday life, and she hardly dared to imagine what she would find at the hospital. On the phone after breaking the news Jess had tried to reassure her, but the attempt was a weak one. Beth interrupted, too sharply. 'I'll see for myself when I get there. Don't take up any more time.'

After she had hung up she bit her lip regretfully. Even today, it was too easy for the two of them to wrong-foot each other. Fighting down a queasy surge of anxiety and guilt, Beth dialled her office and left a message on her boss's overnight answering machine to say what had happened. She packed a bag and headed for the station.

On the way north she huddled into her seat in her damp raincoat, staring out of the train window at grey sidings and fields and factories. Instead of Danny, because that was too fearful, she thought about Sam. She spent too much time thinking about Sam, she knew that, but the central question never diminished in urgency.

Would he leave his wife for her?

Beth had been having an affair with a married man for more than a year. Originally, in her second job after secretarial college, Beth had been Sam Clark's secretary. He was forty to her twenty-two, the good-looking and urbane editorial director of a publishing house, and within three months of her arrival in his office they had become lovers. He had taken her to a book launch party after work one evening, then to a restaurant, and – much later – to a hotel, because in those days Beth's flat was shared with a friend from college. The next day, back on opposite sides of their desks, Beth had been surprised to remember her compliance in all this. But Sam was used to getting what he wanted, and Beth was deeply flattered to discover that what he apparently wanted was herself. Within days, she had fallen incontrovertibly in love with him.

There had been difficulties from the beginning, of course. Sam's job was a demanding one, and his wife and young family took up almost all the rest of his time. Beth had to be content with the few hours a week that he could spare for her, after fulfilling all his other obligations. But she knew that these hours were what mattered most to him. The handful of people at work who knew about the affair seemed unsurprised by it, yet Beth had judged it best to sacrifice the pleasure of being near him all day in favour of the discretion of a different job. With Sam's glowing recommendation she had moved on to the rights department of a rival publisher, a job that suited her well. She was on the way to becoming modestly successful. Sam had helped her to find a little flat of her own, in a suburban north London red-brick terrace. The relationship that had seemed so breathtaking at first had settled almost into a painful routine.

Of course Sam would leave his wife; to doubt that was to doubt her entire life. But *when*? When would he tell Sadie the truth? Beth's bones felt brittle with the strain of waiting for it to happen, before everything else in her life could begin. She had grown thin, and her skin seemed to stretch too tightly over her face.

The train pulled in to Ditchley station. Nothing looked any different since her last visit home, in the summer. To her relief, a line of taxis waited outside the blackened stone entrance. On the way to the big Midland Hospital she gazed at the numbingly familiar streets without seeing a yard of them, only willing the traffic to move faster. She was afraid of what she would find, but longed for the slow journey to be over. The Asian driver tried to chat to her, then gave up after a glance in the mirror revealed that there were glassy tears on his fare's cheeks.

At the doors of the IT unit, a nurse intercepted Beth and led her into the waiting room. Beth saw her mother sitting with Lizzie. Jess's body was rigid and her face was transparently pale except for black shadows under her eyes. With a wash of sympathy that was still tainted by resentment Beth thought, *This is the worst for her. If it was me lying in there instead of Danny she would be unhappy, but she wouldn't look like this. Always, Danny was the one.*

She felt sometimes that she had made her escape to London just to avoid this simple truth.

As they jumped up Lizzie saw the pleading, hungry, uncertain look that Beth darted at her mother. The two women went to her and held her between them.

'Mum, what's going to happen?'

Jess hugged her close. 'We don't know yet. They're doing everything. Everyone keeps saying so. We're waiting to see the neurosurgery consultant after his round.'

'I got here as quickly as I could. It took for ever.'

'It's all right. There's no change. I'm so glad you're here,' Jess said, as she had to Lizzie. She stood with her daughter at arm's length, studying her face, then touched her cheeks with her fingertips. 'You've been crying.'

'I'm okay now I'm here. I want to see him.'

'We have to wait until after the surgeon's round.'

The scope of the waiting was only just becoming plain to them. Every minute that painfully stretched into an hour had to be waited through.

'Is Dad coming?'

Jess nodded. Ian's response had been immediate. '*I'll be there as soon as I can get a flight.*' He loved Danny, of course.

At last Beth stood beside the bed. Dispassionately the machines did their work. Then she leaned close so her cheek almost touched his and whispered, 'Dan. It's me. It's Beth, can you hear me?' When the only response was the sound of the respirator and flickering traces of the monitors she straightened up again.

Looking across at her mother and aunt she thought for the millionth time how alike they remained, even though they had evolved so differently. They were close in a way that excluded everyone else; in the whole world only Danny was more important to Jess than her sister was. Almost all her life, Beth had understood that with her mother she came a poor third.

Now she said coolly, 'Can I talk to him on my own for ten minutes?'

Jess was going to protest but Lizzie restrained her with a touch on the arm.

'Come with me, Jess. We'll get a coffee or something.'

After they had gone Beth sat down on a stool at the bedside. She held Danny's hand.

To begin with '*I'm sorry*' was all she could think of to say.

It was only recently she had begun to think of her brother as an ally instead of a rival. When they were children Danny had always been quick and handsome and strong. She had been shy and serious, lacking the self-confidence that Danny revelled in. In everything except schoolwork she had been slower and weaker. She had longed fiercely to be his equal, but in Jess's eyes she never could be. Her mother had shielded her from his mockery and bullying, and defended her against the world, but Beth knew she was never admired the way her brother was.

'*Mummy's girl,*' Danny used to jeer at her.

But it was the opposite of the truth. Beth was closer to her father, and Jess was eternally seduced by Danny's bright, careless energy. She forgave her son everything, even though he was often in trouble.

Beth thought of these things as she held Danny's hand and tried to convey to him that none of them mattered now.

After Beth had left home, Danny and she had begun to grow close in a way they had never approached before. It was as if, once their parents' uncomfortable marriage had ended, the two of them had been set free to like each other without competing. Danny had lately even been down to stay with her in her flat in London. She had taken him to the theatre, and he had taken her clubbing.

'We had a good time, didn't we?' she asked him aloud. 'We can do it again. I won't complain about techno music if you don't complain about boring theatrical crap.'

'Can he hear me?' she asked the nurse.

'We believe all our patients can hear.'

Beth fixed her eyes on his waxy face. He seemed almost hidden by the tubes and bandages.

She whispered urgently to him, 'Come on, Dan. Come back. Don't leave me alone now, after all, after everything.'

After examining Danny the consultant took the three women aside.

'I'm afraid he isn't responding very well,' he said gravely.

'What does that mean?' Jess asked.

'His reactions to stimuli are less marked than they were last night. The outlook may not be very bright. I wish I could tell you more, or something different, but for the moment we can only watch him and wait.'

Jess looked straight into the man's eyes.

'You are doing everything you can?'

'Everything.'

Unable to bear the familiar confines of his room any longer, Rob went out into the rain. Exhaustion and hunger, as well as shock, began to make him feel disorientated; he knew that last night he had been under arrest, that today he must go to the police station with a solicitor. There was a duty solicitor available; the police had informed him of that. But some independent instinct made him want to appoint his own legal representative.

He stood on the corner of the street, measuring in his mind the distance he would have to walk into the centre of town. It was quite a long way. In his head there were repeating images of his van smashed into the bridge, of Danny lying on the verge. All Rob's tools for work were in the back of the van; what would happen to them? Even as he thought of this he was ashamed that he should consider it worth worrying about.

He began to walk, pushing himself into a rapid clockwork stride although his body felt disjointed, almost dismembered. An hour later he was waiting in a legal aid solicitor's reception area. The solicitor's girl receptionist took one look at him and hurried into a back office.

A man came out to see Rob. He was young, dressed in a tie and a clean shirt, Hugh Grant hair. A public schoolboy, Rob thought, as the solicitor held out his hand for Rob to shake awkwardly with his left one. He introduced himself as Michael Blake.

'You'd better come and tell me what's happened,' he said, showing Rob into an office.

In a flat monotone Rob described the previous evening and Michael Blake listened without interrupting.

At the end Rob said, 'I'm in trouble. How bad is it likely to be?'

Blake put his head on one side, thinking before he spoke. Rob warmed to him a little.

'It depends partly on what happens to your friend. And on what charges the girls decide to press relating to the earlier part of the evening.'

Rob nodded tiredly. 'I've got some form,' he admitted.

'You'd better tell me about it.'

It had happened in an empty car-park, three years ago. He

had been taking a short cut across it on the way to meet a girl. He had been nineteen, Danny's age. He remembered the exact shade of the summer twilight, the tarmac blotched with oil, cinema and gig posters peeling off a hoarding. There had been three of them sitting on a low wall, a big shaven-headed boy, pink and bristly as a prize pig, school bully grown up, and two of his smaller, feral-looking mates.

The big one crooned, 'Look 'ere, it's Bits. C'mon, Bitty. What you got in your lunch box, Bits?' The others laughed and Rob crossed over to them, pushing his face close to the big one.

'Shut the fuck up,' he said.

He thought he had grown out of both the nickname and the shame of it. They belonged to the time when he was much younger, when he was being shuttled between the children's home and foster care. 'Bits' referred to the clothes he was dressed in and the food he was fed on, and also to a day when he was hungry and envious of another boy's packed lunch. 'Give me a bit,' he had demanded.

By the time he was sixteen Rob had become big and tough and independent enough for the old name not to stick any more. To hear it again after so long stripped him down to a discarded version of himself.

'Who are you telling to shut up, Bitty?'

There had been a fight, in which he came off badly. As he hauled himself out of the car-park Rob heard his attackers laughing. A thick, red pall of anger dropped around him like a curtain, overcoming all restraint. Suffocated by rage, he saw a short length of scaffolding pole in a skip at the roadside and armed himself. He crept in a wide circle back to where the three men were sitting on the wall, drinking canned lager. Then he came out of the shadows and hit the big one on the back of the head with the pole. He went down like a pig in an abbatoir.

Rob was charged with common assault. He was fined and placed on probation.

Michael Blake nodded. 'I think I can understand the provocation,' he said.

Rob did not discuss his fear of violence, most of all of his own which seemed buried in him like some atavistic threat.

They went to the police together, in Michael Blake's car.

'We were about to come looking for you, my son,' said the officer who met them.

Rob was interviewed under caution and not re-arrested. In an interview room a police inspector tape-recorded Rob's account of the day before. As Rob talked he could hear Danny's voice, his laughter, as if he and not Michael Blake were sitting beside him.

Before he came to the crash itself the inspector interrupted him.

'You can have a break for a cup of tea, if you want.'

Rob drank the thick brew gratefully. When the interview began again he sat with his head bent, trying to remember. The opaque spot at the centre of his recollection had thickened and spread. One minute he had been racing away from the police, the next Danny was lying on the grass and the whole world had changed.

'Do you have any more to add?' asked the inspector.

Rob shook his head. Nothing.

The inspector told Rob and Michael Blake that the breath test performed at the roadside had shown an immediate positive. The result of the blood test would not be available for some weeks, and in the meantime the police would collect evidence and statements. Officers would interview Cat and the other girl, and statements would be prepared. After that a report would be submitted to the Crown Prosecution Service, with a recommendation as to what the charges should be. Until that time, Rob was free to go.

'By the way,' the inspector added, 'it seems from the accident investigator's preliminary report that your nearside rear tyre deflated before the crash.'

Rob nodded his head again, too numb to make much of the information.

'Is there any more news from the hospital?' he asked.

'There's no change.'

Michael Blake said, 'Mr Ellis is a self-employed carpenter and cabinet maker, and all his tools necessary to conduct his business are in the back of the van. When can he expect to have them back?'

The inspector looked at his notes. 'After the examiner has finished with the vehicle the contents of it will be put in our store. Mr Ellis can collect them once they are approved for release. Probably in about a week's time.'

Outside, Michael said, 'You'll be able to work when the plaster comes off, at least.'

A bus filled with shoppers passed beside Michael's parked car. A boy with a school bag slung over his shoulder ran and jumped on to the platform.

'Yeah,' Rob said softly.

'Can I give you a lift somewhere?'

'No thanks,' Rob told him. He walked away, in no particular direction, only wanting to place himself somewhere else.

The waiting stretched into the next day and the days that crept after it. The ward and the stuffy waiting room became as familiar to the women as their own bedrooms. They sat on the plastic chairs and held one another's hands. When they spoke they talked about the past, editing it for one another so that it seemed to consist only of happy times. For the present they watched the hands of the clock and the nurses and the flickering screen above Danny's bed. They tried not to consider the future at all.

Lizzie drove home to Sock for part of each day, and when they could stay awake no longer Jess and Beth took it in turns to snatch a few hours of sleep in the cramped bedroom near the unit.

Danny's condition did not improve. He did not stretch out his arms again, or clench his fists when the nurses pinched his bruised flesh or pressed on his sternum. The machines did their busy work and Danny lay inert between them.

In the middle of the third day Ian arrived from Sydney.

It was more than two years since Jess and Ian had separated, and over a year since she had last seen him.

In the shabby hospital surroundings he looked fresh and fit, even after the long flight, and his sun-tan was incongruous beside the women's strain-etched faces.

Beth leapt up and ran to him with a cry of relief. She clung to her father.

'I'm here,' he soothed her with his mouth against her hair. 'I'm here now.'

As if the mere fact of his arrival altered everything, Jess thought, then let the thought and its bitterness slide away from her. She had no capacity now to focus on anything but her fear for Danny, and beyond it the dark bulk of awakening grief that was beginning to diminish even the fear.

When Ian looked to her she awkwardly extended her hand, but he pushed it aside and took her in his arms. They stood without speaking as the old familiarity of touch and shape and scent reasserted itself. Jess resisted a sudden blind impulse to give way and hide her face against her husband's shoulder. She would not allow herself to weep here, not yet.

'How is he?' Ian asked.

She shook her head, unable to speak.

In the ward the Indian family were clustered around their daughter's bed, and the grown-up children of a heart-attack victim waited silently beside their father.

Ian went straight to Danny.

'Hello, son,' he said.

He bent forward and gently stroked his cheek, and touched the hank of black hair that protruded from the white bandage. Danny lay wax-faced and motionless.

'Hello,' Ian whispered again.

54

Jess watched and listened to him murmuring to her son. Her dry eyes were wide and staring.

Later, when the grey light was beginning to fade, Ian and Jess went out to walk for a few minutes in the damp air. Cosy yellow lights were coming on in the buildings on the opposite side of the road, and as they passed under a street lamp it kindled with a blood-orange glow. They walked in silence, a little way apart. In the last months of their marriage, when Ian had met Michelle, they had become used to opposition, then to acrimony. But any expressions of regret or attempts at self-justification were choked by the desperation of this moment. There seemed to be nothing to say about the past that mattered any longer.

At length Jess said dully, 'I think they are preparing us for the worst.'

'We don't know that. They may not know themselves.'

Ian would not anticipate the worst before it befell him. At times his optimism was almost wilful. Jess recalled the tired old differences between them, the way that their separate needs and shortcomings had chafed each other for so many years. Their mutual failure seemed merely sad now, belonging to some long-ago time. She stopped in the middle of the pavement and threw her head back.

'What can we do?' she cried, a wail of anguish escaping her.

Ian put his hands on her shoulders. The extreme familiarity of his face only reminded Jess that they were hardly more than strangers now. She didn't know anything about his new life.

'We can't do anything,' he told her patiently. 'Not even us. Only the doctors, and Danny himself.'

Looking beyond the man who had been her husband, into the lighted windows and the rooms containing remote ordinary life, Jess told herself with simple certainty, *If he dies, everything will end.* And her thoughts spun away to the beginning, to when Danny was born, and back before the beginning, as if to another life.

*

Lizzie had come back from an afternoon with her baby and had taken her place beside the bed. Beth was in the waiting room, drinking a plastic beaker of tea. She looked up as soon as the door opened, as everyone confined in the room always did.

Rob's leather jacket was slung over his shoulder, concealing the plaster cast on his arm. The right side of his face had darkened with bruises and scabs. His eyes met hers and Beth knew at once who he was.

'You're his sister, aren't you?'

'Yes.'

The girls' school she had attended was separate from the boys', but Beth was almost the same age as Rob Ellis. She knew from somewhere, from long-ago whispered gossip of girls, that there was a strangeness about him. Something to do with his past. The cloudy associations had regathered as soon as her mother had told her who had been driving the van.

'What do you want? What are you doing here?'

Brusquely he dismissed her questions with his own. 'How is he?'

'In a coma still. On a ventilator. Do you care, since you put him there?'

He had almost turned away but now he rounded on her. His face made her step back, wishing she could take back the words as well. But he only said, 'Yes, I do.'

Lizzie was sitting beside the bed. The registrar had just made his routine visit to Danny. There was no change. She heard the footsteps and looked up. Rob was standing a yard away from her, wrapped in his jacket, his eyes fixed on Danny. He came closer, until he leaned over him. His hair fell forward over his shoulder and the leather of his coat creaked as he stretched out a hand.

Beth had followed him in. She signalled to Lizzie, *This is him*. Lizzie leapt to her feet.

'What do you want?'

Rob gave no sign of having heard her. He was watching Danny, his good hand resting on the edge of the bed. Lizzie

56

ran round to him and shook him by the elbow. He turned very slowly. He was tall, looming over her.

She repeated more loudly, 'What do you want?'

The boy shook his head. He had long hair in thick coils caught back in a rough tail. She heard the rustle of it against his collar. He was unshaven, his cheeks unevenly pricked with a reddish stubble. His lips were cracked and there were dark patches beneath his eyes. A fresh dressing on one side of his head looked startlingly white.

'To see him. What do you think?'

His voice sounded rusty in his throat, as if he had not done much talking lately. Lizzie pushed his arm with the flat of her hand.

'You can't stay here.'

'You can't tell me what I can do.'

His effrontery amazed her. There was a glaze to him, a carelessness, that seemed utterly repellent. What if Jess should come back and see him here? Lizzie pushed harder, anger rising up through her exhaustion and anxiety.

Rob grabbed her wrist. His fingers were like steel, making her wince.

'He's my friend. See? Who are you?'

'His . . . aunt.' She felt frightened now as well as angry.

'Yeah.'

Beth was at Lizzie's side, trying to separate them. The Indian family timidly looked on. Rob flung away from the two women and turned back to Danny. He bent over him for a moment, his lips inaudibly moving. Beth saw it and hesitated but Lizzie was already bringing across the Irish charge nurse.

'I'm afraid you can't stay without the family's agreement,' the nurse said. He was much shorter than Rob. Two doctors looked up from the desk in the middle of the ward.

At the same time Jess and Ian came back.

Ian recognised in an instant who this was, and saw the way that Lizzie and Beth squared up to the intruder, fending him off.

'Come on. Out of here,' Ian said sharply. His hand was already raised.

The director of the unit was on his way across to them, wearing a plastic apron like everyone else who came into the room. Except for Rob.

'I'm sorry, this is too many people around one bed. It's disturbing for other patients.' To Rob he said, 'You are an infection risk. You will have to leave.'

No one had been looking at Jess. But now she said, 'Let him stay. Just for a few minutes.'

She went to the dispenser beside the door and pulled out a disposable apron. She held it out to Rob without looking at him. He took it from her and Danny's nurse helped him to pull it over his head and tie the strings.

'We can go outside,' Jess said.

They went into the empty waiting room. Jess crossed to the high window and stared out unseeingly. It was almost dark.

'Mum,' Beth began.

Jess didn't look round. 'It's what Danny would want. What does anything else matter?'

Rob stood at the bedside without moving. The nurse frowned at him, then returned to writing on the charts. The doctors resumed their low-voiced conversation and the eyes of the Indian family turned back to their child. Rob looked at Danny's face. In his stillness he seemed hardly recognisable. The tube taped sideways into his mouth looked incongruously like a dog's bone.

'Dan,' he said softly. But Danny didn't turn his head or open his eyes.

Rob began to shake. It had taken courage to come here and now it was deserting him.

The hiss and sigh of the ventilator and the flicker of coloured traces across the screen above the bed were nothing to do with Danny. Danny was not here. But all of this hardware was real and present, and the ward and the waiting room and the people trapped in it. And it had taken on its lurid and threatening hyper-reality in the short days since the crash and he could do nothing to banish it again. He closed his eyes and opened them, and bit the inside of his mouth to suppress the groan of horror that rose up in him.

*Wake up*, he silently begged. *Just for a minute wake up and look at me. Be yourself again and let me not have done this. Or let it be you standing here and me lying with the thing in my mouth and the machine breathing for me instead. Go on. Why don't you?*

But Danny's absence and stillness only proclaimed the futility of wishing. Nothing would make the past into the present again. The wasteful truth ignited Rob's anger. He said more loudly, 'Danny, mate, can you hear me?'

Nothing. Rob stepped back from the bed, still staring at the face that injury had unshaped.

'I'll see you,' Rob said. 'I'll see you around, right?'

And then he turned and ran down the ward. At the door he tore off the plastic apron and aimed it at the bin but the air caught it and it floated, like a sloughed-off dry skin.

Rob ran past the closed door of the waiting room and down the deserted tunnel of the corridor towards the lifts. But someone standing in a shallow alcove formed by some cupboards saw him coming and stepped out to block his path.

Danny's father. A stocky, sandy-haired man with a freckly tan and gingery hairs on the backs of his fingers. The fingers were balled into fists now.

'Don't you come back here ever again,' Ian Arrowsmith said. 'Don't you think it's enough to get pissed and smash our boy into a wall, without coming back to look at what you've done?'

Rob was still shaking. He made an effort to swallow but he was dry-mouthed with anger. He saw red flashes of light around the man's congested face.

'What do you think it's like for his mother and sister, seeing you here, knowing what you did?'

Rob clenched his left fist ready to hit him. But then he made his fingers slacken again. Rob ran away, his boot soles squealing on the polished hospital lino.

The surgeon asked to see Jess and Ian.

He said gently, 'Mr and Mrs Arrowsmith. We are going to perform some tests on Danny. These tests will determine for us if there is some hope of a partial recovery, or if the damage his brain has suffered is irremediable.'

Jess looked down at her knees, at her hands tidily clasped and resting there. For a panic-stricken instant she thought she couldn't recall Danny's voice or summon his face. But then she saw and heard him, and lifted her head.

'When?'

'This evening. Mr Barker, my senior registrar, will do the tests. And first thing tomorrow morning I will repeat them myself. We don't want to draw any conclusions until everything has been looked at twice.'

'I see,' Jess whispered. 'It's bad news, isn't it?'

Ian reached out and touched her arm. Jess barely felt it.

'We don't yet know for certain,' the doctor answered. 'But I'm afraid it may be. I'm very sorry.'

He was as kind and sympathetic as it was possible to be. Jess shook her head, understanding that even as the news worsened she had until now nourished the hope, even the expectation, that Danny would recover.

The registrar came to do the first series of tests. Screens were placed around Danny's bed and his family waited outside. Jess imagined what the tests might involve and forbade herself to ask, for fear of what she might hear.

Mr Barker came to see them afterwards. He shook his head sombrely.

The night crawled past. Beth went home with Lizzie after they had assured her that nothing would change before the morning. Jess and Ian alternated in their watch beside the bed. Ian's face had already lost its ruddy colour and taken on a grey pallor.

Jess could not look at him to see his pain. She left her place to the nurse and went to lie stiff-limbed on the narrow bed in the rest-room.

The morning came inevitably and Lizzie and Beth returned. Beth was white-lipped and red-eyed, and as soon as she saw Ian she began to cry again with her father's arm around her. Lizzie had brought a croissant for Jess, wrapped in a linen napkin, and a flask of proper coffee. While they waited Jess drank the coffee and crumbled the flaky richness of the croissant into the napkin. The everyday luxury of it seemed utterly foreign in the here and now.

They heard the coming and going of the morning's business on the unit, and then the consultant arriving.

It seemed a long time that they sat in their familiar positions, listening without speaking.

Beth said at last, 'I want to hear too. Don't go off to see him without me, like yesterday.'

Jess was sitting between Lizzie and Beth. She needed them both with her; Beth's instinct was right. Their closeness excluded Ian and emphasised her sense of separation from him more sharply than ever before. His plain suffering stirred the currents of guilt in her.

Then the surgeon came to them. Jess found herself wondering if he had had breakfast this morning with his own children in some warm pine-fronted kitchen. She imagined two neat little girls in private-school uniforms.

He said, 'I have just done the brain stem tests on Danny myself. I'm very sorry I have to tell you this. But I am quite sure your son is dead.'

'No.' It was Ian who loudly contradicted him. 'He's alive, and moving. I can see it.'

'The movements you can see are reflex contractions. Danny's brain stem remains technically alive so long as we continue artificially to feed and drain and ventilate him, but the thinking part of his brain is dead.'

'Has anyone ever recovered from this state?'

Mr Copthorne looked at Jess. 'No one has. Ever.'

Beth made a small animal noise and turned her face into her father's shoulder. Lizzie was crying too, big tears rolling glassily down her cheeks. Her weeping was theatrical, Jess thought, with the first cold detachment of her grief. And when she turned her eyes to Ian she saw that he was ashamed. Embarrassed by their loss. It was or would become a part of their mutual failure, the final terrible emblem of it.

Danny was dead. He had gone away somewhere while the machines hissed and flickered pointlessly around him. It came to her that she had known it all along and her insistent hope had been only a subterfuge.

Dry-eyed, Jess faced the doctor.

And it was to Jess he said, 'What I'm about to ask you is an imposition and an intrusion into your grief. But terrible and unfair as it may sound, other people can live through your son's death. Could you find it in yourself to make his organs available for donation? I believe there is even a kind of solace in the giving, if you were able to do it.'

Without hesitation, without looking at Ian because Danny was hers now, not his, Jess answered, 'Yes. Take what will help someone else.'

'Thank you,' the man said.

'May we see him first?'

'Of course.'

With Ian walking slowly ahead of them and with their arms linked round each other, the three women went back to the ward for the last time.

In the end Jess was left alone with him. Ian helped Beth away and Lizzie stayed for only a moment longer. She groped her way between the white screens that surrounded the bed, blinded by tears.

Jess sat in silence, watching Danny's motionless face. A continuous ribbon of thoughts ran through her mind, bright images from the past punctuated by a conversation with Danny that she knew must not end now. She would talk to him – how could she not? – and he would answer. She possessed him within her head and the sudden certainty of it was like a light flashing on after days of darkness.

She stood up now and gently lifted the blanket from his shoulders, folding it back so that she could look at him. With an effort of will she made the white discs taped to his chest invisible, and the tubes and wires running out of him. She closed her ears to the gasp of the ventilator and the subdued noises of the ward.

Danny's shoulders were broad and there was dark hair on his chest and forearms. The slow rise and fall of his chest was steady, as if he were sleeping. His skin was smooth and still coloured by the residue of his summer tan. His mother looked at the knitting together of muscles and sinews and the hollow at the base of his throat and the strong arch of his ribcage, and thought how beautiful he was. While she looked at him he was a man and not her child any longer. She would have liked to stretch herself out beside him and take him in her arms. The flush of longing for him made her skin shiver with tiny currents of electricity, as if she were a girl, as if he were her lover.

Jess touched the tips of her fingers to his warm shoulder. She bent down as if to whisper in his ear, and then put her lips to the tiny scar on his jawline.

Then, tenderly, she folded the blanket up again, patting it in place around him.

All the time the conversation ran on in her head, threads of talk they had shared about Danny's college work, his girls, small speculations about the future. She heard his voice again and saw him moving, smiling, moving on as he would not, now.

Jess straightened up, stood back a step.

She did not articulate the word goodbye.

She opened the screens and walked down the ward, somehow placing one foot in front of the other. She saw the faces of the unit director, a nurse, one of the doctors, waiting to help

her. She even smiled her thanks at them, feeling the movement
of it spreading lopsided over her face. The nurse put an arm
round Jess's shoulders. They guided her away from the unit
and the hateful waiting room, so that she would not see or hear
when they came to wheel the body down to the theatre.

# Four

Ian was in the dining-room laying the round table for dinner. He found the white cloth in its usual drawer and shook it out over the table. The stubborn creases revealed that it had been folded away for a long time. Probably Danny and Jess had eaten their meals in the kitchen, if they had eaten together at all. It was almost three years since they had shared·a meal in this room as a family foursome.

The understanding *never again* weighed like a stone beneath his heart. He swallowed, in a confused attempt to dislodge it.

Ian lifted a pair of carved wooden candlesticks off the dusty mantelpiece and set them on the cloth. It seemed important to mark the day of Danny's funeral with proper ceremony. When he had laid five place settings he stood back. The dining-room looked almost the same as it had on the day he'd left. He remembered that he had put his two suitcases down in the hall and glanced in, briefly, as if to check that nothing of himself remained. Then he had put the suitcases in his car and driven away to Michelle's flat.

Years before that, Jess and he had papered this room together over a week of his summer holiday. Today the Laura Ashley pattern of tiny brown flowers looked dingy, and the matching curtains hung limply beneath their gathered pelmet. The brown carpet was worn, and so were the green tweed seats of the second-hand Sixties Scandinavian wooden chairs. Jess had made no changes or improvements to the home they had created together; Ian clumsily understood that she had probably lacked the emotional energy as well as the money.

From the kitchen drifted the scent of frying garlic. James was cooking dinner, and the three women were upstairs somewhere. Ian was glad of the interval of quiet. The house had been full of people for hours.

Everyone had come back to the house from the crematorium. They had eaten the food prepared by the caterers that Lizzie swore by, shaken hands with Ian and Jess and whispered their assurances that if there was anything, *anything* at all, they only had to ask. There had been a parade of faces: neighbours Ian had almost forgotten, teachers from Danny's school, and friends of Jess's, including a woman from her work who had brought flowers picked on the nursery – viburnum and winter jasmine and strong-scented daphne. And there had been solemn, tongue-tied mates of Danny's whom Ian had last seen as little boys. Dozens of faces, and none of them Danny's.

Ian swallowed hard on the sensation within himself that was not quite a yawn, not quite nausea. He didn't know how to express his grief for his son. He hadn't cried, yet. Crying was for women. The acknowledgement made him think of Michelle, who cried as easily as she laughed.

'When are you coming home?' she had asked him. The telephone strengthened her Australian vowels, or maybe his ears were already re-tuned to the Midlands accent.

'I'll be on the Qantas flight the day after tomorrow, love. I want to get back to you, you know that.'

'I'll come and pick you up at the airport,' she'd said at once. 'Do that.'

He missed her. Life with Michelle was comprehensible, comfortable. From the beginning, that had been one of the problems with Jess. He had never felt that she gave herself to him; there was always a little distance, a measure of holding back that was at first tantalising, and finally disappointing.

Ian clicked his lighter to the candles. Points of flame flickered and then steadied in the still air. He watched them for a minute before walking through to the kitchen.

James was standing at the cooker. He looked up and waved a wooden spatula at a pan on the heat. He said, 'It's a bit hit and miss. I wasn't sure where to look for things.'

James enjoyed cooking and was good at it; Lizzie could barely fix a sandwich. It was one of the ways they fitted together. He had tied Jess's striped apron over his unfamiliar dark clothes.

'I'm sure it'll be good,' Ian said automatically. He thought James looked like a poof, fannying around in his pinny. But he knew enough about Lizzie to be sure that couldn't really be the case. For an actress, Lizzie had always been quite definite about liking proper men. For a year or two, long ago, when she had been spending a lot of time in and out of their house and Jess had begun to withdraw, Ian had fancied her himself, although it had never come to anything. It would have been too difficult, that.

'Drink?' James nodded at an opened litre of red wine.

'Scotch for me,' Ian answered. He took a bottle of Bell's out of the usual cupboard and poured himself a full glass. James opened a tin of tomatoes and slopped the contents into a pan. Once he had stirred down the splutter of it, he reached for a cloth and busily dabbed the crimson speckles off the margins of the stove. Tidy, Ian noted.

'Jess still resting?'

'I suppose,' Ian said. 'Do her good.'

After the last mourners had gone Jess and Beth had separately retreated into their bedrooms. Lizzie had given Sock his bath and put him to sleep on the living-room sofa. No one went into Danny's room.

Ian sat down at the table and drank his whisky. He couldn't think of anything else to say to James.

They had met a handful of times at the end of the awkward period before Ian went to Australia with Michelle. James was naturally defensive of Jess; Ian assumed that Lizzie had spared her new boyfriend none of the details about Jess's husband's misbehaviour, but he had felt too embattled to bother trying to justify himself. Moreover, Ian never felt quite at ease with men who were more successful than himself, and he knew that James headed his own accountancy firm. He also knew that when he had married Lizzie James had bought her a substantial Victorian house in a prosperous village surrounded by rare unspoilt countryside. Ian hadn't seen the house but he imagined a cedarwood conservatory, a quarry-tiled kitchen and acres of pale sculpted carpets. His own home, *Jess's* home now, seemed to reproach him with its relative shabbiness.

To his relief, he heard Lizzie emerge from the bathroom upstairs. She crossed the landing and tapped gently on Jess's door.

'They'll be down in a minute.'

James nodded. 'This is ready now.'

The three women came downstairs together.

'He's gone off properly at last,' Lizzie explained, about Sock. 'I thought he wasn't going to.'

'Have a drink.' Ian picked up the uncapped Scotch bottle and poured a measure.

'Thanks.'

'Beth?'

'Give Mum one.'

Jess leaned against the dresser, obediently nursing the glass he put into her hand. Lizzie put a set of dishes to warm and Beth scraped potato peelings into the pedal bin. They were each of them occupying themselves with the tasks to hand, in order to contain the mess of grief. Realising this brought the sudden tears to Jess's eyes. She pressed the back of her hand into her face.

'Sit down, darling. Here, come on.'

Lizzie guided her to a chair. In the folds of her clothes as they held each other Jess smelled cigarette smoke. Lizzie had succumbed.

'Thanks,' Jess murmured. She saw Beth's white face and shadowed eyes, and the way Ian's thin hair had crept back from his forehead. They had loved Danny too; how could they not have done?

She said, 'Thank you for being here tonight.'

'Where else would we be?'

Lizzie's jacket was broad stripes of scarlet and black satin, like a winter deckchair. She had worn it that afternoon at the funeral, with a black fedora hat pulled down to shield her eyes. A costume.

'I can't wear black for him,' she had whispered to Jess. 'As if he was old.'

Jess hadn't thought about her clothes until an hour before the cars came. Although incongruously while she was still married to Ian she had sometimes imagined how it would be if he were to die and leave her a widow. Picturing herself at the graveside, the cut of her black dress.

She had read somewhere that women in unfulfilling marriages fall in love with their sons.

She bent her head, drank some of her whisky.

'Let's eat,' James said.

At once there was a little rush to fetch plates and carry serving dishes.

They sat down in the dining-room. Beth tilted her head as if she were listening for something. She was thinking that the front door should slam now to announce that Danny was home. He would push his way into the room, shrugging his coat off his shoulders, and wolfishly peer into the dishes to see what there was to eat. They were still a family around the table. They couldn't begin to miss Danny yet because he was still so vividly with them. She was afraid of the real start of missing him.

'Do you remember that party he had?' she said quickly. 'You left me in charge of him and all his little mates?'

Jess put down her fork. 'I'll never forget the party. He made us go out for the evening, Ian, do you remember? We came back to find the house detonated. Wreckage strewn everywhere. Like a bombing.'

Ian nodded. 'We walked in through the front door at eleven thirty. To see some kid *puking* into the phone.'

'Dad, he was trying to call a taxi. I'd told him he had to go home.'

'That was Danny's sixteenth birthday,' Jess said. 'It took us a week to clear up. Don't ever let Sock have a teenage bash in your house, Liz.'

James put out his hand to cover Lizzie's.

Nobody spoke for a moment. The scrape of knives and forks grew loud. Then Jess said gently, 'He will be all right. It doesn't mean anything will happen to Sock.'

But for all the affection that underlay her attempt at reassurance, she felt a bolt of anger wildly shooting through her. It clenched her fingers and tightened her throat. Why her boy, why *Danny*, who meant so much to her, and not some other woman's son, even – the guilty black whisper of it – her own sister's?

Lizzie began to cry. Her face turned into the mask of tragedy before the tears began to run. She sobbed, 'This is so awful. It's so final and such a waste.'

Ian and Beth glanced at each other. When she was still quite small Beth had asked her father, 'Why does Aunt Lizzie make such a show of everything?'

He had answered, 'Because that is what she does.' And Beth had understood that her aunt's life was acting, just as acting was her life. Her failure to partition the two had probably meant that her career had never been as glittering as she wished, and her life the same, until James came along. Beth turned watchful eyes on her mother. Jess was always so calm in her gestures and direct in her words. You knew what she meant, as if you could read her mind. If you could *act* that, you would be the greatest. And Jess was strong, even today.

Beth realised how much she needed her mother to be strong. The fingers of dread squeezed at her heart, making her breathless. What if something should happen to her mother now, how would she bear that? She wanted to run to her and hide her head in her lap.

'Did you see him?' Lizzie was asking them all. 'That boy was there this afternoon.'

Jess had stopped eating. One by one they abandoned the pretence of wanting food, but they drank the wine. Ian refilled the glasses. Lizzie rubbed her fingers across her cheeks, leaving black streaks of mascara that James tenderly stroked away for her.

Jess said, 'Yes, I did see him. I thought it was right for him to be there.'

She had only caught a glimpse. Rob was sitting alone at the back of the chapel. It had been no more than a noting of his presence along with all the others.

'I bloody well didn't.' Ian's face reddened. His pained eyes were bloodshot. His grief could only express itself in noisy belligerence. 'If I had done, I'd have got rid of him. Dan's killer, sitting there with all of us? Why should he be free to have another piss-up tonight and slaughter someone else's kid?'

The police had explained to Jess and Ian that once all the evidence and statements had been collected, a report would be submitted to the Crown Prosecution Service, with a recommendation of the charge that should be made against Robert Ellis. The process might take six weeks, or maybe a little longer until his first appearance in the magistrates' court.

'And until then he walks around as free as I am?' Ian had demanded.

That was how it was, they were told.

Tonight Ian had had wine on top of plenty of whisky, but he wasn't drunk. He just looked exhausted and baffled, like a large animal in a pen. Beth stared at the tablecloth. Jess leaned across the table to Ian.

'Don't be angry. Not tonight.' Ian had been angry too often, all through their marriage. With her, with their children, with the disappointments of his life in Ditchley. At least he had put that behind him now.

'He didn't come back here, lucky for him. I'd have found it a bit hard to pour a drink for him.'

To divert the conversation from Rob Jess asked, 'Was today the way these things are supposed to be?'

Jess couldn't remember any funerals except Ian's parents', and her mother's, who had died of cancer when she and Lizzie were in their twenties. Their father had made the arrangements for that one. He was still alive, but he was in a residential home near York. He had been ill, and was too frail to make the journey to Danny's funeral.

The wine had made Jess's head swim. Her thoughts skittered back and forth, as if there was too much pain for them to be pinned for long in any place.

The service had been simple, just a reading and a hymn and two or three of Danny's friends who had offered their memories of him. The priest, who had not known him, had said kind, vague things intended to console without raising the controversy of God or an afterlife.

And after that the gathering in the house, and the inching progress through this evening. After this was over, what would come next?

It was James who answered. 'It was just as it should have been. And you were brave, Jess. All of you were.'

James had shown his unobtrusive strengths in the last days. They had all relied on his cooking and telephone answering and attendance on Sock. 'And I also think it was brave of the boy to turn up.'

Jess smiled her gratitude and affection at him. Seeing his greying hair and plain features, and his kind eyes behind his glasses, she felt envy of Lizzie's happiness twisting the thread of her own loneliness. She began quickly to gather up the congealed plates. She wasn't brave herself, unfortunately. She only felt that she must appear to be, and that was quite different.

Beth stood up. She was shivering because the room was cold, and she was still listening for Danny to slam the front door, and the reality of what she knew refused to dislodge the longing expectation.

'Let's talk about him, not the funeral. Let's get the photos out or something. I'd rather think about when he was alive.'

Lizzie swept her arms around Beth. 'You're right, darling.

All the photos. The christening and the infants' play and the Cornish holidays, the whole lot. Shall we do it, Jess?'

'Yes. Yes, why not?' She bumped softly against a chair in her laden circuit of the table, glad of the muzzy distance that alcohol laid over the sharpness of loss. If she drank some more, might it briefly obliterate the pain? She became aware that Ian was watching her; it seemed incredible that he had once been her husband, that they had shared this house and the responsibility for two children. He took the pile of plates out of her hands.

'I'll get the photos,' Jess said.

Rob rang the doorbell and when there was no answer he pressed his thumb viciously against the plastic button and held it there. A train passed up on the embankment beyond the high wire fence and he turned his head to catch a glimpse of the chain of light as it threaded away. The door swung open without warning, making him jump. There was a black girl in high zippered boots and a short skirt.

'Yeah? D'you have to ring like that?'

'Cat. Is Cat in?' He couldn't remember her other name.

The girl shrugged her indifference and walked away, leaving the door open. Rob closed it behind him and tramped up the stairs to the door he remembered as being Cat's. He hesitated, then knocked.

Her head appeared, wrapped in a towel, in a shaft of yellow light that shone down the dingy hallway.

'It's *you*.' Her eyes darted past him, looking for help.

'I'm not going to hurt you.'

Slowly her gaze returned to him. 'What do you want? What are you doing here?'

'To talk to you for five minutes. It's important.'

She hesitated, chewing the corner of her lip. He hated the fear of him that clearly showed in her face. At last she said, 'Wait a minute.'

The door closed and he heard the bolt slide. He waited in

the dark hallway. When she opened it again she was dressed in jeans and a jersey. The door was on the chain.

'Well?'

'I can't talk about anything through this gap.'

'You think I'm going to let you back in here again?'

'Please,' he begged. He could see her struggle with herself for a moment. Then reluctantly she unchained the door, holding it just wide enough for him to edge past. It was trusting of her, he thought.

He remembered the room. Only it looked ordinary and smaller now, with things like knickers and tights hanging on a little plastic line by the sink, and a portable television on the table. She had been watching *Brookside*.

'I heard what happened,' she said. 'The police told Zoe and me, and we read some more in the paper. It was today, wasn't it? The funeral?'

'Yeah. It was.'

Neither of them knew what to say next. Cat looked younger and more vulnerable than she had done in the club and afterwards. Her eyelashes were colourless without mascara and there were tiny crusts of chapped skin on the full curve of her lower lip. Her damp hair hung in coils against her neck.

To break the silence Rob made a stab at saying something. Anything. 'How long have you lived in this place, then?'

She hunched her shoulders, expressing indifference. 'Bit of a dump, isn't it? I was living with my boyfriend from home, we had a flat together. I came up here from Croydon, you know, to be with him while he was at college. Got a job word processing in the estate agent's in Galloway Street. And then I find out what a loser he is, don't I? So I got this place and moved out again. I didn't fancy going back home. It's all right here. Friendlier than London, isn't it?' She stood with her head on one side, appraising him. 'You want a coffee?'

'All right. Thanks. I thought I hadn't seen you around before.'

'Know everyone, do you?' She was taunting him but he answered her straight.

'It feels like it. I've been stuck here all my life. What do you expect?'

Cat took two mugs out of the sink and spooned Nescafé into them. 'Why don't you go somewhere else, if you don't like it? What work do you do?'

'Carpentry. Kitchens, cupboards. Not building site work. It's word of mouth and local contacts, mostly. Hard to start up from nothing in a new place.'

She was looking more closely at him. Then, to his surprise, she reached out and touched the empty sleeve of his leather jacket.

'What happened to your arm? Was it in the crash?'

'Yes. Cracked elbow.'

'Why *did* you come here?'

Rob began haphazardly, 'I'm going to be charged with causing death by driving under the influence of drink. Lucky I hadn't had any of Danny's spliff or anything else that night, or I'd be up for that as well. I could get five years as it is.'

Her mouth crimped at the corners, showing her concern.

'What do you want with me?'

'I want to know what you told the police. About what happened before we left here.'

She turned away, her head bent.

'Listen.' He stopped himself from reaching out to shake her. 'You know what happened. What did you tell the police? Am I going to be done for assault, as well?'

He regurgitated the events as he recalled them, brutally pushing the facts at her, wanting her confirmation that, yes, that was how it had been.

Not looking at him, Cat said, 'Zoe doesn't remember it the same way as you.'

'It wasn't me who did anything,' Rob insisted. At the same time he felt that he was betraying Danny.

Cat nodded. 'I suppose not.'

Rob picked up his coffee and drank it, hardly noticing that it was much too hot. He was glad that he had come here, to

75

make even this rudimentary contact with another human being. In the two weeks since the accident the rhythms of his old life had faltered and then ceased altogether.

He had not worked because his van had been taken apart by the police vehicle examiner and was in any case too seriously damaged to be repaired, and because his tools had been held by the police, although the coroner's officer had now informed him that he could reclaim them, and because his arm was in plaster. And more than for any of these reasons, he had not worked because he could not bring himself to think of the steady everyday business of constructing dovetail joints and fitting sweet brass hinges, and planing and sanding wholesome wood until it was satin smooth after the destruction he was now guilty of.

He had telephoned the woman whose kitchen was half completed and told her abruptly that he would not be coming back. She had not been pleased. He had not earned any money for more than two weeks, and as a self-employed carpenter Rob did not have very much saved.

As the days after the accident went by his regular contacts with people grew less frequent. At the beginning he had seen one or two of his friends, but, whatever they said, he believed or imagined that Danny's death had shocked them and altered the easiness of their friendship. He took to walking long distances to pubs he had never visited before, and sitting over a single drink, listening to the mutter of the television over the bar. He went to the gym and worked obsessively on his legs. A sweaty cloth twisted round his neck supported his plastered arm while he did set after set of leg and calf raises. He avoided conversations with the other weightlifters, and the sight of his own reflection in the wall mirrors. In the last day or so he had stayed in his room, speaking only to shop assistants when he went out to buy something.

Then there had been the funeral, and Danny's mother had seen him sitting there, and had quickly looked away again.

Cat's face had changed. He half believed she might have

followed and understood something of what he was thinking. She hesitated, then said, 'It's awful for you. But it was
an accident.'

It was not as bad for him as it was for Danny.

Rob came up against the same truth everywhere. This was
what had happened, this was what he had done. There was a
death in his past a long way back before this one and he knew
that old endless finality. The obscene, shameful and mocking
irrevocability of someone being alive one minute and dead and
gone the next.

That was what he thought about when he looked at Danny's
mother.

'I can't remember what happened. Not the actual moments
before,' he said vaguely.

'You didn't seem that trashed. He was, I knew that.'

'Danny. His name was Danny.'

'I know.'

'Say it then.'

'Danny.' Her mouth stretched at the corners making the
word.

He wanted to get away now, before this girl worked out too
much about him. 'I've got to go,' Rob said, standing up.

As he reached the door Cat said, 'You can come back some
time, if you want. You know, if you need to talk.'

'Yeah, I might do.'

James came out of the living-room carrying Sock wrapped in
a blanket. Jess stretched over to kiss the baby's head and
breathed in the sweaty damp scent of his hair and scalp. Then
she stood back to let James carry him on out to the car.

'Will you be all right?' Lizzie asked, repeating herself.

'Yes, I will.'

'Do you promise?'

'I'll be all right. Ian and Beth are here, aren't they?' A
flutter under her diaphragm, like fear or the beginning of
sickness.

The sisters kissed each other and Jess cupped Lizzie's face in her hands.

'Don't worry about me.'

She loved Lizzie, and was much more used to looking after her than the other way around.

'I do. Will you call me? Any time, the middle of the night, whenever? I'll come straight away.'

Jess tried to smile. 'I know. Thank you.'

They hugged again and Lizzie stumbled out after James.

Jess went slowly up the stairs. Beth was in bed, lying curled on her side with her hand beneath her cheek, in the way she had done when she was a little girl.

Jess sat on the edge of the bed and stared at the framed photographic prints on the wall.

'I don't think it's properly sunk in yet,' Beth whispered.

'I know.'

'He didn't seem the kind who was going to die, did he?'

'No. Danny was always interested in getting a bit more life.'

Beth's face was hidden. She demanded suddenly with a spurt of bitterness, 'Have you been wishing it could have been me instead?'

'How can you ask that? No, I haven't. You're mine. You and I have to go on living now.'

She did not know how: she thought that tomorrow would be like setting out from the beginning of time with the necessity to relearn the world in the absence of Danny.

'I'm sorry. I've always known you loved him best.'

'No, I love you both the same,' Jess lied. Beth had always been the vulnerable one and Danny the brave. She cared for Beth, and protected her, but she knew that she failed her too.

'I love you, Mum. And Dad as well. I wish you weren't divorced.'

'I know you do.'

Jess held her hands and rubbed them between her own, thinking how narrow the margin was that separated her adult daughter from childhood.

'I just meant that if you weren't divorced you would have someone to look after you now, when you really need it.'

'You and I and Lizzie all have each other, don't we? We can look after one another. Take it in turns.'

Beth nodded. 'I suppose.'

'Can you sleep, do you think?'

Beth lay back and Jess drew the cover over her shoulders and smoothed the thin fine hair back from her ear and cheek. Jess kissed her and turned out the light, as she had done so often.

'Sleep well.'

When Jess came downstairs again Ian was tidying the photographs into the boxes and envelopes in which they had been stored. They had never been an album family.

'Is she all right?'

'I think so.'

Silence seeped through the house. Jess sat down, letting her head fall back. Ian fanned out a last sheaf of pictures, then dropped them face down like a poker player folding a losing hand. They were wedding photographs; Jess in a white dress and a big hat and Ian in a tight-waisted suit with a huge shirt collar.

'Are you very disappointed in me?' he asked.

They had furnished and decorated this room together too; their mutual failure seemed embedded in the cushions and the carpets.

Wearily Jess shook her head. She knew that Ian wanted to be absolved from having left her for Michelle, for having finally taken the initiative and walked out of a marriage that had failed long before. It was not Ian's fault, and she owed him that acknowledgement. If it was anyone's fault, it was her own. Before Danny was born she had stopped loving Ian and in the end, although she had devoted so much energy to hiding the truth, it had become too obvious for him to ignore.

'I miss some of our life together. I don't want to belittle the importance of our marriage but I miss the ordinariness of it. The everyday little routines. It wasn't a grand passion. How many marriages are? I'm sorry we failed, but I'm not sorry you've found someone else.'

Was that what he wanted to hear?

They had married too early, too young. That was partly what had gone wrong. Jess was nineteen when they met, and still at horticultural college. Ian was two years older, making a precocious success of a job as a photocopier salesman. After a year of spending all their time together there seemed no reason not to marry. Both sets of elderly parents had been eager for them to regularise their relationship. Jess had found a job as under-gardener at a nearby estate; Ian grandly told her that she need only work if she wanted to, otherwise he would look after her.

'Do you remember the couple from Yorkshire?'

They spent their honeymoon in Majorca, and in the hotel there had been another pair of newly-weds. On the second day the other bride had succumbed to a stomach upset and never re-emerged from their room, and her bridegroom devoted himself to beer instead. They would meet him swaying red-faced in the bar or nightclub and loudly insisting, 'It's dead here, it is. Tomorrow I'm renting a car and bloody driving to Madrid. See some action there. You coming with me, or what?'

Long ago. Jess smiled at the memory, grateful to Ian for offering this safe piece of their joint currency.

'It's like remembering two different people,' Ian said.

'I was younger then than Beth is now.'

Beth was born a year after the wedding and Danny three years after that.

'We were happy. I know we were. I can remember exactly the way the world looked. Sharp, with clear edges, and bright as though the sun was always out.'

Jess had no reason to deny it because it was the truth.

For what had come after that she wanted to offer some apology, but there were no words she could think of that were not double-edged. It was simply that Danny's coming had altered all her perspectives.

'I'm glad we looked at all those pictures of him,' Ian said.

'Yes.' Only they were mere glossy coloured images that didn't contain more than a whisper of Danny; already she was afraid that the memories that animated them would fade and leave her with nothing of him.

Awkwardly Jess reached out, and Ian took her in his arms.

He patted and stroked her shoulders with familiar hands and the detail of his weight and shape renewed itself in her mind, bringing with it sharp recollections of how they had lived together. From being unable to imagine how he had ever been her husband, it became hard for an instant for Jess to remember that he no longer was. Would they go upstairs together, treading on the step that always creaked, reveal what each of them already knew, only now freighted with loss?

Ian was right in a way, they had disappointed one another. By slow degrees and tiny irreversible steps, imperceptibly, beginning not so long after the days in Majorca. Of course they would not go upstairs together.

If we had not parted already, Jess understood, we would have to do it now.

They held on to each other without speaking. Then Ian leaned forward and carefully kissed her forehead, and the touch itself was like an absence, a ghostly negative of a kiss.

'Shall we divide the pictures so you can take some back to Sydney with you?' Jess offered.

She began to sort through them again, shuffling quickly through the boxed memories, overtaken by fear that reality and truth were no longer superimposed. She wanted to tuck the truth away, behind the coarse screen of present reality, from where it threatened to escape.

Ian's relationship with Danny had never been quite as easy as his with Beth. Ian was a flatly conscientious man, unimaginative and as intolerant as careful people often are. Danny had regularly made him angry, with his easy negligence and flashes of irresponsibility that were redeemed for most other people by his charm. Jess had sometimes seen Ian look at Danny with an expression of blunt incomprehension. So the family had divided, mother and son, father and daughter. Yet Ian had loved him. His inarticulate, unchannelled grief at the loss of him was proof enough.

She pushed the boxes towards Ian.

'Have whatever you would like. I want you to.'

'I would stay longer, Jess, if I thought I could do anything useful here.'

'If I thought you could I would ask you to.'

They bent their heads simultaneously to the photographs.

'Would you like to come out to Sydney for a couple of weeks' holiday? Over Christmas or something? I'll handle the airfare.'

His offer touched her, but she didn't want to go. She couldn't imagine doing anything except staying here, in this house.

'Are you sure you won't?' Ian persisted. 'If Beth came too?'

'I'm sure. But I think it would be a good idea for Beth. Ask her, anyway.'

The pictures were fairly divided. They sat for a few moments longer in the shabby armchairs on either side of the hearth.

'Danny,' Ian said, on a long breath.

Jess feared the spillage of his grief. She kept her own balanced within herself, lapping the edges of her self-control. She stood up now, touched Ian lightly on the shoulder.

'I'll let you go to bed.'

He had slept every night on the sofa. Upstairs there was only the big room they had once shared, and Beth's, and Danny's. Jess thought of his dark bedroom now, and the darker outlines of the furniture and his belongings held frozen within it and the thin veil of dust over all the things he would never pick up again.

'Good-night then,' she said abruptly to Ian.

When she looked in on her, Beth had fallen asleep, her arms tidily at her sides. Her breathing was inaudible; carefully Jess leaned over her until she felt the faint warmth of an exhalation on her cheek.

The day after Ian flew back to Sydney Jess drove Beth to Ditchley station. They peered through the streaming rain at the strings of coloured bulbs twisting in the wind that funnelled through the shopping precinct. Stronger gusts lashed the branches of the early Christmas tree mounted on the roundabout. It had been raining for days. Jess drove slowly, her eyes fixed on the road and the back of the mud-splashed bus ahead.

Ian would be safely in Sydney by this time, in the bungalow with a view of the blue harbour.

In the station car-park they struggled with Beth's suitcase and an umbrella that the wind snatched and tore into a tangle of black ribs, then stood side by side on the platform to wait for the London train.

'Are you sure you're ready to go back to work?'

'I can't think what else to do. Can you?'

'No.'

'I'll come home at the weekend.'

'If it's just for my sake, you know, you don't have to . . .'

'Mum. I want to come home.'

'Good. It'll be good to have you here.'

Even their voices sounded thinned out, drained of conviction.

Jess began carefully, because Beth had always been reticent about her private life and because she had been warned off the subject before, 'Isn't there anyone in London, anyone, you know, to look after you . . .?'

'There's no one at the moment,' Beth said flatly. 'Here's the train now. Will you be all right, Mum?'

*You have to be.*

'Yes. I will.'

They clung to each other, the constraints dissolving for a moment.

'I'm sorry,' Jess whispered.

'For?'

'For not being able to change anything.'

'I don't want you to say sorry for anything. It makes me feel worse. Look, I'll be home on Friday night.'

'Take care.' Empty words.

After Beth had gone Jess drove home to the empty house.

Sam Clark sat in his office, half turned from his desk in his padded swivel chair. It was dark outside and he could see himself partially reflected in the plate glass of the window wall. Subconsciously he admired his well-cut but longish hair, cobalt-blue shirt and loosened Armani tie. He was talking to his wife, who was also at her desk in the features department of one of the tabloid newspapers. They were arguing, in reasonably good humour, about who should go home to see their three children for an hour before they met up again at a literary party.

'I'm up to here, darling,' Sam said pleasantly. 'I've got an author coming in tomorrow first thing and I haven't read his book yet. If I whip through it now I won't have to do it later, and I can take you out to dinner after the party. Would you like that?'

'You're a snake, Sam. You manage to make ducking your turn to go home sound like you're giving me a big treat.'

'Where do you fancy? Ivy? Caprice?'

Sadie Clark gave a short laugh. 'Christ. All right, I'll go back tonight but do try and remember you were there at the conception all three times. They're your kids as well as mine.'

'And I'm almost as proud of them as I am of you.'

'Christ,' Sadie groaned again before she hung up.

As soon as she let herself into her flat Beth stepped over the scatter of mail on the doormat and went to the telephone. She dialled a number and while she listened to the ringing tone she stared unseeingly at her own face in the gilt-framed mantelpiece mirror.

'Sam Clark, please.'

The receptionist trilled, 'Who may I say is calling?'

Using the formula she had agreed with Sam, Beth murmured, 'Sarah Sharpe, Forward Communications.'

She waited with the breath catching in her throat. Sometimes, in his egalitarian way, Sam answered his own phone. If his assistant intervened, doing the job she had once done herself, it was always much more difficult. Her face suddenly sprang forward out of the mirror's murk, white and tense, the anxious eyes narrowed against the possibility of disappointment.

'My darling. My poor little girl.'

The blessed warmth of his familiar voice. Beth relaxed a degree.

'When did you get back?' Sam asked.

'Today.' She wouldn't admit to only two minutes ago.

'How are you? I've hardly stopped thinking about you. Imagining what you must be feeling.'

She didn't want to talk about any of these things on the telephone, although sometimes the telephone was their only connection for days at a time.

'Can you come round?'

She heard the intake of breath and saw as clearly as if he were sitting in front of her his frown as he made the quick calculations that would enable them to steal an hour together.

'Beth?'

'I'm still here.' Of course.

'Expect me about six. It'll only be an hour, darling. Sadie's got us down for some drinks do later on.'

Beth had met Sadie two or three times in the days when she still worked for Sam. She was American, abrasive in manner, always impeccably turned out in tailored jackets and red lipstick. Beth was too intimidated by her style and success to feel much guilt about deceiving her with her husband.

While she waited for him, in the flat he had helped her to find, Beth showered and changed her clothes. She put a bottle of the white Sancerre he liked in the fridge, lit the gas coal fire and put on some music. As she took out the wine glasses she was thinking that it was at these times, when she knew for certain that Sam would be here with her soon, that she was happiest of all. Perhaps they were the only times when she was really happy. His actual arrival only foreshadowed his inevitable departure.

But while she was waiting for him she thought that she could bear everything else, even that Danny was dead.

It pleased her that the two men had met, just once. On his visit to London she had persuaded Danny to come to the theatre with her, knowing that Sam and one of his authors would be in the audience too. They had bumped into each other in the stalls bar during the interval, and Beth had introduced them.

'Seemed like a nice bloke,' Danny said afterwards.

'He is,' she agreed. Beth did not tell him that Sam Clark was her lover.

At ten past six he came in from the rain in his big coat. Taking her two hands between his and rubbing them gently, he led her into the lamplight.

'Let me look at your face. My poor girl.'

Beth was comforted but she wanted more. She wanted to wind herself around him and have him hold her and tell her that he would never let her go. But she made herself look directly back at him and smile.

'You're wet, darling. Give me your coat. Now, here's a glass of wine. Sit here with me.'

When he was comfortable she let herself cuddle up to him, resting her head against his chest. The demands she permitted herself to make were rationed out like food in a famine.

'Do you want to tell me about it, or just talk? I can't believe he's dead. He was so incredibly young and vital. How old was he exactly?'

She had told him before. 'Nineteen.'

Sam shook his head. 'My God. It's so tragic.'

With his arms around her and the wine in her hand, and

86

the tidy flames to gaze at, Beth did tell him a little. She talked about her mother and father and what the funeral had been like. Sam listened with his mouth against her hair, and then she felt his shoulder and arm make the small movement that told her he was freeing his wrist in order to glance at his watch.

'What time is it?'

They were always counting the minutes.

'Six thirty-five. I wish I didn't have to go anywhere tonight.'

There was always somewhere he had to go, with Sadie or for business or with Alice or Justin or Tamsin, their children.

Beth twisted and tilted her head so that she could look up at him. Their mouths were almost touching. She curled her arm around his neck and shifted herself in his lap.

Sam sighed longingly and closed his eyes. When he kissed her his fingers slipped to the buttons of her blouse and undid them. He looked down at the exposed quadrant of one breast.

'You don't want this now.'

She didn't, and she did. She wanted to be absorbed, over-whelmed, made not to think. She couldn't bear to be left alone yet and the only way she could ensure that Sam stayed a little longer was through sex. He was close to her; she could see the glitter of grey and even silver in his thick dark hair, a patch of rough skin at the corner of his nose, the dark colour of his full mouth. She didn't answer, but loosened the knot of his tie and then moved quickly so that she sat across his lap, her back turned to the fire.

She bent her head slowly so that he couldn't see the clock.

Sometimes Sam would lift her up and half carry her through to her bedroom. Tonight he undressed her where they sat, and they slid awkwardly and greedily, half-way between the cush-ions and the floor.

Afterwards he was late, and hurried. Beth pulled her clothes around her again and watched him blankly as he made ready to go.

'I know. I'm sorry, I'm so sorry,' he mumbled when he kissed her again. 'I'm going to make something happen soon. I promise you. Listen.' He tilted her chin with his finger. 'Do you hear?'

'Yes.'

'I hate leaving you tonight. Will you be all right?'

'Yes.'

'I'll call you tomorrow. I love you.'

'I love you too.'

After he had gone Beth stood by the window looking down into the street. It seemed that half the people passing by in the rain were Danny's age, hurrying somewhere with all their lives to lead.

# Five

The incessant wind had damaged the polytunnels and the screens protecting the nursery stock beds. Almost every morning Jess came in to find the alleys a tangle of spilled pots and branches, and jagged skins of polythene sheeting snapping free from the tunnel skeletons. Today was no exception. With her head down into the spitting rain she worked crabwise along the avenues, righting the pots and tucking spilled compost back into place around exposed roots.

At the end of a row she saw Graham Adair, the owner of the nursery and her employer, crossing from one of the tunnels towards the warmth of his office. When he caught sight of her he came back up the path.

'Damn wind.'

Jess nodded, with her hands around the muddy plastic pot of a Ballerina apple.

'And there's another sheet loose on the end tunnel, if you could have a look at that when you're done here.'

It was back-breaking work trying to hold the heavy sheeting in place against the wind and peg it securely over the hoops.

'Couldn't Tony do it?'

'He's gone with the van to do a delivery.'

'Gary?'

'Off sick again.'

Jess swore under her breath. There was no likelihood of Graham tackling the job himself while there was anyone else on the nursery, including Joyce in the shop.

'I'll do it when I've finished here.'

'Thanks. I'd better get back to writing the catalogue. It's a never-ending task, that one.'

Jess watched him stroll back to the office with his hands in the pockets of his Barbour and his tweed cap well pulled down to cover his bald head. For most of the year she loved to be outdoors, but today she would have jumped at the chance to sit inside and tap out flattering plant descriptions on the word processor.

The torn sheeting took half an hour to replace. When the job was done she was ready to begin the regular work of the day. Yesterday she had brought across from the tunnels a trolley-load of stock plants of acanthus and Japanese anemone, and they were still waiting for her on the propagation bench. The propagation shed was open to the yard on one side, but at least it was sheltered from the wind and rain.

Jess pulled forward a pile of plastic trays and released a hillock of prepared compost from the hopper centred over the bench. Out of habit she reached up to the little transistor radio on a shelf and switched it on. Voices swam around her but she didn't try to interpret them. She worked in a bubble of silence and isolation.

With a trowel she half filled a tray with compost. Gently she released an acanthus plant from its pot and teased the roots free. Using a sharp knife she cut off a long section of root and sliced it into six parts, through the gnarled brown coat to reveal the pearly white interior. She laid the sections on the bed of earth in the tray and covered the shining cuttings with a blanket of fresh compost.

She felt that she was performing an act of burial. There was no hopeful sense that each of the cuttings would bring forth a new plant, even though experience told her that it certainly would. She firmed the earth and pushed the tray aside, as if condemning it. She repeated the sequence with the next tray and found that there were tears running down her face. Rubbing her cheeks and nose with the back of her cold hand smeared her face with dirt. She had to stop work and grope in the pocket of her coat for a tissue. The radio voices faded into the sound of children singing a carol. It was exactly a week before Christmas.

Jess worked on until half the trays were done. She wrote out and dated a white plastic label for each one before walking across the yard to the rest-room for her coffee break.

Joyce was already there. 'Hello, my duck,' she said.

Jess made an effort to smile and slumped in a chair with her hands hanging between her knees. Her fingers were numb with cold and she felt too weary and disjointed even to fill the kettle.

Joyce rustled and creaked behind her, then put a mug into Jess's hands. It was steaming hot tea, made with Joyce's own cache from her locker.

'Joyce, you didn't have to do that. I'd have made myself some once I'd thawed out.'

'It's only a cup of tea. Are you eating and sleeping, my girl?'

'Yes,' Jess lied. The night hours, infinitely drawn out and silent, were the worst of all. And when she slept there was the waking again, and the momentary disorientated struggle to identify the shapeless dread that possessed her, and the blacker moment when memory flooded back.

'Doesn't look like it to me,' Joyce said. 'Punishing yourself won't bring him back, you know.'

Jess would have turned on anyone else for saying it, but she was easier with Joyce. Sometimes she was even able to talk to Joyce about how she felt.

'Nothing will bring him back,' she agreed baldly. Her fingers stung as the blood began to circulate once more. The pain made her eyes water and she was afraid that she might be crying again.

'It's your afternoon off, isn't it?'

Somewhat uncharacteristically Mr Adair allowed each of his employees half a day before Christmas in which they could do their shopping. The idea was that staff would then not take sick-leave in order to do it, although this had plainly not worked in Gary's case.

'Yes.'

'Why don't you go and forget everyone else and buy yourself something really nice, expensive, a nice jersey or some scent, and then get a box of chocolates and eat the whole lot in the cinema? It's what I do on my home help days.'

Once every three weeks the local authority provided an extra few hours of care for Joyce's mother, so that Joyce could have a whole day off.

'Does it work?'

Joyce laughed, putting her head back and letting out a surprisingly joyful gurgle.

'She's still there when I get home. But at least I smell nice and I've had all the soft centres to myself.'

'Perhaps I'll try it. How is she?'

'The same,' Joyce said.

Jess nodded. 'Thanks for the tea.'

She finished the acanthus cuttings and made a start on the Japanese anemones before leaving for her half-day's shopping. Jess drove the twenty miles to the city centre, and after queuing in a long snake of cars she found a place near the top of the multi-storey park. She stood in the lift with half a dozen other people, holding herself rigid as if brushing against another person might breach her defences.

The sky was already darkening when she emerged into the shopping street. Star-shapes of white bulbs were suspended overhead, and the shop windows blazed in the murk. A Salvation Army silver band was playing carols outside Marks & Spencer.

Jess went into a toyshop. It was hot and crowded with shoppers, and the primary colours of pyramids and towers of boxes jumped and vibrated in front of her eyes. She came to a display of wooden toys and picked them up one by one, absently following the smooth varnished contours with her fingertips. There was a chunky engine and linked waggons loaded with red and-yellow blocks, and she took a box with a picture of the same train on the front and carried it over to the queue at the cash desk. While she waited her turn she stared through the window into the street. The crowds washed past, a dark tide of them bobbing with bags and packages to the distant music of 'Good King Wenceslas'.

Jess emerged from the shop with the train in a paper carrier bag. The list of presents to be bought was folded in her coat pocket, but the effort of acting on it seemed incalculable and she stood motionless in front of the toyshop, looking towards the bandsmen. The lights reflected in the polished surfaces of their instruments and the curved peaks of their caps.

Then she saw Robert Ellis.

He was further down the street, standing just as she was, washed up against a shop window by the surge of shoppers. He was watching the musicians too, his shoulders hunched forward against the cold. He was holding a bag of shopping.

Jess was shaking. He had been out buying Christmas presents like everyone else in the world. There were Christmas lights and carols and decorated windows just as there had been every year and would be all the years to come, only now Danny would never see them.

The boy had turned a little aside, and he was looking at her. He was thirty yards away but she saw how he hesitated, then began to move towards her. He threaded his way between the people. Jess wanted to turn and run but she could not.

At the hospital, even at the funeral, she had somehow been ready to see him. His presence was explicable; it was disturbing but within the realm of her expectations. Now, in the lit-up street with the jingle of music, it was fearful.

He came quickly, taller than most of the passers-by and so seeming larger than life once more. He stopped a yard in front of her.

Jess looked down at his shopping bag. It was printed with

the name of a local supermarket. She could see the wrapping of a loaf of bread.

'Are you all right?' he was asking her.

She shook her head, shocked, staring at him. He came closer, awkwardly put out his hand to steady her.

'Can I do anything?'

The reaction came quicker than the flicker of thought. Jess jabbed out her hand to push him away. But he resisted the pressure and so she swung her other fist backwards, weighted with the bag containing the boxed wooden train. The bag smashed into the arm that he held protected against his chest, and in a red-lit instant of pure vindictive pleasure at his hurt Jess saw his wince of pain and heard him gasp aloud. But the wild double lunge had unbalanced her on the slippery pavement. She skidded with her arms flailing and stumbled forward. She hit the ground on her knees and the bag flew out of her hand. She crouched for a second with her head down, absorbing the shock of the impact. When she looked up there was a staring circle of faces and Robert Ellis in the centre.

Indignant voices broke out.

'Was he going for your bag?'

'Are you hurt, love?'

Jess struggled to her feet in a tangle of inquisitive helping hands. The boy's face was a white block punctured with imploring dark holes.

Turning her back on him she broke free of the knot of passers-by. The street opened in front of her, a shiny corridor leading round the corner to privacy. Head down she began to run, away from the prying eyes and the stricken boy, leaving her toy train lying in the gutter and ignoring the voices that called after her.

Her house, when she reached it, was silent and dark, a place of painful refuge.

Jess did not turn on any of the lights. She preferred the

darkness. Moving by touch and instinct she went into the kitchen and sat down at the table. Slowly her eyes accommodated and the familiar outlines of cupboards and chairs solidified within a soft grey pall. The unwashed plates and clutter of food that she had left on the table were almost invisible, but the faint rank smell that emanated from them crept around her.

She sat still at the table. Once she reached out with her right hand and felt the contours of a loaf on the bread board, and the greasy slick of the butter dish. She had always scolded Danny for leaving the kitchen in a mess. She sat with stale crumbs gritty under the tips of her outstretched fingers.

Later, the telephone rang. It was Lizzie.

'Darling, how is it? How was your day?'

Jess found her voice with difficulty. 'Not too bad. I went into town this afternoon and bought Sock his Christmas present.'

'Did you?' She could hear that Lizzie was smiling.

'A wooden train and coaches, red and yellow, loaded with blocks. But . . . stupidly, I somehow left it in the shop.'

'They'll keep it for you. Or I can call in and pick it up over the weekend if you want.'

'Yes. Yes, I suppose so. Don't worry, I'll do it.' The prospect seemed enormously complicated.

'What else have you been doing?'

'Just work. Nothing very rewarding. It's a bad time of year on the nursery. Everything dormant. What about you?'

Had she said dead, or dormant?

'Jess, do you really want to go off to this place, wherever it is, for Christmas?'

'Of course I do. Julie and I will have a good time together.'

Jess and Julie had met at horticultural college. Julie had even been there the night Jess and Ian met at a pub disco. The two women had remained friends but they saw each other only rarely now. Julie worked in the tropical house at Kew Gardens and lived in a west London suburb.

Jess had booked a Christmas break, the brochure lay on the dresser somewhere away to her left, within the soft grey-black blanket of darkness. Four days in a comfortable country hotel, with log fires and tastefully restrained celebrations and probably discreetly congenial company, other middle-aged single people and quiet couples. But the booking was for herself alone. Assuring Lizzie and James that she was going with Julie seemed the only way to avoid spending the holiday with them and Sock. Jess knew that she couldn't bear the warmth and intimacy of a family Christmas, feeling as she did. She wanted the refuge of being alone with her grief.

'Are you sure?'

Why were people always asking her if she were sure of everything, of anything?

'Yes, I think it's what I need. A change of scenery, some peace and quiet. It's only four days, isn't it?'

'You'll definitely come to us for New Year?' Kind Lizzie, who could not help.

'Promise.'

'What are you doing now?'

'Going to bed, I think. Early night.'

'I'll call you tomorrow, darling. Sleep well.'

Then there was the night, the lowest ebb when loss seemed as infinite and as vertiginous as space, followed by the chafing confinement of yet another day.

The next evening, just after Jess arrived home from work, two police officers came to see her. One of them was the WPC who had taken her to the hospital on the night of the accident. Jess showed them into the living-room, but not before they had caught a glimpse of the kitchen. She felt not exactly ashamed but startled by an outsider's appraisal of it. Then she dismissed her own concern. It didn't matter, any of it.

'How are you, Mrs Arrowsmith?' the policewoman asked.

'I am all right. Thank you.'

'Mrs Arrowsmith, we are trying to establish a clear picture of what exactly Daniel and his friend did and where they went in the hours before the accident.'

'I understand.'

'We know they drove a young woman named Catherine Watson back to her home, together with another girl called Zoe Hicks.'

'That sounds like Danny.'

'Does it?' It was the policeman who asked, sharply.

Jess was bewildered. 'What do you mean? He was nineteen, he liked girls. Girls particularly liked him.'

The policeman said, 'Miss Watson has made a statement to the effect that, on the night in question, your son and Mr Ellis assaulted her. She had made it clear that she did not wish to have sex, but they would not take no for an answer. Miss Hicks's statement bears this out. Following the disturbance, the police were called to the house by another tenant, but Daniel and Mr Ellis had already run off. A panda car picked them up on the bypass because they were speeding. They were accelerating, trying to get away, when the accident occurred.'

Jess shook her head, her mouth tightening.

'There's a mistake.'

The young policewoman was looking sympathetically at her.

'There's some mistake, Danny wouldn't have done that. It was the other boy, Robert Ellis. It must have been.'

In her mind's eye, Jess saw Rob's face, as it had been outside the toyshop. Confusion and uncertainty scratched at her before she reiterated, 'It wasn't Danny.'

'I'm afraid that is at odds with the girl's statement, Mrs Arrowsmith. Have there been any similar incidents or complaints about Daniel in the past?'

'None whatsoever.'

'I see.'

'Is that all?' She wanted them to go and leave her, and take their ugly untrue accusations with them.

'Yes, thank you. I'm sorry we've had to come to you about this, but it is very important for the case against Mr Ellis for us to establish the truth about what happened that evening.'

Jess's mouth threatened to crack out of her control. It was too late for Danny, the truth or otherwise could not affect him now.

'I understand.'

When the police had gone she groped her way upstairs to Danny's bedroom. Standing in the middle of the floor, she howled out his name, but she couldn't hear his voice or even see his face. He had been taken away from her and lies and accusations threatened to distort even her memory of him.

'No,' Jess shrieked into the silence, denying the police. '*Nonononono.*'

But a seed was sown, nevertheless.

Beth came home for the weekend, the last before Christmas.

Before she arrived, Jess washed up the dishes and sketchily cleaned the kitchen.

On Saturday they drove over to see Lizzie and James and Sock, and exchanged their Christmas presents. Jess had not been back to the toyshop; she chose a different gift for the baby and deflected Lizzie's questions about it. Nor did she mention the visit from the police to either Lizzie or Beth. It was a mistake. It was to do with Robert Ellis, not Danny.

At the end of the day Beth and she came home again, and they moved about the quiet house with listless consideration towards each other. Jess knew that Beth kept herself and her grief too contained, but she could not find a way to unlock her. When Beth went upstairs, Jess came to sit on her bed again. She looked small and defensive under the covers.

'Do you want to talk?'

Beth shook her head. 'What can we say? I hate the world

for not having Danny in it. Sometimes I forget he's gone, perhaps for an hour, and then the memory comes back and it's like having to go through the loss all over again.'

'I know. It's the same for me. I suppose you get used to what's happened, in the way you can get used to anything in the end.'

'Is that how it is? I don't want to forget Danny.'

'We won't do that. But we could talk about something else. Anything you want. What about the trip to Australia?'

Beth had agreed to make a three-week Christmas visit to Ian and Michelle in Sydney. 'I'm looking forward to it, of course I am. But it's a long way to go. From you and . . . everything.'

As she said it, Beth was shocked to realise that she was as deeply and sharply hurt by her love for Sam and by his unavailability as she was by Danny's death. For an instant, Beth was tempted to spill out everything to her mother but she stopped herself. If she did confess, Jess would offer sane advice in her calm way. She would tell Beth that she was worried for her, that she would make herself even unhappier than she was now, that she would soon meet someone who was free and fully deserved her.

Beth did not want to hear any of these things.

Sam had telephoned her before she'd left yesterday to say that he would drive her to the airport for her flight, and added in his husky voice that he did not know how he was going to negotiate three whole weeks without seeing her.

She loved him so much she was afraid that she might split open. The plushy weight of devotion within her obscured everything else, even Danny's death.

'I understand. Or at least, I think I do. But it's a good thing to do, Beth. To go and do something, rather than just stay here with me.'

*Separately immersed in our separate losses,* Jess thought. *We can't help each other. Why is that?*

Beth didn't answer. The idea of putting half a world between herself and her lover seemed unbearable.

Jess waited for a moment, then mutely patted her daughter's shoulder and went away to her own room.

The last days before Christmas trickled away. Outside, Jess held herself together. She moved the barrows of bare plants and checked the stock plants and the tunnels and greenhouses, and worked some shifts in the shop so that Joyce could have a little time off. But beyond the hours when she was able to numb herself with work Jess occupied an unmarked space of empty time. She stopped trying to measure out the void with meals and sleep and chores. She ate what came to hand when the necessity arose, often standing at the kitchen counter with unfocused eyes, spooning cold food out of a tin.

The nights were the worst times because of the withheld promise of sleep and because, if sleep did come, there was always the moment of waking and remembering again. She stopped going to bed. She roamed the house instead, picking up books or magazines and reading a dozen words before putting them down in a different place. She dozed on the sofa for brief intervals, before waking up chilled to wander through the rooms again.

The deliberate solitude and the letting go of the tight threads of normality were a kind of solace. She did not have the resources for giving out care or reassurance to anyone, even herself. When her friends telephoned Jess insisted that she was all right, just being quiet. Even Lizzie she convinced that she was managing well, handling her loss in just the calm reflective way that they would have expected her to.

On the morning of Christmas Eve Jess telephoned Beth to wish her *bon voyage*. Beth was waiting for Sam to arrive. The hour that it would take for them to reach the airport together would have to contain all the nourishment she needed to survive the next three weeks and she was more conscious than ever that as soon as he did arrive the seconds would be racing past towards the moment of separation.

'I'll call you from Sydney,' Beth said. With ears sharpened by endless waiting she was listening for the car drawing up outside.

'I'll be at the hotel, remember, with Julie? It'll be easier if I call you.'

'Okay. Mum? I love you.'

'I love you too,' Jess said, with a renewed sense of having failed her child at some point in the past that had gone unnoticed, and was now irretrievably lost.

After they had said goodbye Jess picked up the small suitcase that she had left waiting in the hallway. She checked the doors and windows of the house and went out to the car. She laid her suitcase on the rear seat and backed carefully out of the gateway. She did not look at any of the neighbours' houses; she did not want to see anybody or to be noticed by them. The street was quiet. Most people who were going away for the holiday would have left already. She drove automatically, taking the route that she usually followed to the nursery. The main roads were busier and she drove with a kind of abstract attentiveness that kept her thoughts separate from her actions. She reached the big roundabout leading up to the motorway before she realised that she was driving in exactly the opposite direction from the route she had planned to the hotel.

She continued to drive without changing her expression, smoothly negotiating the roundabout and doubling back in the direction she had come.

She retraced the route exactly, back to the quiet street. She stopped the car a little way from her own gate and quickly walked the short way to her house, praying that she might not meet anyone. Jess shut the front door behind her and double-locked it. She leaned back against the shield it provided, closing her eyes, breathing hard as if she had been running. The new sourish smell of the house swam forward to welcome her. Until this moment she had believed completely in her own intention to spend a quiet Christmas alone in a country hotel, and now she felt relief and guilt in equal proportions at having evaded it.

With the back of her hand pressing to her mouth, she made her way slowly to the kitchen at the rear of the house. She sat down at the table, listening. There was nothing to hear except the faint creak of the walls and floors and the wind in the trees outside.

Rob eased his arm into his leather jacket. The plaster had been removed the day before and the elbow joint felt weak and unpredictable, as if the arm might suddenly fly out in some unpremeditated direction.

Holding his forearm close against his chest he stood beside the table in his room, looking down at a present wrapped in shiny paper and a box shrouded in the remains of a paper carrier bag. The present was for Cat. He had been surprised to find himself thinking of her when he saw the little Victorian water-colour on a market junk-stall. He had bought it, thinking it would look interesting amongst the posters and cards tacked to the walls of her room, and spent a day making a little carved wooden frame to fit. He had no idea what Cat would be doing tonight. He imagined a noisy skein of sisters and brothers in the family house in Croydon.

Rob picked up the shredded bag instead, and tucked it and its contents under his arm.

He could not blot the white face of Danny's mother out of his mind, nor could he get away from the ache of a misunderstanding. There was an injustice that he burned to explain to her, and to Jess alone, and so be relieved of some of the weight of it.

He left his room. The other flatlets in the building were deserted; everyone had gone somewhere else. It did not occur to him to wonder whether Jess Arrowsmith might also be away for the holiday. He was certain without even posing the question to himself that she would be in her house, that he would find her and talk to her.

He could have caught a bus across town, but in the last weeks he had become used to walking. He set out with his head down, the package under his undamaged arm. Under the damp and misty sky there was a slick glow of orange light oiling the streets and late bright shopfronts. The stillness of Christmas anticipation that scented and weighted the air excluded him entirely. Most of the people who passed him were smiling, many of them seemed to be drunk. Rob kept his head bent and walked fast enough to make himself breathless.

There were coloured lights wrapped round a tall fir tree at one end of her street. A little knot of teenage boys on bicycles were wheeling and braking at the corner. They stared an uneasy challenge at Rob but he passed by without looking at them. As he walked towards Danny's house his isolation contained him like a steel box. The windows facing the street were all dark.

The bell rang in shrill bursts. Then the fading echo of it was overlaid with staccato banging.

Nobody knew she was here, Jess thought. There was no light to betray her. Whoever it was would surely go away soon.

But the knocking continued, stirring up sharp reminders of the night the police came. At last, in order just to silence it, she plodded the length of the hall and slipped on the chain.

She opened the door a narrow crack and peered out to see Robert Ellis.

A trickle of fear crept down her spine. She had guessed even as she opened the door who was waiting outside, and had recognised him immediately even though he was no more than a black outline against the street light.

She would have closed the door again but with the faster movement he slid his fingers inside and gripped the edge. To slam the door would only be to smash it on to his knuckles.

He inclined his head towards the opening and Jess saw that the metallic coils of his hair were darkened with rain. She stepped back, away from him, her fingertips still resting on the chain stay.

'What do you want? Why are you here?'

'I just thought . . .' He held up something she had not noticed before, a package. Nursery artwork in primary colours was visible through torn paper. It was Sock's train. Jess stared at it, then looked into the luminous slice of Rob's face visible through the narrow aperture.

'Will you let me in, just for a minute?'

Her mouth tried to frame the reasons why not.

*You killed my son, now you want to come visiting?* She shook her head.

'Please,' he whispered. 'It's important.'

'Go away.' She knew that her voice was barely audible and she raised it with difficulty. 'Go away. Now.'

'I want to talk to you about Danny. I need to tell you what happened. Please,' he begged her.

She thought of the police, and their mistaken accusation.

This boy knew the truth. She would make him tell her.

A car passed slowly along the road, the lights swelling and diminishing in the mist. Jess watched it disappear, then she fumbled, stiff-fingered, with the chain. It swung loose with a series of tiny clinks. The gap between door and frame widened by an inch, then another inch, until it was just wide enough to admit him. He stepped into the house.

Rob held up the torn bag. 'I thought you might . . . might need it, to give to someone.'

'It was for my sister's child. Dan's baby cousin. It's all right. I bought another present for him.'

But Jess took the bag and secured the door again behind them. She turned back to the kitchen and he followed her. She was used to moving in the familiar dimness but he bumped against the corner of the stairs and almost stumbled. He put up his good hand to feel the way. The complex layers of smell in the kitchen contained stale bread and cold grease and confined air. Unthinkingly, Rob felt for the switch at the left of the door and turned on the blinding overhead light. He glanced around him, blinking, then he crossed to the table and held out a chair for Jess to sit down.

To her surprise she took it, meekly sitting and shielding her eyes with her hand.

She had not given any thought, in the last few days, to the further silting up of her refuge. She had stopped regularly cooking and eating meals, just as she had stopped going to bed to sleep, and she left the remainders of her haphazard snacks cluttering the counter tops and blocking the sink. There seemed to be no point in holding steady the repeating patterns of domestic life for herself alone. If she had once scoured tiles and polished pans and poured bleach down drains for Danny and Beth, because that was what mothers did, then there truly was no reason to do these things any longer.

Because Danny . . . And because Beth was grown up and had moved into a place where it seemed that Jess could no longer reach her.

The mess that crept out of the corners of the house was a sour and tangible confirmation of the truth and solitude that winged and swooped around her like some black bird of despair.

The boy was moving around the room. She heard water running, then the rattle of the kettle as he filled it and set it back on the counter top. He opened a cupboard door and closed it again. Jess frowned and jerked up her head.

'What are you doing?'

'Making you some tea.' Like Joyce, wanting to do something, however peripheral.

He stood still with his hands cupped around her cold teapot, waiting for what she would say.

There was a long, silent moment when she might have unleashed her anger against him or given way to fear or to a rush of tears. Jess knew that there was only the thinnest skin of defiance stretched over her desolation. And then, in an instant's clear perception, she understood that Robert Ellis felt exactly as she did.

She did not shout or allow herself to cry. Drily she nodded her head. 'There are teabags in the cupboard to your left.'

He made the tea and poured a cup for her, placing it on the table at a little distance. He left his own filled cup on the draining board and turned to the sink. Jess watched him as he cleared a double handful of teabags and eggshells and soaking crusts and dropped it into the bin. He ran hot water and squirted an arc of washing-up liquid, releasing a sharp lemon scent. He began to wash up, scraping plates and plunging them into the water, then deftly rinsing them and slotting them into the drying rack.

Jess drank her tea. She watched him working with his back to her. His leather jacket creaked faintly as he stretched out an arm. He was very large in the confined space between the sink and the table and there was an edge of controlled clumsiness in his movements, in the way that he bent his wrist to lift a dripping plate, that reminded her of Danny. It was like watching Danny wash up after she had cooked dinner for him.

Jess stared at Rob. A clean and unconfined tenderness for her son slowly washed through her. For a moment it took away her grief and bitterness so that she felt a kind of natural relief that this large boy had come here, to fill the empty aching space.

'Why are you doing that?' she asked.

'It looked like it needed doing.'

He did what Danny would not have done, cleaned the burned pan that she had set on the ring and forgotten about two days ago.

'Your tea will go cold,' she reminded him.

'I didn't really want tea.'

'Stop washing up now.'

He turned reluctantly. Jess pointed to a chair on the opposite side of the table. When he sat down Jess noticed his hands and the way his hair hung in a thick weight against his neck and the purplish shadows beneath his eyes. In truth he was nothing like Danny.

Suddenly he demanded, 'I suppose you're wondering how I dared to come here?'

He went on, not waiting for her to answer, 'It wasn't so much daring as not being able to stop myself. I felt like I was pulled here. I've kept on thinking about you ever since it happened, and more since the afternoon in town when you fell down. I keep seeing your face. He looked like you. Not in the hospital when he didn't look like anyone, just like something carved out of wood. But before that, when we were friends.'

'Friends,' Jess echoed.

The boy didn't resemble Danny but still images of them vividly collided in her head. It was the cadence of their voices and the posture and the half-truculent, mumbled, sidelong rush of their confidences.

'We were, you know. We liked each other, we were mates. And then I drove into the bridge and he ended up in that bed.'

Jess had watched him coldly, conscious once again of the oscillation within herself between anger and pain and of the fragility of the shell containing both, but then she saw that his hands were shaking and remembered her conviction that he felt exactly as she did. She got up from the table and went to one of the cupboards, took out the whisky bottle and two glasses and poured him a measure. He looked blankly at her.

'You're giving me a *drink*?'

'What else should I offer you? Hemlock? A cup of bleach?'

A twitch of disbelieving laughter changed his face, momentarily, beyond recognition. He picked up the glass and took a gulp of Scotch. His mouth tightened again and he put the drink aside.

'The police came here a few days ago,' Jess told him. 'They said they were preparing the case against you.'

'Yes.'

Their eyes met. Rob's were narrowed and sharp with pain.

'What did you and Danny do, that last day?'

'We went to the gym. Danny liked the gym and we worked out together sometimes.'

It hurt Rob to recall the day. Every hour of it was lodged in him, sharp like splinters beneath the skin. But he laid it out for Danny's mother while she listened, her eyes like Danny's, fixed on his face. He described the snooker in the pub and how Danny had beaten him, and the café where they met the girls and the unwinding of the evening afterwards. Jess sat without moving, except to reach for her drink.

'I gave him and a girl and one of her friends a lift back to the girl's place.'

'The police told me so. What was her name?'

'Is. Her name's Cat. Danny really liked her.'

'Girls always like Danny.' Jess held her glass next to her mouth, rolling its coolness against her cheek. 'Do they go for you too?'

Rob nodded his head, slowly, not knowing how he would answer the next questions. 'Um. I do okay. Used to.'

It was the way he said it, *used to*, that opened up a vista for Jess of how everything in his landscape must have changed too, gone dark, just as it had for her.

In a different voice she asked her intended question, 'Will you tell me what happened with the two of you and the girl? The truth, please. It's important.'

'It was, it was just . . . Nothing really. One of those things that got out of hand. No one, no one's fault.'

'Who are you trying to protect, Danny or yourself?'

Rob hesitated. 'Neither.'

'So tell me the truth.'

Rob thought, *Easy. I could tell her what Danny was like sometimes.* But what was it he said, once, about his mother? She worships the ground I walk on, that was it. Grinning as he said it. She didn't know he could go mad if he didn't get what he fancied.

Why should she have to hear about this now he was dead?

'Go on,' Jess said flatly.

He reached back for the memory. It was sharp enough in his mind, the difficulty was how to convey it.

'Danny was just kissing her. Flirting, then pushing it a bit further. The way he did. He told her he loved her.'

Jess was looking down at her hands, sitting very still.

Something about the quietness of her posture, the vulnerability of it, made Rob want to tell her the truth. As softened a version of it as he could manage, at least.

Danny had held the girl down while he was kissing her. The more she tried to resist him the more brutally he pinioned her. He had forced his hips between her legs and she had kicked wildly, twisting her head from side to side. Zoe had lurched upright, her mouth open as she stared at them. As Cat squirmed, Rob threw himself sideways off the bed and grabbed Danny's shoulders. He tried to haul him off, hearing some piece of the girl's clothing ripping and Danny's panting breath.

Rob was yelling, '*Get off her. You fuckhead, Dan.*'

Danny was strong, and he was suddenly and completely out of control. He pinned Cat with one hand round her throat and swiped the side of a clenched fist backwards into Rob's teeth.

'What's up with you?' he gasped. 'This one's mine.'

Cat was helpless under their combined weight. Her head rolled from side to side and a frightened little noise came out between her bruised lips. Zoe was on her feet, staggering a little.

Rob locked his arm round Danny's neck and jerked backwards. As Danny's back arched Cat twisted herself free. The two boys fell in a tangle of fists and feet, a chair crashing with them. Zoe opened her mouth and began to scream, a long, undulating cry that woke the house.

Danny was on all fours, panting, with Rob looming over him.

Someone began hammering on the door and Zoe's scream faded into a whimper as she lurched to open it.

'Get the police,' she sobbed. Footsteps turned and galloped down the stairs.

Rob pulled Danny to his feet. Danny's face was smeared and his eyes were unfocused, although he turned his head to look for Cat. She was on the bed, bundled against the wall. Tears had made black mascara streaks down her shocked face.

Rob shouted, 'Run! Danny, we've got to *move* before the fucking law arrives.'

They broke for the door. Zoe flung herself out of the way and they pushed out and down the stairs, past a terrified-looking girl stammering into the payphone in the hallway.

All this Rob described, as shortly and as unemotively as he could. He kept out of his voice and eyes the fear that violence stirred in him by reminding him of his father.

'It was all over in a couple of minutes. We ran for it, and the next thing we were out on the bypass with a police car behind us.'

'And then you lost control of your van and smashed into the bridge.'

'Yes.'

Jess stood up, went to the bottle, poured herself another whisky. Had Danny tried to rape a girl when he was drunk? Every fibre of her being made her long to reject the story outright, but the way the boy told it, it sounded like the truth. Yet he could easily be lying. She shuttled the notions in her mind, trying to accommodate them. She felt the boy's eyes on her back.

After a minute she swung round to him.

'Why are you here on Christmas Eve? Where's your family? Your mother?'

He stared at her before he answered. He thought he had suppressed every nuance of his history. He was used to doing it; over the years he had made a completely new person of himself. So how could this woman have made the connection so rapidly, unerringly?

'My mother's dead. My dad moved to Scotland, about seven years ago. We lost touch. There's only me.'

'I'm sorry,' was all Jess said, very gently. She didn't try to ask how his mother had died, or why his father had gone. She understood that she would be given no satisfactory answer. Not now, not yet.

Rob's glass was empty. He stood up quickly and his chair almost overbalanced. The clatter startled them both.

'I'd better go.'

From her place at the table Jess looked up at him. 'You don't have to go. You can stay if you like and have something to eat.' As he stared at her she laughed suddenly and then shrugged. 'Actually there isn't anything to eat now I come to think of it. Plenty to drink.'

'There's always the Chinese takeaway. Even on Christmas Eve,' he said tentatively.

He was right. The Golden Palace in the shopping parade would be open, even tonight.

Jess stood up too, steadying herself with the back of the chair. She looked down at her white knuckles. She felt stiff and dirty, and cold with sitting too long in one place.

She said, 'I'm going to have a hot bath. Afterwards we can have Chinese, if you want.'

He didn't respond and she moved quickly towards the door to cover the awkwardness. Rob didn't really want to go. He wanted to stay here and go on talking to her.

'Shall I do this while you're in the bath?'

He meant the kitchen and the mess that remained.

'If you like.'

He called her back when she was already out of the room. He was pointing to the transistor radio, Danny's radio, which sat on the window-sill. 'Can I listen to something?'

Images collided again.

'Why not?'

Jess ran the bathwater, as hot as she could bear it, and lay back under a pall of bubbles.

The bathroom was directly above the kitchen. She could hear the music rising in muffled surges. Danny always moved at the eye of a hurricane of noise.

Perhaps Danny had assaulted a young girl when he was drunk.

Tears squeezed out beneath her closed eyelids.

She was grateful that the other boy was downstairs. She was glad of the noise, and the space that his clumsy shape partially obliterated, and that she would not be alone this evening.

# Six

The empty tinfoil dishes still lay on the table. They had eaten everything last night. Jess picked up one of the dishes and dipped her finger into the viscous pool of cold sweet and sour sauce, all that remained. She licked her finger clean, with the realisation that she was hungry again. She made herself a pot of coffee and found some biscuits in a tin.

It was Christmas afternoon, and she had slept for twelve hours.

The house seemed still to contain the noise that Rob Ellis had brought in with him, and the kitchen smelled of bleach and lemon cleanser, as well as Chinese takeaway.

While they'd eaten the food they'd talked about Danny.

Jess recalled his childhood and Rob listened with an odd kind of greed that surprised and puzzled her. In turn, Rob had offered her a different perspective of Danny, as an adult and an equal. 'He was, how can I describe it, optimistic? There was a natural upside to him, and it made him popular. Everyone wanted a piece of him. Women, other blokes, me. He kind of believed everything would be right, and somehow it nearly always was.'

He thought the world owed it to him, Danny did. Rob studied Jess's face, so that she half turned away, wanting to conceal herself. 'Did you help him to be like that?'

'I think he was just born that way.'

These flattering memories were safe enough. It was easier simply to remember how Danny had been. They did not talk any more about the evening of the accident or its aftermath.

But for all that she was grateful for his company and for the image of Danny that he offered, Jess was amazed to find herself sitting at her kitchen table with Robert Ellis. Last time she had tried to hit him. She couldn't work out for herself whether this latest reaction was the madder or the more perfectly sane.

After they had eaten, Rob stood up politely. Jess went with him to the front door and they shook hands. The rain had stopped, and the sky was miraculously clear and starry. They looked up at it for a moment, their breaths clouding together.

'Thank you,' Rob said, before he walked quickly away.

'Thanks for coming,' she said to his back.

There were more questions she should have asked him, Jess thought, as soon as he was gone.

She retreated into her house and went to bed, and slept the clock round.

Jess said aloud, as if someone had asked her a question, 'I liked him. Although there is something not quite right about him. I don't mean wrong. More like, incomplete.'

The echo of her own words startled her into the realisation that she was alone, and the sociable scent of fresh coffee was wasted on the aching house.

Jess went into the living-room and dialled Lizzie's number. James's warm voice asked her solicitously how she was feeling, whether the hotel was comfortable, if Julie was enjoying herself.

'We're fine,' Jess gabbled. 'Yes, this is just what I need. A real rest. Shall I just speak quickly to Liz?' James's elderly and difficult mother was staying with them for the holiday. They must be about to start lunch, or maybe were already in the middle of it. 'Happy Christmas, James.'

She repeated her assurances when Lizzie came on the line.

'Yes, it is, it really is fine. Our room's comfortable and there are plenty of people to talk to. I'm going down to lunch with Julie now, and after I've eaten too much I'll fall asleep in an armchair in the lounge, isn't that what you're supposed to do? Tell me about Sock, did he like his presents?'

Lizzie was relieved to hear from her, but she was in a hurry, flustered by the demands of the day.

'I'm so glad, darling. Sock's going to start screaming any minute. I miss you. Promise you're okay?'

'I am, of course I am.'

'Happy Christmas,' they wished each other hopefully. 'Happy Christmas.'

Jess understood that she had just crossed a boundary. She had lied in order to preserve a separate place for herself, and in doing so she had turned her back on the rational behaviour that everyone knew her for. It was as if she had reached back to some other, wilder version of herself that had been long buried. From the trough of grief she swung high into a kind of fierce and solitary euphoria.

She telephoned Beth in Sydney. Michelle answered the call; Jess wished her a cordial happy Christmas and asked how they had spent the day.

'Thanks,' Michelle said, with a touch of surprise in her voice. 'It was thirty-two degrees here this arvo. We had a beach barbie.'

'Sounds great.'

'Beth enjoyed it. Hold on, I'll give her a shout.'

Beth came to the phone. 'Mum? Oh, I'm pleased you've called at last. I thought you weren't going to. What are you and Julie doing? Is it snowing or frosty? It's so hot here, it's not much like Christmas.'

She sounded forlorn. Jess assured her quickly that she was fine, that it was a cold, glimmering English winter's day, and that she missed her.

'But you aren't too lonely, Mum?'

'No. I promise.'

'Do you want to talk to Dad?'

'Just quickly.'

With Ian she exchanged brief greetings. The sense persisted that they were further apart even than the great distance between them.

*

After Christmas lunch, James's mother sat down to watch the Queen's speech and promptly fell asleep. Lizzie took the exhausted Sock upstairs and laid him in his cot, fully dressed. He began a scream of protest, but his eyes closed midway. He fell asleep too, with his wet eyelashes glued to his crimson face. Lizzie turned round to see James in the bedroom doorway, finger to his lips.

She had not had time to make their bed that morning. The creased sheets and pillows looked disreputable, inviting. She pushed her hair back and let the fingertips of her other hand rest at the vee of the cream cashmere tunic he had given her for Christmas.

'Yes,' James whispered. 'Time for a lie-down, wouldn't you say?'

The dining-room and kitchen were still littered with washing-up. Separately they made the same choice, and smiled at each other like conspirators. James softly drew the curtains and then took his wife in his arms. He peeled off the tunic and stroked the lace stretched over her breasts.

The crumpled nest of their bed received them. As she wound her legs around her husband Lizzie felt dazed and honeyed with lust and happiness. Already close to coming, she shivered with pleasure as he entered her. Over James's shoulder she saw her son stirring in his sleep and faltered in her rhythm for a moment. James covered her eyes with his hands.

With his mouth against her ear he insisted, 'It's time we put him in his own room. I want you to myself in here again.'

'Yes.'

They rocked together, listening to the joint rasp of their breathing.

'Wait,' Lizzie begged.

'No,' he said brutally. Lizzie particularly admired James's talent for being apparently complaisant everywhere except in bed.

Afterwards, as they lay wound together listening for the signs of James's mother waking from her nap, Lizzie asked, 'Did Jess sound all right to you?'

James frowned. 'Yes.'

'I thought she sounded odd. Strained.'

'It's not surprising, is it? Don't worry about her so much.'

'She worries about me.'

'She doesn't need to do that any more.'

Jess was out walking. The cold that had suddenly descended had bleached all colour from the world. Roofs and tree branches and street walls were dead black under a white sky, and blocks and wedges of intermediate grey piled in the space in between them. It was the interim time of the brief day when lights blazed in every window but the curtains were not yet drawn. Jess moved slowly, looking in.

Every yellow square, it seemed, framed a neat family tableau. Mother and father, children and grandparents and cousins, excited dog, and cat asleep on the hearthrug.

Outside, passing from one to the next, Jess felt disembodied. It was not an unpleasant sensation.

She thought how her family must have looked as happily ideal as these did, softly lit by candlelight and enclosed by the sentimental glitter of tinsel, but she also remembered the reality. Christmas had never been a happy time. The prolonged intimacy of the holiday had only made her even more aware of the shortcomings of her marriage. The day had always ended with her wearily determining that next year would be different, and better. It never was different, but the children were her best compensation. They had always loved Christmas, looking forward to its arrival and celebrating its overindulgence with unbroken delight, even into their late teens when Ian left with his Michelle.

Only this year, Danny had sighed in nostalgia. 'It was so fantastic when we were kids. You made it pure magic. And Dad was always home and it was exciting and completely safe at the same time.'

Ian's sales jobs never took him away at Christmastime.

'You're right. It was. Weren't we lucky?' Jess had gratified his nostalgia and pressed her own sadness into its box, and she was thankful now that she had done so.

She turned a corner into another street, with yet another set of golden tableaux. Speculating about appearances belied by reality was making her melancholy, and she was relieved when the curtains began to be drawn against the luminous twilight. She walked on more briskly through the suburban avenues and crescents, until she came to the edge of open country and the darkness lost the orange opacity of the town and became complete. Reluctantly she turned and began to thread her way towards home again.

She was thinking about all the husbands and wives now hidden behind curtains. Happiness was a fancy extra to marriage, she thought, like power steering or tinted windows. It wasn't supplied as a basic. She did not any longer regret the end of hers. She only wondered how the loss of Danny and her grieving for him might have been altered by sharing it. Although Danny himself had not been shared. Danny was her own.

Jess made a wide circuit and came into her street from the opposite direction. She had walked a long way and her face was flushed from the cold air. She let herself into the house and turned on all the lights, pulling the curtains tight to keep her own tableau private.

When the knock came at the door she did not have to ask herself who it might be. She moved slowly to answer it, knowing that she was crossing another boundary.

Rob stood on the step, holding something out to her. She looked and saw a bottle of wine and a box of chocolate mints shop-tied with a rosette of red ribbon.

'You can tell me to fuck off if you want.'

She did not say anything. There was a mixture of aggression and extreme vulnerability in his face that made whatever he said irrelevant.

'I sat in my room all day and thought about you. You're

here on your own and I thought . . .' The speech tailed off and he made a visible effort to continue. 'I should have said more than I did last night. I don't know what happened in the accident, I can't remember the moment, but it *was* an accident.

'If it could have been me it would have been better. Only it wasn't. What can I say to you? *What?*'

He made an angry sweep with his fist, still holding the wine bottle by the neck.

'And I'm standing here, like I've come to a fucking party. I'm sorry, all right?'

Jess saw now that he was either partly drunk or high, probably both. To her own surprise she was neither angry nor afraid of him, only conscious of the effort it had cost him to come back here again.

'I'll go.' He pushed the offerings at her.

Jess ignored them and took hold of his wrists. For a split second she was aware of his resistance, and how strong he was. Then he sagged into compliance and she drew him into the house. She closed the door, took the things out of his hands and set them aside. She put her arms round him as if he were Danny.

'It's all right,' she lied. And added, 'It will be all right,' in the hope that against all the odds it might be.

He was taller and broader than Danny. She felt diminished, overbalanced, her maternal reassurances misplaced, and yet an awkward pity and affection nudged her. She noticed then that his smell was clean and complicated, and in a distant way familiar. She turned her head aside, resisting the impulse to press her face against him.

His jacket creaked as he moved stiffly, not knowing what to do with his hands.

Jess let her arms drop.

'You've got all the lights on,' he said.

'Yes. Isn't it good?'

He followed her to the back of the house. She had brought the wine and chocolates, and now she put them on the table.

'Thank you,' she said. It was Christmas; they acknowledged it silently, and the truth that mutually separated them from the universal celebrations.

'Can we drink this?' She pointed to the wine. 'There's only whisky, otherwise. Are you hungry? I don't think even the Golden Palace is open tonight.'

'Did you hear what I said out there? I'm not a *killer*.' His mouth twisted. 'I was pissed, not that pissed. We'd had a night out, yeah, like you do. We were getting away from the girl's place because we knew the police'd be coming. But it could have been the other way round. You know? Easily. Dan could have been driving. I lent him the van sometimes.'

Distractedly Jess opened the freezer compartment of the fridge. There was a lone foil dish under a drift of frost crystals. It was a Marks & Spencer lasagne, two servings, so she must have bought it before Danny died. She didn't often buy food there because it was too expensive. It would do for Christmas dinner.

'But it wasn't the other way round, was it? You are alive and my son is dead.'

She caught herself, precariously rocking on the lip of a pit of black anger. She put the lasagne in the microwave, slammed the door and twisted the control.

Rob put his hands to his head. His fingers were hooked as if he would claw himself. 'You don't have to remind me. As if I could, could *unburden* myself of it, by making you listen to me.'

'As if,' Jess said stonily.

She moved clumsily around the kitchen, opening a drawer to take out knives and forks, rattling them down in a bunch on the table, dealing plates without looking at them. She knew that Rob was watching her. Her hands and feet felt oversized, the nape of her neck ached with the effort of holding her head up.

'I've got the return date coming up.'

'What does that mean?'

'Don't the police tell you anything? They'll have all the statements and evidence. I'll go back there and they'll notify me of the charge. I'll be given the date of my court appearance.'

'Yes. Yes, I knew about that.'

He sat with his face hidden in his hands. Jess stopped beside him, then reached and let her fingers rest on his shoulder. He felt the same as she did, she remembered.

The oven pinged. She took the dish out and put it on the table.

'Are you hungry?' she repeated.

He nodded his head, unwillingly. She sat down and they faced each other again, over the food.

'You had better tell me. What you remember. About the accident. If that's what you really came here for?'

'What's your name?'

'My *name*?'

'What do I call you? Mrs Arrowsmith, or something else?'

'It's Jess.'

'All right. Jess, then.'

He told her about running away from Cat's house.

'We knew we were in trouble, right?'

She didn't press him for any more details about that. Only inclined her head, painfully.

'We jumped in the van. Drove around like crazy trying to find our way in all those fucking back streets. Then got out on the bypass and the next thing there's the cops behind us. I put my foot down.'

'What did Danny do?'

'Shouted. Something like, *Go, man*.' Rob remembered now. Danny was *laughing*.

'I saw some lights coming at me. I was dazzled.' He dropped his knife and fork, rolling his head as if it hurt him. 'Next thing I'm looking at the concrete pillar. It's too close because the front of the van is all squashed up against it. The seat beside me's empty with the door burst open and Danny's out on the verge lying on his side like he's asleep. That's all I can remember.'

'I see,' Jess said.

He turned on her. 'Do you? Do you know what it feels like to cause someone's death? I'm surprised.'

'I didn't mean that.'

Rob's left hand chopped through the air and caught the rim of a plate in front of him. The plate bounced and twirled off the table to smash in fragments on the floor. He shuddered and pressed his hands to his ears, but he also saw that Jess shrank backwards in her chair.

'Oh, don't worry. I'm not a real danger to anyone. Except myself.'

He was only a kid like Danny, Jess thought. Unable to see much beyond himself. The pathos in him touched her again.

'I'm sorry about your plate.'

He gathered up the shards of it and put them in the bin next to the sink.

'It doesn't matter.'

Jess left her seat. In the cramped space of the kitchen between the counter and the table they hesitated, with their breath catching, then took hold of each other. They did it blindly, out of need. Jess did put her face against him now. The rough wool of his jersey corrugated her forehead and the tip of her nose. After a moment he lifted his hand to cup the back of her head, holding her close to him. They stood for a moment in amazed stillness, listening to themselves.

'What can we do?' Jess asked, her voice muffled.

'Just carry on, I suppose. What else?'

Somehow she was comforted by this flat acceptance of continuing existence, even though to continue might seem impossible. Rob must have just carried on at other times in his life, she thought. It was what she had been doing herself.

She broke away from him.

'Finish this, won't you?' She pointed at the lasagne dish, and gave him another plate, wanting to see him eat. For herself she poured more wine.

'Have you got a solicitor? You must have. What does he say?'

He hunched his shoulders. 'Not much. He's a bit of a prat. He hasn't seen the case against me yet. I'll have to stand trial in the Crown Court. That's all I really know.'

'Do you want me to come with you to see the solicitor?'

Rob gave her a hard look, disbelieving. Then, seeing that she meant the offer, he smiled.

Jess heard the surge of blood in her inner ear. She could not remember having seen him smile before. Seeing it made her admire what she saw, and when she made the instinctive and shameless step in her imagination beyond that she became aware that he was taking the same measure of her. She put her hand up to her face.

He said quietly, 'No. But thanks for the offer.'

They stood up at the same time, making the same moves to clear the perfunctory meal. They stepped carefully around each other, anxious to avoid accidental touching.

'Come in the other room,' Jess said. She had not lit the fire and the grate looked dead and cold.

'Shall I?' he asked, pointing at it. A minute later the yellow flames that leapt from the firelighter blocks softened and warmed the room.

The fish eye of the television blankly regarded them.

'*Christmas Night with the Stars*?' Rob murmured.

'We could just sit here by the fire and talk,' Jess countered. The curtains were still open; if there was anyone outside looking in they would look like mother and son, a part of one of the Christmas families.

As if he read her mind Rob stood up and pulled the curtains closed. The awkward intimacy of the room tore a sudden cry out of Jess. She moaned as if the words were wrung out of her, 'I wish he was here. I want him back.'

Rob took hold of her wrist. 'I know you do. But he's dead.'

'You have to talk to me. Tell me the truth.'

He shook her hand loose and took it in his own. 'I'll tell you anything you want.'

'Was it Danny or you, that night?'

There was a silence.

'Was it Danny?'

Jess already knew the answer. Stiffly she withdrew her hand and turned it over and back again, staring down at her skin.

'Why?' she asked in bewilderment.

'Sometimes when he wanted something and couldn't get it . . . he *had* to have it.'

Yes. Whether it was her attention, a game of Monopoly or one of Beth's toys . . .

She had protected Beth, but she always gave Danny what he wanted. She couldn't deny him.

A slow, unpleasant recognition inched in on her. *You can't unlearn something once you've found it out*, she thought.

'And what did you do?'

Rob shrugged. He was embarrassed.

'Cat was upset and the other girl starts screaming. I know we had to get out of there.'

'Why?' Her dark eyebrows rose.

Rob said abruptly, 'I've already got a record, all right?'

'What for?'

He told her about the pig boy, and the nickname.

Afterwards she said, 'I see.' Then added quickly, 'I don't mean I know what it felt like. Tell me some more about it. If you want to.'

He found that he did want to.

'My mum's dead, right, and my father's gone. When I was thirteen I was fostered by some people called Purse. By name and nature, as another older kid who lived there pointed out. On the night I arrived I was given a bag with some pieces of toilet paper in it. It was my ration for the week.'

'What if you needed more?'

'You pinched someone else's. Or improvised. You don't want to hear this, do you?'

Jess nodded, slowly.

He had lasted six months at the Purses'. Even now he could

124

remember the smell of the house and the taste of Mrs Purse's potato hotpot. After that he had been returned to council care.

'How old were you when your mother died?'

'Ten.'

There had been a series of foster homes, alternating with longer intervals back in the children's home.

'Why didn't your father look after you?'

'He couldn't. Now I've told you all about that, you have to tell me something in return. Go on.'

Jess considered. Nine years ago. She had been thirty-five, Danny ten.

Her life had been ordinary, at least compared with what Rob had baldly described. She had had a part-time job in those days, as a keyboard operator with a manufacturer of plumbers' supplies. It was boring, but better paid than horticulture. Ian was often away, Danny and Beth were turning from small children into adolescents.

She could not even properly remember how she had felt. She supposed that for safety's sake she had deliberately made a colourless version of herself, and kept a guilty and flamboyant Jess securely hidden.

Rob listened to the pallid story with the greedy attentiveness she remembered from the night before.

'It sounds safe,' he nodded at the end.

'I suppose you're right. It was safe. Not very exciting.'

'Excitement is terror and threat for safe people. It's adventure holidays, and drugs on weekends. I'd have changed places with Dan any day.'

'Yes. Were you threatened and terrified?'

He looked hard at her, as he had done before.

'I can't remember.' Or would not tell, she understood.

It was late when they finished talking. Jess looked at the little gilt clock on the mantelpiece and saw that it was one in the morning. Christmas was over.

'I'll be going,' Rob said.

Without looking at him Jess said, 'You can stay the night here if you want. You can have my daughter's room.' Not Danny's.

Rob lay on his back in Beth's bed. His throat felt dry with talking. He couldn't remember how long it had been since he had last talked so much. He liked the way Jess had listened without interjecting herself. She didn't ask for approval all the time as women of his own age did; she was herself, and the sympathy she offered had been real but restrained. There had been no look-at-me-being-sad-for-you. He hated that.

The mess in her kitchen yesterday had disturbed him. It had stirred memories and his first thought had been to eradicate it. It was only belatedly that he had realised how unlike her it was and therefore how expressive of her misery. Then, when he looked closer, he read the misery in her eyes. He had put it there; he couldn't clean that away with bleach and a floor-cloth.

She had reddened hands with short nails. Hair the same colour as Danny's, emphatic dark eyebrows that made her look stern.

The daughter's room had pink-and-cream curtains, framed photographic prints in a careful arrangement on the long wall and a collection of china animals in a grid of small shelves beside the window. The quilt cover was pink and cream stripes. The daintiness of it all made him feel a clumsy, sweaty intruder. He silently swore and turned to lie on his front, pressing his face into the pillow. He wouldn't sleep. The house crept with memories and nuances and his guilt stalked him, a gaunt huntsman.

He knocked on her bedroom door.

'What is it? What do you want?'

She was still in bed, the thin morning light barely penetrating the closed curtains. She half sat up, defensively pulling the covers closer around her.

'I thought you might like some tea.'

He put the cup on the bedside table, backed away again.

'Um, yes. Thanks. What time is it?'

He told her. 'Do you want me to go?'

*Expecting the answer yes,* Jess understood. *Out of habit.*

'No, stay. If you can. Do you want to?'

'Yeah. I mean, yes.'

Later, when some warmth crept briefly into the colourless midday sun, Jess drove them out into the country. They left the car at the side of a lane and went for a walk up a long slope of fields that gave way to a bare crest of moorland. From up on the high ridge they could look down in either direction on an undulating landscape of hills with grey-blue deposits of houses and tall chimneys in the hollows. Jess walked fast, turning her face deliberately into the wind. The villages were too distant for them to be able to distinguish people. The few vehicles on the hedged ribbons of road were only visible as moving specks in the stillness. It was easy for Jess to imagine that she and the boy were the only individuals alive in the post-Christmas stupor.

'I love it up here. I used to bring Beth and Danny when they were small.'

'Did they enjoy it?'

Rob looked incongruous, too long-legged, uncomfortably hunched in the short leather jacket. He was pale-faced and urban in the rainwashed light.

Jess grinned. 'Not much. They complained enough.'

'Didn't your husband come?' The sandy, belligerent little man he had seen in the hospital corridor, making a nuclear family foursome.

'No. He was away or busy, usually. The way men often are.'

'Don't you like men?' he challenged her.

'Yes, I do.'

They walked in silence for a few hundred yards. A flock of nervous sheep jostled away down the hill.

'My father was a drunk,' Rob said. The wind caught at the words so Jess only just heard them.

'What did he do?'

'He *drank*.'

Rob did not revisit the past if he could help it. Sometimes it visited him; the miasma of it had crept around him more persistently since Danny's death. This particular corner of the territory came back to him most fearfully in smells and noises. Occasionally even the whiff of a bar-room was enough to materialise his father, huge and meat-fisted, blurry-eyed and reeking of whisky and beer. Or the unseen sounds of violence; breaking glass – even a plate smashing like last night in Jess's kitchen – made him also hear his mother's voice in the next room, imploring, *No, Tommy, please, don't do this now.* Then he heard the impact of a backhanded slap, and another, and the muffled swearing and pleading and the tangling crash of furniture as someone or something fell over.

He hid under the bedcovers, absorbing with his fear the certainty that he should have gone to defend his mother.

And yet before the worst time, at the end, there had sometimes been a different version of his father. A big, clumsy man who liked cards and patiently taught his son to play whist and rummy. The three of them had played at the kitchen table with the television turned off. But there would always come a night when Rob woke up to hear the shouting and smashing again.

'Did your mother leave him?' Jess asked.

'Not exactly.' Then he added, 'I'm not like that. Not like him.'

'I know you're not.'

The sun was setting. As it sank, the white sky turned green, then flushed reluctantly with a faint, chilly pink. They descended from the ridge and reached the shelter of the trees, and discovered that in the lanes the twilight was already thickening into darkness. As they plodded the last mile back to Jess's car she thought of yesterday's walk, when the black beyond the town's orange glow had beckoned her away from all the

Christmas windows. She was glad that the boy was with her tonight. The careful but matter-of-fact descriptions of his childhood constantly changed her understanding of him. It was better that he should be here, she assured herself, than that they should be separately eaten up with grief.

She put her arm through his and he held it in place, matching his step to hers.

In the next village the pub was a blaze of light.

'It's opening time. We could stop for a drink,' she suggested, unwilling to go back to the silent house.

It was early and the bar was almost empty, but there was a log fire and no piped music. There was tinsel wound through the horse-brasses and a coloured sign over the fire read *Jack and Aileen wish all their Customers a Merry Christmas and a Prosperous New Year*.

Rob and Jess sat in a corner with their pint and a half of beer. The cosy ordinariness of the pub reminded them that they were not after all the only people in the world, and made them differently and sharply conscious of the currents between them. One or two of the people who came in glanced speculatively into their corner.

Jess stared absently into the fire. She had taken off the knitted hat and scarf she had worn on the walk and her flattened hair framed her face. There was colour in her cheeks. Rob thought, she doesn't look like anyone's mother. She looks like a woman. He felt a twist in his belly that made him shift on the wooden bench so that Jess turned to look at him and their eyes met.

'I'll get another drink,' he mumbled. Jess had bought the first ones.

While he stood at the bar, Jess saw Danny with him. He playfully punched Rob's arm in a greeting, and said something that made them both laugh. She felt the cold shiver of loss and another sensation, even colder, that was to do with the distance between herself and the two boys and the mislaying of her own youth and freedom.

Then he came back and stood looking down at her and everything changed again; he was not her son or her son's friend but a man she already knew. She couldn't get back her safe ignorance of him, any more than she could get back her untarnished version of Danny. Rob and she were not consoling each other or trading bitterness or blotting out reality. They had slipped into something else, and that was becoming reality.

They continued to sit in the pub, admitting nothing, talking only a little. They ate a meal that neither of them much wanted because it was a way of holding off whatever might come next. A big man with a red face approached their table.

'Excuse me, you two,' he said. Their faces turned up simultaneously and Jess felt hers burning. You two. *You two.* The words seemed loud and then grew deafening in their echo.

The man was staring at them. 'Is this free?' he repeated, pointing at a chair.

'Yeah, mate. Sure. Take it,' Rob mumbled.

Jess said, 'We'd better go.'

He helped her to her feet. The touch of his hand on her arm seemed too intimate. It made her think how long it was since anyone had touched her in that way.

But then in the car he sat silent with his head turned away. Jess thought, *It's nothing. My imagination. I'm old enough to be his mother. You two?* She almost laughed at herself. Relief was tinged with the heat of disappointment so that she savagely bit her lip to counter it, twisting her mouth as she drove.

When they reached home she said, 'I'm tired, Rob. I'm going straight to bed.'

He waited in the doorway looking up to where she stood on the stairs.

'Do you want me to go?'

'No.'

She shut herself in her bedroom, undressed and lay on the bed. By listening hard she could just hear the sound of him moving about downstairs, and the faintest ripple of music.

*

Rob slowly climbed the stiars. Outside her door he stood for a moment. There was nothing to hear, not a movement. Slowly he reached to the doorknob and circled it with his fingers.

Then he snatched his hand back. Her imagined exclamations of outrage, anger, jarred in his head. He stood for a moment longer with his arms hanging at his sides, then crept like a thief into the daughter's empty bedroom.

Jess didn't know how long she had slept. Her eyes opened and she went through the stages of remembering what had to be endured each time she woke up. Now the recollections were layered with sharp awareness of the boy asleep only feet away from her. She turned over and tried to will herself back to sleep but she knew at once that she was too wide awake. Her skin felt thin and hot as if she had a fever.

Impatiently she pushed back the bedclothes and wrapped herself in her old tartan dressing-gown. Barefoot for the sake of silence, she stole down to the kitchen. At the sink she filled a glass with water and sipped it, staring at her reflection in the black window glass. The overhead light was too bright, making her blink. In the living-room she knelt and blotted her fingertips in the film of ash that spread over the hearth. Christmas night. *I want him back.*

*I know you do. He's dead.* That's what the boy had said, and that was all there was. Danny was dead and they were not.

'Danny?' Jess said aloud. She looked around for him but there was only the completeness of his absence. No answer, no embodiment, not even the sharp image of him in her mind's eye.

Jess got slowly to her feet.

Carry on, that was what had to be done. Rob said it. She did know him, she thought. Somehow he had occupied her, pitching his camp, lighting a fire and partly unrolling the history that went with it. Welcome or unwelcome. Or maybe even to think whether she wanted him or not was an irrelevance because what would happen was inevitable. She touched her face with her fingertips but even the contours of it felt unfamiliar.

She went quietly back up the stairs, pausing on each step.

Outside Beth's door she stopped again; then she twisted the knob and opened it.

'Come here,' Rob's voice said out of the darkness.

# Seven

The darkness was a blessing.

Jess felt her way, her hand stretched out. He was holding back the covers to allow her to lie down beside him. She fumbled with the belt, then dropped her robe on the floor. The air was cold on her shoulders.

She lay down in his arms. The touch of him was foreign and yet familiar.

'I nearly came into your bedroom. I stopped myself. I could only think of you being outraged.'

'I woke up. I knew I wouldn't sleep again.'

He kissed her. 'Can I touch you like this?'

'Yes.'

'And like this?'

'Oh. Yes.'

The scent and feel of him was so young. Clean and unused. She was glad of the dark that forgivingly hid her lines and pouches. Rob moved his hands, finding that her flesh was loose but also soft, seemingly soft enough to dissolve, certainly to bruise if he was too clumsy with her. She smelled womanly and complicated, and so enticing that he wanted to bury his face in her like a child in his mother.

'What do you like?'

This considerate eagerness excited her. 'I like all the usual things.'

'This?'

'Yes.'

Her hand was on him. His mouth moved over her face, from her eyelids to her throat.

'And you?' she whispered.

'Like that. More. Turn on your side.'

They didn't talk for a while, allowing a different language. The bedclothes coiled around them and they pushed them away, freeing themselves.

'Have you got something I can use? In your bedside drawer?'

Jess laughed, a touch wildly. 'I don't. I don't do this.'

In the years since the end of her marriage there had been one or two mild dinner dates, exchanged flirtations. Tepid possibilities that she had dismissed. There was nothing she could remember that came near this imperative, instant connection. The urgency of it.

'It's safe, anyway. I had my tubes tied.'

Wanting no more children, after Danny. There would be no more. Too late now, and too old.

'I meant Aids. What do you want me to do?'

'This. Just as you are.'

'Yeah. I know I'm okay. All right. Now. There. And *there*. And . . .'

Jess smiled, holding him in her arms, winding her legs around him. She *had* forgotten, the fluency and the comedy and the brutality and tenderness of it. Now she remembered, easily becoming amphibian again after a long time on dry land.

'Jess. Oh, Jess. Wait. No. Yes, oh. *Ah*.'

She held his head against her. There were coiled strands of his hair in her mouth and wound over her eyes.

'I'm sorry. Hey, are you smiling? I can feel your mouth crinkle. It's all right. I'll be ready to go again in a minute.'

'I'd forgotten. That's what you do when you're twenty-two.'

He said, 'I like it when you laugh. I really like it. All right, now you.'

'No, it's fine.'

'Yes. Hands, or mouth? Or we can do it together. Give me your hand, here, like this. Like this?'

'Oh. Yes. Just like that.'

Once they had begun, they understood now, there was no ending. They were driven over and into and around and under each other. Their night stretched into a week, dwindled into a matter of minutes.

'Again.'

'Now?'

'Immediately. Sooner.'

'There. And there. Turn over. Put the pillow there, what do you feel?'

'I feel,' Jess said, 'unwrapped. Bare. Nothing to hide.'

'Good. So do I. Don't talk any more now.'

The bed became confining. They transferred their greedy explorations to the floor, the armchair beneath the window. When the first grey light of the morning came they watched themselves in the mirror of the wardrobe. Their skins swam luminously pale in the dimness, their faces were alike, as if in family resemblance, swollen-mouthed and wide-eyed in astonishment.

'It's daytime.'

'I don't want it to be. In the light maybe this shouldn't have happened.'

He put his hand over her mouth. 'Shh. Come back into the bed.'

'That hurts.'

'Yes. We've done it too much.'

'Hold me instead.'

'I am holding you. Are you tired?'

She nodded. 'But I've never felt so alive.'

'Nor have I. It's like discovering a sixth sense. No, six extra senses.'

'I'm sleepy now but I'm afraid to go to sleep.'

'Don't be. Close your eyes.'

She lay on her side and he fitted himself into the curves of her back and knees. She felt his exhaled breath innocently warm against her neck, slower and deeper, as they voyaged into sleep.

When she woke again Jess broke through the layers of dread and recollection, but now, as she came closer to the surface, they were interleaved with different sensations. There was warmth next to her, a rhythm of breathing different from her own.

As soon as she was fully conscious she knew she was happy that the boy was here. Loneliness and sadness had begun to undo her.

But to be happy was unthinkable. The shock of realising it made Jess jerk upright. To be happy with this boy in her bed?

Rob opened his eyes and looked at her. She wrapped her arms defensively to cover herself.

'You're hiding from me? After what we did last night?' There was disbelief and a touch of scorn in his voice, and the beginning of resignation. 'Are you sorry it happened? It *did* happen, didn't it?'

'Yes.' Jess unfolded her arms. She rested them on the twisted covers and he propped himself on one elbow, looking at her.

Something in their positions, or his expression or the angle of the light, awakened a memory and for a moment it took hold of her so forcefully that it was more vivid than the reality. She was a young woman, only in her twenties. Her skin was sun-tanned and as elastic as Rob's. It was the hottest hour of a Mediterranean afternoon and a wedge of sunlight struck through the half-open shutters, dividing the room like a fallen pillar. The man in the bed beside her turned to rest his head on one arm and his features were as clear as if she had seen him yesterday. She was stroking his black hair, telling him that it was time to go, the baby would wake up soon.

And just as she did now she felt the charge of sex, and a confusion between doing wrong and yet feeling right as she did it.

The boy's long hair hung over his shoulder. She resisted the impulse to touch it.

'I'm going to get up,' she said.

Jess reached out of bed for her dressing-gown and pulled it round her. She wanted coffee and silence and time to think.

'I'm not sorry,' she told him candidly.

Nor was she sorry for what she had done twenty years ago.

'But I don't know what to do now. I've lost Danny and I thought the only way to help myself through it was to live in a very plain, bare sort of way. Can you understand that? Without doing anything too quickly or even moving too much until I've got used to him being dead? I thought if I closed everything down, I could survive until the pain wore off a bit. I just wanted to keep *still*.

'But then there was finding out about what he did that night. It changes him, and so many other things too.' She was thinking of Beth. She must talk to her, but how to begin?

'And now there's this. It isn't a very straightforward or minimal connection we've made, is it?'

Rob shook his head. 'So do you think we should have stopped ourselves? Should you have gone past the door? Should I have pretended to be asleep when you opened it?'

'I don't know. No. That wouldn't have been honest.' Was honesty what mattered, then? 'Look, I'm going downstairs.'

She added silently, *Don't follow me now. Let me just think, will you?*

Rob lay back, lacing his arms behind his head. The tricep muscles were developed, sharply defined. The skin of his right elbow and forearm was still dry and flaky from the plaster cast. Jess turned sharply away. She could not escape the certainty that they had already crossed into new territory together. Even if she wanted it they could not retreat or unlearn what they had already discovered.

In the bathroom she took off the tartan robe and looked at herself in the mirror. She had lost weight; the fragile arch of her ribcage stood out above the contradictory spread of her hips and stomach.

But otherwise, she thought, although she had given it no

137

consideration for so long, the spectacle was not too bad.

Her eyes were bright and her face had softened. The soft-
ness came because she was smiling.

You poor old thing, she told herself coolly. To have your
head turned by a boy of twenty-two, to do what you did last
night.

With *this* boy.

She tipped her head forward, rested her forehead against
the mirror. She had turned the shower on and the water
splashed busily behind her. Breath and steam condensed on the
glass, mercifully obscuring the reflection.

Shocked dismay and a wild, guilty, bitterly defiant kind of
pleasure fought within her.

Down in the kitchen, dressed in jeans and a shirt, she made
coffee and put away the plates they had used the night before.
The evening seemed to belong to long ago and recalling what
had intervened deepened the dull flush over her throat and
cheeks.

Jess sat down at the kitchen table to drink her coffee. She
worked out how to tell the boy that he must leave, and rehearsed
the assurances she would give and extract about not seeing
each other again, about there being no further contact between
them.

There was no sound from upstairs. He must have the same
ability as Danny to fall asleep at will, anywhere. She imagined
him sleeping with Beth's covers rucked up around him.

After a long time she heard the bathwater running. He did
not have any difficulty either in making himself at home, she
thought. Stiffly she stood up from the table and washed her
cup and the cold coffee pot, using small, tight movements, keeping her resolution clearly in the front of her mind.

There was another long interval before she heard him come
slowly down the stairs. She stood facing the door with her hands
at her sides. Her fingernails dug into her palms.

His wet hair was dark. He had combed it flat and tied it
back in a knot that left his face exposed, the skin seemingly

drawn tight over his prominent cheekbones. He was wary, his lips pressed in a tight line.

'You're going to tell me now that I must go.'

'Yes, that was the idea.'

He didn't deserve chilly flippancy. If she was going to send him away she must do it gently. Trying to begin again she said, 'Rob, listen to me, I can't let you stay here, not because of Danny . . . Oh *God*, what do I mean, of course because of Danny . . . but also because I'm old and you're young and I need just to be left alone, and because you need what I can't offer and . . .'

'Jess.'

He put his hands on her shoulders, made her look at him although she tried to turn her face away.

'You don't have to do this.'

'Yes, I . . .'

'We can help each other.'

She was caught by the words. She stopped trying to evade him and listened to the echo of them. The notion of being helped was so large and luxurious it wrapped around her like a cashmere blanket. And yes, the boy needed helping as much as she did. They felt the same. She knew him now. So who better to offer it?

Jess let her shoulders sag. She was balanced on the sharpest edge between longing and grief. She rested her face against Rob's shoulder and found that she was weeping.

'Stay then,' she said.

'The door of your airing cupboard upstairs is too heavy for the hinges, you know. It's pulling them out of the frame. I'll fix it if you like.'

'All right. I'll cook you some breakfast in exchange.'

'Deal.'

He wiped her eyes for her.

'You look about fourteen this morning.'

'Add thirty years.'

He kissed her and the erotic charge that had skewered her

the night before spiked her again. Against all her inclinations Jess made herself step away from him.

'Why, Rob?'

'Because I want to. Obviously.' His face was still close to hers and she examined the contours of his mouth as the tiny facial muscles worked it, and the reddish-gold stubble that stopped just short of the full line of his bottom lip. She was tight-throated, with her breath catching at the top of her lungs. Shameless, she thought. 'And because I need you.' She lifted her eyes to meet his. 'Does that turn you off?'

Jess considered. To be needed, and therefore desired. It was like the answer to a riddle with the question missing.

'No. Mothers get used to being needed,' she answered softly. She kissed him back, deliberately, liking the way his arms roughly tightened around her.

In the cupboard under the stairs Rob found a small box of tools that Ian had left there. He took off the cupboard door and replaced the hinges. He carried Jess's transistor radio with him and played it at full volume while he worked, and the noise filtered into the corners of the house, so that his presence seemed to fill it.

'Come and look. It's done.'

She admired the neat job. 'That's good. Hey. The door even closes properly, it hasn't done that for years. You're good at what you do, aren't you?'

He shrugged, leaning back against the cupboard with his hands in the pockets of his worn jeans.

'I haven't done very much work lately. Wood and joints, making things fit and comfortable, it hasn't seemed as easy to do or as logical as it did before.'

The same tragedy had skewed their lives in the same brutal fashion. The plain orderliness of every day had been snatched out of their reach and would not be given back again. Jess stared at him, feeling the bitter, visceral pull of their connection. Only the intensity of it made her sure that it was rooted further back in their separate histories, before Danny's death.

'I know how that feels,' Jess said.

A moment of clear insight made her understand that her life had been meaningless even before the accident, and that she had deliberately made it so, to protect herself. It must be the same for Rob; they must recognise it in each other. They could not feel this affinity otherwise. Her eyes searched his face for confirmation, then she went to him, stepping over the clean curls of woodshavings scattered on the bathroom floor.

She took his face between her hands and kissed his mouth.

She needed to touch him, and more than that. It was a sexual imperative but it went deeper. She wanted there to be no barrier between them: sex was a way of dismantling the barriers, the most direct and least subtle way of breaking them down, but what she longed for was the perfection of intimacy itself. She craved it, like an addict groping for a fix.

'Come with me,' she commanded.

In the bedroom the curtains were still drawn, but Rob had made the bed, a little awkwardly with the covers drawn up crooked, as Danny would have done it. There was a shade of confusion in Rob's face.

'Are you afraid of me?' Jess asked.

'Christ, no. I just don't know what you want.'

She undid the buttons of her shirt and twisted it off. She took off the jeans and her underthings and stood in front of him, her hands loose at her sides, unselfconscious of her body's imperfections. She felt a huge sense of freedom swelling and lifting her up, and it lit her face and widened her mouth into a smile.

Rob saw that her belly was heavier than his memory of it from last night, with a single crease below the weight of it that shadowed her white skin. Her breasts were slack, with blue veins fanning from the dark nipples. There was a simplicity and inevitability about the evidence of her ageing that touched him more directly than a younger, more obvious beauty could have done. And there was something in the way she offered herself to him, without any of the complications or uncertainties of the night before, that was safe and reassuring and yet triggered the strongest response in him.

He fumbled with his own clothes, dropped them in a heap. Her skin against his was cool, then burning hot.

Their coupling was as urgent as before, and more so, this time almost brutal.

Jess craned back her head so she could speak. 'Stay with me today, stay tonight.'

'Is that what you want?'

'Do *you* want it, Rob?'

Was that the first time she had used his name?

'Yes, yes. It's what I want. I don't know anything else but I know this.'

The telephone rang on the bedside table. Jess lifted her hand to it, then let it ring with her fingers curled over the receiver. It rang for a long time, and when at last it stopped she reached over and ripped the jack out of the plug. She looked down at Rob. His hair spread bronzy metallic threads over her pillow.

'I don't want to let anyone else in here.'

'What if it was important?'

Angrily she smothered his mouth. 'I don't want to have to take care of anyone else. Anyone at all except the two of us. Okay? Just for a day, two days. The day after tomorrow I've got to go back to work. Just until then.'

'Okay.'

They were setting themselves back-to-reality deadlines, and their looming reminders made the present seem all the more intensely precious.

Lizzie carried Sock out of the house, while James reversed the car. It took the efforts of both of them to open the passenger door and fit the sleepy baby into his car seat, to strap him securely in place and wedge him with his comfort blanket and his toy rabbit, and to load his pushchair and holdall and spare toys into the luggage space. They were red-faced and panting when they stood upright again.

'Are you sure you want to do this?' James asked as he eased himself into the driver's seat. It was early in the morning, the last day of the Christmas holiday.

Lizzie scrambled into the front passenger seat and snapped the tongue of her belt into the lock. She turned her smudged eyes accusingly on him.

'What else can we do? She never went to the hotel, there's no answer from the house. I'm scared to death for her.'

'She's a grown woman, Liz. Maybe she just wanted some time to herself.'

'Without saying so to me? That isn't Jess. I know her. I'm certain something's wrong.'

'She wanted you to think she was at the bloody hotel, or she wouldn't have telephoned and pretended to be there.'

'That worries me all the more. What if she's . . . done something stupid?'

James looked steadily at the road. 'I don't see Jess as a suicide if that's what you mean. She's too strong.'

Lizzie gave a small cry of fear and crammed her knuckles against her mouth.

'What has happened to her? Where has she gone?'

He sighed, then put his hand on her knee to reassure her. 'We'll find out. But don't necessarily expect her to be happy about it, will you? If she wanted to put some space between herself and everybody else, she won't want it removed until she's ready.'

'It's just that she's always been there. All our lives, there's been Jess and me.'

'I know,' James said, so that she hastily put her arm around him and he had to brake to avoid swerving.

'Jess was always the most important person in the world to me, until you and Sock came along.'

'Do you think she doesn't know that?' he asked her sombrely.

*

Jess's house looked as it always did when they reached it after the twelve-mile drive. Her battered Citroën was parked outside, the bedroom curtains were drawn tight.

James pulled into the kerb and switched off the engine. Sock had slept all the way but now he rolled his head against the seat restraints and began a half-hearted cry.

'Shh, lamb. Look, here's Rabbit. And your drink. Are you thirsty?'

'I'll go,' James said. 'You stay here with him.'

There were two pints of milk waiting on the step. Through the open downstairs curtains he could see the more or less tidy living-room, the ashes of a fire in the grate. James pressed his finger to the bell. He could hear it shrilling inside, cutting through the retentive silence. He lifted his finger again and waited, gazing backwards to the car where Lizzie was attending to Sock.

There was no answer, no sign of movement in the house. He pressed his finger to the bell for a longer interval and shifted his attention to the panes of opaque glass in the door, wondering how difficult it would be to break in.

Lizzie hauled Sock out of his seat straps and hoisted him against her shoulder. He craned his head to look around him as she hurried up the path.

'Car,' he said equably, now that he was no longer confined within it.

James rang the bell even longer and harder the third time. They crowded together on the narrow step, peering urgently at the shadows behind the glass.

'Jess, where are you?' Lizzie whispered. 'She's not here. How can we get in?'

James held his hand up. 'She is here. I can hear something.' He picked up the two bottles of milk and held them in the crook of his arm. One of the shadows moved within the house, then swayed closer to the glass. It defined itself as a head and shoulders and a hand raised to the latch.

The door opened and Jess stood there, one hand holding

her dressing-gown wrapped tightly around her, the other pushing her hair back from her face. She looked blankly at them and the pints of milk and Sock with his rabbit.

Lizzie blurted, 'Jess darling, where have you been? The hotel said you never arrived and I couldn't get any answer on the phone and I thought something had happened to you.'

Jess's face betrayed impatience and anxiety and alarm, before composing itself into determined blankness again.

'Nothing has happened to me, you can see. Here I am.'

They were on the doorstep like a surprise party gone wrong. Only Sock, babbling his version of Jess's name, was unaware of the awkwardness. 'Can we come in?'

'Um, yeah. Sure. Of course you can. Come on.'

They trooped into the narrow hall.

At the head of the stairs behind her Rob appeared.

They looked up at him from an angle that made him seem immensely tall and broad, legs planted apart like a Colossus. He was naked except for a towel tucked around his middle.

The doorbell's insistent ringing had woken them from an entwined deep sleep.

Lizzie gasped. Sock's small voice chattered on in the stunned silence.

Jess found that she could only twist her mouth into a smile. There was no use trying to explain away what was already obvious at a glance to all of them.

'It's my sister and brother-in-law,' she explained to Rob. And to Lizzie and James she murmured, 'I'll make some coffee.'

Open-mouthed, Lizzie watched Rob's broad shoulders and muscular legs turn back towards Jess's bedroom. Sock did his special fist-clench wave.

In the kitchen Jess didn't look at any of them. She went deliberately about the business of filling the filter machine with water and measuring ground coffee into the paper cone. Lizzie set Sock on his feet and he stumped straight to the nearest cupboard, wrenched open the door and began to drop saucepans on the floor with a crow of pleasure. No one took any notice of him.

Lizzie snatched the coffee tin out of Jess's hand. 'What's going on? What's *he* doing here?'

Jess stopped what she was doing, turned to face her sister. 'I think that's pretty obvious, isn't it?'

Relief at finding Jess safe and a shock for which she hadn't prepared herself ignited in Lizzie. She began to shout her anger at Jess. 'How could you? With *him*, after what he did? Here in your own house? Has he done something? You've got to tell me. Has he threatened you? Jess, he must have done, you couldn't have just let him.'

'Couldn't I?'

Jess looked past her sister to James. His pleasant open face was stiff with embarrassed disbelief. Jess looked away again.

'Couldn't I?' she repeated. To defend herself and Rob became the most vital thing. 'How about if it's me who wants it? How about if we want each other, like you two, like anybody else? Maybe we're taking care of each other because we're the only people who know how to do that? Can't you imagine?'

Lizzie was still shouting. 'No. I can't imagine. It's unnatural, immoral. It isn't you, Jess.'

'How do you know?' she asked coldly.

'Liz,' James murmured, warning her.

Sock clashed two saucepan lids together. Liz rubbed her mouth with her fingers and stooped down to him. It was a pivotal moment. The sisters knew that they were already divided; a few minutes and a handful of words and the boy had come between them as nothing had ever done before.

'What about Beth?' Lizzie pleaded.

'Beth is twenty-two years old. An adult woman. And before you say it, before you invoke him, Danny is dead. You shouldn't have come here this morning. James, you shouldn't have let her come.'

Rob appeared in the doorway. He was fully dressed now, with his leather jacket slung over his shoulders.

To Jess he said, 'I'll be going.'

A plea rose in her throat, *don't*, but he turned and went before she could articulate it. The front door slammed behind him. Sock was startled by a noise not of his own making and his face crumpled threateningly.

'Why did you do that?' Jess said bitterly. 'I wanted him to be here.'

Lizzie's angry disbelief was tinged with a jealous sense that Jess was lost to her. 'And we shouldn't have come?'

The silence ticked between them. Jess took back the tin of coffee, shrugging. She did not care to make this better now. She was angry too, and did not want to smooth and reassure or dissemble. She wanted to be herself.

'Hi,' Cat said.

She had thought carefully about it, then found her way to Rob's place. She was pleased to find him in. 'I thought I'd, you know, come and like check you out. Are you okay?'

'Yes, I'm okay. Why not?'

He let her in and she wriggled out of her shiny short mackintosh and dropped it on his bed. She was wearing a suede miniskirt and a jersey in some sort of fluffy pale wool that increased her resemblance to a perky kitten.

'What did you do at Christmas?' she asked inquisitively.

Rob shrugged. 'I was here.' To deflect her curiosity he said, 'What about you?'

She crinkled her face. 'I went home to my mum and dad in Croydon. My sisters and my two brothers were there as well, and my mum's parents. Bit of a crowd, but it was quite a good laugh.'

'Must have been.' He remembered the picture he had found. 'Actually, I got you something.'

Her triangular face flushed in surprise. She was extremely pretty today, he noticed. She seemed to change each time he saw her.

'What for? I mean, why?'

'I don't know. It was just something I found.'

He gave her the little water-colour of a winter country scene in its new carved frame. As he handed it over he realised that something about the picture's smallness and neatness had reminded him of Cat herself. She gazed at it, turning it over to examine the back as well as the front.

'It's really pretty.'

She was disconcerted. And the picture would only look odd hanging on her wall amongst the swingbeat band posters and drawing-pinned postcards.

'Do you want to go and have a drink, or something?' he said hurriedly. 'Now you're here?'

Her cloudy eyes lifted to his. 'Yeah. That'd be nice.' She tucked the picture tidily into a carrier bag unfolded from her little handbag.

In the pub, over their drinks, Cat confessed to him, 'Actually, I thought a lot about you. You know, over Christmas. About how you might be feeling. And I thought about him as well. Danny. It's sad. I feel sad about him even though . . . you know.'

Her PVC coat creaked as she stretched to pick up her lager and she glanced at Rob from under her eyelashes.

He thought suddenly, *She fancies me. Out of sympathy or curiosity or a sense of drama, she's fixed on me.* But he did not attach much significance to it.

All day, since he had walked out of her house and left her with her nosy sister, Jess had been with him. He had not so much thought about her as been colonised by her. Now an immense weight shifted inside him, making his ears ring and his hands twitch on the beer-puddled table. Someone edged behind his chair to get to the cigarette machine near the door. A fresh burst of music crackled out of the speaker wedged in the corner over their heads. Rob tried to reconnect himself to this familiar mundane environment but he felt entirely absent from it, as if he was still in the house with Jess.

He wanted to go on talking to her, never to have to stop. She was old, older than his mother would have been, and the age difference had never seemed less relevant. Whatever they said, and did with one another, did not go through any conduits of deception or pretence. It was all direct, decoded, bare face to face. He could not explain to himself the fascination, the electricity that stabbed and at the same time soothed him, any more coherently than that. He had the sense of being lost and miraculously found again.

And she had been so great, so surprising – he fumbled with the words and images in his head – in bed. Direct there too, all hot hands and mouth. Nothing like the half-dozen or so girls he had had before. The thought of it made him suddenly hard.

'You all right?' Cat was asking him.

'Yeah. Sorry.'

Their glasses were empty. She said, 'I'll get this one in, shall I?'

He watched her slip through the crowd to the bar. He noticed that two or three of the other drinkers watched her as well. Not surprising. She was worth looking at. Danny always did have an unerring ability to pick the best one of any bunch of girls.

And he was dead.

The horror and despair of it thumped in his brain and belly again, as it did a score of times a day.

Jess knew. It was nothing to do with sex; not really. His erection had already collapsed. Jess did not dissemble or submerge her misery, but he had begun to cherish the hope that she did not blame him for it either.

Cat was threading her way back towards the table, biting her lower lip in concentration, a pint and a half of lager in her fists.

Afterwards he walked her back to her house.

'D'you want to come in for a bit?'

Rob shook his head. 'I won't tonight. I've got to get back.'

'You will ring me?' She had written the number down for him.

'I will, yeah. This week some time.'

She reached up and kissed his cheek. 'If you want anything, you know?'

He supposed that he could have pressed her for a withdrawal of her statement to the police, but the police and the case against him seemed to have been nudged into irrelevance by everything else that was happening.

'Thanks,' he said, and walked away, wondering if the plummy-voiced sister was still at Jess's house, calculating how he might go back and be with her again.

The house was in darkness once more. Like a ghost Jess flitted along the landing to Danny's bedroom. She inched the door open and slipped inside, then felt for the switch of the reading lamp on his table. A circle of greenish light spread over his undisturbed belongings. Jess had barely been in here since the funeral.

She sat down at the table and touched the rack of cassettes and the scatter of loose change he had left there, then turned her head to look at the bed. The covers were smooth. His books were on the shelf above and his clothes hung in the wardrobe. She breathed in, trying to detect the scent of him, but the room smelt only of dust and a trace of the joss sticks he burned to disguise his marijuana smoke.

Jess slowly exhaled, tilting her head back. There was no stronger a sense of Danny in here now than there was anywhere else. She couldn't conjure him up, either the sight of him lounging on his bed or the sound of his voice, and it had been easy before Rob came. The loss of the ability made her feel panicky. This room would have to be cleared, sooner or later. She didn't want a shrine that contained nothing of him.

She would ask Rob to help her, she decided. He would know what to do with all these belongings, and as she contemplated this another thought came to her. The first days and weeks of grief had made her feel suspended, as if she was hanging in some hideous space and waiting for something to happen that she couldn't imagine or reach out for. Now something had happened. She had been forced to view Danny from a different perspective. And Rob had come.

Jess clenched her fists and bent her head, suddenly overcome with longing for him.

# Eight

Lizzie said, 'I don't know whether I should be asking this of you. It's kind of you to do it. But you always are kind to me, aren't you?' She pushed back her hair, and re-rolled the sleeves of her big jersey. When Jess said nothing, she demanded, 'Where is he, anyway?'

They were passing bags and toys from hand to hand. Sock was asleep in his buggy.

'Do you mean Rob?' Jess asked.

'Of course I do.'

'How would I know? You saw him leave the other morning.'

'That was three days ago.' Lizzie's relief was evident. 'You haven't seen him since then?'

'No. I don't know where he lives.'

But then the anguish in Jess's face was so clear to see that Lizzie tried to break the constraint between them by putting her arms round her sister's shoulders.

'I suppose the police might tell me where to find him, if I asked,' Jess added, not yielding to Lizzie's embrace. 'I haven't got to that yet.'

But I will, she thought. If he doesn't reappear soon, I will.

'Jess, I don't know what to say. It's wrong, that's all. I just think you should leave it alone. You'll look back and wonder how you . . . what you were doing. He's just a boy. He was driving the van, wasn't he? It's because of him . . .' Lizzie broke off uncertainly. 'Do you want to see him again?'

There were white lines tightening Jess's mouth. She broke away from Lizzie.

'I know what he did,' Jess said. She kept to herself what else she knew about that night. 'And I do want to see him again.'

She said it defiantly, because it was the truth. The distance between herself and Lizzie widened with every word.

'How do you know it's wrong? What if it's right? Perhaps you shouldn't interfere, Liz. Of course I'll look after Sock. Any time you want me to, I will.'

James was at a conference and Lizzie was going to London, summoned at a day's notice by her agent to try for a role in a new television serial. She had told Jess, 'It's a peach of a part. A real proper grown-up woman with wrinkles and quandaries. I've got to get it.' And Jess had responded, as she would, 'Of course you must. I've got a couple of days off due to me because I did extra before Christmas, I'll take them now.'

As a result, Sock and all his requirements for a forty-eight-hour stay were piled in the hall. But Lizzie was hesitating, clearly wondering if her sister's home was after all a place of safety for her baby.

'Don't worry. I'll look after him as if he's my own.'

The bitterness of this caught at them both.

'This is awful. I don't mean anything,' Lizzie mumbled. 'I just don't want you to be hurt any more.'

'I know you don't.'

'Be friends?'

'We are. We haven't quarrelled.' Jess was afraid that what had happened went deeper than a quarrel. The sisters stiffly hugged each other, trying to generate what had always been instinctive.

'Go for the part, don't worry about Sock.'

'Okay, don't give him too much Ribena.'

'You warned me about that already.'

After Lizzie had gone Jess took the baby out for a walk. She pushed him, still asleep in his buggy, along a side-road to a point where a high-backed bridge humped over a canal. She aimed the buggy down the steep slope to the towpath, letting the weight of it briefly pull at her arms.

She had not been down here for years, but the scenery was entirely familiar. Tufts of frostbitten grass and dead stalks snagged the pushchair wheels as she walked, and colourless puddles holed the muddy core of the path. A line of starlings perched on a wire fence, before flurrying upwards as she drew level with them.

She had regularly brought Beth down here for walks when she was a baby, sometimes on her own and sometimes with two or three other young mothers. She had lost touch with all those women now their children were grown-up and there were no more sandpit excursions or school parents' evenings to bring them together. Ahead, Jess knew, under another bridge and around a bend, the canal widened into a basin. There would be an untidy flotilla of narrowboats undergoing renovation and peeling cabin cruisers with drawn window curtains and hopeless, semi-submerged barges with oil-slicked stagnant water in the bilges. And when she turned the corner Jess saw that the view was, indeed, almost unchanged. A pair of moorhens busily skidded away from her across the water.

Sock had woken up. He rolled his head and caught sight of the moorhens dragging their V-shaped wakes behind them.

'Duck,' he said. He waved at them, rotating his mittened hand from the wrist.

This baby gesture reminded her so much of Danny that Jess stopped walking, bending her head and hunching her shoulders to accommodate the pain. The hurt had a pervasiveness that broke down the dimensions of time; the roundness of Sock's head in his bobble hat and the resistance of the hooked buggy handles and the smell of oil and water brought back the long-ago afternoons so vividly that Jess slipped out of the present moment and became the woman she had been then. Each step she had taken had been an effort to contain her feelings. Every forward glance, an attempt to narrow her horizons. She was a woman in love with a man who wasn't her husband. She knew all over again the wild beating of longing kept inside a box of silence and denial.

'Duck,' Sock said again, conversationally.

'That's right. Little black ducks, aren't they?'

There was a bench set back from the towpath on its own puddled semicircle of bare earth. The wood was scrawled over with black graffiti, *Zoe 4 Mick* and *Karen is a slag*. Jess sat down on it, swinging the buggy round so she could look at Sock's profile. His boneless button of a nose was pink with cold but the rest of him was warm in his zipper suit. Jess leaned back and stared unseeingly at the reflections in the canal water.

She had met Tonio in Italy.

Ian and she had been on holiday there, the summer that Beth was a year old. They stayed in a quiet *pensione* overlooking a cream-coloured square where the window shutters had faded to a sun-blistered amalgam of green and grey. The ample widowed *signora* who owned the *pensione* had a pert, confident teenaged daughter, and one of the mother's ambitions was for her daughter to learn to speak good English and get a management job in one of the big hotels in Venice or Rome. And so Tonio Fornasi came three times a week to exchange English conversation with Vittoria and correct her grammar and vocabulary. Jess remembered the first time she saw him: he was standing in the narrow foyer of the *pensione* with Vittoria flirtatiously hanging on to his arm. He was wearing a navy and white striped T-shirt with a hole in one sleeve, loose trousers with a drawstring tie and sandy espadrilles; his habitual outfit, as Jess was to learn. His hair was so black that it looked blue; his face and arms were deeply tanned as if he worked out of doors. Jess's first assumption was that he was one of the fishermen who worked out of the tiny harbour below the square.

'So Viti,' he was saying, 'learn the words I've written down for you, and practise them. Try them out on your mother's guests here.'

He had smiled across at Jess, who was staring at him for no reason, yet, except the broadness of his Irish accent.

'Hello there,' he grinned as he passed them on his way out into the evening sunshine.

The next day, in the evening *passeggiata*, they saw Tonio sitting at a café table with a drink and a closed book in front of him. He lifted his hand to greet them. Beth tottered towards him and fell over the bag at his feet.

'Join me, why not?' he asked, when they had picked her up and stopped her wails.

The day after that he came with them to the beach. Over lunch in the little café where everyone knew him, Tonio told them that his Irish mother had met his Italian father before the war, when she had been brought by an aunt to see the paintings and frescoes in Florence.

'That was it. There in front of the Baptistry doors, love at first sight.'

Brigid Doherty returned to Florence in 1938 to marry her Italian love. He was killed in the fighting against the Eighth Army in Tunisia in 1943, and after the war Brigid took their son back home to Cork.

'There I stayed until I was eighteen and went to Trinity. And since then I've been here and there. All kinds of places, let me tell you.'

It was his history that touched the first chord in Jess, although it was not just the romantic story or even Tonio's embroideries on it that woke her up to him. It was more that listening to Tonio, and talking to him, peeled and sharpened Jess's awareness of a world she was missing. And he listened to her, when Ian stopped talking about his work and ambitions, as if there were no other words in the universe.

At the end of the day on the beach he shook Ian's hand and kissed the tips of Jess's fingers. The humorous curl of his mouth made the gesture a parody but the intention of it remained. With a sense of shock that tightened her scalp over her skull, Jess looked into Tonio's black-coffee eyes.

'I have to teach all day tomorrow,' he said. 'Perhaps we'll meet the day after, when I come to see Vittoria.'

It was a statement, not a question.

When the day after came, it happened that Ian was suffering from too much sunshine. In the early evening he lay down and covered his reddened skin with the cool bedsheet, closing his eyes against the light. Beth lay fast asleep in the cot at the foot of the bed.

'Can I do anything to make you more comfortable?' Jess fretted.

'Just leave me in peace,' he moaned.

She put on a pale-green dress and loosely pinned up her hair. The mirror in the tiny bathroom beckoned her but she stopped herself looking in it. It did not – should not – matter what she looked like.

Ian lay on his side with his back to her, feigning sleep. She touched his shoulder gently, wanting to say something to draw them closer. But he didn't move and Jess slipped out of the bedroom and down the shallow stone stairs of the *pensione*. And as she had known he would be, Tonio was waiting for her.

'The poor man,' he said lightly, when she told him about Ian. He extended his arm to her. 'So, shall we go?'

As she walked out on Tonio's arm, Vittoria glowered at them. Jess felt as if her eyes and ears had been cleared and her tongue untied. With her sharpened eyesight she saw how the street glowed with busy warmth; every window offered a tableau and every cranny of the little town contained a story. It was invigorating to find herself a part of it with Tonio.

Tonio took her to a tiny restaurant and fed her *spaghetti alla vongole* and dark-red Tuscan wine. She ate as if she was starving. He looked at her in her thin green dress and at the way strands of her hair lay over the skin of her throat.

'You are very young to be a mother already,' Tonio said.

'I'm twenty-two. It's not so young.'

He tilted his head on one side. 'And are you happy?'

'Of course I am.' Too quickly.

'Of course?'

After the challenge he waited. Jess bent her head and turned her wine glass in spirals on the tablecloth. It was her own doing, she knew that. She had married Ian; he had not turned into anyone different once the rings were on their fingers. It was Jess herself who had changed. She had wished for security, for a child, and as soon as they were hers she had felt locked in by them. It was not that she was unhappy, more that she was left gazing at unfolding perspectives that she couldn't now reach. These possibilities seemed as intricate and as untouchable as a Chinese paper flower blossoming underwater.

Yet everything she had done she had done voluntarily. She kept herself busy with the effort of containment and compromise.

'I have a beautiful daughter. I love her very much.'

'I see that.'

But she did not love her husband. The months of their marriage, too much intimacy and too little, had made her aware of it. She didn't think Ian knew, but there was a hollowness between them that left him confused. And in his confusion he became angry.

Now, in Tonio's company, Jess felt unbalanced. It was like standing on the brink of a precipice, fearing and longing to pitch forward into the windy abyss.

Tonio took out his money to pay their bill and counted out crumpled 500-lire notes. At a glance Jess saw that there would either not be enough or he would have nothing left, and lightly insisted on paying. His acceptance revealed another truth about him to add to her store; he had no money and the lack of it did not concern him.

They walked back through the velvet night to the *pensione*. Looking up, Jess saw that Ian's bedroom window was dark behind the shutters.

'Do you truly have to go home on Saturday?' Tonio asked. His mouth was an inch too close to hers.

Jess allowed herself to think, longingly. It was the middle of

September and the season was nearly over. Already the *pensione* was emptying out. At home Ian worked long hours; Beth loved the beach and the sunshine.

She heard herself say, 'If I could change my flight maybe Beth and I could stay on a few days longer.'

'That would be a fine thing.'

He didn't touch her, only smiled so she saw the whiteness in the dark. After a minute he stepped back, leaving the space of air between them, and strolled away.

*I only said maybe,* Jess thought, as she went slowly up the stairs. In the bedroom Ian and Beth were both fast asleep, lying in the same position, legs wide and arms flung out.

Jess remembered how it had been. Her grief and her recollections of this place and Sock's presence all put her back inside her earlier self.

After a year had gone by she found herself walking along the towpath with another baby in his pushchair and Beth toddling beside her, hand to the hem of her mother's skirt, eyes fixed distrustfully on the canal as if it might suddenly rise up and engulf her. Beth was always frightened of falling in and she steered a cautious route on the side of the path well away from the dun-coloured water.

After the walk Jess would go home to the house she shared with Ian and make tea and bath the children and talk to her husband, and day by day she would get more used to the deliberately narrow focus and the containment of her feelings. This was her choice.

The restrained pattern of her life did not weave or flower around Tonio. She was doing what she imagined to be right, even though the mere thought of the alternative made her heart knock against her ribs.

And in order to keep on doing what was right, the business of expressing longing and venting feelings somehow became what other people, like her sister Lizzie, did, while Jess protected and supported and – she supposed – lived a sort of vicarious life through them.

'How sad and pale. How *wasteful* of me,' Jess said aloud. She thought, as she had begun to lately, that she had tried to do what was right, only to discover that it was wrong.

Somehow, with the best intentions, she had failed her children. Until only a few days ago she might have argued that at least she had done well by Danny by giving him everything she had. Only now it seemed that everything was much too much, in a way that she would probably never quite be able to fathom or measure or put right, because he was dead. The sadness of it made the other failures, of her marriage and her understanding of Beth, seem diminished and drained by comparison.

The baby turned his head to look at her. It was now, not then. This was Sock, not Danny, and Beth was on the other side of the world, not clinging to her skirt.

Sock stuck out his legs and began to strain in his straps, twisting his head. Jess recognised the warning signs and jumped up from the bench.

'Come on, let's go back home, shall we? Let's see what we can do.' She began to push, walking fast so the wintry grass swished against her legs.

By the time she reached the end of her road the baby was rigid, and already crimson in the face with yelling.

Then Jess saw, as if they had rehearsed it, that Rob was waiting outside her door.

He was sitting on her front path, his back against the fence and his knees drawn up. He was tossing gravel chips, making a deft flick of his wrist each time, at a beer can lying in the gutter beyond the gate.

The mere sight of him made her fears seem absurd, but she had been imagining that he had disappeared or died. The ordinary continuity of life seemed so precarious after Danny's death that Jess was full of terrors for everyone she cared for. It was only her own existence that went grinding inexorably onwards.

Relief at the sight of Rob washed through her, but it was grained with irritation at his casualness, at the truculent look he shot up at her, even at his bony wrists. She stopped in front of him, so that Sock's contorted red face was on a level with his.

'Christ, what a noise.' Rob scowled.

'He's hungry and thirsty. If you can't handle it you know what you can do,' Jess snapped.

She trundled the buggy on up to the step and groped for her keys. Rob scrambled to his feet and lifted the buggy into the house for her. Jess carried the howling baby into the kitchen, found his spouted cup and filled it with water. She put it up to his wide-open mouth but Sock flung it away from him and gathered his breath for louder screams.

'For God's sake,' she muttered.

The Ribena bottle was at the bottom of his bag of supplies. Jess dug for it one-handed until Rob hoisted the baby away and awkwardly rocked him as she mixed the drink. Between them they got the spout into his mouth and the noise abruptly stopped. Sock sucked between shuddering sobs and his eyes fell shut.

Rob and Jess supported the bundle of him between them. Jess reached for a banana and unpeeled it so that as soon as Sock's thirst was quenched she could plug it into his mouth.

It struck them both at the same moment that they made a picture of a dissonant family. They looked at each other and Jess began to laugh, then Rob was laughing too. She set the miraculously restored Sock on his feet and he stumped away, greedily mashing banana into his mouth.

They stopped laughing and Rob took Jess by the arms and held her face in his hands. He lowered his head and kissed her, hard, his teeth biting and bruising the soft tissue of her mouth. Weakly Jess clung to him, her irrational anger burnt up by greedy longing.

At last she drew back her head so she could see his face.

'Where have you been?' she whispered.

Sock found the saucepan cupboard. He pitched the pans on the floor and turned a banana-smeared smile on them.

'What are doing? Naughty boy,' he chortled rhetorically.

'I didn't know whether to come or stay away.'

'I was afraid. I thought . . . I thought you were dead, too.'

He looked straight into her eyes. 'I worked that out. Not soon enough but I did. I'd have gone on waiting outside until you came, however long it took.'

Jess nodded. 'Don't go.'

'I'm not going.'

Rob's mouth travelled over her face. His thumbs pressed into her cheeks and his fingers tangled in her hair. She had forgotten Sock before a new wail began.

'What's the matter with the little fucker now?' Rob groaned.

'He's a baby. It's what they're like.'

'Where's your sister?'

'Gone to London for two days. I've taken some time off to look after him.'

'Hmm. Good news and bad news. Why couldn't she take the blob with her?'

'Because she couldn't. He's not a blob.'

Unwillingly they relinquished each other and Rob bent down to put his face close to Sock's. The child stopped in mid-yell and stared back, round-eyed.

'That's better,' Rob said to him seriously.

'Man,' Sock answered.

'You bet your life.'

'Just watch him while I make his tea, will you?' Jess ordered. Rob hoisted the baby up and wandered into the next room. When Jess found them again Rob was sitting on the sofa watching the television, with Sock straddled on his chest. Jess thought, they're more the same generation than Rob and I. They could easily be brothers. They could both be my kids. Instead of Danny. Danny is gone.

Rob saw her face. He swung Sock under his arm and came to her. 'It's okay,' he said.

'Is it?'

'No. But it is how it is. We can help each other, can't we?'

Again, the seductiveness of the notion. Wearily Jess tried, and failed, to unravel her feelings. Rob seemed to blot out the light so she couldn't examine them properly, but there was comfort in that too. And there was a burning ache inside her that he set off; she couldn't deny or ignore it.

'Yes, I suppose.'

'What have we got to do with him now?'

*We* made them the odd family again, mother and father and baby. Jess's mouth trembled, then pinched in an uncertain smile.

'Give him his supper, bath him and put him to bed.'

'And after that can we do the same for ourselves?'

'Yes.'

'Come on then, Blob.'

In the kitchen Jess watched him spoon mashed carrot into the soft triangle of Sock's mouth.

'You like babies, don't you?'

'I don't know any.'

He had no brothers and sisters; Rob had told her that much. She couldn't imagine him as a baby himself. There was a wary, too adult, contained quality about him.

He put his arm round her waist now and held her, feeding Sock one-handed. Gently Jess let her hand rest on his hair and stroked it. A reservoir of tenderness was tapped between them.

Beth stood at the window looking down the garden of her father's bungalow in the Sydney suburb. If she peered away to the left she could just see a narrow slice of one of the lobes of the middle harbour, but mostly the view consisted of the thick leaves of unfamiliar vegetation and the walls and tiled roofs of the neighbouring houses. The windowless blue-painted wall of the next-door house was only two metres to her right, over a low fence. Everything was very close together. The suburban bungalows rolled on for miles, up and down the hills around the harbour, each set in its tongue of garden. She had expected more space, more room to move and breathe.

Her eye was caught by the flickering dart of a lizard on the concrete patio as Michelle came round the corner of the house.

'Hi, honey.' Michelle smiled as she stepped in through the patio doors. She was a nursing supervisor in the accident and emergency department at the district hospital, and she was still wearing her white nurse's overall. She had sandy-blonde hair, tied in a prim plait for work, and a sun-freckled complexion. Her colouring, or perhaps something about the shape of her head, troublingly reminded Beth of her father. It was as if the second time around Ian had chosen a version of himself, rather than a copy of Jess. Nothing at all about Michelle was reminiscent of Jess.

'Hi. Busy night?' Beth asked politely.

'Not too bad. But I'm bushed now.'

Michelle kicked off her white rubber-soled shoes and sat down on the biscuit-coloured tweed sofa with a sigh of relief. Beth poured a cup of coffee and handed it to her.

'You're an angel. Thanks.'

The two women tried hard with one another, but proximity hadn't made them close. Beth felt like a grey-skinned intruder in the square, tidy white rooms, even when she went to ground with relief in the spare room across the passage from Ian's and Michelle's. And she missed Sam. Every time the telephone rang she willed it, with wild illogicality, to be him. But it was always one of Michelle's girlfriends making a date for tennis or to suggest they all came over for a barbie.

They heard Ian's station wagon drawing up at the front of the house. A minute later he came in with the newspapers and a brown bag of shopping.

'I'd have gone out for that, Dad,' Beth protested.

'I thought you were still asleep. Hello, darling.' He kissed his wife on the tip of her nose and tickled her cheek with the end of her plait. Beth gazed out at the coarse leaves of the tree that dappled the glare of the patio with a corner of welcome shade.

'What are you two doing today?' Michelle asked cheerfully, her wide grin clearly absorbing a yawn. She would have to sleep, of course, before the next night shift. Beth knew her irritation with her stepmother's wholesomeness was unfair, but a prickle of it ran up her spine just the same. Her father smiled heartily across at her.

'I thought we might take a drive up to one of the northern beaches. Since it's such a great day. Have a picnic, do some swimming. What do you think, Beth?'

Beth thought she couldn't bear another day of having the sun probe her eye-sockets and burn her brain-pan.

'I don't know. Don't feel you have to make an expedition for my sake, Dad.'

She knew they were exchanging exasperated glances. She hadn't been the most enthusiastic guest, although she had tried her best.

'Well, okay, if you don't want to do that. Perhaps we can just take a walk and have lunch by the harbour.'

'That sounds perfect. I'd really love to.' She had overdone the eagerness this time, but at least the day was settled. It had to be lived through, only in order to get to the next, and the one after. Beth pressed her mouth shut. *Sam. Sam, oh Jesus, Sam, why aren't you ever here with me?*

Beth walked with Ian on a narrow strip of shingle beach. Behind them a ferry nosed out of Manly and headed across the dazzling breadth of water towards the harbour bridge.

'I like having you to myself like this,' Ian attempted. 'Reminds me of when you were a tiny girl. You were always such a thoughtful little thing. Always looked before leaping.'

A bit of a weed, in other words, Beth silently translated. Scared before I knew what to be scared of.

Her father had eternally been her defender, loyally championing her against the noisy glamour of Danny. But it was always Jess's attention she had wanted to attract. Her mother's love was elusive, like Sam's. Ian confronted her with his, and with his bafflement and disappointment when she found herself unable exactly and explicitly to return it.

Beth put her arm through Ian's, deliberately pinching it against her ribs. She looked over the water at the sails of the yachts and windsurfers, and the crowded decks of the harbour tour boats, towards the distant green slopes of Double Bay dotted with the white cubes and towers of lovely homes. She thought, *Where the fuck am I and what am I doing here?*

Aloud she said, 'I love you, Dad.'

'I know you do.'

They came to the end of the crescent of beach and climbed some concrete steps in front of a parade of surf shops.

'How is your mum, do you think?'

Beth had spoken to her on the telephone two or three times since Christmas night. Jess had sounded odd. She had asked staccato questions and not listened to the answers, then her voice had trailed into silence as if something else commanded her attention.

*Nothing. Nothing's happening here*, she had insisted, when Beth had asked her.

'Grieving,' Beth said. 'It was the worst thing that could have happened to her. Losing Danny.'

'You or Danny, yes.'

*No*, Beth thought. But she kept the amendment to herself.

They reached a restaurant with tables set outside under a blue canopy. The menu promised the best fish in Sydney, as most of them did. The waiter who came over to take their order wore his longish black hair tied back in a pony-tail. He bore the most superficial resemblance to Danny. Since his death Beth was always seeing boys who looked like him. A greasy balloon of grief inflated itself in her stomach, smothering the vestiges of her appetite.

'Why did I always look before leaping?'

Ian turned the ruddy width of his face towards her, startled by the edge in her voice.

'Were we always so different, Danny and me?'

'You were different for me. You came first, you made the biggest change to my life. I remember I used to tiptoe upstairs when you were asleep to check that you were still breathing. Like a little hedgehog under the cot sheet. Your mother didn't; she always knew you were breathing.

'You were a careful little girl, I meant. Clever and wary. I always thought you were checking me out before loving me, to make sure I deserved it. Does that sound ridiculous to you?'

'No.'

He was right. Jess and Danny took her adoration without thinking.

'Danny never considered anything of the kind.' Ian echoed her thoughts. 'I suppose Jess gave him that arrogance. I used to think sometimes she loved him indecently.'

He added quickly, his face reddening further, 'Not that way, I don't mean like that. But too nakedly, somehow. Over-eagerly.'

'I know.' Beth bent her head. A plate of food was put in front of her as she listened to her father talking about her childhood, over which innocent days a darker, coarser patina was being laid. She picked up her knife and fork, dissected white strips of fish from the springy bones and rearranged them under the vegetables at the side of the plate. She was thinking that it was just that intense way Jess had loved Danny that she had longed for herself. Ian must have wanted it too. The lack of it would have undermined her parents' marriage.

The food was taken away at last. She had made it look as if she had eaten some of it.

Ian sat sideways in his chair and hummed a couple of meaningless notes; it was his way of announcing a difficult topic.

'You don't much like Michelle, do you?'

'Of course I do. I think she's great.'

'She's great for me.' He said it firmly, and gratefully.

He remembered the first time he'd seen her. She had been sitting at her keyboard in the general office, the sandy gold of her hair like a sunny halo in the gloom. She had the broad shoulders of a swimmer and a smile that was wide enough to include the rest of the room as well as him.

'Who's she?' he asked the office manager.

'Temp wp operator. Not bad,' was the ambiguous answer.

It was a week before he spoke to her, and a month before he saw her outside the office. There was a night when some of the secretaries came to the leaving party for one of Ian's salesmen. Michelle was amongst them. Jess would have recoiled from the raucous atmosphere, but Michelle pitched straight in as if she belonged there.

'I'll have a beer, thanks,' she said in answer to Ian's question. 'Or better make that two, save pissing about.' She told him that she had trained as a trauma nurse in Sydney. She was taking a long break from the rigours of the job and working her way round Europe.

'How long are you staying here?' he asked. The question took on a level of significance unimaginable an hour before.

Michelle grinned, and shrugged. 'How long's a piece of string? Actually, I'm thinking of moving on soon.'

The threat determined him. 'Have dinner with me before you do?'

She had given him a hard look, then nodded. 'Yeah. Why not? Thursday good for you?'

There was a directness about her that he loved from the beginning. Michelle knew her own value and was a shrewd judge of other people's. She worked out what she wanted in life and wasted no energy in wishing for what she could not have. As she said to him later, 'Doing the job I do, you learn there's no point pussying around. Tomorrow may be too late.'

He told Jess he was working and took Michelle to a country-house hotel for an elaborate dinner.

Over the *feuilleté* of wild mushrooms she said to him, 'I know you're married, Ian. What's the game plan with me?'

For his previous affairs the answer would have been simple, although he would never have stated it. An interval, discreetly managed, lasting perhaps a year. Midweek nights in hotel bedrooms, occasional longer trips together. Before anything became stale or threatened to grow beyond manageable limits, a regretful break. Ian usually picked married women who had plenty to lose if their secrets were discovered. But he knew from that evening onwards that Michelle was different.

'I don't know,' he answered humbly. 'I don't have a game plan.'

'I see.'

He had booked a room upstairs, but he didn't even try to corner her in it that night. Instead he drove her home to her shared flat, and fantasised for days afterwards about what it would have been like to have her under the canopy of the creaking four-poster bed, and on the glass-topped table with its brochures for similar hotels elsewhere in the Midlands, and in the mirror-and-marble-lined bathroom amongst the complimentary shampoos and bath gels.

It was Michelle who called him.

'So?' There was a teasing challenge in her voice.

'So I'll see you this evening.' He tried to match her.

This time they did go to bed.

Michelle's undressed body astounded him with its glow and its firmness. She showed him how she liked to have her hands and ankles tied with the towelling belt of her bathrobe, and to have her luscious bottom mildly striped with the belt from his trousers. She also showed a liberating disregard for what her flatmate might be thinking on the other side of the thin partition wall.

She sat astride him, rocking her hips, her mouth curved in a sweetly triumphant smile. 'We're just having fun. Everybody does it; you poms just like to pretend otherwise.'

'Why me?' he kept murmuring afterwards, his lips against her ear. 'Why do I deserve you?'

Michelle became serious for a moment. Their faces were pressed together and her wide eyes squinted as she gazed into his. She stroked his hair with the tips of her fingers.

'You're a good bloke, Ian. I don't think you're very happy, are you?'

'I don't know,' he lied.

After that came the acknowledgement and the separation. Michelle was what Ian wanted. He knew her and understood her and she held nothing back from him. Whereas Jess was opaque; she had evaded him for so long that he hardly knew her. Even in bed they avoided one another, allowing their touching only to follow a ritual that minimised the possibility of sudden pain. Their retreat through recrimination into bitterness into separation and then divorce had such an inevitability that it was like stepping through the formal measures of a dance. Michelle remained in Ditchley and Ian moved in with her. It took two years for them to reach Sydney together. Ian knew how unhappy he had made his wife and family; he also felt there was nothing else he could have done.

Beth was staring out at the blue water and the jaunty scraps of sail belonging to windsurfers and dinghies. All the resentment that she had kept pinned down through her visit suddenly swept up inside her. Ian was her father, Jess was her mother. They belonged together. Michelle was an outsider, an orthodontically overpowering interloper who reflected Ian's own face back at him. Blotting out Jess's, and all their joint history, and replacing it with tennis and beers and bloody barbecues at the beach.

'You belong with Mum,' she blurted out, too loudly. The couple at the next table swivelled their heads. 'For me you do still. With us. You say I made the biggest change but you still went and left me, didn't you?'

She wanted to leap up and load her arms with ammunition, with cutlery and plates and bread rolls, and pelt him with them, hitting him and shouting out her buried hurt at his having abandoned her for Michelle.

*Like a kid*, she thought dazedly. *Like a kid having a tantrum. I'm nearly twenty-three. Why this, now?*

Ian put his hand over hers. The fine hairs on the backs of his knuckles and the patches of freckles beginning to merge together were so familiar, so nearly but not quite reassuring.

'I was married to Jess, not you. I'm your father, not hers. I wanted to change the first; nothing in the world will ever change the second.'

'That's all *shit*,' Beth shouted at him.

Now the waiter who looked a little bit like Danny turned to peer at them. Tears rolled out under the rims of Beth's sunglasses and slid down her face. Ian left his chair and came round to her. He squeezed her shoulders and stroked her hair.

'It's grief,' he whispered to her. 'Just grief. I feel it too, only it comes on me differently. I want to swear and punch holes in people.'

'Do you?'

'Of course. Of course I do. I miss him so much. I loved him as much as you and Jess did. He was my son, my boy.'

Beth tried to stop her tears. Ian and she might as well have been invisible now, so tactfully and intently had the waiters and the other diners begun to ignore them.

'I'm sorry,' she managed to say. 'I'm selfish.'

But she was thinking, *My son, my boy*?

She looked through the altered patination of her life into the grain of the past, and a rogue cell of doubt seeded itself in the established tissue of her belief. It took root and began to divide and redivide.

'Sit down again,' she whispered gently to her father. 'I'm sorry to make a scene. You're right, it's probably nothing really to do with Michelle.'

Ian took his seat again with relief. He ordered coffees, and two brandies that he wanted and Beth did not. Looking at his daughter with the comforting fume of the spirit at the back of his throat he saw her tight mouth and hungry eyes. Clumsily, but wanting to reach out and touch her with something, he said, 'You need someone, love. I wish there were someone over there to look after you for me. Some decent bloke.'

Beth lifted her head, stared through him. 'Don't worry about me. I don't need anyone. But someone will turn up, just the same. They always do, don't they?'

He did not understand that her optimism was unfounded; he only knew that something in it touched him deeply.

He mumbled awkwardly, aware of his inarticulacy, 'You deserve to be happy. If anyone does, Beth, you do.'

# Nine

The court anteroom was sour with the press of too many people and their apprehensive sweat and cigarette smoke. The tiled floor was littered and dirty and the rows of seats were all occupied. The noise of anxious conversations and whispered consultations made a dull commotion over which the ushers shouted names to summon offenders before the bench.

Rob sat and stared at the floor. From time to time Jess stood up and went outside for a few breaths of fresher air, but Rob didn't stir.

The solicitor, Michael Blake, had another client listed, charged with taking and driving away, and he wove between Rob and the other boy and his family, apparently impervious to the noise and overcrowding.

'Is it always like this?' Jess asked him. She had immediately warmed to Michael Blake when he hid his amazement at the sight of her with Rob. He shook her hand and politely made no comment.

'Invariably. You get used to it, if you're unlucky.'

He opened his battered briefcase and frowned at a sheaf of papers including Rob's legal-aid forms. The three of them were sharing a row of bolted-together plastic chairs with a pair of teenage Rastafarians and their voluminous mothers, one of whom was shouting incoherently at a portly and unimpressed solicitor.

Michael explained to Rob, 'Your legal aid's in place now, which means we can get on with preparing the defence. Once the committal date's set we can push to get the papers from the prosecution, and as soon as I've had a chance to look at the forensic we'll have a better idea of whether to maintain that it was an accident or to settle for a plea of careless driving.'

'It was an accident,' Rob repeated. He didn't glance up.

Michael Blake could not help turning a look on Jess. He had taken off his suit coat and slung it over the back of his chair, revealing sweat rings in the armpits of his shirt. Jess had washed and ironed a shirt for Rob and insisted that he wore a tie. He had shrugged and capitulated, but her efforts had been misplaced. Everyone else was routinely scruffy and Rob looked as if he was trying too hard to please.

Under the solicitor's scrutiny Jess felt bizarrely partisan. She was on the wrong side for the bereaved mother. Her place was behind the prosecution, but her awareness of it only made her more determined to protect Rob. Danny's death had been an accident. How could she be here otherwise, if she were not convinced of it?

'It could only have been an accident,' she said. Her voice was low, so that Michael had to lean forward to catch the words against the mountainous woman's ranting.

'Is that why you are here, Mrs Arrowsmith?' he asked.

'I'm here because Rob asked me to be.'

It was true. 'Please come to the court with me,' he had begged her. And she had promised him, 'Of course I will.'

'I see.'

'Robert Ellis?'

The usher had emerged from the door to the court. He consulted a list and roared Rob's name again.

'Let's go,' Michael said.

After the long wait it was the briefest appearance. The bald charge, of causing death by careless driving while under the influence of drink, was read out. Rob looked down at the ground and Jess watched the back of his head. The solicitor for the prosecution requested a committal before the Crown

Court in six weeks' time. The magistrates conferred briefly behind their spectacles. A committal date was set and Rob was remanded on bail with the condition that he sleep every night at his home address.

The magistrate regarded him across the bench. Jess felt an extraordinary sensation, the hairs of her neck and spine standing up as if she were a mother animal defending her cub.

It had been an accident. Nothing, none of this, would bring Danny back.

'If you do not comply with this order, Mr Ellis, you will be in breach of bail and liable to be remanded in custody. Do you understand that? Mr Blake, will you make sure that your client understands me? Thank you.'

They were dismissed. Jess stood up and followed Rob and Michael out into the anteroom. The next case up was the Rastafarians.

The noise and overcrowding outside the court were, if anything, more intense.

Michael Blake looked satisfied. 'No secondary charges,' he said.

'Why?' It was Jess who asked.

'Lack of evidence, I imagine. Or charges withdrawn.'

Danny's girl and her friend must have decided, or been advised, not to press any charge of assault.

Rob thought of Cat for the first time that day and found himself wondering if she had put the little picture up yet on the wall of her room. He imagined how she would search in her perspex boxes and jewellery tray for a drawing pin and press it into the wall and string the picture on it, and how the pin would then pull out while she was standing back with her head on one side to judge the effect. The picture would fall face down on her bedcover and she would mutter '*Fuck*' and begin to hunt for a proper nail. When she found one she would hammer it in with her shoe.

The anteroom and the lawyers and defendants and the smell of tension grew doubly ugly and repellent.

Danny's mother touched his arm.

'Can't we go?' Rob snapped.

Outside, on the steps, they hesitated before the arterial current of heavy traffic heading towards the bypass. It was a windy day and rags of newsprint and balloons of plastic bags whirled overhead.

'About the conditions of bail,' Jess began. She had to raise her voice and turn aside from the road to make herself heard. Over the last two weeks Rob had spent almost every night at her house.

'Yes,' Michael Blake said. 'Do you want to help Rob?'

Again Jess felt the incongruity of her position. She did not need to explain it; she guessed the solicitor was more than shrewd enough to have deduced it for himself.

'Of course I do. Couldn't we tell the police that he is living with me?'

Rob stood between them. The gritty wind had made his eyes water. Jess knew that she was clumsy but she wanted to define what they were allowed to do.

'I wouldn't advise that,' Michael said.

'Why?'

'It would be useful, when the case comes before the judge, if you were to make a brief plea to the jury on Rob's behalf. To say, as Danny's mother, that you would not wish further unnecessary pain to result from what you believe to have been an accident. If that is what you do feel, of course. But the effect might be diminished if the court were to understand that there is, ah, perhaps another dimension to your relationship.'

'That we are lovers.'

It was Rob who said it. The plain statement of fact without embarrassment or prevarication seemed to Jess to be extraordinarily gallant, and immediately she thought that gallant was the oddest word to apply to Rob. He was plain, not ornate, lacking the guile for calculated gallantry. Standing in a huddle in the ugly street she was granted a momentary perspective of the infinitely different constructions and configurations of love.

She was bewildered by it and at the same time reassured. To try to define it or even analyse it for herself was senseless. The absence of it left by Danny had been partly filled by the presence of it with Rob. That was all. No more complicated than that and yet, she thought dizzily, how momentous.

Then, as quickly as it had come, the understanding was gone. But a confused, defiant kind of happiness stayed with her. She shifted, realigning herself between the two men, so that she stood close to Rob.

'It doesn't matter. You can stay at my place,' he said to her. He was pale-faced, ill-looking, but there was a defiance that matched her own. And to Michael he added, 'It's nothing to do with anyone but us. We don't have to defend or explain ourselves, do we?'

'Of course not,' the solicitor said suavely. 'The magistrate just asked me to be sure that you understood the conditions of bail.'

He shook hands with Jess and Rob. 'I'll be in touch.' Then he walked away towards the car-park behind the court.

'Pompous cunt,' Rob said.

'Just doing his job.'

'Let's walk somewhere for a bit. I don't want to be inside.'

They set off parallel to the stream of traffic, heads down against the stinging wind. The January cold was mean and sharp, and as they moved across the backdrop of a giant advertisement hoarding depicting Father Christmas and his reindeer and sleigh, and a sack spilling electrical goods from the discount store on the nearby trading estate, Jess suddenly longed for warmth and abundance. To be where there was no rain or frost, under blue skies, with the splashy leaves of a fig tree to shade her from the sun. The idea was so remote from this reality and so unattainable it almost made her laugh out loud.

She looked at Rob and saw the tight set of his mouth and the pallor of his skin showing up a crescent of reddish bristles the razor had missed.

'Are you all right?'

He shook his head: one sharp jerk. 'I hated that. That place. Waiting. The smell of it. It makes me remember.'

'Remember what?'

He ignored the question. 'They're going to put me inside.'

'No.'

'Five years, max, that's what the law said. I know I did it, I know Danny's dead but I don't want to go to prison. Jesus.'

He put his hand up to his mouth. He was wild-eyed, and his pallor had turned greenish, as if he might be going to vomit. Jess remembered the protective rush she had felt in court. He was more vulnerable then she knew. We can help each other, she thought. He had told her that much.

She took his arm. His hand was absolutely cold. 'Come on. I won't let you go to prison.' It was like saying to Beth, *I won't let you fall in the water*. 'Walk. Keep warm. Talk to me about it. What is it you remember?'

'Court. My mother took out a restraining order against my father. I must have been eight, or something. The magistrate looked the same as that bloke today. The smell was the same. I remember sitting in a side room with some biscuits on a plate and being asked questions and hating him and wanting to cover up for him at the same time. He was all right when he wasn't pissed. Not that that was often.'

They had turned off the main road and walked the length of a street lined with small shops, most of them closed and boarded up.

'What happened?'

He turned to stare down at her.

'What?'

She saw that he was absorbed in contemplating the spectres within his own head. On the corner of the street there was a lit-up window. As they came closer Jess saw that it was a café with lanterns in the window and red curtains, the brightness of it looked optimistic in the barren landscape. The promise of warmth made her realise she was shivering with cold.

'Come in here. Get a hot drink. We can't go on walking the streets.'

There was a group of painters in spattered white overalls at one table, a pair of pensioners at another, some middle-aged women – enough people for their conversation not to be overheard. She steered Rob to a table and ordered coffee and eggs and toast.

'Tell me what you remember,' she said again.

His mouth had loosened, lost its definition. The words came out of it, surprising him.

He remembered lying in bed. There was a front room and a back room, and in the back room were his parents' bed and his own, a mattress wedged between the foot of the big bed and the wall. There was a landscape of imaginary continents and archipelagos contained in the peeling patches and remaining pattern of the wallpaper, picked out by the street light shining through a gap in the curtains. He would lie still under the covers, mapping the territory in his imagination.

There were often arguments in the front room, in this streetlight time when he was supposed to be asleep. He could hear them clearly; the shouting was a counter-theme to his numb explorations of the wallpaper country.

'Your dad had a few drinks,' his mother would lamely explain. 'It's the way it takes him.'

'I wish it didn't.'

'I know that. I wish it as well, Robbie.'

This night was different. Obsessively thinking back over it later, at the Purses' or in the children's home or wherever else he happened to be, Rob fixed on this night as the beginning of the worst time. He heard the shouting and then his mother whimpering.

'Don't, Tommy. Ah Tommy, no.'

And another noise. A defensive clatter followed by a thump, the sickening unreverberative sound of something hard hitting something soft that absorbed the impact into itself. It took him a moment to work out that the soft thing was his mother. He heard the sound of another blow. The instant's quiet that followed was far worse than the shouting.

Rob pushed back the covers and squirmed out of bed. He stood up, and in the cold room he felt spindly and afraid. But he ran out of the bedroom and hesitated by the front room. He could hear his mother crying now, so he threw open the door. She was sitting on the brown leatherette sofa in front of the television, one hand to her face and the other crossed over her chest.

His father stood over her. His big arms with clenched fists looked like fleshy hammers. He turned his head slowly to Rob, and his eyes focused like red darts in the bristly grey and purple slab of his face.

'What are you fucking doing? Eh? Who asked you in here?'

'Tommy, not the boy. Leave him alone.'

She removed her hand from her jaw and Rob saw that the corner of her mouth was puffed and bleeding and her eye was half-closed around a reddish swelling.

'Don't hurt my mum.'

But he was already retreating, taking steps backwards away from his father. He remembered thinking how huge the man was, thick-shouldered and wide-legged with a belly that hung over the waistline of his low-slung trousers. Rob could smell his breath. By the time he was backed against the wall Rob was whimpering exactly as his mother had done.

His father hit him across the side of the head. His skull struck the door frame and the impact made noise blaze in his ears as the pain broke through his terror. Rob slid downwards until he was sitting in a heap against the wall.

'You keep your snotty little snout out of what isn't your business.'

Tottering in a semicircle and almost falling over, Tommy turned back to confront his wife. He recovered himself and wagged a thick finger at her.

'The pair of you, you make me puke. I'm getting out of here. But don't think I won't be back. Don't you think that, for one second, you bitch. Stinking bitch. I do what I want, I do. Nobody tells me what.'

He was heading for the door now. He made a kind of zigzag rush towards it. Rob sank further into himself, protecting his head with his arms. His father tried to kick him aside, but missed. Rob rolled away and crawled to his mother, reaching her as the door slammed shut.

'He's gone,' his mother whispered. 'He's gone for now.'

Rob brought a bowl with some hot water and Dettol, and a towel. He helped her to clean up her face but they didn't say much to each other. She seemed smaller, insubstantial, disfigured by the facial cuts and swellings so that she seemed barely to be the mother he knew. She examined the side of his head where the blow had connected, making him turn his jaw from side to side and nod his chin up and down. Her fingers lightly touched the bruise.

'I think it's all right,' she murmured. 'I think we'll both be all right.'

He kept quiet, not asking any of the questions that simmered inside him. He already knew that she couldn't or perhaps wouldn't give him the answers he deserved: that was how she was. She always seemed in the end to accept what Tommy meted out to her, and expected him to do likewise.

Afterwards they went to bed. There was a tiny bolt on the bedroom door and she slid it to. This minimal defence only made Rob think how easy it would be, with how little effort his father might kick the door and tear the screws from the splintery wood.

Without asking if it was allowed he curled up in his parents' bed, lying against the curve of his mother's back. Their positions made him think of a teaspoon and a tablespoon. His mother was wearing her old candlewick dressing-gown and he breathed in the grainy, sweetish scent of it.

After a while he became aware that his mother was crying. She was trying to keep it quiet and not to move, but he could tell just the same. He lifted his arm from his side and rested his hand on the ridged cottony material rucked over her hip. He stroked her, making little movements at first, then bigger ones that reached up her curved back to her hunched shoulder. He was struck by the bigness of her, the meaty swell of her buttocks and the width of her back. But at the same time she seemed hardly there, gone away from him, sucked into herself as she wept.

The feeling it gave him was unbearably complicated.

He wanted to kiss her and comfort her, he wanted her to stop crying and be herself, he wanted her not to need his reassurance but to turn round and offer him hers. And there was another disturbing feeling that was to do with the round swell of her and the rough-smooth texture of the candlewick under the flat of his hand. He did not even know what it was but it made him feel guilty and changed, as if he had stepped out of one version of himself and into another, and would never get the old one back again however much he longed for it.

It was a long time before he fell asleep.

The waitress brought the eggs and coffee. Rob was not hungry but he was terribly thirsty. He drank the coffee so quickly that it scalded the roof of his mouth.

'What happened?' Jess asked. She buttered a triangle of toast, pinching it in her strong fingers and rotating it briskly on the plate. He noticed again that she did not try to console him with ineffectual sympathy, or to reflect any of the import of his revelations back on to herself. She just listened and waited.

'My mother did try to do something. She was quite determined to begin with. She seemed to gather up her intentions as if she knew that it'd be too late if she left it any longer. We went off the next morning with a suitcase, a long way on the bus. To a big, smelly house with a garden that looked over some playing fields. There were a lot of women who sat around smoking, and kids crying.'

It had been a women's refuge. But Rob and his mother had only lasted there a week. She had hauled him and their suitcase back to the rooms again, complaining that she couldn't bear the lack of privacy in the refuge, or the rules. Tommy had been waiting for them, sober and full of contrition. Then, a week after that, there was another bout of drinking and shouting and Rob lay in his bed with his eyes on the shadowy continents, the fear of violence squeezing his heart and lungs until he could hardly breathe. He wasn't brave enough any longer to climb out of bed and try to intervene, and the shame of that added to his despair and disgust.

One bad night his father broke his mother's jaw in three places. He staggered out of the room and disappeared, and Rob did creep out of bed then. She was lying semi-conscious, half on and half off the leatherette sofa. He called an ambulance from the public call-box down in the street because their phone didn't work any longer.

While his mother was in hospital, Rob was placed with a short-term foster family. Not the Purses, yet, but not much better. It was bliss when he was finally returned home to his mother and the two rooms. But this time the police and social services were involved, and his mother was being persuaded to take reluctant legal action against his father. Rob remembered her weakly protesting, 'It's only when he's been drinking. He only does it when he's had a drink.'

His own feelings for his father had turned into a cold, fixed kernel of loathing anchored within a shell of terror. His fear of the sudden eruption of violence, the way it could spring red-hot from nowhere, became his strongest sense. He could understand how the same fear made his mother seem smaller than her real self. During that time she went on shrinking and withdrawing; when he touched her now to try to reassure or console her he was surprised that he had once found her big. He was determined that he would not be separated from her again.

There was the business with the court. It was something to do with restraining his father, and with a place of safety for himself. He remembered particularly the sonorous, reassuring rolling cadence of the words. A Place. Of Safety. He repeated them longingly to himself, but they did not deliver any such reality.

There were several interviews with kindly officials, who tried to make him explain his history and his feelings. Fear of his father and a bigger, unnameable fear of the unknown future tied his tongue. He denied as much as he could and when he did have to talk he mumbled, and hurried, and understated. He understood his mother. He felt closest to her then, when they got back to their rooms and were waiting in dread and longing for Tommy to reappear.

Rob stopped talking. His tongue felt as if it might stick to the roof of his mouth. Jess buttered toast, put it on a plate and pushed it towards him.

'Can't you eat something?' she asked.

He took one of the triangles and bit into it. 'That court-room. The smell and noise, smoky and sweaty and people shouting. It makes me remember. It makes me feel like I'm a terrified kid again.'

'I understand why you went so white.'

He looked across the table at her. She was calm, neither shocked nor pitying. It was a release to talk to her, and much more than that – there was a force field of attractions that pulled him to Jess, some of them straightforwardly to do with her strength and honesty, others that lay deeper within him, in a muzzy buried core that responded to scents and skin textures, and half-spoken endearments, and hands that covered his ears and cradled his head. As he thought of these things he put his fingers on Jess's sleeve and stroked it. She was wearing a dark-red jacket in some sort of chenille yarn. And as his fingers smoothed the nubbly surface a current flowed up his arm. It spread like a shock to his shoulders and stomach, and made the blood roar in his head.

At the same instant he saw that she felt the current too. Her eyes widened and her mouth opened a little, so he saw the red inside of her lip and a glint of saliva.

His fears and the memories and associations from the past turned inside out to reveal a new set of imperatives.

Danny's mother. Rob longed equally for oblivion and the fierceness of gratification. As Jess did too. As he stared at her in the café he thought he knew her as well as he did himself and it was only an accident of physical configuration that kept them divided.

'Let's go,' Rob said in a low voice. 'Let's go home now.'

The house was cool, almost chilly, and utterly silent.

Jess double-locked the door behind them. All the way back they had not touched each other, not even brushing hands. But now they fell together. They were rough, clawing with their fingers and brutally kissing the cold skin that the wind had touched. They were both gasping for breath.

Rob took hold of her hand. He pulled her up the stairs, both of them stumbling, bumping against the walls in their haste. The bedroom looked chaste with the covers drawn up smooth and the flat winter's-afternoon light draining the colours to shades of grey and brown. Jess pulled the curtains haphazardly together to shield them from whatever lay outside.

When she turned back to the room they hesitated another instant. Their faces swam together in the grey shadow. Then they pulled off their own clothes, in too much haste to do it for each other.

When he was naked Rob reminded her of how he had looked in the hospital, in the waiting room, the first time she saw him. Bigger-seeming and broader than an ordinary man, and also wild and threatening, and burning with the electricity of life.

He pushed her down on the bed. She opened her legs to him and he entered her, without preliminaries.

It was the most intense love-making Jess had ever known. And also almost the shortest.

Afterwards, when they lay still with her arms and legs

wrapped around him, she thumped her fist weakly on his shoulder.

'I don't understand,' she whispered. But the truth was that she did. This bout of passion was as much an exorcism as a collision of desire and within the labyrinth of it there were the black alleys of mothers and sons as well as the wider, easier avenues of men and women. And there was temporary oblivion for both of them in the exhaustive mechanics of sex.

Rob didn't answer her.

She tapped her fist once more. 'Again,' she murmured. 'Again, again.'

Afterwards, when they had briefly slept and woken up again, Jess disentangled herself from Rob's arms and the twisted bedclothes and went into the bathroom.

The dimpled, opaque window glass admitted the last of the daylight. On the white-tiled window-sill stood an innocent line of bottles and cosmetic jars, with one or two of Rob's basic toiletries amongst them. She frowned at the ordinariness of it all. Then she picked up an aerosol container of his shaving foam and squirted a soft pyramid into her cupped hand. The synthetic, ferny smell of it was reminiscent of him before it mingled with the other bathroom scents. She rubbed the foam 'off on a towel and bent down to take a long drink from the cold water tap. Then with both hands she raked her hair back from her face, not looking in the mirror. She took a deep breath, preparing herself. Then she went back into the bedroom and lay down again. She put her arms around him.

'What happened to your mother?' she asked.

'If you want me to tell you, I will.'

'Wait. Did Danny know?'

'Yes. I told him. Because he was important, I wanted him to know. We were friends.'

'Go on.'

It was two years after the start of the worst time. It had begun as it always did.

He had been asleep, then his subconscious alerted him and he snapped into wakefulness even before he heard his father coming up the stairs. He sat up on his mattress and peered over the footboard of the big bed. The covers were flat; his mother wasn't there. He lay down again and now he could hear it. It was the sound of heavy irregular footsteps and the sliding, brushing noise of his father's shoulder pushing off from the stairway wall as he struggled to propel himself upwards. There had been a low murmur of voices, but now there was a rustle and a tiny click. His mother had been watching television but she had switched it off. Rob had a clear picture of her. She would be sitting motionless on the edge of the brown sofa, hands between her knees and head bent, waiting for Tommy.

The door of the other room slammed open. Rob heard the first shouted question and the patient, conciliatory mumble of his mother's answer.

The pattern was familiar enough; his mother's meekness only enraged the man further. The shouting became a roar, a chair overturned, the banging overhead began as the woman upstairs registered her protests at the noise. Rob put his hands over his ears and gazed hard at the wall. He had given names to the continents and oceans.

He could still hear. His father sounded different tonight, worse, like a goaded animal. Rob thought confusedly of a bull-fight poster he had once seen, and the black bull maddened with a fan of bloodied darts sticking out of its shoulder while the fancily dressed matador danced in front of it. Only his mother was no matador. She didn't dance. So the picture didn't work. Why was he thinking of it?

There were words and jumpy drumbeat rhythms winding round in his head. He made them repeat themselves, increasing their insistence, in a vain attempt to block out the noise.

He even opened his mouth and began to sing, the sound coming out as a thin, monotonous wail.

*No. Tommy, for Christ's sake no.*

His mother was screaming. He knew he should have got out of bed, but he could not. He could not even move his fingers. Terror and revulsion induced paralysis.

He heard something clatter, then a scuttling sound like a rabbit or even a mouse clawing into a corner.

*Bitch, fucking little bitch, I saw you, I know where you've been.*

*Tommy, no, I swear to God. I've been here all night, ask Robbie.*

Those were the last words. There was a scream, a long rising screech that raised an echo after it abruptly ceased, and a complicated soft thump. The silence fell on Rob like a blanket's weight. He lay and waited for the next outburst, although he knew nothing so simple could happen now. Instead he heard his father panting like a dog, and mumbling his mother's name over and over.

*Kathleen, all right now, you're fine, Kathleen. Do you hear me?*

Moving slowly, as stiff as an old man, Rob uncurled himself from the shelter of his bed. He crossed the lino floor and opened the two doors that separated him from her. He saw his father kneeling down and his mother fallen in an awkward heap with her head in the hearth. The brass hearth tidy that usually stood to the left of the fire had fallen over. There was no open grate, it had been boarded in and filled with a two-bar electric fire, but his mother had still liked the hearth tidy in its place. She kept the brass stand polished, and the poker handle and the brass trim on the brush and pan.

He had hit her with the heavy poker.

*Kathleen?*

His father turned to stare at Rob as if he had never seen him before. He got heavily to his feet. Rob took his place beside his mother. Her face was white and there was some bloody froth on her mouth. He knew as soon as he looked at her that she was dead.

He went down the stairs, barefoot and in his pyjamas, and out to the call-box in the street. While he talked into the receiver he saw his father emerge from the house. He shuffled away down the street, his steps always carrying him at an angle until he hit the wall of the nearest house and lurched away to begin the zigzag again.

There was a silence. Jess was crying. The tears ran backwards out of her eyes into her hair, into the pillow.

'They found him, of course,' Rob said. 'There was a trial. The court was cleared when I gave my evidence. Guilty of manslaughter. He did five years, in the end, that's all. He lives somewhere in Scotland now. Glasgow, I think.'

'I'm so sorry,' Jess said. There it was after all, the sympathy and the tears. He wished, momentarily, that he hadn't told her. 'I understand more now, better.'

He tilted his head back to look at the ceiling. 'I'm not different from him, really, am I? I killed Dan, didn't I?'

The vehemence of her response astonished him. 'Don't you dare to say that again *ever*. It was an accident. It could have been the other way round. You said so yourself.'

'I wish it had been.'

'You said that too. Listen to me.' Her fingers hooked into his upper arms, hurting him. 'I loved Danny more than anybody or anything in the world, and he's never going to come back to me, or grow up, or marry and have children. Nothing will replace him for me, his death was a tragedy but it *was* an accident. I forgive you for the part you played in it.'

'Because of history? Because of what I've just told you?' It seemed that he might almost laugh, deriding her.

'No. Because it could have been Danny who killed you. Because of what I've seen and heard since he died. And because I want to.'

Rob asked harshly, 'Do you think that violence is inherited? Do you think it lies buried inside us, waiting its chance to burst out, like some hereditary disease, only more fatal?'

'No,' Jess answered. 'I don't believe that.'

He was surprised by her ready dismissal of his fear. He had voiced the worst, and it seemed that she hadn't heard it.

'It's what I'm afraid of,' he whispered. 'I feel as if it has happened already.'

She put her hands over his ears now, cradling his head, and he moved closer to her, shutting his eyes and willing himself to be reassured. The combination of the maternal gesture with her loose nakedness was confusingly erotic. He twisted his head free and examined her face in close-up, letting his hands slip over her shoulders to her breasts and the dip of her waist.

Jess breathed, 'It hasn't happened. It won't. You are not violent, you are gentle. We can help each other, do you remember?'

The skin of her inner thighs was soft, almost powdery. As he parted her legs again he heard the faint exhalation of her breath.


That night, mindful of the magistrate's warning, Jess drove them both to Rob's room. She brought with her a carrier bag containing her night things and working clothes. She would have to be at the nursery very early in the morning; Graham Adair had already warned her that with looking after Sock and accompanying Rob to court she had taken far too much time off. 'We're not in Easy Street here, you know,' he had told her darkly.

Jess had seen the place where Rob lived before, but she had never spent more than an hour there. Now she put her bag of belongings on a chair and tried to convince herself that she could feel at home. It was not dirty or even very untidy. The shelves covering one wall were beautifully made; on her first visit she had examined and admired the smooth surfaces and impeccable joints. Rob was good at what he did.

But in fact the room made her feel old.

It was the temporary shelter of someone in transit, who had not yet collected much of life's baggage and who did not need to take much interest in its arrangement. The room was weatherproof and acceptably warm and that was all that was required of it. It would be abandoned without a thought as soon as the owner moved on. It was a young person's stopping-place. She compared it with her own house, silted up with the material accumulations of the years and the memories that snagged around them. Her house still contained her husband and her small children; they lurked in the dim corners and sprang at her from photographs and their discarded possessions. It was painful. Jess felt a sudden sour impatience with the constraints of it, and a twist of envy of Rob, who was still young and able freely to move on to the next place and the next episode. Whereas she had concluded her own episodes, long ago.

Rob felt the awkwardness between them. He was silently tidying up, tipping things into drawers and raking clothes off his bed.

Jess told him, 'It's all right. You don't have to do anything because of me.'

'I'm not doing.'

*It's no good*, Jess thought. *The two of us can't live here for any length of time. Why did I imagine we could, just because I don't want to be parted from him?*

Rob had picked up something from a dingy chair that occupied one corner of the room. He folded it unnecessarily and Jess saw that it was an angora jumper, so small that it was almost child-sized. Dove-grey and fluffy, like a baby's toy or some cuddly animal.

'I'm sure it suits you.' She smiled, only meaning to tease him a little.

He scowled. 'It belongs to Cat. She left it here.'

Cat had come to visit him. She had peeled off her shiny mackintosh and dropped her rucksack and her scarf and gloves in different corners. She'd kicked off her ankle boots, and when the room warmed up she had taken off her jersey and sat in her little ribbed top, arms bare from the elbows down wrapped around her skinny black legs as she talked.

Jess watched him put the jersey away out of her sight. He hadn't told her that he had seen the girl.

She thought of her as Danny's girl, but that was a mistake.

A different colder perspective made her look around the room once again to see if there were any other signs that she had failed to interpret. It was a young man's place; inevitably he would have girls there. No wonder she felt old and incongruous.

'Does it matter?' Rob challenged her.

'No. Of course not.'

They went to bed. Jess cleaned her teeth and face in the chill bathroom Rob shared with another room on the same landing. The basin was speckled with dried foam and beard-shavings.

When they were lying together in the dark under the faintly musty quilt Rob asked suddenly, 'What are we going to do?'

'I don't know,' she answered truthfully. Evidently it was becoming imperative to do something.

'I've got to get some work. I need to. I've got no money and I hate sponging off you.'

'You aren't sponging. Your arm is only just better.'

The mended elbow was still stiff. Rob was supposed to go to physiotherapy at the hospital, but didn't.

He was grateful for her attempt at reassurance, but it didn't lessen his fear. The thought of his committal and the trial and whatever lay beyond that made him feel powerless, like the small boy lying in his bed watching the wallpaper. And as soon as he was grown-up he had promised himself never to be help-less again.

Jess's thoughts moved in a different direction. She was sink-ing towards sleep, and the awkwardness of being in Rob's room made her imagine that he would prefer it if she were not there.

She said blurrily, 'Beth is coming back this weekend. I'm going to meet her at the airport. She'll come home with me for a couple of nights. I'll need to look after her, Rob.'

'Of course. Don't worry. I'll keep well out of the way.'

'I didn't mean that.'

'Whatever you meant.'

Jess put her head on his shoulder. He stroked her hair and

waited his turn to go to sleep. He remembered how Beth had looked at the hospital and the glimpse he had caught of her at the funeral. No resemblance to Danny. Not much of a likeness to her mother. Tidy bobbed hair, neat working-girl clothes. A little pale face transfigured by shock, but still with a touch of petulance. Her daddy's arm round her shoulder.

He didn't like the look of Beth. He was jealous of her.

# Ten

Beth pushed her luggage trolley through the customs barrier at Heathrow.

She saw him immediately, standing out from the crowd of relatives and limo drivers as if a spotlight beamed down on his head. Sam, wearing unfamiliar weekend clothes, waiting for her. It was eight o'clock on a Saturday morning, she hadn't thought he would even remember what flight she was on, and yet he was here to meet her.

Joy dispelled the exhaustion of the twenty-four-hour journey. She whirled towards him and a second later she was in his arms.

As they kissed she was exulting. *He must have told Sadie.*

She saw in her mind's eye an instant yet complete picture of how they would live together, marry when his divorce was finalised, in time have their own children. Happiness ran through her veins like molten gold.

Sam tilted her chin to look into her face.

'Wow. Sun goddess,' he murmured.

'Sam, tell me? How come you're here?'

He shrugged easily and smiled. It was a smile she recognised, cautioning *Don't crowd me with too many questions.* At once the sinews in her throat warningly tightened.

'Sadie's taken the kids to Devon for the weekend. I came on the spur of the moment. You look great.'

'Do I?' The current of happiness froze. Nothing was any different after all, any different from the way it had been five minutes ago, except that he was here. And so must have been thinking of her when he woke up this morning. That was something, except there had been only the one thought which hadn't taken account of any of the other parts of her life or even the possibility that she might have someone else to meet her.

Which she did. With the ecstasy of seeing Sam already fading Beth remembered that it was her mother who was supposed to greet her. She looked around and only then saw Jess, standing fifteen feet away behind the press of arrivals, staring straight at them.

'But my mother's here.'

She pulled herself out of Sam's arms, replaying the last seconds in her head. What had Jess seen? And what were they all supposed to do now, have breakfast together and admire her photographs of the harbour bridge?

'Your mother?' He sounded surprised, even annoyed, as if she had no right to a connection with anyone except him. She turned to Jess.

'Mum, hello. How are you? Thanks for coming.'

Jess enveloped her with the warmest hug, ignoring the confusion for a second. As they clung together Beth knew how pleased her mother was to have her home again and she responded as eagerly as she could, making an effort to balance the unreconcilable demands.

'This is a friend of mine, Sam Clark. Sam, this is my mother.'

They were shaking hands. Jess looked different. It was not just that she was surprised or disconcerted by what she had just seen; more that her face had opened up in a way that only now told Beth that it had been closed before.

'All my fault,' Sam was saying charmingly. 'I woke up too early, remembered Beth was coming home, thought I'd come down and take her out to breakfast. I can never go straight to sleep after these long-haul flights, can you?'

'I've never done one,' Jess said coolly.

There was a small silence. Beth was thinking, *I can't let him go. I can't possibly kiss him goodbye here and go on home with Mum.*

*And the three of us can't go anywhere together*. The only variable was Jess.

'Mum, you must have got up so early to be here.'

'Not really. I stayed the night at Julie's.' And Jess suddenly stuck her hands in her coat pockets, stood up straighter. 'Listen, since Sam is here, why don't you go and have breakfast with him? I didn't get to Julie's until very late last night . . .'

*Why?* Beth wondered. *What kept her at home?*

'. . . and so I can easily go back and spend an hour or two with her. I can do some shopping and pick you up from your flat this afternoon. Will that do?'

'I'd love to borrow her until then.' Sam smiled. 'That is, if you really don't mind.'

Sam drove her home in his Saab. Beth had looked up and down the rows of cars in the short-stay car-park for a glimpse of Jess's old Citroën, for a brief sight of her mother's quick, determined stride towards it, but she had seen neither. Now that it was too late she was angry with herself for having chosen Sam before Jess, and she was angry with Sam for having caused the dilemma. She kept her head turned away from him, and stared out at the massive grimy façades of London as they swept along the Euston Road. The bare branches of trees in Regent's Park made black scribbles against the dirty sky. Even in anger she was affected by his nearness, by the warmth of the corduroy ribs curving over his bent knee, by the blue cuff of the shirt enclosing his wrist.

'Sorry,' he said.

He touched her hand and she softened at once, as he had known she would. Beth thought, *How easy I make it for him, out of fear that difficulty might discourage him altogether.*

'It doesn't matter,' she lied. 'It's only that she didn't know about you and now I'll have to explain.'

'I just wanted to see you.' He was like a little boy caught out in some piece of mischief, a resemblance he fostered deliberately.

'And I wanted to see you.'

They had almost reached Beth's street.

'You look like your mother. If I'd been watching for anyone but you I'd have recognised her standing there.'

'Danny was even more like her.'

'Yes.'

His agreement briefly startled her. She had forgotten their meeting at the theatre, and her forgetfulness twisted with further dislike of what she was doing.

'And are you happy to be home?' he asked, when they reached it. Beth looked around her first-floor rented rooms, seeing that they looked dusty and cluttered. She wanted to sweep the dried-flower arrangements and framed photographs into a bin bag and throw open the windows to let in cold air.

'Yes,' she told him. 'Because you are here. Otherwise the place looks like a dump.'

'Spoiled by the Antipodes.' He laughed.

He had brought their breakfast with him, one of the little love feasts they enjoyed creating for one another, croissants and fresh orange juice and a bottle of champagne. Beth lit the gas fire and they curled up on the sofa in front of it while she told him about Australia. Sam took off her shoes and rubbed her cold feet, and she let him feed her and refill her glass, and gradually the champagne did its work. Her head fell against his shoulder and she sighed with relief and gratitude at finding herself here with her lover. Her bones ached with the strain of being separated from him.

'Better now?' he murmured.

'Much better.'

They kept up the pretence that he looked after her and that she benefited from his care. Sam leaned closer to her, so that she saw the faint web of laughter lines creasing the skin around his eyes, and smelled his clean, particular scent. She let him hold her face between his hands, knowing that it was the truth when he said how much he had missed her. Why should he not miss her, when she made everything easy for him?

And when he kissed her, love for him made her turn milky and acquiescent. She could not have done anything this morning other than bring him home; this was what mattered. It was only when he was absent that it seemed so little to fix her life upon.

'Come to bed,' he ordered.

They pushed her suitcases aside and he began to undress her. He kissed her tanned shoulders.

'How is Sadie?' Beth asked cruelly.

'The same as always.' It was not easy to make Sam feel uncomfortable. 'Let me look at you. Jesus, you are beautiful, you know. Look at this, and these.'

And as he always did, when he gave her his full attention, all of himself, Sam made her feel that she really was beautiful and in the right place. In bed he did what he wanted, just as invariably, but because he made it easy for her to abandon herself to him it became what she wanted too.

'It's the best sex I've ever had,' he had told her once, and she had believed him, forgiving his slight incredulity. His experience was much wider than hers. For herself, even at her bravest and most optimistic, Beth did not think she would ever find another lover like Sam.

'I love you so much,' she said helplessly. By way of an answer he pressed his face into the hollows of her armpits, against her belly, between her legs.

Afterwards, comfortable in every corner of herself, she fell asleep in his arms. She woke to find him dressed in his shirt and trousers, sitting on the edge of her bed with one shoe in his hand.

'You're going?' The betrayal was somehow worse for being so predictable.

'Darling, I'm really sorry. I've got to go home and do some work. I didn't want to wake you,' he said. 'I'll call you at work next week.'

He bent over to kiss the top of her head, then he went, and left her.

*

Jess drove northwards up the motorway with Beth beside her.

'Are you exhausted?' she asked. They had spoken very little so far. The latest constraint between them seemed to intensify their awareness of the old ones. It had begun to rain; the flat landscape beyond London looked drab and exhausted.

'I slept for a while after Sam left.'

Jess stared at the road ahead, not knowing what questions to ask, if any.

'I didn't expect him to be at the airport,' Beth said at length.

'I saw you both before you saw me.' Jess meant that she had seen the intensity of their embrace; there was no use Beth trying to suggest that Sam was a mere friend.

'I haven't told you about him . . .'

'No, you haven't.'

'. . . mainly because he's married.'

Jess sighed, unsurprised. 'Oh, Beth. Men like that are always married.'

She had not intended to make any judgement, even to offer any comments unless Beth asked for them. She had never felt in less of a position to judge or advise anyone.

'What does that mean?'

'I mean that good-looking, self-satisfied men of his age always have wives, and still want something else as well. Something that doesn't inconvenience them too much.'

*Or threaten them too much either,* Jess thought. Beth's vulnerability irritated her, but she also felt a deep, protective tenderness, and regret that her daughter had not wanted to confide in her. *I* have *failed her,* she told herself. *I continue to fail her.*

'I didn't tell you about him because I knew that was what you would say. Please, let's not talk about it.'

That was so like Beth. She withdrew, whereas Danny would have leapt in a blaze of fervour to justify himself and his passion. Jess's fingers tightened on the wheel. She must stop comparing them. She was coming close to losing Beth too. The comparisons stretched back, bony fingers digging into the past.

'Listen, I didn't mean to say that. I didn't mean it to sound so dismissive of him. Does he make you happy?'

'Sometimes.'

The flat answer overlaid such depths of pathos that Jess had to blink in order to see the road. She had no power to change anything for Beth; now her own secrets made another thorny barrier between them.

She made herself say neutrally, 'Then I'm glad, if that's enough for you.'

To fill the silence that followed, Beth leaned forward to the cassette player. A tape protruded from the slit and she stabbed it with her forefinger into the play position. She listened absently to the music for a moment, then her attention focused.

'What's this?' She pressed the eject button and studied the tape in disbelief. 'How long have you been listening to Portishead?'

The tape was Rob's. Jess had cleared the house of every trace of him, but she had forgotten the car.

'I gave someone a lift. He left it behind.'

Jess had not been able to work out what she would tell Beth. And now, taken by surprise, her first and only instinct had been to deny Rob. Beth was looking curiously at her. Jess took the tape, one-handed, and dropped it without a glance into the door pocket. She picked up another, at random, and fed it into the tape slot. Innocuous music seeped into the draughty space between them.

'Look at them,' Jess said.

She was standing with Beth beside her, looking out of the bay window of the living-room. Lizzie and James were walking Sock from the car to the gate. He lifted his arms without looking up and a parent on either side obediently took hold of a hand. They swung him in the air and his mouth made a circle as his face creased with amazement and delight.

The two women smiled, but separately.

Beth had avoided any subject that might lead back to Sam, and Jess tried to suppress even the briefest thought of Rob, in case some hint of the truth leaked into the air between them.

'Did something happen while I was away?' Beth asked once, curiously.

'Nothing,' Jess answered.

They had spent the weekend being elaborately and emptily polite to one another and now it was Sunday lunch-time, time for family gatherings. The shoulder of lamb with garlic was roasting and the table laid.

Jess and Lizzie had barely seen each other since Rob had been discovered at the house. Jess had made sure that he was elsewhere when Lizzie collected Sock.

Jess opened the front door to them. She covered the awkwardness between Lizzie and herself by lifting Sock and rubbing his head, too urgently, so that his smile buckled and transformed itself into the beginnings of a wail.

'Hush now. Silly Jess,' she murmured to him. 'Silly old aunt.'

Everyone followed her into the kitchen, all of them talking determinedly, Lizzie the loudest.

'Beth, it's done you good. Hasn't it, Jess? She looks so well. God, what I'd give for a tan like that. I want to hear about everything, darling.'

'Mum told me about the part. Congratulations. It sounds wonderful.'

Lizzie grimaced to convey her nervous anxiety. It was true, she was nervous, and it was her way to exaggerate her feelings in order to control them. Ever since Sock was six months old she had been worrying about the stalling of her acting career. She didn't want to leave her husband and child to go out and tout for work as she had once done, but she was afraid that if she didn't have a career she would slowly become invisible. It wasn't what had happened to Jess, exactly, because Jess could never be invisible, but Lizzie was intuitively aware that her sister must have suppressed her wishes and dreams for the benefit of her children and her husband, and so had become a paler version of her true self.

And *now*, Lizzie thought in grim parentheses, look at what

has happened in reaction. Everything has come bursting out of her in a passion for the terrible boy.

Her disapproval and her anxiety for Jess made her even more aware of their lives in contrast and her own dilemma. James had fallen in love with her as an actress, a woman with a life. If she became someone else, someone less than she had been, might she risk losing an element of his love and admiration? However much James insisted otherwise, she thought she could hear a hollowness in his assurances.

It was precisely because James and Sock were so precious to her that she had to go out and prove to the world that she deserved them.

Nervousness gnawed at her. Anxiety made her hungry. She was putting on weight, and smoking too much to try to curb her appetite.

To Beth, who was sun-tanned and as slim as a wand, Lizzie said over-brightly, 'I'm scared to *death*. I haven't done anything for so long. Jasper, he's the producer, saw me in the Dickens and thought I'd be right for this so I went down and did the reading for the director, and then a video.'

Auditioning had been so familiar, and at the same time so alarming after her long absence from it, that Lizzie had felt almost strangled with fright. Nervousness had toned down her performance to the point where it had become unstudied, almost understated.

'And I didn't in the least expect to but I got it, and God, we're into rehearsal in ten days' time and shooting a week after that.'

It was a police serial, a six-parter. Lizzie's role was not the lead, that was for a young actor, but it was a leading support. She was to play a hardened police pathologist with a soft heart. A good part for a woman of almost forty who hadn't worked for two years.

'You'll be very good,' James said. 'You know you will.'

'But there's Sock to think of. Rehearsals are in London, Beth, and shooting's on location in Wales, as well as at Pinewood.'

James assured her, with the air of repeating words that were fast becoming a mantra, 'I can manage Sock easily. We're getting a reliable temp nanny, Beth, to look after him during the day while I'm out.'

'And you know I'll do whatever I can to help, Liz.'

Jess spoke quietly. And the way that Lizzie half turned but did not quite look at her told Beth what she already suspected, that there was some serious breach between the sisters. In all her life she had never known them to have a real quarrel. Lizzie's stream of talk was her way of trying to cover it up. James looked embarrassed and Jess herself was preoccupied, as she had been ever since she had collected Beth from her flat.

'Well. Does anyone want a drink?' Jess asked, breaking a little silence.

Each of them made separate, thankful manœuvres to do with opening bottles and finding glasses. Lizzie asked Beth some question about Australia, and the talk about it carried them to the table. James carved the lamb while Jess handed the vegetables, and Sock beamed impartially from his ingenious chair that clipped to the table edge.

The sour-milky winter sun shone briefly through the dining-room window, making a pale lattice of light and shade on the cloth and the best plates and dishes that Beth had laid in honour of Lizzie and James. The sun's weakness made Jess try to measure the interval that still separated her from spring. On the nursery the earth lay frozen, and above and below ground the roots and stalks of all her plants remained black and stubborn. Graham Adair was irritable, criticising everything she did. Joyce had murmured during Friday's tea-break that he might be in trouble with the bank. *Business doesn't look good*, she had mouthed over her tea mug. *Don't think about it now*, Jess resolved. She pushed that anxiety to one side and concentrated on the table. The sun faded behind the clouds and an easier, brownish gloom crept inwards to replace it.

*Sunday lunch*, Jess thought, *family time*. This family had dutifully gathered to support one another with the props of meat and two veg, but the reality was exactly the opposite. A space had opened between the three women as if Ian and Danny had been a busy male glue that held them by preoccupying them. Without its binding force they became insubstantial and untrue to each other.

It seemed much longer ago than Friday evening that she had last seen Rob. She wondered what he was doing, if he was sitting in his room amongst belongings that had become familiar to her, or if he had gone out somewhere with people she did not know, people of his own age who would understand aspects of his life that she did not. She became aware that Beth was watching her.

'You're very quiet, Mum.'

Beth wouldn't let her withdrawal go unremarked; she was already angry with her because of Sam. All unfair anger, Jess thought.

'Am I? I was just worrying about work. Graham Adair's got money problems, Joyce says.'

Beth continued to look at her, eyes pale in her sun-tanned face, probing Jess's deflection for the truth behind it.

Diplomatic James did his best to lighten the atmosphere. 'Did you see the Botanic Gardens in Sydney, Beth?'

After they had eaten Lizzie and Beth began the washing-up. Jess looked out at the houses opposite, and their rows of prim front windows and net curtains hiding the families within. Some of the nearest neighbours she knew, but more were strangers now. Ten years ago Ian and she had been friendly with several of the couples. Then one of them had also divorced and two others had moved away. The fourth family was still there but the children had grown up and left home, and Jess seldom saw the parents now. The last time, she remembered, had been after Danny's funeral.

The sight of the Sunday street and the closed windows bred a feeling of extreme restlessness in her, a dull ache between her shoulder-blades and an itch beneath her feet that made her curl her toes inside her shoes.

'Let's go out for a walk,' she suggested, too loudly.

'No thanks,' Beth replied.

'I won't either,' Lizzie said. 'Too bloody cold.'

James offered, 'I'll come with you if you don't mind me bringing Sock in the buggy. He might go to sleep.'

After the customary lengthy preamble of dressing the baby in his padded suit and bobble hat and mittens they rolled the pushchair out of the house. Jess drew in a breath of air and began to walk. James had to hurry to keep up with her, jiggling the pushchair over the uneven pavement.

Lizzie established herself on the sofa with the Sunday papers. She was wearing suede ankle boots and black velvety leggings, and a caramel wool tunic that clung to the undulations of her belly and bottom. The vee front dipped to reveal the line between her pushed-up breasts.

What is it with this family, Beth wondered, that makes its siblings so unalike?

She balanced on the edge of the hearth, rocking her determination into place.

Finally she demanded, 'What's going on?'

Lizzie looked up from the culture pages, eyes outlined with mascara and a touch of kohl, blinking at Beth's fierceness.

'Going on? What do you mean?'

'You know quite well. Don't bother playing dumb.'

Lizzie looked guiltily aside, giving everything away. *You can't even* act, Beth stormed within herself. But she said patiently, 'You and Mum have had a big disagreement. I've never seen you like this with each other before. What's been going on while I've been away?'

'Nothing much.'

'That's not the truth. I want to know, Lizzie. Is it Danny?'

'Yes,' Lizzie said quickly.

'Well, I don't fucking believe you.' Beth began to shout. 'I saw how she was before I went. That was grief. This isn't, it's more like, like defiance. Like, up yours, world. And you and James, she's saying up yours as well about whatever it is you know and don't like and won't tell me about. And there's something else, the staring into space and not hearing when she's spoken to, and then making herself concentrate politely on what's going on. If I didn't know better, I'd think she was in *love*.'

'If only it were as forgivable as that,' Lizzie breathed.

Beth bent down, seized her aunt's wrist. A coil of bracelets bit into her fingers.

'Tell me. *Right* now.'


James and Jess walked a few streets to a little playground. The fenced-in enclosure looked over a wedge of open countryside towards the concrete curve of the motorway in the distance. Soon, in less than an hour, it would be getting dark and the lights of cars would begin to make cone-shaped holes in the murk. Jess stood at the railings, fists grasping the vertical bars, following the line of the road with her eyes. It was the route she took to work every day, but in her imagination she continued far beyond the nursery. She went north, through the Midlands and Manchester and Carlisle, the Scottish border. Would she have to cross the Pennines to get to Scotland? The realisation that she had no idea was surprising, oddly disturbing. How limited I have been, she thought. Where have I been, and what have I done? She turned her back on the road and the dim beads of cars threaded along it.

Sock had not fallen asleep. James lifted him out of the pushchair and fed him into the bucket seat of the baby swing. The chains suspending it creaked gently as he pushed. Sock's padded legs stuck straight out as he leaned back, momentarily bewildered. But as soon as he understood the idea he let out a thin shriek of pure ecstasy. His face turned red and his mittened fists grasped the orange plastic rim of the bucket. The air itself seemed to vibrate, then to turn in a giddy vortex with Sock at its centre, such was the intensity of his pleasure in discovering swinging.

'This is wonderful. It's a first,' James said.

'Think of all the discoveries ahead of him. And you.'

'I'm sorry. Was that clumsy of me?'

Jess shook her head. 'I wasn't thinking of Danny then. Not at that moment. Although he's there so often. In one shape or another.'

James pushed Sock and Jess stood watching. Every contour of the park was familiar, just as the canal-side had been, even though she had not visited it for years. Danny and Beth chased each other between the slide and the swings and she heard their shouts and disagreements loud in her head.

'James? Do you disapprove of what is happening between Rob and me as bitterly as Lizzie does?'

'It's none of my business.'

It wasn't an evasion. Jess knew that James meant exactly what he said, and it suddenly became important to her to know what he did think.

'Are you shocked, then? Surprised at me?'

He considered, then said carefully, 'I'm not shocked, no. I was surprised, until I thought about it. I can believe, without understanding the details of it, how a love as powerful as yours for Danny might transfer itself to the other boy. If you are bereaved it is probably a way of bearing what might otherwise be unbearable. You are living through what's likely to be the worst time of your life. Who am I, or Lizzie for that matter, to make a judgement on how you do it?'

An understanding of the finality of her loss came back to Jess. Sometimes, mercifully, she couldn't quite stretch her mind around the immensity of it; at other times, as now, it was clear and total. She had told James that he was often there, but she understood that Danny would never exist again except in the shades of her memory. The absence of him would never lessen or change.

But now in the centre of the dark landscape she saw Rob, and instead of whirling in the windy abyss of loss her thoughts fixed quietly on him. She and Rob were helping each other.

She said to James, 'I think that is partly how it is.'

He left the swing to the diminishing arcs of its own momentum and stood facing her.

'Be careful, won't you?' he said kindly.

'I will.'

She did not know whether she would or not, but she loved James for his grave sympathy.

He turned back to lift Sock out of the stilled swing. The baby's howl of protest split the air like a cleaver.

'I said, I want to *know*.'

'Then ask Jess yourself.'

'You know she won't tell me.'

'I don't.'

Lizzie stood up and Beth closed in, trapping her with her back to the wall.

Lizzie tried to laugh the moment away, putting up her arms like a shield. 'What is this? The Inquisition?'

Beth's face didn't lose its tight lines. The fierce light of her imagination swung like a following spot on a darkened stage, too slowly at first, always just missing the figure that slipped aside into the shadows. She was groping for a truth that was coming closer but still just evaded her.

As she stared into Lizzie's face she suddenly saw beyond the concealing smile. A glimpse of something like dread in her eyes made her think of the hospital. And then of Jess. What had she said about her mother to Lizzie?

*If I didn't know better, I'd think she was in love.*

Sometimes, when she was younger and full of jealousy, she had imagined that her mother was in love with Danny and had been stricken with shame merely for having the thought.

There was a lover now. She was certain of it.

'Who is he?' she demanded. '*Who?*'

'I don't know what you mean.'

But Lizzie did know. Beth saw it.

The spotlight of her imagination swung again, cruelly fast,

and suddenly the shadow she had been chasing was captured in its full glare. Beth felt the yawning pitch of sudden nausea. Once the figure was revealed there was no hiding it again, although as soon as she recognised it she longed for it to be gone.

It was the worst, the most unwelcome speculation, but immediately she was sure of it. The very impossibility explained Lizzie's fear and Jess's strangeness.

She remembered how the door of the hospital waiting room had opened, and he had been standing there in his leather jacket. The right side of his face was darkened with bruises and scabs.

'It's Robert Ellis,' she whispered.

And then she screamed it into Lizzie's face, willing a flat denial out of her, 'It's Robert Ellis, isn't it?'

Lizzie said nothing, and her silence was eloquent enough for Beth.

She stepped back, whispering in belated disbelief, 'My *mother?*'

Lizzie's hand groped along the mantelpiece for her cigarette pack. Beth turned away from her and ran up the stairs, not fully understanding where she was going. Outside Jess's bedroom she hesitated, then threw open the door.

The white cover on the bed was tidily drawn up over the plumped pillows. On the dressing-table were bottles of scent and a tube of handcream, and the *découpage* box made by Beth long ago as a Christmas present, in which Jess kept her few pieces of jewellery. There was a chenille jacket over the back of a chair, a paperback novel on the bedside table.

Beth opened the wardrobe door. Her mother's clothes hung in a neat line, shoe boxes were stacked on the shelf at the bottom. The first drawer she flung open was the same, revealing only folded underwear, white at one side and black at the other. Jess was tidy, Lizzie was not.

Guiltily she slid the drawer shut. She sank down on a corner of the bed, feeling sick. She had been looking for some evidence of Rob Ellis's occupation of her mother's bedroom. There was nothing. Nothing to be seen, at least.

Beth groped her way to her own room. The bungalow in Sydney had contained the low murmur of her father's sexual engrossment with Michelle; most of the time Beth had been able to blank it out, and when it had become too noticeable it was explicable. Unwelcome, but at least comprehensible.

This was different. If it was true. It stirred the depths of disgust and anger within her.

Beth sat for a long time. She heard Jess come back from the walk with James and Sock. The scratch of heated talk was audible from downstairs but she couldn't distinguish any words.

Then Lizzie and James left, retreating to their car again under the camel-loads of baby equipment.

Beth sat in silence, stiff-necked and unmoving, until Jess knocked on her door.

'Yes.'

Jess came in, bringing Beth a cup of tea on a round tray.

'Thank you,' Beth said, but she didn't reach to take it. Jess waited, then put the tray on the table beside her. The teaspoon made a faint clink in the saucer. Beth hadn't taken sugar in her tea for years.

'Can I sit down?' Jess asked. The basket chair at the foot of the bed creaked under her weight.

'Is it true?' Beth demanded. Her eyes burned.

'You are so angry.'

'Is it *true*? Answer me.'

'It depends what you are asking.'

'How can I say it without throwing up? Are you involved in some way – Christ, in any way – with *him*? With Robert Ellis?' She spoke his name with the greatest difficulty.

'Did Lizzie tell you this? It doesn't matter if she did. I just want to know.'

'No. Lizzie wouldn't say a word. So I thought of the worst possible thing, and there it was. I guessed, okay? The way you talked on the phone. The way you looked as soon as I saw you in the airport, like you were holding something, hiding it. The tape in the car. You've said nothing in all the words you've uttered since I've been home. Keeping your secret, and it was worth trying to keep from me, wasn't it? The worst possible thing. I'm right, aren't I?'

*Tell me I'm wrong. Go on, deny it. Please, Mummy.*

'Yes, you are right. As far as the bare facts go.'

'You've . . . had him here, in our house? Lived with him? Cooked for him?'

Jess had kept her head bent, but now she looked fiercely up at Beth.

'What else would I do? Although the terms of his bail now say he must stay at his own address.'

'How could you?'

'How? He came here one night. Christmas Eve. We talked about loss. He wanted to tell me that Danny's death was an accident. I knew that already but Rob made me listen to the truth instead of my own roaring pain. I understood something too, which was that he felt the same as I did. I was comforted by that.'

'You were comforted, so you went to bed with him, is that it? He killed Danny. He's the same age as me.'

'Which is worse, Beth?'

'What would Danny think?'

Jess said sadly, 'Do you imagine I haven't asked myself the same question? The truth is, I don't know. All the certainties I had about him are fading away. Perhaps he would hate it as much as you do. Or maybe he would judge me less harshly. Rob was his friend.'

Beth slowly shook her head.

'You say *Rob* in a special voice. I can't take it in. I think it's disgusting.' She pronounced it with bitterness, biting the word off as it emerged.

'You think that? What if it's valuable to me? Because I am your mother, I shouldn't acknowledge myself or my own needs?'

Beth clenched her fists in her lap.

And then the accusations burst out of her, shrill with her loss and all the boxed-up resentful bitterness of the years.

'What about me? My brother's dead, as well as your son. You always loved him best, I know that. But I need you now. *I* do. I don't want to share you with Dan's killer. I want you for myself now, at last. Don't I deserve that?' she shouted at Jess.

But when she had finished she began to cry, silently, and her mother took her hand.

Jess said softly, 'I know. I am here, Beth.'

Beth knocked her hand aside.

'Leave me alone.'

She took her canvas holdall off the chair and swept the contents of a drawer into the slack mouth of it. She threw another handful of her belongings on top.

'Where are you going?'

'Back to London; where do you think?'

'Please stay. Until tomorrow, Beth. Like we arranged. Please, I want to talk to you. Don't go off like this.'

Stone-faced and stiff-lipped, Beth said, 'I'm going. You can't stop me.'

'I know I can't stop you. Can't I persuade you?'

Jess tried to catch her arm and their flailing wrists caught the cup and tray balanced on the table. A stream of cold tea ran down to the floor.

Beth ignored it. She went downstairs to the telephone and ordered a taxi to take her to the station.

Jess went heavily into the bathroom, found a cloth and filled a bowl of water. She went down on her knees and sponged up the spilt tea.

Within seconds, it seemed, the cab was hooting outside. Beth went out at once, carrying her holdall. Jess tried to follow her, the pink bathroom cloth still furled in her hand.

'Wait, Beth. Don't go like this.'

'What about *me*?' Beth repeated. Those were the last words. The engine was running. The cab driver put her bag into the boot and she got into the back seat of the car, slamming the door. Jess gazed through the misted glass that cut her off. She couldn't see her daughter's face properly.

'Wait,' she repeated.

Beth was staring straight ahead of her. If she heard the entreaty, she gave no sign. The driver shrugged and the car moved forward and away.

Jess left the Citroën double-parked with the lights blinking. She ran up the steps to Rob's front door, jabbed her finger to his bell-push and kept it there. At last he opened the door.

'Come with me,' Jess demanded.

'Where?' He was wearing sweatpants and a grey T-shirt, torn at the shoulder, revealing a triangle of smooth skin.

'Just come.'

He followed her without another question.

Driving soothed her. She took the motorway curve away from the town, past the wedge of open ground with the playground in the distance, now hidden in the darkness. Being one bead in the endless necklace of Sunday evening traffic drained the agitation out of Jess. Rob leaned forward to the radio and pressed the buttons to find music that suited him. Jess responded by driving faster, chopping from lane to lane, chasing the techno beat he had chosen. She braced her arms and gazed into the lights of oncoming cars.

'Slow down,' he ordered her. His left foot pressed vainly at the floor.

'Play something else then.'

He glanced down at the jumble of tapes in the well between them, picked one up and peered at it.

'So this is where it went to.'

He put his Portishead tape back in the slot.

'Better?'

'Sort of.'

She drove on, past the turning to the nursery.

'Where are we going?'

'I don't know. I just wanted to drive away, away from home, with you.' The road signs flashed up, Stafford, The North, Manchester, North Wales, and whirled into the darkness behind them. How many miles to Scotland? How many hours' driving? She could feel the threads that tied her to home straining, then breaking. The sensation that freedom gave her was dizzy, uninhibited, like drunkenness.

Jess kept one hand on the wheel and with the other reached for Rob's. Their fingers linked together and Rob's head dreamily fell back against his seat. How many spliffs had he smoked today, Jess wondered, sitting alone in his room?

When they had listened to both sides of the tape and travelled fifty miles through the black-wrapped and orange-lit centre of England, Rob asked gently, 'Are you going to tell me what's happened? Or are we going to drive on to Gretna Green?'

'Is that what you're afraid of?'

He rolled his head, breathing out something between a sigh and a laugh. 'No.'

'Beth knows. She took it very badly.'

He listened while she told him. At the end he said, 'I don't know what to say.'

Jess thought, *How could he know?* He had experienced none of the sad complications of parenthood. He had not even set out on the journey yet, encumbered with the shiny beliefs that would slowly tarnish and buckle into compromise and misunderstanding. She wondered whether Beth had reached London. Maybe she would call Sam for comfort, although it was more probable that Sam was at home with his wife, immured in Sunday evening domesticity. Jess's heart ached for Beth in her isolation.

'So this is running away?' Rob asked.

Jess straightened her arms on the wheel. 'It feels right. It felt like I was burning up at home.'

Another road sign luminously expanded in their lights. A service station lay just ahead.

'Pull in here,' he said.

Obediently Jess indicated, swung the wheel. They rolled under the trees into the gridded parking lot. All around them overweight families disgorged themselves from cars and plodded heavily towards self-service pots of tea and plates of food. Rob and Jess sat in silence as the Citroën subsided with a series of small metallic clicks.

She turned to him. 'We've got to go back, haven't we?'

And when he didn't answer she nodded. 'Your bail. My job. I've got to go to the nursery tomorrow, and the day after, and the day after that. I need the money.'

Rob leaned closer to her. In the dimness she saw his head silhouetted by the lights of another car. When he kissed her she closed her eyes. She put her hand on his shoulder, found the tear in his T-shirt with the tips of her fingers. The skin beneath was very warm.

'I've got about two quid on me,' Rob said. 'I could probably buy you a coffee. Keep you awake on the way back.'

Jess smiled. 'Okay. Do that. Then we'll go home.'

They would go back to his room, to the neat shelves and the double mattress under the Indian spread, and the faint odour of joss that reminded her of Danny.

# Eleven

Rob stood up in the dock and gave his name and address.

He remained standing while the clerk of the court read out the charge against him once more. Watching from behind the plexiglass grille of the public gallery Jess saw that he stared straight ahead of him, not flinching at the words. *Causing death by careless driving when under the influence of drink.*

The lone magistrate was a stern-faced man with a dark moustache and heavy spectacles. He looked up from the sheaf of papers in front of him. Rob's case was the fifth of the morning. The court officials and solicitors and security officers shuffled and murmured routinely amongst themselves under the white overhead lights. The court smelled of polish.

'How do you plead, Mr Ellis?'

'Not guilty.'

The magistrate transferred his gaze to Rob's solicitor.

'Mr Blake.'

'I'm not requesting any of the prosecution evidence this morning, sir.'

The clerk of the court began to read a list of names.

'Police Constable Farrell.'

'Full witness order,' responded Michael Blake.

'Anthony Sumner.'

'Full witness order.'

'Michael Frost.'

'Full witness order.'

They were the policemen who had attended the scene of

the accident, the motorists who had witnessed the accident, the medical examiner, the police vehicle examiner, forensic experts. Those whom Rob's barrister wished to cross-examine were placed under a full order, to appear at the trial.

When the list was concluded the magistrate told Rob, 'You are committed to stand trial at the Crown Court on a date which will be notified to you. If you fail to present yourself on that date you will be arrested and sent to prison. Is that quite clear?'

Rob said in a low voice, 'Yes.'

'Conditions of bail remain the same.'

The committal procedure was complete. It had taken seven minutes. Rob left the dock with a guard at his shoulder who opened the side door of the court and waved him out.

'I don't want to go to jail.'

'You won't.'

'*Shit.*'

Despairingly Rob rolled his head and pressed his forehead against the window glass. A surprising March sun glittered in his eyes and drew a shimmering layer of hot air off the roofs of cars idling at the traffic lights.

Jess was driving him from the court to a new estate on the southern edge of the town. He had begun on a job in one of the raw houses, building shelves. Jess was in a hurry, reckoning up the time it would take her to drop off Rob with his tools and drive back the way she had come, all the way to the nursery.

'It will be all right,' she promised.

'Will it?'

'Yes. Somehow.'

He rolled his head back again, grabbed her hand so she almost swerved. She frowned and corrected the wheel.

'I'm starting to piss you off, aren't I?' he asked.

'No.' It was the truth, only she felt caught in a mesh of interwoven anxieties that twisted around Rob and Beth and Lizzie, and sometimes left her wanting to cut herself free. Do I dream of freedom, she wondered, or do I dread it?

The turning for the new estate was coming up. She indicated left and pulled out of the line of traffic, then negotiated a roundabout and the access road. New trees were staked and fenced along the verge. The gingery brick houses stood close together in small plots of churned-up ground. Jess thought as she had done often enough before that she should set herself up in business, making gardens for houses just like these. Nothing complicated, just the right plants in the proper arrangement, something that would give each house its individual signature. But she never did more than play with the idea, and she believed now that she never would.

The house Rob was bound for was identical to its neighbours. He got out of the Citroën and hauled his tools from the boot. Every movement and all the sharp angles of his body announced to Jess his anger and frustration. He was so young. He was so like Danny. The resemblance was for a moment sharp enough to make Jess smile and draw in her breath, pressing the heel of her hand to her mouth.

He asked her, 'You okay?'

She nodded, not able to speak.

Rob put down his bag and knelt, so his eyes were level with hers.

'It's the waiting I can't bear. You see? It's not knowing what's going to happen and not being able to do anything about it.'

'I understand.'

'I know you do.'

They leaned towards each other and kissed. Jess wondered who might be watching from the windows of the houses, but Rob was as oblivious of onlookers as always. He never cared who saw them, never gave any hint that they made an incongruous couple.

'Tonight?' he asked.

Jess shook her head. 'I'll have to work late to make up for this morning. Tomorrow night.'

He stood up. Abruptly he said, 'You're a good person, Jess. You do much more for me than I'm worth.'

'How do you measure worth?' she asked over her shoulder, as the car slid away from him.

The nursery was open again to the public after the winter closure. There were three cars in the car-park when Jess arrived, and she saw a pair of grey heads nodding in consultation beyond the beech hedge. She had hoped to slip unnoticed into one of the greenhouses and start work, but she was only half-way up the cinder path at the rear of the garden when Graham Adair popped out of his office.

'Another morning off,' he announced lugubriously.

'I had to go to court. I did explain that.'

'We've been very busy. I had to help out in the shop.'

Jess looked around for the throngs of eager purchasers of hardy perennials. 'Three carloads?'

He stared at her, eyes bulging. 'Earlier on.'

'Well, I'll get started, shall I?'

'There are some people in one of the tunnels.'

Jess sighed. 'I'll deal with it.'

A couple in green padded anoraks were poking about in the stock beds, even though a notice at the tunnel entrance clearly indicated that it was private. The man was holding up three pots of Jess's favourite ivy, Hedera *Melanie*. The garnet-tinged leaves were exotically crimped at the edges like the lacy hem of a ball-dress.

'We'd like to take these.'

'They're not for sale, I'm sorry. They've only just been potted up so they're not ready.'

The woman's face fell. 'Oh, what a shame. And they're so lovely. Look at the edges of the leaves, the little frills.'

Jess softened at once. As well as the plants, it was the gardeners, the single-minded enthusiasts with their notebooks and lists, who made up for Graham Adair and the unheated propagation shed and the long, frozen winters.

'Come with me, then. I'll see if I can find a couple of more mature specimens for you.'

She shepherded them out of the tunnel. Outside there were flowering clumps of hellebores bordering the path, some white-veined with green and others deepest plum-purple, and beyond them a sheet of white and lilac crocuses unrolled beneath the trees. There were no leaves on the trees yet but the buds were thickening. Jess turned her face upwards, letting it unfold in the treacherous warmth of the sun. Soon, the winter would be over. There would be more nights of frost and weeks of cold to dim the prospect, but the end of it was believable now. She could smell the spring. The faint sharp scent of it gathered in the scrolls of bone and membrane at the back of her nose and flooded the tender passages that had been clogged with despair. Behind her, the couple crowded on her heels, eager for the trophy of uncommon ivy.

'This way,' Jess directed them.

Rob sat back on his heels, surveying his work. The woman wanted shelves in her chimney-breast alcoves and he had measured up and ordered the wood, and the timber merchant had delivered it. Before – so much of his life, it seemed, now lay on the other side of the cruel bracket, *before* – he would have collected it in the van, and he would have made sure that the wood was free of knots, and cut to the proper length. It was difficult to work without the van. Jess lent him the Citroën whenever she could but she needed it to get to the nursery. And he didn't like driving any more. Danny sat in the seat beside him; Rob sometimes felt his presence so strongly that he turned his head to look at the empty place.

After the trial he would be disqualified from driving. It didn't matter but he wondered, how many years? Two at least. Two was the minimum. That, and whatever other sentence he would be given.

He pressed his shoulder to the frame of the shelf, and ran his hand over the splintery wood. Nothing fitted any longer.

The grain seemed to twist, buckling the plank.

'How's it going? Would you like some more tea?'

The woman of the house was in her mid-thirties, fluttery, too given to looking into the room to check his progress.

'No thanks. In fact I've got to go now. I'll be back first thing in the morning.'

'But . . .'

'Will it be all right if I leave my tools here? In the bag, like this? I'll only have to carry them home and back, otherwise.'

The customer was not pleased. Rob left the house and almost ran down the deserted road past the gingery houses. He had a long, long wait at the stop for a bus into town.

He stepped off in the main street, opposite the toyshop where he had seen Jess before Christmas. He wished that he were going back to her house now. It was still light, with the residue of the day's warmth coating the sticky pavement. It was a Thursday and the shops were open late. Crowds of people, mostly young women, circulated through the wide-open doors.

Rob worked out that he had three choices. He could go and sit in his room, or walk to the gym and spend an hour lifting the surly weights, or he could go to the nearest pub.

The pub on the corner of the shopping precinct had been given a country and western theme. He sat on a fake buffalo-hide stool at the bar and ordered a pint from a barmaid wearing a stetson and fringed buckskins.

'Hi. It is you, isn't it? I mean, how are you?'

There was a girl standing beside him. He didn't recognise her at first.

'It's Rachel. From that night. Don't you remember?'

He did remember now. The plain one of the foursome of Cat and her friends, who had been ill at the club and had been taken home.

'Yeah, right.'

She was standing staring at him. With a mixture of curiosity and apprehension and sympathy. I don't need this, he thought.

'Can I?' Rachel gestured at the seat next to him. She had a glass of lager on the bar. 'Only I'm waiting for Cat and Zoe. They'll be in just now.'

Rob had been about to stand up and carry his drink away to the farthest corner of the room but the prospect of seeing Cat was enough to keep him where he was. He had not made any attempt to get in touch with her since the time she had called on him and left behind her little fuzzy jersey, nor had she made any further efforts to see him, even to retrieve the jersey.

'So,' Rachel said gamely. 'What are you doing with yourself these days?'

'I'm waiting for my trial.'

'Oh. Right. Course.'

Rachel was still searching for a different direction the conversation might take when Zoe and Cat appeared. They jostled through the saloon doors, laughing, laden with shiny carrier bags.

'Rache. Cat spent next month's money as well,' Zoe exclaimed. Then she saw Rob. 'God. It's you. What are you doing here?'

Cat said nothing. She let her arms drop and her bags slipped around her feet. Rob left his stool and picked up the biggest one for her. It was pale blue, with red hearts and the word Babe printed on it. The pale-blue silky twist of the cord handles looked incongruous in his hands. He held the bag out to her.

'Thanks,' she said, then confided to him, still laughing, 'I did, too. Spent all the money I haven't got. What am I going to do?'

He shrugged, but he wanted to laugh too. The need surprised him.

'I've still got the jersey you left at my place. Don't you want it?'

'Ooo-*oo*,' Rachel said.

'Shut up, Rache. Here, you can get the drinks in,' Zoe muttered.

Cat steered Rob to one side. Her cheeks were flushed with the heat of chain-store changing-rooms and her damp fringe stuck to her wide forehead.

'I thought I'd leave it. You know, see if you wanted to come and find me. Obviously you didn't.'

'I did want to.' He realised it now. 'Only, you know.'

Her eyebrows went up, catching the spikes of her fringe.

'I mean, if you were going to press charges. It would have been kind of inappropriate, don't you think?'

Zoe overheard and interrupted. 'Cat never was going to, not really. Not the next day, when the statements started. Only once the law was on to it, it was hard to stop it all happening. He did try it on though, didn't he? It was him who started it. He was out of order, right?'

'Danny,' Rob corrected her automatically.

'And then he was dead. The solicitors and the police told us . . .' She shrugged.

'That there was no point. Because he was dead,' Rob finished for her.

'Yeah. But he did do it, you know. He would have done if he could.'

It was how he was, sometimes, Rob might have said. Just once or twice, when he didn't get what he wanted. He could have made some plea on Danny's behalf, but he looked into the girl's stony, knowing eyes and said nothing.

'It wasn't your fault,' Zoe said.

'No. Not for that, anyway.'

Cat was loading herself up again with the shiny bags. She held out two to Rob and he took them.

'We're not stopping here, are we?' she asked him.

'Um. No, not if you don't want to.'

Signals passed between the women. Zoe and Rachel leaned back against the bar.

'See you tomorrow then,' Cat told them. She manœuvred Rob out into the whitish evening, her hand under his arm as she looked around them. 'Now. What do you want to do?'

'Do I get a say?'

She smiled, showing her teeth. 'You do if you say what I want.'

'How about, let's go back to my place and dump these bags and pick up your jersey, then have a drink somewhere?'

Her smile widened. 'Just what I was going to suggest, as it happens.'

On the bus, cramped in a seat with the shopping heaped on their laps, Cat's warm thigh pressed against his. Rob remembered the drive in his van, from the club to Cat's house. The rain and the windscreen wipers and the whisper of sex. That had been *ordinary*. It was what came after that distorted everything, like a black glass set in front of his eyes, and cut him off from the whole world of before. And yet now, this moment on the bus with Cat leaning against him and smiling sideways through the soft curtain of her hair, this was also ordinary as well as pleasurable. The connection lifted him for a moment into happiness.

'D'you fancy that?' Cat was asking.

'What?'

She repeated some suggestion about letting her buy him a pizza for supper. She bit the corner of her lower lip and he noticed how the colour ebbed around the indentation and then flooded back again.

'Okay. Sure.'

When they reached his room she dropped her shopping bags with a predictable sigh of relief. She wandered from the shelves to the table, as if she was looking for something without knowing quite what it might be.

'Here.' He opened the drawer and handed over the fuzzy jersey. When she took it, he realised that he had never pressed his face to it to try to catch her scent and regretted the missed opportunity.

'Thanks.' She went to the window and stood with her back to him, her weight resting on one hip. The curve of her body lifted the hem of her short skirt on one side and revealed the

224

line of her thigh. Without any warning, desire for her flooded all through him.

'I saw you with his mother,' Cat said softly. She was still looking out into the sooty garden.

Rob said in bewilderment, 'What?'

'In the supermarket. You were doing the shopping together. You pushed the trolley and she put the tins and washing-up liquid and toilet paper into it. And at the checkout you packed it all into boxes and she wrote the cheque.'

'Danny's mother,' he corrected. 'Jess. Yes, that's right.'

He remembered the day. They had driven to the big Tesco on the ring road, and he had felt angry and cramped because he had been unable to pay for anything. After that he had made himself go out and get some work. The shelf job had been the first opportunity he found.

Cat turned from the window. She came very close to him, thoughtfully pinching the front edge of his leather jacket before she finally lifted her head and met his eyes.

'Where were you?' he asked. 'Hiding behind the baked beans?'

'I didn't hide, exactly. You just didn't see me.'

'No.' He could believe that.

'Rob, isn't it kind of . . . weird? You and his mother?'

Looking down into her wide-set eyes Rob knew that the naïve question was deliberately so, and that by association all of Cat's naïvety must be a deliberate mask for a much cooler intelligence and determination than he had given her credit for. Suddenly he found her slightly formidable as well as sexy.

'No. Well, okay, yes, a little. Jess is a very . . . good person.' It was a lame definition and he owed her a better one. 'It happened. Is happening, Cat. I don't regret it, right?'

'You're looking after each other.'

'Yes.'

She nodded, assimilating that. Then she reached up and curled her arm around his neck, drawing his head down so that she could kiss him very thoroughly on the mouth. He

225

hesitated, holding himself back from her. But then his hands lifted, unweighting themselves, to rest on her shoulders. They slid down over the narrow cylinder of her ribs and came to rest at her waist, drawing her against him.

After a while Cat tipped her head back and regarded him. 'Shall we go out for the pizza now?'

'Is that what you want?'

'It's what I think we should do.'

'Then we will,' Rob said, his assumed meekness mirroring her deceptive naïvety.

Beth woke up early on Saturday morning. She had intended to stay asleep, to swallow up as much of the day as possible, but when she opened her eyes and looked at the clock it was only half past seven. She turned over but she knew she would not sleep again. Her outstretched arm lay across the empty half of the bed. Sam had been there last night, but he had got up before midnight.

Beth had sat up, bitter-eyed, the covers falling off her shoulders, to watch him dress. She had promised herself that she wouldn't keep asking, but she couldn't help it.

'When are you going to tell Sadie about us? When?'

He had sighed and touched her cheek. 'I don't know, darling. I can't yet. The time isn't right. It isn't easy for me, this, either.'

Much easier than it is for me, Beth had thought. But she'd kept it to herself.

Now, in the morning, loneliness folded around her. Usually, most of the time, she convinced herself that Sam, when she did have him, was more than enough compensation for the times when she did not. When the certainty abruptly failed her, as it did now, her days seemed a waste of waiting and emptiness.

She pushed back the covers and got out of bed. She began to think about Jess and to wish she could talk to her. There had been two or three conversations on the telephone since the day she had guessed the truth about Rob Ellis; each time it had been her mother who had called Beth. They had reassured each other that they were both well, stiffly exchanged small pieces of news with a wary politeness that did not enable them to mention Rob or Sam. Beth had not been home again.

On an impulse Beth picked up the telephone. Jess was an early riser. She would be up by this time, even if she was not going to work.

There was no answer. Beth let the ringing go on and on, but there was still no reply.

She decided at once. She would go home for the weekend. If she caught an early train and took a taxi home from the station, she would be there by the middle of the morning.

Jess drove back with Rob to her house. When Beth was willing her to pick up the phone she had been asleep with him in his room. They lay with their faces almost touching, his arm heavy across her shoulder and the dark and copper strands of their hair in a damp tangle beneath their heads.

'Are you sure you want me here when you do this?' Rob asked as they came home again.

Jess nodded. 'I do. I can't do it on my own.'

They went up the stairs and paused outside Danny's door.

Then Jess turned the handle and they went in. The curtains were half closed and the room swam in a soft gloom. The walls were a collage of pin-ups and football posters and gig flyers, the clutter on the desk and shelves still lay as Danny had left it. A thick layer of dust masked everything, making the room look as if it had been captured and frozen at the instant of his death.

Jess moved slowly, gently touching his possessions.

'I don't want it to be a shrine,' she said. 'I know some mothers want to keep the room just as it was left. But I don't think I can bear the stillness of it. I don't want a dead place left where he lived. I can keep some of his belongings, can't I? I can change the room, it won't make any difference to the memories of him.'

She opened the curtains and sunshine revealed more of the dust.

'It's too sad like this. It looks as though I've neglected him,' she whispered.

Rob wiped his mouth with the back of his hand. 'If it's what you want. Where shall we begin?'

Jess opened a cupboard and took out some of Danny's clothes on hangers. The scent of him lingered in the folds.

'Would you like any of these?'

Rob shook his head. He couldn't look at her. 'I don't think they would fit me.'

They began the work. It was a relief to focus on the practicalities. Methodically they emptied the cupboards and the drawers and Jess sorted Danny's possessions into boxes or neat piles; to save or to give away, to sell or throw out, to leave aside for Beth to decide what she might wish to keep.

Jess had dreaded this necessary moment but now that it was here she was glad of it. She found there was nothing threatening or fearful or ugly about Danny's belongings, only her fear of the grief that they would unleash in her. However intimately connected with him they had once been, the books and clothes and records were only things. And the handling of them, the unwrapping and the refolding, had another effect. It brought him closer, stirring small, mundane memories of him in both of them that the scale of his tragedy had obliterated.

Rob dusted the books – there were not very many – and stacked them in a box for her. He disconnected the stereo and amplifiers and neatly coiled and clipped the leads. He worked deftly, without asking questions. Jess found reassurance in his closeness. They became absorbed in the task; slowly they dismantled the shrine, exposing rectangles of unfaded colour on the walls as they unpinned the posters, leaving the chipped shelves bare. They shared the memories that were awakened, talking in quiet voices.

On top of the wardrobe was a stack of photographs. Rob found them but hesitated to lift them down, guessing they might be Danny's stash of porn. The rest of the room had been quite innocent. It might easily have belonged to someone much younger than Danny.

'What's that? Let's have a look,' Jess asked.

When he put the small pile on the bed Rob was relieved. They were not porn but school pictures. The biggest, a long pasteboard rectangle filmy with dust, was a photograph of the entire comprehensive school. Long rows of boys, hundreds of faces above white shirts and striped ties, mugging their various adolescent attitudes at the camera.

'Look,' Jess said, pointing.

Danny was in the front row, a tidily dressed child with a mass of untidy black hair. He stared expressionlessly straight at the camera.

'Looks a proper little spod,' Rob said.

'I remember that day. I made him take his shirt off in the morning so I could iron it again. Where are you?'

'Let's see. Here somewhere. There's Brett and what's-his-name, Gibson.' And the pig boy, red-faced and bristle-haired, although he wouldn't indicate him. 'Yeah, there.'

He had a brutal haircut then. It was the colour of his hair that made him stand out in the row, that and his contradictory expression. His jaw was set but he was glancing down and away, defensive.

'Danny was eleven, so you were fourteen. Look at you. Where were you living?'

'With the Purses.'

Jess ran the tips of her fingers over the two faces, as if she could coax them into life or comfort their pains.

The other pictures were Danny's form groups and team photographs. He always posed somewhere close to the middle, curling his mouth or angling his eyebrows, aware of his good looks. In the football team he sat in the centre with the ball between his feet.

'Kenny Dalglish of the fifth form,' Rob murmured.

Jess laughed, a sudden soft giggle like a young girl's. Rob

laughed too, out of affection for his friend and because Jess's laughter was so good to hear, and also out of private gratitude that he was no longer the child in Danny's picture.

'Why did he keep them hidden away?' Jess wondered.

'Nostalgia. His guilty secret, an innocent past.'

The other pictures made them laugh too. They didn't hear the taxi drawing up outside, or Beth's key turning in the lock. She was on her way up the stairs when she saw the open door and heard the murmur of voices and laughter. She trod more softly, up the remaining stairs and along the landing.

The bedroom floor was heaped with Danny's things. Her mother and Rob knelt amongst them, their heads bent and their shoulders touching. Beth felt suddenly that the house was full of secrets, like Chinese boxes, one fitting inside the next. If she could only uncover the truth, Jess and she might understand one another better.

Jess looked up and saw her. She sat back on her heels, her face flushing with colour, one of Danny's photographs still in her hand.

'Beth. I didn't hear you.'

'You were too busy, obviously. I called earlier as well.'

'I wasn't here. I was at Rob's.' Jess didn't want to lie, or to pretend otherwise. It came to her that she was glad that Beth had arrived, like this, without giving any of them a chance to hide. It was better that she should see the reality than smoulder in London, imagining it.

Rob had eased himself backwards, away from Jess's side. Now he sat on the edge of the bed, his hands loosely hanging between his knees. Looking at him, Beth saw that at least he had the grace to appear embarrassed.

'What were you laughing at?'

Jess gestured at Danny's things. 'Just the old photographs. We . . . I thought it was time to sort things out.'

Beth stared at her brother's belongings, the posters and tapes and folded clothes. Then she ducked her head. Filtering through her anger with Jess, her jealousy of Rob and the queasy dismay at the thought of them together came another sensation. She felt guilty, because she should have been here to help Jess with this. If she had offered, even thought about it instead of huddling in her flat with her gnawing longing for Sam, Jess might not have had to turn to Rob Ellis.

The realisation stopped the flow of her resentment. She had been going to demand, bitterly, *Time to forget him already, is it?* But the words dried in her head and she hesitated, her eyes on Danny's school pictures. Then she edged a little further into the room, keeping as far from Rob as possible.

She knelt down opposite Jess and picked up a double cassette case. It was empty, and when she examined the sleeve she saw it belonged to a Rolling Stones greatest hits compilation. Danny had lent her the tapes the last time she had been home before he died. The memory of him leaning against the door of her room made her blink, and the indrawn breath rasped painfully at her lungs.

'What can I do?' she asked Jess. 'There must be something I can do here.'

'I put some stuff aside for you. I didn't know what you might want to keep. You could look through it.' Jess spoke too briskly. Beth knew it was because she could not deal with this work in any way except by treating it as a job to be completed, and that her own arrival had caused some alteration. Before, Jess had been laughing softly with Rob.

On top of the pile lay Danny's baseball jacket, dark blue with pale leather sleeves. Beth had worn it once or twice. She picked it up and folded it on one side, wanting but unwilling to put her cheek against it with Rob Ellis watching her.

'I'll go,' Rob said.

'No. Stay.' Jess caught him by the wrist. 'I want the three of us to do it together.'

Beth bit her lip. It seemed that Rob now had rights here that were equal or superior to hers.

What did he know? What had Jess told him?

The sense of secrets that were denied to her intensified.

Caught in the race of her thoughts, Beth found herself staring at Rob. And in spite of her hostility, she clearly saw the conflict in his eyes. He was staying for Jess's sake, because she had asked him to and because she needed him. For himself, Beth understood, Rob would have found it easier and much more comfortable to leave.

She bent to her task once more. After a moment, doing her best not to sound grudging, she asked Rob, 'What about you? Do you want to keep something of his?'

Rob shook his head, then hesitated. 'Well. I'd like one of the team photographs, perhaps.' Not the whole school, with the unwelcome faces, but the soccer team. He had never been in any of the teams himself, even though he had probably been a better player than Danny. It had been enough of an effort for Rob to negotiate the course of the days. There had been no spare will to win left in him.

Jess glanced at Beth and Beth made a small shrug.

'Take any one you want,' she said to Rob.

In the end, the job did not take very long.

Surveying the bare walls and shelves and the bundles on the floor, Beth thought how little Danny had actually possessed, how meagre the remainders were to represent a whole life. Even a life as short as Danny's.

'I'm going to put this load in the car. I'll drive it straight down to Oxfam, and then it's done,' Jess said.

'Let me carry it,' Rob said.

'All right. Just out to the car. Thanks.'

Rob and Beth were left to watch her drive away. Their hands and faces were grimy with dust. Turning back to the house, without Jess to contain their concern and to hold them apart, they both wondered dangerously if they were going to attack each other.

Instead Beth said stiffly, 'Thank you for helping her.'

'It's more the other way. She helps me.'

Suddenly enraged by the idea she hissed at him, 'Do you deserve her help?'

'No. I don't deserve anything.'

His admission unbalanced her again.

What was it she had once heard about him? Girls had whispered, and the boys had smirked in their offhandedly cruel way. Some crucial detail once known and now forgotten scratched at her.

'What has my mother told you?' She blurted out the jealous question without intending it.

'What? Nothing. What would she have told me? I don't know what you mean.'

She stared into his face. His green eyes were opaque, unreadable. His proximity made her unwillingly note that he was attractive and the realisation made her shiver and step back.

'Something I don't know,' she murmured.

'Nothing,' he repeated flatly.

Beth retreated into her room. She sat reading, or trying to read. Jess came back and she heard the mutter of voices downstairs. After another interval Jess tapped on her door.

'Beth? I'm just going to drive Rob home. I'll be back in about an hour, okay?'

Once again the Citroën started up outside and moved away.

Beth put down her book, carefully marking her place even though she had not taken in a word of what she had read. Silently she crossed the landing to her mother's bedroom and went quickly to the window, moving the curtain aside a little so that she could look down into the street. Jess's car was gone and the road was quiet.

She turned back to look at the room. Last time she had crept in here it had been to search for signs of Rob's occupancy. Now she was hunting for something else, something even more significant, and she didn't have even the faintest idea of what it might be.

Beth worked quickly, her ears always sharpened for the sound of the returning car. The drawers in the chest were blameless, as well as the shallow ones in the dressing-table. The shelves yielded nothing that struck her as important, even though she flipped out some of the older, fatter books and shook them to see what might have been slipped between the pages.

The wardrobe was last. She ran her eye quickly over the clothes on their hangers and the shoe boxes that stood in the bottom corner, neatly stacked exactly as they had been last time.

Beth flopped down on her knees and removed the whole stack from its resting place. The top four boxes contained Jess's summer shoes and her one pair of strappy evening sandals. The fifth was heavier. She weighed it briefly in her two hands and then jerked the lid off.

Inside were dozens of letters, small sheaves tidily parcelled with rubber bands. Frowning, Beth stared at the different piles. The certainty that she was on the point of a discovery faded away. The bulk of the letters were from Ian. His handwriting was immediately recognisable. Flipping quickly through them Beth saw that they had all been written long ago. Another substantial package containing as many postcards as proper letters was from Lizzie. Her huge, undisciplined script looped over the envelopes and often filled the message half of the cards with a single sentence. 'Why did I ever say yes to bloody Malaga with bloody Richard??' And more of the same.

The last two thinner packages were made up of Danny's notes and postcards, and her own. Beth saw that her mother must have kept just about every line she had ever written to her. The last item in the pile was a home-made Mother's Day card with a crayoned yellow-and-purple flower and a message in laborious letters, *Mum I love you deth*. Always the trouble with b and d, Beth recalled.

Her hands were shaking. She felt like a thief. She snapped the rubber band round the sheaf of her own letters and was about to replace everything hastily in the box when she saw that it contained one more thing. Lying flat on the bottom, unnoticed before because it was dusty white against the dusty white lining of the box, was a folded sheet of paper.

Beth picked it up, her hands suddenly steady. Inside the paper there was a single photograph.

The colours were fading, but they were still bright enough to convey the intensity of Mediterranean sunlight. Against the background of a strong blue sea stood a young man. He was wearing a striped T-shirt and loose trousers and the wind off the sea blew his dark hair in long curls around his tanned face. He was looking into the camera and laughing. The picture made him so alive that Beth could almost hear the laughter.

She had no idea who he might be. She had never seen the man, or boy, or even the photograph of him.

But he looked familiar. And the familiarity of the stranger alarmed her, and fascinated her, and made her determined to find out who he was and why Jess had hidden him at the bottom of her wardrobe.

Quickly she slipped the photograph into the pocket of her jacket. It fitted there snugly. She refolded the empty paper, replaced it in the shoe box and slotted the sheaves of letters on top. Then she put the boxes back in their place in the wardrobe, in the correct order.

She gave the room a last glance to make sure that everything was in place, then tiptoed back into her own bedroom. Ten minutes later she was still gazing into the face of the man in the photograph, when she heard Jess come back into the house.

Beth hid the picture temporarily in her own drawer, and waited for Jess to come upstairs.

# Twelve

Beth didn't ask Jess about the photograph.

There wasn't any way to say, 'I was just going through your belongings and I found this. Who is he? I know he's important, and I want to know why.'

And the longing to talk to her mother that had brought her here from London in the first place also faded. Now she was mute and defensive.

'I'm glad you came this weekend,' Jess said when she returned. They sat in the living-room, which looked dusty and unused. On the mantelpiece a bunch of daffodils had dried to papery buff in an earthenware jug. Beth fixed her eyes on them and didn't answer, so Jess tried again.

'I wish we could share our lives a bit more than we do. I never seem to see you nowadays.'

There was still no answer. 'Listen, I know it's hard to understand about Rob and me.' Jess's voice was shaky, betraying her nervousness. 'I don't think I understand it properly myself.'

'How much time do you spend with him?' Beth attempted a crispness that she didn't feel.

'Quite a lot.' She was going to add that she admired him, that he had become important to her, but she knew Beth wouldn't want to hear anything of the kind. Instead, clumsily, she muttered, 'I'd feel very lonely otherwise.'

'So you *do* think I should spend more time at home with you?'

'Beth, I don't think you should do anything. I just want you to be happier.'

Grief had only pushed them further apart, when it might have brought them closer.

Beth nodded. 'When I got home this morning you were laughing, you and him. In Danny's room.'

'I did try to tell you why. The pictures were so innocent, and Rob said that an innocent past was Danny's guilty secret. I had been so afraid of going through his things. Afraid of looking at them, you know, in case it hurt too much to bear. But in the end it didn't hurt, it was a relief. It made me remember little things about him that I might not have thought of otherwise.'

'But when I arrived it was different, wasn't it?'

Jess thought back, frowning, wanting to tell her exactly and truthfully how it had been.

'Rob was there with me. I would rather have spared you that. But it was more that seeing you made it harder to have those memories of Danny. Just at that minute, realising how much I love you made me aware of how much I loved him.

'And I do love you, you know,' Jess finished in a whisper. 'I love you so much.'

Within herself, deep inside, Beth knew that it was true. But nearer the surface, where resentment and jealousy still seethed, she couldn't suspend her disbelief. She said nothing.

Jess waited, but the silence stretched until it became chilly. She asked at last, 'How is your friend? Sam?'

'The same,' Beth answered, cutting her off.

Later, Beth asked if she could borrow the Citroën for a few hours.

'Of course you can.'

'I thought I might go over and see Lizzie.'

'Good idea.' Jess didn't even try to suggest that she might come with her.

Upstairs, putting on her jacket, Beth took the photograph out of her drawer and slipped it into her pocket once again.

*

Lizzie had put on weight. Her face was noticeably rounder and there was a little cushion of flesh under her jaw.

'Stress makes other women get haggard and angular. Not me, wouldn't you know it? I put on pounds on my hips and belly and I look like I'm wearing a pork sausage under my chin.'

They sat at Lizzie's pine kitchen table with mugs of herb tea between them.

'Bloody camomile and spearmint. What I'd really like is a triple Scotch and a box of Black Magic.'

'Have them, then.'

'Can't. Wardrobe are complaining about letting out my waistbands every other day.'

Lizzie was not enjoying the big part she had been so pleased to get. The role was more difficult than she had imagined from a read-through. She wanted to play her police pathologist character sympathetically, as a middle-aged woman with a difficult job and a complicated private life. The director wanted her admirable but unlikeable, and their clashes were daily becoming more open and more serious.

'He wants ambitious and steely,' Lizzie sighed. 'There's nothing in the script, so I'm trying to do it out of the air. Hard-boiled and hard-hearted but still with a heart, if you get me. I'm making a lousy job of it.'

'I'm sure you aren't.'

'Thanks, darling, but I really am. They keep changing my scenes. I'll probably never work again. And the way I feel now it'll be a big relief.'

She had slipped out of the rhythms of working. She had also underestimated the difficulty of being parted from Sock. Location work on the Welsh border was distant enough to mean that she couldn't get home during the week, and even when they were shooting in the studio it was too far to travel home and back overnight. She didn't trust the temporary nanny, even though James patiently assured her that she was efficient and reliable. When she was supposed to be concentrating she was worrying about her child.

'Are you with us, Elizabeth?' the campy director would sigh. 'Or not?'

In the past, Lizzie would have turned to Jess for emotional reassurance and practical help. Jess would have discussed with her the nuances of the director's attitude until they had worked out what she must do. And Jess would have stepped in to look after Sock, understanding that Lizzie's life was not a series of watertight compartments, that anxiety flowed from one into the next. James did his best, because he was kind and he loved her. But he was baffled by the tight wires that strung Lizzie up and he was growing impatient with difficulties that he couldn't properly understand, much less make better for her. James would have much preferred it if Lizzie could have devoted herself to being his wife and Sock's mother, but he was prepared to support her as far as he could if she insisted on working as well. He understood that she had been her own woman when he married her, and that they were probably both too old now to change themselves even to benefit each other.

He asked, 'You do want to make a success of this part, don't you?'

'Yes. God, yes.'

'Then go and do it. You know you can.'

The trouble was that she didn't know anything of the kind. Motherhood seemed to have severed her from what certainties she had ever had about her work, and the responsibilities of both halves of her life felt too heavy to lift at once. *I can't put everything I've got into doing the part*, she thought. *If I do, what will happen to Sock?*

In her worst moments of panic, in the thin-walled stuffy hotel bedroom on the Welsh border during the pitch-black small hours, the thought came. What if something happens to him because I'm not with him? What if he dies?

Fear would dry her throat and set her heart pounding, and she would get up and empty the mini-bar of brandy miniatures, and in the morning she would be hopeless.

She thought a lot about Jess and Danny. It was only now,

after their first serious rift, that the extent of her reliance on her sister was becoming clear. She was racked with pity for her too, made more aware of the scale of Jess's loss by the grip of her own anxiety.

Lizzie lit a cigarette and abstractedly rolled the packet end to end in front of her.

'How is Jess?'

Beth's mouth crimped with the effort of containing a different response before she asked tonelessly, 'Haven't you seen her?'

Lizzie shook her head. 'Not since I began work on this thing. I suppose that's quite a long time, isn't it? A month, anyway. We've talked a couple of times on the phone.' Conversations that admitted nothing and avoided everything. 'She's with that awful boy all the time.'

'He isn't awful,' Beth said abruptly. She had seen that he wasn't, in Danny's room, but still she was surprised to hear herself defend him. Lizzie's eyebrows went up into the exotic fall of her hair and the hand holding her cigarette froze in mid-air.

'It's just inappropriate, him and Mum, that's all.'

'Oh. I see.'

Lizzie poured more tea into Beth's cup, making it plain that she didn't see.

Beth took the photograph out of her pocket. She slid it face-up across the table.

'Do you know who this is?'

Lizzie picked it up, frowning and tilting it towards the light. Then she shrugged.

'No. Why?'

'I . . . found it at home. It's Mum's. I thought it was important for some reason. I can't quite remember why, really. I just thought I'd ask you. I was sure you'd recognise him.'

'Hmm. Some old boyfriend, I suppose. There were one or two before your father. The look's about right for the early Seventies. Flared trousers and sideburns, and all that hair.'

'Unless it was taken last week and he's a retro freak.'

'You mean your mother's running a whole string of boys?'

Their attempts to strike some humour out of their concern seemed creaky and tasteless, and they were glad when James came in with Sock. Lizzie took the baby in her arms, but he writhed and kicked until she set him down. He began to roam the floor, busily snatching at cupboard knobs with his starfish hands.

'He won't let me do anything with him,' she sighed.

'You're imagining it,' James assured her, as he kissed Beth in greeting.

He came and sat at the table with them and poured himself a cup of tea. Idly he picked up the photograph and glanced at it, then looked more closely.

'Who's the pin-up?'

Beth reached across and took it.

'It's just a picture I came across when I was clearing out at home. I wondered if Lizzie knew him.'

'Never seen him in my life.'

James made a face as he tasted his tea. 'Ugh. How long ago was this made? Funny. I thought at first glance it was Danny.'

At home, Jess laid out some scraps of paper on her dressing-table. There was a ruled sheet torn from a pocket notebook, with Danny's scrawl across it. There was a girl's name, Paula, and a telephone number and the words Copa Club. Beside her name Danny had written in block capitals, FIT!! To help him remember exactly which girl out of so many, Jess imagined. She wondered if he had ever called Paula, whoever she might be. The other papers were college work, disconnected sentences that might have been lazily taken lecture notes. And there was a small black engagements diary, last year's. She opened it and looked at the scribbled reminders, most of them no more than names and places. The entries stopped altogether in mid-March.

There was no particular reason why Jess kept these fragments, rather than any of the others she had found in Danny's room. Only that they seemed to stand for him and also for the darker, faultier version of Danny, the one that had begun to shadow her golden son. Jess was trying, painfully, to be honest in her memories.

She folded the sheets of paper around the diary, making a neat rectangle. Then she opened her wardrobe and slid the bottom box out from the stack of shoe boxes.

She took out the sheaves of letters and cards. Slipping the rubber band from Danny's sheaf, she put the diary package at the bottom and squared the edges of the pile by tapping it on the box lid. The topmost item was the first birthday card Danny had ever made for her, but she didn't want to look at these mementoes now. The dismantling of his bedroom had taken enough of her strength.

Jess snapped the rubber band back into place. As she was about to replace the papers she looked down and saw the folded sheet lying at the bottom of the box.

She took out the remaining contents and picked up the piece of paper, then flipped it open. The photograph of Tonio was gone. It was perhaps a year since she had looked at it, but she was as certain she had put it back in its old place as she was of her own name.

Jess knew it wasn't there, but still she searched through all the letters and cards. She hunted through the boxes of shoes, and on the floor of the wardrobe, and in the pockets of her clothes on the hangers. Then she reached up to the bookshelf on the wall beside her bed and took down an old Michelin green guide to Italy. It fell open readily to reveal a picture postcard that might have been used as a bookmark. Jess did not need to read the few words on it, nor the address the writer gave, because she knew them by heart. She had only wanted to make sure it was still there. She stood with it in her hand for a moment, frowning. Then she put the card back and slotted the guide into its place on the shelf. She stacked the sheaves of letters back on top of the folded paper and made a neat tower of the boxes once more. She closed the door of the wardrobe and clicked the catch.

*

'How was Lizzie?' Jess asked, when Beth came home that evening.

'She was okay. A bit worried about the part. It's not going very well.'

Jess waited, but Beth did not volunteer anything more.

'Is he here?' she asked coolly.

'No. If you mean Rob. It's one of the conditions of his bail that he must sleep every night at his own address.'

The women's eyes met. It was Beth who looked away first.


Sundays in spring were always busy at the nursery. Jess arrived well before noon when the gates would be opened to the public. She made a circuit of the stock beds, checking the plants lined up on their Mypex blankets ready for sale. She made a mental note to move some showy Bergenias that were just coming into flower to a more prominent position. There were plenty more in the tunnel, and it would be good to shift some of them today. In the shop she found Joyce in her nylon overall, racking some new wildflower notelets next to the floral biscuit tins.

'How are you, my duck?'

'Not bad,' Jess answered, meaning it. The weather had turned mild and there was a soft and milky sweetness in the rinsed air. She felt a curl of hope brush inside the drum of her chest, barely perceptible but still unmistakable, like the first quickening of a child in the womb.

At the same moment she heard a voice in her head. All would be well, it said. Not yet, but in good time.

She smiled at Joyce. 'And you? How's your mum?'

'Not too good. She cries. You know? She doesn't recognise me, or where she is, or what's happening to her. And she's so unhappy. She sits there in the chair with tears rolling down her face and I don't know what to say to her to stop them.'

Jess put her hand on Joyce's arm.

'I'm sorry,' she murmured.

Joyce went heavily round the end of the counter and sat at her stool behind the till. There was no more to add.

'Have you seen him, by the way? He was in here earlier on, looking for you.'

She could only mean Graham Adair. Jess sighed. 'He can't be complaining already. I'm not due on until twelve. I'd better go and see what he wants.'

She went out into the sun and crossed the yard towards the office. Mr Adair was standing at the window and beckoned to her.

Jess knew what it was as soon as she crossed the threshold.

'Shut the door, could you?' He frowned. The yard was empty.

'I'm sorry,' her employer said in his fussy, portentous way. 'I've looked at this in every possible light. Believe me it's even kept me awake at nights, but there's no getting round it. With the recession and the overheads and the competition from the garden centres being what it is.'

Jess gazed at the squares cast by the sun on the dusty lino-tiled floor, listening to him telling her that he would have made this staff economy earlier, if it hadn't been for her sad personal circumstances. Wanting her thanks, presumably, for his untoward generosity in keeping her on this far.

She needed this job. The loss of it was a serious blow.

'It's a month's notice, of course,' he said, bringing his clean hands together with a gesture of finality and relief.

Jess wondered why she had never told him how much she hated his toothbrush moustache, and his unsoiled stiff wax jacket, and his bank-manager's prissy diction.

'I see,' she said, wondering why she wasn't telling him even now. And then, when the silence lengthened, 'Well, then. I'd better go and get ready to open up. If that's all?'

'It is,' he said, with a stiff nod.

She went out again, passing the tunnels that were clouding in the sunlight with tiny beads of condensation. In the car-park there were some couples waiting in their cars, no doubt with the Sunday papers and a Thermos of coffee.

Joyce was still in the shop.

'I'm a staff economy,' Jess told her flatly. 'A month's notice.'

Joyce's eyes and mouth made round holes in the pinky slab of her face.

'That bastard. That little slimy idle toe-rag.'

'Yeah,' Jess agreed with her. 'That's about it.'

'I . . . Well. I don't know what to say. I've a good mind to tell him to stuff his job as well.'

Joyce's job was even more necessary than Jess's. Jess tried to smile at her, then put one hand on her nylon sleeve.

'Thanks. But don't do that. I'll find something else, don't worry.'

She went out again, down to the propagation shed to collect a plant trolley. Then she filled it up with the glossy fat-leaved Bergenias and trundled the load around to the display stand beside the entrance. She arranged the plants and sold a dozen of them before her lunch break.

At the end of the day she drove home, lost in a train of uncomfortable thoughts. Beth was watching television in the living-room. She aimed the remote to switch it off as soon as Jess came in.

'How was your day?'

'Bad. I got the sack.'

Beth's eyes rounded. Then she uncurled her legs, stood up and hesitantly came to Jess. They sidestepped in front of each other, almost in a little dance, before connecting in a brief uncertain embrace.

'It wasn't good enough for you. You'll find a better job.'

'Will I? Yes, I'm sure I will.'

'I'm really sorry.'

'Don't worry. It'll probably turn out to be a good thing.'

They were already moving apart again, neither of them knowing who had begun the disconnection.

'Is there anything I can do?'

Not be angry with me, Jess thought. Not blame me for my undeniable mistakes. Not lie to me.

'No. Thanks. Everything will be all right.'

Their words were as flat and as dislocated as they felt themselves to be.

'What have you been doing?'

Beth's sidelong glance, no more than a flicker beneath her eyelashes, betrayed her unease. 'Not much. As you can see.'

'Well. It is Sunday. I think I'll just go upstairs and get changed.'

Jess went up to her bedroom. From beneath her she could hear the mumble of the television and she knew that Beth had subsided into the corner of the sofa again. She opened the wardrobe door and removed the bottom shoe box from the stack. She took out the letters and unfolded the white paper and saw that the picture of Tonio was back in its place again. What she had hardly believed was proved to be true – it was Beth who had found it and taken it, and Beth who had replaced it once more.

Jess sat down on the bed and looked at the photograph for a long time.

No inspiration or direction emanated from it: there was nothing to tell her what she should do next. But Jess had the sense that the most rigid and established bonds that had kept her plodding the same channels for years were at last breaking up and dissolving.

The truth that she had suppressed was rising closer to the surface; it was barely a secret any more. The old fear of its being known was suddenly counterweighted by a fierce longing to set herself free of the burden.

If she asks me, Jess resolved, I will tell her the truth. If she asks.

The decision itself was a kind of freedom. She put the picture away in its box. At once she began to think, not of Beth or Tonio or her lost job, but of Rob.

She lay back on her bed, letting her clenched fists fall open. Open-eyed, she imagined the close warmth of his skin and the blue-white hollow at the small of his back, and the pleasing scent of his sweat. A longing to lose herself in the intricate, demanding and therefore obliterating mechanisms of sex crept over her. And she hazily smiled because it was incongruous to find herself middle-aged and yet still so susceptible. She had been amazed that sex was so good with Rob; it had begun in need and despair and it was getting better, and simpler, as her shock at finding herself doing it at all faded away.

Jess lay for a moment longer, allowing herself to bask in the chain of recollections. Then she rolled over to stretch out for the telephone beside her bed. She dialled his number and let it ring, long after he would have picked it up if he were there, if he were going to answer.

Rob and Cat bought a bag of chips at the shop midway between the pub where they had spent the evening and Cat's house. They walked slowly, dipping into the bag in turn. As they turned into her street a train rattled over the embankment beside it, the yellow windows forming a smudged chain of light that failed to make them lift their eyes.

Rob took her keys and opened the door for her.

'Come in,' Cat said. They went up the damp stairs to the door of her bedsit.

He was reminded all over again of the first night as she slid a disc into the player, as she rummaged in the cupboard under the sink for something to drink. The recollection froze him and Cat looked over her shoulder to see him hunched, white-faced, inside his leather jacket.

'It's okay,' she said. She touched her fingers to his cheek.

'I dream about it,' Rob told her.

He had not admitted as much to Jess, but now he blurted out to Cat the repeating terror of crashing metal and blood and the thwacking roar of the helicopter as he crouched in its terrible eye of light.

'I'm not surprised,' she soothed him.

'I don't dream about Danny. Only about blood and noise; then I wake up, and I'm like fighting to escape from the nightmare, from the grip of it, and then I'm properly awake and I remember all over again that it was real. That it happened and it's still happening.'

He would turn over to Jess so that she stirred in her sleep and held him, and the close cottony scent of his mother closed around him again.

'It'll get better, I'm sure,' Cat said. 'It's just time, isn't it?' She stood behind him and massaged his temples with her fingers. 'Do you like this? I always do it to my mum when she's got a bad head.'

Rob let the rigid stalk of his neck loosen and fall back a little. Cat bent forward and kissed the top of his head. Then she reached around and undid the buttons of his shirt and slid her small hands in against his chest.

'Try and forget about it for a bit,' she whispered, her mouth warm against his ear. 'You can't go on blaming yourself.'

'I do blame myself. Even being in this room reminds me of what I did.'

'And what about being with his mother, then?'

She was still standing behind him. Rob couldn't see her face.

'That too,' he muttered.

But with Jess he felt immune. There was nothing further to admit to her, nothing worse or more fearful that could happen between them, and still she had not rejected him. It gave all their dealings a lightness that was almost hallucinatory. More, Jess satisfied a need in him that had gone unmet for so long that it had grown within him and alongside him to become a part of his anatomy.

No wonder, Rob thought, that what they did to each other was so powerful. He thought of her now with longing and a spurt of desire caught him and stiffened him.

Cat was too cunning to press him any further about Jess. With her precise instinct for achieving what she wanted she slipped around to face him and then sat down across his lap. Her small skirt rode up her thighs and she shifted forward so that her forehead touched his. The corners of her mouth curled upwards in satisfaction as she discovered his erection.

She kissed him and, shifting her weight, he kissed her back.

'Try not to think about the accident all the time,' she breathed. 'You're going to have to go to court, aren't you? The police and the judge and all of them will do what they're going to do and you'll have to take it from them. Perhaps go to prison like you said. That's their, like, what do they call it? Retribution? Only you'll be doing double, Rob, because you're punishing yourself so hard as well.'

*No*, he thought. But he didn't try to contradict her now.

'Look,' she said, in a softer voice. 'We're here this minute, the two of us.' She slid her hands from his shoulders, down his arms to catch his wrists. Her hair fell against his mouth and he lifted their joined hands to brush away the strands. 'What do I have to say to you? Let's go to bed, okay?'

It was ordinary, and normal, Rob thought as they stood up. This was what his life had been like, on the other side of the brackets, before.

Cat's body seemed childlike after Jess's ampleness. Her skin was tight and smooth and as he kissed her again he could feel tiny shivers of pleasure and happiness rising in her like bubbles.

She took him by the hand and led him to her bed. Her cat-eyes slanted as she looked up at him from under her fringe. She took off her clothes and he followed suit, dropping them to make a heap with hers.

'Better,' Cat murmured. 'Now you're getting the idea.'

Her sheets smelled of the scent counter at Debenham's, rather than of clean laundry and ironing, like Jess's did. Cat lay back and spread out her arms, tilting her head back to expose her throat and the tender hollow at the base of it. Rob knelt over her and put his tongue in the soft place.

'Ahh,' she sighed.

'Cat.'

'That's me.'

A little later he asked her urgently, 'Are you okay? I've got nothing with me.'

249

Dreamily she put her hands either side of his face, holding him still so she could look into his eyes.

'It's fine.' She lifted her hips towards him. 'Everything's cool. You don't have to worry about anything. I promise.'

'You don't have to promise me things.'

'I do, because I want to.'

She was whispering, guiding him into her. He could see the lovely obliqueness of her smile. 'That's right. Like that. Yes. *Rob.*'

# Thirteen

Beth had imagined doing this often enough. But now she was actually here she felt alarmed, as if her self-control had all evaporated and there was no way of predicting what she might be capable of doing next.

She was sitting at the window table of a café bar on the corner of Sam's street, looking diagonally across the road to his house. It was white stucco, like the others in the terrace, with three steps up to the front door and elegant little iron-lace balconies in front of the raised ground-floor windows. The front door was painted bright red, the same colour as one of Sadie's power suits.

'Hi. What can I get you?'

The waiter was done up in a long white wraparound apron and a black T-shirt with the name of the bar printed across the chest. He was Australian, muscly-armed, with blond surfer-boy looks fading in the London murk.

'Just – oh, a glass of wine. White.'

She listened without hearing while he recited the Sancerres and Chardonnays, and picked the last one he mentioned. He whisked about with glasses and ashtrays and she peered around him, not wanting her view of the house obscured.

'Will someone be joining you?'

'What? No. No, no one else.'

'Uh-uh. You haven't been in before. Are you local?'

The bar was almost empty and he was being friendly, maybe even preparing to flirt with her. Beth pressed her lips tightly together and stared out into the street.

'No.'

Sam's Saab was drawing up outside the house. It was driven by Sadie; Beth could see the gloss of her dark hair.

'I see. Right. Well, enjoy your wine, won't you?' Offended, the waiter withdrew and left her alone.

It was Wednesday evening. After her weekend with Jess Beth had called Sam on Monday and again on Tuesday, until she was afraid that his secretary was becoming suspicious. Sam hadn't returned her calls. This morning the secretary had told her that Mr Clark was working at home today. Beth had waited through the long afternoon in a state of indecision, but as soon as six o'clock came she walked out of her office and caught a bus to Kensington. She had never been to Sam's home, but she had long kept the exact location of it pinpointed in her head. Her journeys to and fro across London were even undertaken in reference to it – such and such a place being quite near to Sam's, or a long way off, or in the opposite direction.

Sam was in the passenger seat of the car. She saw him climb out and say something across the roof of it to Sadie. They were both smiling. Beth almost spilled her wine. She put it down and hid the lower half of her face with her hands.

The children were in the back. Sam opened the rear door to help them out and they spilled on to the pavement. Alice in a red duffle coat and Justin in a padded anorak raced each other up the steps, and tiny Tamsin scrambled after them.

Sadie was wearing leggings and a big plaid shirt. She was smiling as she followed her children up to the red front door, looking softer and younger than on the few other occasions Beth had seen her. As she searched for her keys the children bumped and nudged around her like tugs with a liner.

Sam was unloading shopping bags from the boot of the car. They had been on some family outing and now they were coming home for supper and bathtime and story-reading. They looked like a happy family.

They *were* a happy family, Beth thought bitterly, as she watched them disappear into the house.

She waited five minutes, then she went to the phone at the back of the bar.

It was Sadie who answered.

'May I speak to Sam Clark, please?'

'Sure. Who's calling?'

Beth made up a name and added that she was from the office.

'Hello?' Sam came on the line sounding puzzled and irritated. 'It's me.'

There was an aching silence. Beth added, 'I'm in the bar across the street. Can you come out?'

'Hold on please.' He put the phone down and she heard him walking away, then voices in the distance. Her stomach felt entirely hollow. When he came back he spoke quickly, in a low voice that she had to strain to hear.

'Walk down the next street. There's a little public garden at the end.' He cut her off before she could answer. Beth paid her bill and scooped up her coat, pulling it on as the waiter came over to help her. She went out into the smoky air.

Sam pulled up behind her in the Saab before she reached the entrance to the park. He leaned over and opened the door, and she swung herself inside. She saw at once that he was apprehensive, as well as angry with her, and the realisation gave her the first savour of power over him that she had ever tasted.

He accelerated sharply, driving fast to get further away from his house. Beth sat back and looked at the well-kept houses and prosperous streets.

'Nice area,' she murmured.

'For God's sake. What are you doing? What exactly was I supposed to say to Sadie?'

'Whatever you did say, you're here now, aren't you? It can't have been so difficult.'

'Beth. You don't understand, do you?' When she didn't answer he took his hand off the wheel and searched for hers. 'You'd better tell me what's happened.'

She was disappointed already. She could force herself on him, but she couldn't make him give her what she needed. She wanted his closeness, not to have him afraid of what she might do next. She kept seeing Sadie on the steps of the house, with their children bumping around her.

Sadly she said, 'You haven't called me. I wanted to see you.'

'Christ, Beth. I've had two really busy days. Justin's been ill and so has the au pair, so I took today off to help Sadie out. We've just got back from taking him to the doctor's.'

He was rumpled and boyish and Beth felt the repetitive pang of love for him. She made herself stare out of the windscreen.

'What are we going to do?'

'Drive around for a bit. I can't be much more than an hour.'

'I didn't mean this minute . . .'

'I know what you meant.'

He didn't offer any more, nor did she try to wheedle it out of him. They had reached an impasse.

After edging forward another few hundred yards in the evening traffic Beth began to tell him about the weekend. She explained about Rob and Jess, and the photograph she had found in her mother's wardrobe.

'You went through your mother's belongings?'

'Yes. Was that a wicked thing to do?'

'I don't know. You must want something very badly. What is it you need to find out?'

'The truth,' Beth breathed softly. 'The answer to a riddle that has eluded me all my life.'

'Ask your mother, then.'

'Do you think she'd tell me?'

'I have no idea. But be direct. Don't go creeping and whispering and groping in the dark.'

'Is that what you think I do?' She turned her head to him now. Sam smiled at her, full of rueful and puzzled charm.

'There is a need in you, I've always known that. A powerful longing for something you can't identify. If you think your mother holds the secret, then why don't you ask her for it outright?'

'Maybe I will,' Beth answered.

Sam took a turning into a side-street and another into a cul-de-sac. He drew in beside a deserted factory building and switched off the engine. Then he leaned across to her. His hand travelled from her knee to the warmth between her thighs. Beth sat very still. Every atom of her longed for him, but she wouldn't let herself give way. That was predictable, the old pattern between them, and tonight had altered the direction.

She lifted his hand and moved it away, and she felt a jolt of surprise passing through him. When she looked into his eyes there was dismay and annoyance, and perhaps a shade of respect. She also thought that he was a little afraid of her.

She said gently, 'You should get back, and so should I. You could drop me at a tube station.'

'All right. I'll call you, though. I'll call you first thing tomorrow.'

At Hammersmith station she stepped out on to the pavement and let him go without looking back. She joined the thin stream of people trickling into the anonymous maze of the underground.

Through the days that followed Jess went to the nursery, did her work and came back again, all the time sensing that a change was coming that would be much more far-reaching than merely losing her job.

Each evening she went to Rob's. There was a new level of need or insistence in him. He knelt in front of her and tilted her face between his hands, studying her expression in the light of the bedside lamp. He took off her clothes and folded each piece before laying it aside, then touched her as if trying to memorise the loose planes of her body. When they lay down he held her tightly, his face pressed against her neck. She could feel the moist exhalation of his breath.

Rob had been to meet the barrister who would represent him, and had come back despondent.

'I *am* guilty,' he said. 'I was driving, I was drunk. Why am I pleading the opposite?'

Patiently Jess reiterated, 'Your tyre blew. It was an accident.'

'If it were Danny instead of me, what would Danny be doing?'

'The same. Defending himself.'

'I wish I knew. I wish he were here.'

'I know. So do I.'

'Oh God, Jess. How can one minute change everything for ever?'

Blindly, then, they reached for each other. Their mouths bruised, and their fingernails and knuckles scraped on the knobs of bone and sheaths of muscle that separated them.

Afterwards they lay breathless and wordless, watching the reflections in each other's eyes. Jess thought she saw images of confusion now in Rob's. She began to dream of ways that they might set themselves free together; there was a desperation in their connection that made her long to follow it as far as it would go, to whatever conclusion might come. Her fingers hooked and knotted in his hair.

'Let's go away,' she breathed. 'Let's leave everything behind and run.'

Rob gazed at her, touching his thumb to the corner of her mouth as if it were clay to be moulded. An answering reck-lessness flared briefly in his eyes, before fading away again.

'Sure. How about the Caribbean?'

'I mean it. Listen to me. We'll go somewhere where it's warm and sunny.'

She was dreaming of Italy. There would be flowers and blue skies, and the first warmth of summer in the air.

'In virtual reality?' he asked bitterly.

'In the flesh.' The stared at each other, trying to gauge

the depth of intention. 'I'll sell the house and we can use the money.'

'Don't sell your house. It was Danny's home.'

Jess murmured, 'I'll think. I will do something.'

Then at the beginning of April came Lizzie's fortieth birthday.

In the days beforehand she insisted, 'I don't want a celebration, I don't want anything. I'm just going to pretend it isn't happening.'

It was James who decided there must be a surprise party. It was time for something to celebrate, he reasoned, and having passed fifty himself he couldn't see that turning forty was anything for Lizzie to feel disturbed about. He telephoned Jess to tell her his plans.

'Will you do me a favour? Will you take her out somewhere interesting on the day and keep her busy until it's time for the party?'

And when Jess hesitated he added quickly, 'I'll pay for whatever it is, of course.'

'It isn't that,' Jess assured him, although she hadn't found another job and anxiety about how to pay the bills once she had left the nursery nagged her constantly. 'Are you sure it's what Lizzie would want?'

'Lizzie adores a party, doesn't she?' James said firmly. 'And now she's finished the filming she'll enjoy a day off.'

So Jess invited Lizzie to spend the day of her birthday with her at a nearby health club. Lizzie was pleased with the idea and accepted immediately. She thought they both deserved a day's pampering, and looked forward to the opportunity to be with Jess without the disagreements that had lately come between them.

'I won't be back from the party until late tonight,' Jess explained to Rob as they prepared to go their separate ways on Lizzie's birthday. It was a Friday and Rob was already dressed in his work clothes, and Jess was putting on her good shirt and jacket.

They had to move carefully around each other in the narrow confines of his room.

'It doesn't matter. I'll wait up for you.'

'I don't want you to, Rob. If I'm drunk I'll stay over at Lizzie's or else I'll go home for the night and see you tomorrow. Why don't you get together with some of your own friends this evening?'

Time was forcibly exposing the differences between them. Rob's withdrawal from his old ways and friends of his own age made Jess anxious, but whenever she suggested and he agreed that he should resume them she was immediately pricked by a kind of despairing jealousy. She could never be young like his friends, so the gap between them could never be closed.

Jess knew that there was another woman who came to his room. Sometimes she found traces of her: a discarded pink paper tissue with a print of lipstick, a dark paint-lick where her mascara wand had tapped against the mirror over the sink. More often it was a matter of intuition, when the room seemed tidier or smelled sweeter than usual. Jess ignored these signs because she didn't want to see them, or recognise what they meant. Yet with an almost unconscious part of herself she speculated about her rival. She would be younger than Rob, or the same age. Everything, she guessed, that she was not.

Rob also knew that he couldn't be properly a part of Jess's life. He couldn't imagine a time ever coming when he would be able to go with her to parties like this evening's, and the thought made him want to hold on even tighter to what he did have of her. To hold on to their hours of freedom and privacy, as if they were numbered. And in another dimension of his life, outside the brackets that Danny's death had set around it, he saw Cat.

Their relationship was all Cat's doing, at the beginning. She was subtle and tenacious at getting what she wanted, then holding on to it. After the first time they slept together he watched her lying in bed, with the certainty that he wouldn't see her again. He regretted it, distantly, but there were too many other much bigger demands pressing on him.

'I'll see you,' she promised, and he nodded without committing himself, before sliding out of the door. But Cat meant what she said. She proved to have a knack for turning up at his place at the right times, when Rob was lonely and filled with dread of the future. Cat was carefully undemanding. They went to the pub together, or to see a film. Once they went to a club, a different one from the place they had been with Danny. Half unwillingly, for odd afternoons or evenings, he let her draw him back into his old life. He discovered an affection for the times *before* that he had not felt or understood while they were still his.

Cat didn't ask what he did when he was not with her and, after the first time, Jess's name was never mentioned between them.

Rob watched Jess dressing up for the day with her sister. She twisted her head, deftly slipping a pearl stud into each earlobe. The strong spring light fell on her face. Her skin was lined and the corners of her eyes were drawn down under a fold of skin, and the evidence of her age struck him with an inarticulate tenderness and a longing to capture the moment and Jess with it, for ever, before she could disappear or desert him.

He spoke her name, so thickly that she turned to him with widening eyes.

'You are beautiful,' he told her.

Her face softened. She reached out and took him in her arms and rocked him against her.

'I love you,' Jess said, and in that moment he meant everything to her, more even than Danny had done.

They were both late. They could hear the whisper of the minutes passing. It was Rob who stood back, touching his fingers to her cheek as he did so.

'Enjoy the massage and the hot tub, and the party tonight as well. I'll go to the pub or somewhere for a couple of hours and I'll see you tomorrow.'

In spite of himself, in spite of everything else, Rob knew exactly where Cat would be on a Friday evening. He also knew that she would be watching for him.

'I can't believe it,' Lizzie sighed, leaning her head back against the dripping wall of the steam room. 'Forty. *Forty.*'

'Try to think of it as an achievement,' Jess murmured with her eyes closed. They had swum against the current in the pool and baked themselves on the sunbeds. Now, dressed in towel togas, they were moving lazily between the steam heat and the white plastic recliner chairs beside the pool.

'Anyway, would you go back to being twenty-two again if you could?'

'Yes,' Lizzie said. 'Like a bloody shot. Wouldn't you?'

Jess shook her head.

'Why not?'

'Live through everything all over again? No, thanks.'

Lizzie regarded her. The vehemence of Jess's words indicated some level of bitter experience that she hadn't shared. What was there in the past that had made her sister close down and stand back from the world? Perhaps, she thought, she had never properly understood her. If she had done, surely, the affair with the boy would not have seemed so shocking, so completely out of character?

The photograph that Beth had produced slipped into her mind for a moment.

Jess was still talking, with the steam vent hissing softly behind her and the clouds of eucalyptus-scented vapour blurring the space between them.

'It is an achievement. You've got James and Sock, and your career, look at all the work you've done . . .'

Lizzie interrupted her. She believed she had understood one thing, even though it was only about herself.

'Bloody police dramas. I was crap, anyway, and I hated every minute of doing it. Listen. When you're forty you've got to be able to look at your life and your talents, haven't you? I've just decided something, sitting here with you.'

'What's that?'

'I'm going to pack it in, darling, and be a proper mother. And if James stops loving me because I'm dull, well . . .' She stopped at the thought, then rushed on, 'At least I'll know what it was he fell for. I'll have to try and make another comeback.'

Jess said, 'I don't think you need worry. James loves you so much it shines out of him. It's nothing to do with you being on the telly or assuring everyone who tunes in to Classic FM that they never need have chapped hands again. It's because you are yourself, and Sock's mother.'

Lizzie leaned her head back in the kindly mist and closed her eyes. Did she deserve the answer to be so simple?

'Maybe. I should be happy to have James and Sock, shouldn't I, and stop wishing for anything more. Stop fearing anything less, too.'

And what did Jess have? Remorse suddenly pinched at Lizzie's diaphragm, leaving her breathless. 'Do you think I'm a thoughtless self-centred bitch?'

Jess laughed. 'Of course not. You're my sister. We're very different, that's all.'

'The family unlikeness.'

The final gasp of steam was exhaled from the vent into dripping silence.

Lizzie reached impulsively across and touched Jess's wet, smooth arm. 'I'm so happy you asked me to do this with you today. It's the best present I could have, our being friends again. Look. There's something I need to say. I'm sorry I made such a thing about you and the boy.'

'Rob.'

'About you and Rob. I didn't understand. I don't understand still, if you want the truth. But if it's what you need it's none of my business, Jess. Will you forgive?'

'You know you don't have to ask that.'

'*Will* you?'

'Yes. I need you as much as you need me, you know.'

Lizzie said humbly, 'I don't think I ever realised that.'

The door opened. 'Mrs Arrowsmith? Mrs Arrowsmith?'

It was Jess's masseuse in a pink overall and a plastic name badge. Jess gathered her towel around herself and went to follow her. The sisters smiled at each other through the dispersing steam.

'Happy birthday,' Jess reminded Lizzie.

They finished their day with a facial and a face make-up. After the various layers of paint had been applied Jess felt as if she was being despatched for the evening wearing a latex mask, but Lizzie was pleased with hers.

'It was all worth it, I feel thirty again.' She pouted at Jess's reflection next to hers in the changing-room mirror. 'And you look great.'

'I look like an old slapper,' Jess corrected her.

'Not a bit. Just entirely glamorous. You're much the better-looking of the two of us. Always have been.'

Jess drove them home to Lizzie's. The story she and James had told her was that the three of them were going out for a celebration dinner together. Lizzie sighed happily in anticipation.

'I'm so glad I'm going out with the two people I love best in all the world.'

Jess smiled weakly, thinking of the feverish preparations made by James and the house that would even now be filling up with giggling, conspiratorial friends. She would not want to be in Lizzie's place.

There were no tell-tale cars in the street when they got there. James had warned everyone to park further away. The house was quiet as they reached the gate. To Jess's relief it was exactly the time she had promised to deliver Lizzie home again.

Lizzie rummaged for her keys, opened the front door. The hallway was dark and silent. Calling out for James, Lizzie flung open the door of the living-room. There was a sudden blaze of light and a wall of beaming faces. Forty people began singing 'Happy Birthday'.

Jess watched her sister's face. After a second's amazed disbelief it broke into a rapturous smile. Lizzie was pleased.

James had been right after all, and Jess's fears were misplaced. *He knows her better than I do*, she thought. It was right that he should.

Lizzie was swamped with kisses and hugs and presents. 'I can't believe it,' she kept crying delightedly. James had done a good job. There were actors and neighbours and family friends and Lizzie's agent. And at one side of the crowd Jess was amazed to see Beth.

'Thank you so much, Jess,' James whispered to her. 'You did it beautifully.'

'I need a *very* large drink.'

'And you shall have one.'

'Champagne,' Lizzie was calling, lifting a bottle in each hand. 'Come on, all of you. If I've really got to be forty let's do it in style.'

Jess took a glass and drained it. She knew at least half the people in the room and it took her a while and most of a second glass of champagne before she reached Beth's side.

'I didn't expect to see you.'

'It's a surprise party, Mum.'

'How long are you home for?'

'Just tonight. I came straight up on the train and I'll go back in the morning. You look different.'

Remembering, Jess put up her fingertips to test her maquillage. 'I had my face done with Lizzie. Does it look awful? I feel as though it's going to crack.'

'No, it's good. You just don't look like anyone's mother.'

'Perhaps that's no bad thing,' Jess answered thoughtfully.

Two more people nudged against them. One was Evie, Lizzie's oldest friend from drama school, and the other was a pony-tailed man in a sea-green tunic whom Jess had never seen before. Evie introduced him as Lizzie's astrologer. He gazed deep into Jess's eyes, then bent low over her hand to kiss it.

'Has anyone ever spoken to you about your aura?' he murmured.

Jess resigned herself to this conversation as one of the waiters hired by James refilled her glass.

The caterers had laid out a buffet supper in the kitchen. It was a warm evening and the french doors were open to let the guests drift out into the garden. Jess saw Beth laughing with the young actor who had played the rookie CID officer in Lizzie's police serial. The circles of conversation formed and re-formed and the talk and laughter grew noisier. It was a good party. Lizzie floated from group to group on a tide of champagne and attention.

Jess looked around the swell of the party and followed the connections between people as if they were links in a chain. Evie's husband had taught briefly at the drama school, had introduced Lizzie to her agent, who years later had married as his third wife the businesswoman through whom Lizzie had eventually met James . . . These connections were life's ligaments, Jess thought, her reverie fuelled by the champagne she had drunk. They held everyone securely suspended in the warm and necessary fluids of family and friendship. Only in her own case, some of the ligaments had been severed. She was isolated where Lizzie was gregarious, and she knew that her isolation had deepened with Danny's death and her immersion in Rob.

Jess drank some more champagne and glanced across to Beth. The rugs had been rolled back in the living-room and the dancing was beginning. James took Beth by the hand and they shimmied across the floor together, laughing at the tangles of their clumsy feet. Jess thought how good it was to be at this party. The connections bound her in place too. Everything was capable of change. For a long time she hadn't believed it, but now she knew she wouldn't feel the same sadness for ever.

'Here is my beautiful dreamer,' a voice murmured in her

ear. It was the astrologer, but Jess felt happy enough not to mind even him.

'God, how much champagne have I drunk?'

Lizzie sat at the kitchen table, legs and arms flopping over her chair. The tears and laughter of the evening had melted her elaborate eye make-up and turned her eye sockets into sooty smudges.

'Just enough.' James tipped the dregs of the last bottle into the nearest glass. Lizzie crooked her arm around his neck and pulled him closer so she could kiss him greedily.

'That was the best party ever and you are the best husband a woman of forty could wish for. So I'm just going to finish this last little drink, my love, and then I am going to take you upstairs to bed. Right?'

'Right.'

She winked at Jess and Beth who were sitting at the table opposite her. They had enjoyed a long post-mortem on the party, and now Jess was thinking fondly of one of the twin beds in Lizzie's spare bedroom.

'Having James here and Sock elsewhere for one night is too good an opportunity to miss. No small-hours cries, no dawn summons.'

'It's past the small hours already, darling.'

'My God, what are we waiting for?'

Lizzie stood up, not very steadily, and James supported her.

'Good-night, you two. Thank you for being here. Thank you for everything. I love you both.'

She blew a kiss each to Jess and Beth and had almost reached the door before she turned back with a mischievous and lopsided grin.

'You never told me, Beth. Who was he? Did you find out?'

'Who was who?'

'The pin-up in the picture you brought to show me.'

A slow, dark flush began to mount in Beth's face but Jess did not see it. She kept her eyes on the table, on the last plates and glasses left by the caterers.

'No. It doesn't matter.'

'Oh well. Dark horse. Jess always was. Night night.'

Jess sat motionless on one of the two guest beds. Her head and hands felt disconnected from her body and she could hear the blood dully surging in her ears. The beds had matching pale-blue floral quilt covers and pillowslips, and a bottle of mineral water with two glasses stood on the table between them. James had thought of everything.

The door clicked and Beth came in from the bathroom. Jess didn't look up, but she heard her turn back the cover and slip into bed.

'Are you ready to go to sleep?' Jess asked. 'Shall I turn out the light?'

'If you're ready.'

Jess lay down and reached for the switch. The darkness enveloped them and the cover of it and the descending silence made her suddenly blurt out the question.

'Why did you steal my photograph? Why did you search through my things and take it?'

'It wasn't stealing.' Beth's voice was muffled. 'I put it back.'

'*Why?*'

'I wanted to know something. I felt that our house, all of our life, was filled with secrets and I thought you were sharing them with Rob and I felt closed out and jealous. I've always felt jealous and excluded, didn't you know that? You and Danny and now you and him. Never you and Dad, that would have been something.'

'I see.'

'No, you don't. God, I wish I hadn't drunk so bloody much, I can't think straight. I wanted to know whatever it was I'm not supposed to know, right? I thought Lizzie might be able to tell me. But she couldn't. So now I'm asking you.'

Just like Sam told me to, Beth thought. She realised with a little shock that she had barely thought of Sam all evening. 'Who is the man in that picture? The photograph you keep hidden under the letters in the box at the bottom of your wardrobe, okay?'

Jess said, 'His name is Tonio. He is a man I fell in love with twenty years ago in Italy.'

There was a long, long pause.

'And so,' Beth said carefully, 'are you going to tell me about Danny and me? The difference between us?'

If she asks me outright I will tell her, Jess remembered. That was what I decided. Not that she doesn't already know the answer.

She said clearly and slowly, 'Tonio is Danny's father.'

Beth sighed. Jess thought she heard relief, even triumph. Suspicion must have seeded itself within her long ago. Perhaps even at some level she had always known.

'Yes, I thought that must be it. Did Danny know?'

'No.'

'Does Dad?'

'No.'

'Does anyone?'

'Nobody.'

'What about Rob Ellis? Have you told *him*? When you were going through Danny's things together, perhaps? Was that what the two of you were laughing about?'

'No. He doesn't know. He has told me things about himself, about his past, but he didn't ask for my secrets in return.'

Beth turned over. Jess knew that she was lying with her back to her. She could picture the curve of her spine, the knobs of bone swelling under the pale skin with its achingly familiar configuration of tiny moles. She wanted to hold her as she had done when she was a little girl.

'Beth? I don't know what else to say. I'm sorry.'

'At least I know, now.'

'Do you want to talk about it?'

With deliberate, wounded cruelty Beth answered, 'I think it may be too late for that. And I want to go to sleep now.'

'All right. Good-night, then,' Jess said humbly.

She lay on her back for a long time, her eyes dry and wide open, staring into the dark. Beside her, at last, Beth's breathing slowed and steadied into sleep.

'What's happened?' Lizzie asked in bewilderment. Even through the blindfold of her hangover she could see that whatever it was was serious. Beth shook her head and finished her coffee. She had refused breakfast, telling Lizzie she had to get straight back to London. There was a train at midday.

Jess had got up very early and had swept floors and washed glasses and ashtrays with grim concentration. Now she sat at the end of the table watching a pair of fat thrushes in the trees outside the kitchen window. The birds took it in turns to guard the nest site or swoop away in search of food.

'I'll drive you to the station, Beth,' James offered. 'I can pick up Sock on the way back.' He had stayed overnight with the nanny who had looked after him while Lizzie was filming.

Beth agreed wearily. She went upstairs and came down again with her coat on, and Jess and Lizzie followed her and James out to the car.

'Can't you stay?' Jess implored, at the same time hearing how repetitive her pleas were becoming. 'Just till this evening? We can talk, at least . . .' She spun round suddenly to James and Lizzie. 'Can't I just speak to her? Privately, for one minute?'

Their immediate backing away told Jess that she must look and sound quite crazy. But she wanted more than ever to catch hold of Beth and keep her, as if the force of her determination alone could break through to her.

Beth looked coldly at her with Ian's eyes. The dry, brittle husk of self-containment kept Jess at a distance.

'I want to think. I just want some time on my own to think about it. I feel as if I've lost Danny twice over.'

Jess stood back again. She felt that she was always saying that she was sorry, and that the need for apologies was only just beginning. She was very tired, and lonely, and all the optimism she had felt the night before collapsed within her.

'All right.' She was going to cry, she couldn't help herself. 'All right. Just remember . . .'

She was going to offer some promise or reassurance, but couldn't find the words. She lifted her hand to James instead, to indicate that everything and nothing had been said, and turned back towards the house blinded with tears.

In the kitchen, now smelling of bleach and cool air instead of the smoky party aftermath, Jess poured herself a cup of coffee with shaky hands. Lizzie propped herself against a corner of the table, legs crossed, fiercely drawing on the first cigarette of the day.

'You'd better tell me, Jess.'

'Had I? Yes, I suppose I should. Are you sitting comfortably?'

'Don't be hard, it doesn't suit you.'

Jess turned her back, went to the window. Both thrushes were at the nest now. They jostled together, heads bobbing like clockwork models.

Amazingly, Lizzie didn't try to interrupt her while she talked. And at the end, when Jess looked round again, Lizzie's eyes were popping and her mouth hung open. She shook her head in slow bewilderment.

'I don't understand you.'

'Really? Couldn't you put yourself in my place, Liz? I fell in love with Tonio. It was as if I was breathing for the first time. It was as if I'd never been touched, or opened my eyes, or seen the sky before. *In love* sounds so banal, doesn't it? The stuff of pop songs and adverts and Sunday afternoon films? But it caught me. I was alive, and before I had only been mechanical. I would have done anything for him, anything to stay with him. But he didn't ask me, and I was already married, and I had Beth.'

Lizzie collected her wits. Her face drew itself together and softened with empathy.

'Yes, I know what being in love feels like,' she said.

'You do. That's what happened to me. And I was pregnant

269

when I came home to Ian. I was only a few days late, but I knew. It was what I wanted. I wanted that baby, I wanted Danny more than anything, and I had him. He was *mine*. My reason, my reminder.'

'Did you ever hear from Tonio again?'

Jess hesitated. Then she said, 'No.'

'Why didn't you even tell me?'

'Because I didn't want you to have to keep that secret for me for the whole of Danny's life.'

Slowly, wonderingly, Lizzie nodded. 'And Ian never knew either?'

'No.'

'I always thought he treated you badly. Never being there, being angry when he was. I guessed there were affairs before Michelle.'

'It wasn't that. We both went through the motions, you know? Of being loyal and responsible and responsive to each other. For all those years. But it never worked. It wasn't working even at the beginning, before Tonio. It would have been better if we'd never married in the first place. Except that then we wouldn't have had Beth.'

'She was very upset. It's my fault; I shouldn't have mouthed off about the photograph last night. I thought he must be just some guy out of your past, I was going to tease you about keeping him secret. Perhaps if I hadn't said anything, none of this need have come out.'

Jess looked at Lizzie's kitchen dresser with its rows of cups and jugs and blue-and-white plates and snapshots of Sock, evidence of an orderly domestic life. She said slowly, as if working it out for herself, 'I'm glad she knows. That there's a source for her to let her anger spring out of. In the end it may even make it better.'

'And what about Ian?'

'Now that you know, and Beth knows? I shall have to tell him the truth. I don't know how. But I owe him that much, don't I?'

Lizzie left her perch on the table and came to stand at the

window beside Jess. She put her arm around Jess's shoulders and held her protectively, and Jess caught the old, familiar waft of perfume and cigarette smoke.

'Thank you,' Jess said softly, then, 'Look at the birds.'

They stood side by side, watching the nest building.

# Fourteen

Jess tried to write a letter to Ian. She tried once, then half a dozen more times. Each time she tore the paper in half or screwed it into a ball.

*Do you remember Tonio Fornasi?*
Probably you don't. Why should you? He was just an Irish-Italian we met on holiday long ago, when we were young. Then, after you went home to your work, Beth and I stayed by the sea for three more weeks, until the end of the summer's sunshine.

And when the three weeks were over I almost didn't come back, Ian. You wouldn't remember anything about that because you never knew what happened.

I fell in love with Tonio. It was as if he just reached out and picked me, like a fig off the tree. I must have been ripe, mustn't I?

At the beginning, in the afternoons when he wasn't giving English lessons, the three of us went to the beach. Beth played in the sand and he built outlandish castles for her and told her rambling stories about the imaginary people who lived in them. He had smooth, tawny skin, and the sea salt crystals dried on the slick black hairs on his legs and forearms and sometimes shot a minuscule rainbow dart into my eyes.

At first I just thought he was beautiful, in the way I might have looked at and admired a painting that didn't belong to me. And I liked him because he made me laugh, and because he listened when I talked and remembered everything I told him, and because he seemed gentle and happy with what he had. Which was almost nothing.

The first evening we spent alone together happened just because you had sunburn and couldn't come too, do you remember that? But as soon as we left the *pensione* it was as if I were Tonio's for the evening. Not in the sense of being possessed, but rather attended to. As if I were precious. For a couple of hours I felt as if I was the most important being in his world. Can you imagine that? I stopped admiring in my detached way and became, well, susceptible.

After that, once I had agreed to stay in Italy and you had gone home, I thought it would be just a flirtation between us. A summer's game, a Mediterranean episode. A kiss or two, perhaps, after dinner under the stars or during a walk on the beach with the moon silvering the sea.

But it became much more than that, because Tonio fell in love with me. He fell in love with Jess Arrowsmith, the calm and rational, the prematurely married and maternal one. I was so amazed by it. I had no idea before then that I might be interesting to a man like Tonio.

Yet it wasn't that I didn't want it to happen, because I did. I dreamt of it. It was so long ago, but I can still remember how it felt. On one day the sea was flat and I could see the uneventful horizon. On the next, a magnificent wave had swollen up out of nowhere, and the crest of it towered over me but there was an instant when I could have turned my back and held my breath and swum away. I didn't. I opened my eyes and let the blue-green water crash all over me; then the wave's undertow caught me and spun me away.

The *signora* in our little hotel had taken a great liking to Beth, do you remember? She was happy to look after her in the evenings although the daughter, the black-eyed pouting Vittoria who was Tonio's English pupil, was deeply jealous of me. Tonio would come to pick me up after Beth had fallen asleep and we'd go out together into the silky warmth of the night.

Tonio lived in one room close to the little port. One night he took me there, and we sat on his iron-framed bed because there was only one chair in the room, and he fed me a picnic of bread and prosciutto and olives and dusty, tough-skinned but intensely sweet little grapes. The grape juice ran over my lips and chin and he wiped it away with the tip of his finger; then he kissed me.

These are the things I remember.

The sounds of the port, men's voices and the creaking of the little boats and the dull putter of the engines as they set out for the night's fishing, rising up to the open window with the mixed reek of salt and cooking and diesel oil.

That night was the first time Tonio and I made love.

The mattress on his bed was thin and hard. The sheets were worn, finely darned in places, but clean and scented with lavender. He left me for a moment and went to the window to close the shutters. His naked back was as brown and smooth as toffee.

I had had the average sexual experiences for a woman of my age and time, I suppose, but Tonio didn't recall any of them.

There was a grace about him, and a reticence that made his advances seem thoughtful, almost reverent. Then, once his reticence was overcome, he became exuberant. Permitted to enjoy it, he took the greatest pleasure in sex. I used to wonder romantically if the duality in him came from the contradictory genes, from the Italian heat and the Irish melancholy.

He kissed the protruding bones of my feet as well as the white strips where my bikini had hidden the pale skin from the sun. All the creases and hollows and nerve-endings of me were valuable to him, as his became to me. Tonio made me feel beautiful, that evening and all the nights that followed, and he gave me the great gift of being uninhibited. Like that, with a man.

I didn't do as much for you, I know. We didn't do it for one another, did we, not in all the years we were married?

You will be thinking, I suppose, that this is all to do with sex.

It was and it wasn't. Sex was important but it was only the key that unlocked a door, and the unlocking of the room of intimacy and what we found within it reminds me of how it is now, with Rob Ellis.

Rob recalls Tonio for me, all the time. There is the same vulnerability, and the opposite face of the coin – a confidence that is all the more devastating because it is unacknowledged. An identical honesty and passion. It is to do with sex, you see, and also it isn't.

Well. That was all the time Tonio and I had together, twenty years ago. It was not quite three weeks; only nineteen days and evenings. At the end of it he didn't ask me to stay with him and I told myself that even if he did, I would refuse. He was penniless and rootless, and he didn't care that he was or wish for anything more, whereas I had Beth and you, and our life together in England. Pallid, anxious Jess, with my prematurely weighty burden of responsibility. I never was going to run off with a wild black-haired gypsy, was I?

The inevitability of our parting didn't make it any easier to bear. Or make it seem any less doubtful, up to the very last moment.

On the final evening Tonio did try to beg me for something. He took hold of my hand and his eyes were black and shiny with grief, but I wouldn't let him speak. I had wound up my determination not to look back to such a point that I was afraid even a word would shatter my resolve. I didn't let him say his word, and every day since then I have wondered what it was that he intended. Some entreaty that I couldn't answer, I suppose, or some promise that he could never have kept. But if I had stayed there – and I so nearly did – and exchanged promises with him, neither of us would have been able to keep them. I knew that then, as surely as I know it now.

We separated for good on that last evening. There were silver bars of cloud across the sky, and the crowds of the *passeggiata* were thinning out. I never looked back at him. Not out of bravery or determination, but out of fear.

That was all. My great love. I am a coward, naturally.

When I came home I knew already that I was pregnant. If I seemed hot and sad and also simmering with mute resentment, perhaps you put it down to the sun and my restless disappointment that the long holiday was finally over. It was easy to cover up. I made the smallest adjustment to the real dates, and my Danny became nominally your Danny too.

It was a bad thing to do, Ian. I don't ask for your forgiveness because I don't deserve it.

Before you ask if I ever saw Tonio again, the answer is no. He sent me a picture postcard once, from a village in the west of Ireland. The people in our old house kindly forwarded it to me here. There was no address but the village name, and the message on the back was only a few colourless words to do with the weather and the scenery. And the last sentence read, *This is a beautiful place to live.* He signed it with his full name, Tonio Fornasi, as if I might not remember him.

I used to imagine that he might have married the plump Vittoria, and fathered a litter of round Italian babies.

That's all, Ian. The whole, complete story.

Jess didn't send this letter, of course. Nor did she send another of the explanatory, self-culpatory versions that she struggled over for hours. In the end she wrote a short note. She was sorry, and ashamed. She had kept a secret for twenty years and now, in grief's unravelling and exposing of truths after Danny's death, it had come out. Beth knew and so did Lizzie, and it was only fair that Ian should hear it from herself.

She was sorry, again.

Ian picked up the letter from England with a sheaf of bills and reminders. Michelle had left them on the kitchen table for him to open on his return from work. He dropped the others and opened the white envelope at once, frowning.

Then he stood in the neat blue-and-white kitchen, holding

276

the single sheet of paper and reading the brief paragraphs over and over again.

'That you, babe?' Michelle called from the bathroom. She came in a moment later, her torso wrapped in one towel, another tucked into a turban around her dripping hair. She held the headdress in place with one hand and slipped her free arm round her husband's waist. Her fingers picked at the buttons of his shirt and when he pulled away she looked quickly up at him.

'What's wrong?'

'What time is it in England now?'

She shrugged. 'I dunno, Ian. You're the native. Some time early in the morning, isn't it?'

'I want to talk to my girl.'

He went into the living-room and stared at the slice of garden visible through the slats of the blind, then picked up the phone and began to dial.

Michelle followed him. 'What's *happened*?'

He gave her the letter and she read it quickly.

'Shit, Ian. Do you believe this?'

He was listening to the ringing tone in London, in Beth's apartment. 'I don't know. I'm going to find out the truth, aren't I?'

'You didn't have to come over here for my sake, Dad.'

'I wanted to come. I couldn't sort this out from the other side of the world, could I?'

They were sitting side by side in front of Beth's gas coal fire; the acid light outside dimmed some of the lustre of the energetic flames. The grudging spring in London had been windy and wet, and only twenty-four hours after leaving Sydney Ian was stricken by the cold. He was sitting in the most comfortable corner of the sofa, that Sam usually occupied. Beth let her father circle her shoulders with his arm and felt the usual bleak twinge of regret that it was not Sam who was here with her. She pushed the thought of him aside. It

277

was getting easier to do, or so she told herself.

'It's not the kind of news you get every day, is it?' Ian said bitterly. His Australian interrogative was becoming more pronounced. 'Your wife's carried a candle for another man all through your marriage. Your son isn't your son. After you've already lost him. I feel as though Danny's been taken away from me twice over.'

Beth stared into the fire.

'I felt that too, when I first knew about it. But Danny's the same person, isn't he? It's like Mum isn't your wife any longer, but she is who she is just the same. Would you rather not have known about this?'

'I wouldn't have minded being left with my memories. What have I got now?'

He was angry. His fists were clenched on the cushions. Beth knew that her father's natural response to whatever might threaten to overpower him was anger. He had come flying back to London in a blaze of it, and now it would have to be directed somewhere, at someone.

'Don't,' she whispered, but he didn't hear her. She felt a prickle of fear, a slow shiver of foreboding, crawling up the back of her neck and into her hair. 'Don't be angry with Jess. I went snooping and I found out what I needed to know.'

'Needed?' He blinked at her, his short eyelashes bleached by the sun making his eyes look porcine.

'I always felt the difference between Danny and me.' She was going to say something like, he was the gold and I was the base metal, but she stopped herself in time.

Ian said roughly, 'There was no bloody difference. You were our kids, both of you. I know that. You were made the same, loved the same. Anything else is a piece of rubbish, whatever your mother says.'

'Dad.' She reached for his hand. The skin on the back of it was reddish and the sinews had grown more prominent. He seemed suddenly older than Jess, and different, almost a stranger. 'Don't judge her too hard, whatever.'

His face contracted between hurt and wrath. 'You defend her, always. You didn't even tell me you'd found out all this.'

'I didn't think I had the right to tell you Mum's secrets. And I don't want to take sides,' Beth protested, but she was thinking, *Yes, I defend her. It's irrational, when I attack her so fiercely in person.*

Ian struggled to take the balanced view for Beth's sake. 'Of course you don't. You're right not to. It's just that Jess and I . . . do you think I don't feel the failure of it all as well? The loss of what we might have been? We were married for over twenty years, for Christ's sake.'

'Does she know you're here? Or are you just planning to turn up at home?'

'I'll call her. I'll let her know what to expect.'

Again Beth sensed the pressure of anger in him like steam building in a sealed chamber. She wanted to find a release valve but had no idea which point to press.

'Be careful,' she implored. 'Be careful, won't you?'

It had been an unusually busy day, for a weekday. There had been a steady stream of cars, and three coach parties.

Jess was the last to leave the nursery, an hour after it closed, at seven o'clock. The day's selling had seriously depleted the rows of plants and some of the specialities were completely gone. Trolley-loads of replacements would have to be brought over from the propagation enclosure to restock, and usually she would have done the job at once. But tonight she decided to leave it until the morning. It was her last week. It wasn't her responsibility any longer.

Joyce had been busy all day in the shop. When Jess came in she offered sympathetically, 'D'you want me to stay another hour and give you a hand? Since you've got your ex coming round?'

Ian had rung Jess that morning. After Jess's first expression of surprise, they had exchanged only the formal minimum of words, recognising that there was nothing to be resolved on the telephone. Jess mentioned afterwards to Joyce that Ian was unexpectedly on his way up to see her. No more than that.

'No, Joyce, thanks all the same. You get on home. You've got enough to do.' Joyce's mother's day nurse didn't like to be kept on late.

Joyce had taken off her overall and put on her coat. She left Jess the safe keys and combination, as she had done often enough before. Jess bagged the day's takings, raising her eyebrows wryly at the large amount of money.

In the safe, Jess saw, were all the takings from the beginning of the week. Graham Adair hadn't done the banking yet. She shook her head and locked up the safe. She was in a hurry: Ian had told her that he would arrive at seven thirty.

There was an added anxiety, also. She had tried to reach Rob at his current job to tell him that they couldn't meet this evening, but he hadn't been there all day long. With these complications twisting in her head she drove home, the familiar route.

Rob was at Jess's house. He owned a set of keys now, and he felt safe there, surrounded by the evidence of normality.

He had gone to work in the morning, but the rough framework of the kitchen he was building changed its dimensions, barring him in and at the same time alarming him with its expanse. The uprights he had installed waited around the margins of the room, anticipating drawers and the shelves and the finish of panelled doors. His hands were clumsy and he found that he was sweating as he handled the plane and chisel. He switched on his radio and listened intently to a talk programme, but when he made a turn that caused him to stumble and pull the jack out of the socket he realised in the sudden leap of silence that he had no idea what the topic of discussion had been.

Carefully, keeping the sense of dislocation at bay, he measured and cut a length of fibreboard to make the base of a worktop. But when he carried it to the intended place he found that it was short in both dimensions. A new sweat of panic broke out across his chest.

He couldn't do this work, he had no idea what he was doing. The place, the glistening familiar blades and curves of his tools, the resiny scent of new wood and the stink of glue, all of these things seemed threatening as well as foreign. Rob leaned against the wall, panting a little, until the rush of air past his head stilled somewhat. Then he packed up his tools again and made his way home, to Jess's house.

He spent the rest of the day enclosed there. He washed down the tiles in the kitchen and vacuumed the carpets and loaded the washing machine with the sheets off the bed. The restoration of order and cleanliness and the buzz of machinery soothed him, white noise briefly blocking out his surges of panic. At the end of the afternoon he took some pieces of chicken out of the fridge, and prepared them in the way that Jess had taught him. It had become their routine to eat a meal together at her house, then to drive to his room for the night, to sleep.

At seven o'clock the doorbell rang. It was too early to be Jess, even if she had forgotten her keys.

From the protective shadows at the kitchen end of the hall-way, Rob looked at the panels of frosted glass in the front door. He saw the outline of a man, a stockily built man with his arm raised, the forefinger pressed to the bell which shrilled aggres-sively. The man's shadow shrank as he waited, listening, while Rob remained motionless. He was thinking of the police, of whatever other nameless authorities might be watching and pursuing him and Jess.

The man, whoever he was, stepped briskly up and rang once more. Rob could see that he was short but thickset, with the outline of powerful shoulders. At last, with evident reluctance, he retreated again. His shadow slid down the glass and disap-peared, and Rob heard the click of the gate closing.

Ian walked back down his old street. It was so much the same, down to the dandelion leaves sprouting in the gritty angle where the brick garden walls met the slabs of the gum-blotted pavement, that he found it hard to hold on to the fact that he no longer lived here. Danny's death was an early-morning dream, and in a moment he would wake up properly to the end of it before the dream evaporated into a morning's undefinable melancholy.

Jess and he would make it. There was no Michelle, he had conjured her out of the erotic shallows of the dream and the incandescent white light of Sydney only lay behind his eyes.

But the street did not fade. Some of the houses had changed hands. There were new neighbours now; their cars and colour schemes and gardens were different. The nearest pub, five hundred yards from Jess's house, was more or less the same, although Ian did not recognise any of the bar staff or early-evening drinkers. He bought a double Scotch and took it to a sticky bench seat under the window, to drink while he waited for Jess.

Jess hurried into the house and Rob came to meet her. Their hands touched and their mouths met eagerly. She noticed that Rob was breathing faster, as if he had been running. She let herself be drawn against him for a moment, closing her eyes with a shiver of longing, then she pulled herself away. She was panting too, with the urgency of what needed to be said.

'I tried to reach you all day.'

'I've been here.'

'I didn't think of that. Why? No, it doesn't matter. Listen, Ian's coming tonight, you mustn't be here.'

'Why not?' he asked automatically, realising at the same moment who the man at the door had been.

Jess's eyes darted around.

'I have to talk to him. He's angry with me, he's come all the way from Sydney.'

'Why?'

'It's about Danny.'

282

'He's angry with *you*?' Rob's shoulders were up, his fists clenched. Jess saw this with a premonitory beat of fear. She tried to speak calmly.

'There's something I should have told you, when you told me about your father and mother. I never did, I don't know why. Partly loyalty to Danny, mostly shame. I will tell you now, but not this minute because there isn't time. Will you just go, and leave me to talk to Ian?'

'Of course I'll go.' His head dropped as he turned away, and she wanted to hold him back.

'Rob . . .'

'Yeah. Will you be okay?'

She faced him, full on. 'Yes. With you. If you're with me.'

'Why are you sending me away then?'

'Just for now, Rob. There's time for everything after this . . .'

Only she had the strongest sense that there was not, that there was no time left.

And it was already too late. The front gate clicked and creaked on its hinges, and Ian's shadow fell across the glass. The doorbell shrilled again.

Without hesitation, now that the moment was here, Jess went to the door and opened it.

Ian looked, and saw. Flickers of suspicion and disbelief and finally recognition chased across his face.

'G'day,' he sneered.

'Come in,' Jess motioned. 'Rob's just going.'

Rob shuffled aside to let him in. As Ian roughly shouldered past, Rob caught the smell of whisky on his breath, and saw the way Jess meekly made way to let this man and the bundle of his aggression into her house.

'Rob.' Jess's voice was firm.

'I'll call you later. I'll call you at ten, right?'

'Piss off, lad, if you know what's good for you,' Ian said.

Rob began to lunge at him but Jess interposed herself. She steered him to the door. 'Go on. Leave it. I'm all right.'

Rob found himself on the other side of the front door. He

listened and waited for a long moment, then went slowly to the gate.

Ian wiped his mouth with the back of his hand. 'Jess. What's that little piece of shit doing here?'

'He's not little. He's six inches taller than you.'

'What's he doing? Christ Almighty, not that?' He gazed at her, rapidly blinking his eyes. 'It *is* that, isn't it? *You* and the, the murderous fucker who killed Dan?' There was a long, painful pause before he stuttered, 'It's porn, that's what it is. It's obscene, Jess. How could you do it?'

Bewilderment had caused his anger to slip out of his grasp for an instant. Jess felt the nudging of compassion for him.

Wearily she said, 'I don't know how. It just happened.'

'Does Beth know about it?'

'Yes.'

'Christ. She never mentioned a word to me.'

'Perhaps she thought it wasn't her business. Have you come from Sydney to talk about this, or about Danny?'

'I don't know. My God, I don't know what to talk about. I was married to you for more than bloody twenty years and it seems I know less about you than the woman next door. How do you think it feels?'

'I don't know. I can guess, I think. Come in the kitchen. I can give you a drink or something to eat, if you want.'

Ian's anger wasn't displaced for long. As Jess found glasses and broke out ice cubes, she felt the heat of it pressing behind her, at the nape of her neck and in the hollow of her back.

'I'm sorry,' she said, an ineffectually generalised apology. Ian took the whisky she gave him and drank it, then poured himself another.

'Are you? He was my son. My son, my son . . .' He rolled the glass against his forehead, the clinking ice making a tiny, inappropriately festive accompaniment. He winced and screwed his eyes shut, but the furious tears squeezed out anyway, under the lashes. He shook them away, rolling his head like a dog in pain. Jess began to calculate how much he must have had to drink. An empty afternoon on the train from London. An hour or so to wait for her to come home, whiled away in the pub. Ian had never been a reflective or temperate man. A spasm of physical fear of him briefly pinched her throat.

Ian snapped his eyes open again. They were burning red-hot, the pupils contracted to specks. 'So. Is it the truth or one of your fantasies?'

'One of my . . . ?'

'You heard. You know. I want the truth. Plain.'

'I wrote it in the letter.'

'Say it. Bloody say it. Look me in the eyes and tell me.' He grabbed her wrist and twisted it, hurting her. 'Whose son? Mine or the nancy Italian's?'

'He wasn't a nancy. What are you afraid of that makes you call him that?'

'*Whose?*'

'His. Tonio's. He was Tonio's son. Let go of me. You're hurting me.'

'He was mine. Can you hear me?' Ian was shouting, the spiritous blast of his breath catching her full in the face.

Sadly Jess shook her head.

'You're a lying bitch.'

'No. Why should I lie to you?'

'You have. That's what you're saying. All the years. All the times I thought . . .'

He drew a single, shuddering breath. There was an instant when he might have swung either way, into sodden tears or incoherent rage. His eye was caught by a movement outside, beyond the french doors that led into the twilit garden. Rob ducked his head but it was too late.

'*Why is he spying on me?*'

The pressure of pain within Ian burst through the leaking seal of his self-control. With one hand he cruelly jerked Jess closer, the other swung back, in a fist, ready to strike her.

Rob ran at the glass door and smashed straight through it, his leather-clad shoulder sending a sparkling shower of splinters through the time-frozen air. He staggered with the force of the impact, then recovered himself. He dived straight at Ian.

Jess ducked to avoid Ian's fist and flattened herself against the kitchen wall, hands pressed to her mouth. It was as if the scene in front of her was on film, slowed almost to a standstill. Rob was out of control as much as Ian. Jess saw it and stiffened with fear.

Ian's head turned and his lips pulled back over his teeth. He swung aggressively to Rob, bracing himself to land a punch with his right hand, his left up in a guard against his jaw.

Rob was younger, and sober, and much quicker on his feet. The wild punch missed his head and he swiped Ian's fist away. He grabbed Ian by the throat and shook him, lifting him right off the floor. Ian kicked up into Rob's groin and as Rob gasped and doubled over Ian sprang on top of him. They collapsed to the floor, kicking and pounding at each other over the stars of broken glass. A chair overbalanced and toppled with them, and as they struggled Jess caught glimpses of first one mottled, rage-twisted face, then the other.

It was a long time, and also only a few seconds.

Rob was strong and fit, and fired by his wild determination that Jess should not be harmed. Ian had only his anger burning, but it was powerful enough to make him fight viciously. His knuckles smashing into Rob's mouth brought the blood springing out over his teeth and tongue. Rob spat and jerked back, breathing in gasps through the streaming blood.

It seemed that the film stopped altogether for a long beat.

But then Rob regathered himself. With all his strength, he smashed a terrible punch into the corner of Ian's eye. Immediately Ian sagged forward like a deflating balloon. As he dropped, the crack of his forehead hitting the kitchen table was a louder echo of the first blow.

Rob stood with his head hanging, shuddering, his hands dangling loose by his sides. Blood still ran freely and dripped off his chin.

Jess gave a little moan and scrabbled towards Ian through

the glass. She knelt over him. His eyes were shut and shallow snoring gasps forced themselves out of his slack mouth. He didn't move when she touched him; when she tried to lift him in her arms his head wobbled inertly and fell sideways. There was a ragged blue-white indentation in the middle of his forehead and a reddening contusion spreading from his temple.

'What have you done?' she cried, looking wildly up at Rob.

Rob began to babble. 'He was drunk, violent drunk. He was going to hit you, I saw him. It was like seeing my mum and *him* all over again. I had to stop him. I had to, I had to . . .'

Jess bent over Ian again, willing him to open his eyes. His breathing thickened and he coughed weakly.

Rob was regaining his senses. As he stared down at the unconscious man he knew that the worst had happened for the second time. The violent loss of control he had always dreaded had finally overtaken him.

'Ian, come on. Wake up. Please open your eyes,' Jess was begging. She hauled herself to the sink and wrung out a cloth in cold water, then folded it over his forehead.

'What can I do?' Rob whispered.

Jess darted a frantic glance at him. 'You'd better go. Go on, just go. I'll do what needs doing here. Get away or you're in serious trouble.'

He knew that she meant it. There was no disagreeing. He melted away, out of the house and into the darkness.

Ian stirred on the floor. Jess swept the glass away from his head with her forearm and a splinter stabbed her wrist. His eyes opened and he stared foggily up at her.

Jess soothed him, 'You're all right. You're going to be all right.' She was patting his forehead with the cold cloth when a sound that shrilled at the periphery of her attention began to register itself as the telephone ringing. To make it stop she jabbed at the receiver and dislodged it from the cradle. As it swung at the end of the cord, she heard Lizzie's puzzled voice.

'Darling, is that you? Jess? Are you there?'

Jess grabbed the mouthpiece with a sob of relief.

'Lizzie.'

'You *are* there. What's going on? Listen, I'm in town. I've had a marvellous facial and a massage and I was going to say shall I come round for a drink . . .'

'Oh please, Lizzie. Just come. Come right now, and help me.'

The sisters helped Ian on to the sofa in the living-room. He was conscious but disorientated.

'Police. I must report this to the police,' he kept repeating.

Lizzie said grimly, 'Just wait a few minutes. Sit there and rest yourself. Leave the reporting to us.'

Jess picked up the bowl of water she had used to bathe his head. Her wrist was roughly bandaged where the broken glass had cut her. She was thinking quickly, images of desperation colliding in her mind. From the mess of what had just happened she tried to pick through the chain of likely consequences.

She remembered about the pig boy. Rob already had a record of assault. He was on bail; he would be remanded, now, if they came for him.

*I don't want to go to jail,* he had whispered.

Why were they here? What reason was there to stay here, where everyone was against them?

Lizzie took her free arm and steered her out to the kitchen, out of Ian's hearing.

'What's going on? What were he and Rob doing in the place together?'

'It was a mistake. Ian arrived in a blind rage, I've never seen him like it. I sent Rob off straight away but he must have climbed into the garden to make sure I was going to be all right. Ian hit out at me and a second later Rob smashed through the window.'

'And bloody well half killed him.' Lizzie blew her cheeks out sharply. 'He's big trouble, that boy. And there's going to be more trouble once Ian gets going on him.' There was a pale tinge of satisfaction in her voice.

'Ian's not half killed, is he?'

288

Seeing her real fear, and remembering the intensive care ward and the waiting room that must be so much more painfully vivid in Jess's memory, Lizzie hurried to reassure her. 'Oh, no. Don't worry about him. He might have some concussion, he'll definitely have a headache. Nothing worse than that.'

Ian called from the next room. 'Where are you? Are the police coming?'

Jess hovered in the doorway. Ian was trying to get to his feet, still holding an ice-pack against his forehead. He was muttering threats, his voice slurred.

Within her, some tethering filament of reason and docility suddenly broke from its roots and whipped free. She gathered herself together, and her random fears and longings focused themselves in a hard, clear beam of determination.

She said, 'Lizzie, will you look after Ian for me? He's not seriously hurt. I have to go somewhere.'

She ran up the stairs and took her passport out of the drawer in which she kept it. Downstairs again, she gathered up her coat and bag from where she had left them in the hall. Lizzie and Ian were both staring wordlessly at her.

Jess went straight out of the house and got into her car. Then she drove, fast, all the way back to the nursery. The gates were locked, but she had locked them herself and the keys were in her bag. She also had the keys to the outer and inner offices.

The safe sweetly yielded its contents to her. She took a nylon shopping bag that Joyce kept in her drawer and tipped the money into it. She lifted it by the nylon handles, frowning a little at the weight. Nearly three thousand pounds. Not a fortune, but enough to tide them over. Then she sat down at Graham Adair's desk and pulled a sheet of paper towards her.

The note she scribbled said, 'I have borrowed the week's takings. I think you owe me something, although I know it isn't nearly this much. I'll pay you back, with interest, when I've sold my house. Yours, Jess Arrowsmith.'

She locked up behind her, very carefully, and got back into her car. She put the shopping bag on the passenger seat beside her and drove a five-mile detour to Joyce's house to drop the keys through her letter-box. Then, in a blur of dismay and delight at what she was doing, knowing that her boats were not quite burned yet but that she longed for them to be alight and blazing beyond all hope of salvation, she drove on to Rob's.

It took several minutes' ringing and knocking to bring him to the door. She was sure he would be here. Where else did he have to go? Jess didn't answer the question for herself, and in any case she was proved right. He inched open the door at last, peering at her, white-faced, his cut lip puffed and distorted.

'I thought it must be the police,' he said dully. His bruised mouth made it difficult for him to enunciate his words.

'Go in and get a few clothes and your passport. Hurry up.'

He did what she ordered without asking one question. Within five minutes he was getting into the car. He removed the shopping bag from the passenger seat, before slumping into it. Then he rested his head tiredly against the window and let Jess take him wherever they were going.

They had reached the ring road curving away from town before he raised his head again. Looking at Jess he saw, extraordinarily, that she was smiling.

'What's funny?' he asked bitterly.

Jess had been thinking that there was a wild, black comedy in the fact that she was with her lover, running away from the police and her husband, on the proceeds of a week's sales of geraniums, lobelias and flowery tins of shortbread.

'Jess, they're going to come and put me inside after what I've just done. It doesn't make me laugh, it makes me think I've screwed everything for good. Where are we going?'

'To the airport.'

'Why?'

'We're going to catch a plane. That's why I told you to bring your passport.'

He was beginning to understand that she meant what she said. 'Christ, Jess. I haven't a penny to my name. And you told me that you don't, either.'

'I'll tell you what's making me laugh. Look in the bag you took off the seat.'

He did as he was told. As they passed the first road sign for the airport he turned on her.

'What did you do?'

'Borrowed it. From the nursery.'

Her eyes were bright. She told him her plan. Rob listened in awe and disbelief.

'Wait a minute. You did this for me? You were prepared to steal, and leave behind everything you care about, and do it for *me*?'

'It's for me too. Are you game?'

He bent his head towards her until his bruised mouth touched her throat and his fingers rested on her thigh. His voice was hoarse when he answered.

'Yes. I'm game.'

# Fifteen

The first flight with seat availability was bound for Frankfurt.

From Frankfurt airport, while Rob sat and waited with Joyce's bag held tight on his lap, Jess telephoned home.

'Where are you?' Lizzie's voice crackled, anger springing out of relief at hearing from her.

'Doesn't matter where I am. Is Ian all right?'

From where she stood Jess could see Rob's face. His lip was bruised and hugely swollen, even though she had wrapped ice-cubes from the drinks trolley in her handkerchief and made him press them against it.

She remembered what Rob had confessed to her, *I am afraid of violence. It frightens me because it is inside me, just like it was in my dad.*

No, Jess had reassured him. But tonight she had caught a glimpse of the demon. And right or wrong, her instinct had been to protect him from it and from the world as well. The notion of escape as they had dreamed of it suddenly presented itself as a reality, fully within her reach, and she had snatched it.

Lizzie said sourly, 'Yes, he's all right. The doctor came and offered to admit him for the night just for observation, if a bed could be found, but Ian said he wouldn't go anyway. He's angry, Jess. Your boyfriend had better keep out of his way.'

'I'll see he does.'

'Where *are* you? It's a bad line.'

'What's Ian doing now?'

'Lying down upstairs. Probably asleep. Someone's supposed to check on him every two hours.'

'Lizzie, I'm going to ask you to help me.'

'Of course I'll help you. When are you coming home?'

Jess took a deliberate breath, slowing her words to make them clear. 'I'm not coming home. I'm staying away, with Rob. Will you look after Ian tonight, until you are both sure he is all right? Will you then arrange to put the house on the market for me? A quick sale. I need the money as soon as possible.'

Lizzie took in the words, then measured their import.

'What have you done?' There were colours in Jess's voice that she hadn't heard for years; had almost forgotten ever being there.

'We are on our way to Italy. I took the money to do it out of the safe at the nursery. I'll pay it back as soon as I get the house money. It's just that you're going to get visits from the police, asking questions. You can tell them the truth, of course. I don't care about Graham Adair.'

Lizzie thought, *She's gone crazy. Demented. It's a breakdown. Delayed reaction, grief and stress.* But then she corrected herself. *That's what I want to think.* The truth was that Jess sounded sane, even joyful. As if she had taken her world into her own hands at last; had decided to live instead of existing. Lizzie was pierced by a sudden dart of envy.

'Will you do it for me?' Jess's voice sang in her ear over the babble of some airport announcement that Lizzie couldn't decipher.

'Yes,' Lizzie said. 'If you're sure it's what you want. It's not too late, if it isn't. Ian will calm down when he's sober and his head mends. He won't kill your boyfriend. You can hand the money back to the nursery. For God's sake, Jess, why didn't you ask James and me for it?'

'There wasn't time. I didn't want to make plans, I just needed to do it. It's better like this. Lizzie, I've got to go. Thank you for everything. I'll call you.'

'What about Beth?'

'I'll talk to Beth. Good-night. Don't worry.'

When she was sure that she had gone, Lizzie slowly replaced the receiver. She waited to feel angry or alarmed, but all that came to her was the bizarre conviction that Jess was happy. And then she corrected herself. It was not happiness, it was too raw and interleaved with pain for that. But for a single instant, standing with her fingertips resting on the telephone receiver, Lizzie could almost scent the passion of Jess's leap away into a different place.

Beth was at home in her silent flat. She picked up the phone on the first ring, wishing she were careless enough to do otherwise. At first, Jess's voice sounded so different that it frightened her. Her heart began to knock an irregular rhythm, *Mum, be safe, you have to be safe . . .*

'I'm all right,' Jess reassured her in the new voice that sounded younger and high-pitched and frightened as well as elated. 'Only I've just done something I have to tell you about right now. I want you to try not to be angry with me.'

'What is it? What's all that noise?'

'I'm at Frankfurt airport. I'm here with Rob.'

'What? Why?'

'Listen.' Jess told her the events of the last twenty-four hours. She insisted that Ian was not seriously hurt, but that any more trouble was serious for Rob. If he stayed in England he would go to jail at once.

'I didn't plan it, Beth, not any of it. It just happened and I did the first thing that came into my mind. It felt right, it felt like freedom, and staying in England meant the opposite.'

'I see.' Beth sounded cold, with her anxiety now all squeezed out of her voice by bitterness. Jess spoke faster to try to make her understand that mere miles made no real distance between them. She felt the wrench of divided loyalty, cruelly pulling her in two directions.

Humbly she said, 'I don't want you to think I've run away and left you behind. I haven't done that, and I won't ever.'

'Does it matter what I think?' Beth's internal voice chimed harshly, *She's finally abandoned you. Cut herself off and gone with Robert Ellis.*

'Beth, it matters to me more than anything.'

'Really? You don't exactly show it.'

'I'm sorry. But I've got to go on now, I can't turn back. As soon as we get somewhere I'll phone and let you know where you can reach me if you need to. I'll write, I'll call every day if you want me to. I love you so much, Beth. I don't know what else I can say.'

'Is that all?' Beth wanted there to be more but she was too hurt and too defensive to ask for it.

'All?'

'Yes. I want to call Dad, to make sure he's all right.'

She wanted her off the phone, Jess understood. She nodded her head, staring unseeingly at the German dialling instructions.

'Yes. Yes, of course. I . . . just wanted you to know what has happened. I'll call again. I love you. Look after yourself, and . . . okay. Goodbye.'

'Mum?' Too late, Beth called out. Jess was gone, and there was only the whisper of the disconnected line.

Jess waited until she was sure that she was in control of herself, then walked slowly back to Rob. He was sitting near a group of stranded travellers who were settling down to a long wait on the airport benches. He looked more lost and directionless than any of them and for a moment her awareness of him blurred with Danny again, a younger Danny, and her step faltered as she wondered where she was, and where she was leading them both.

When she reached Rob's side she said, 'It's okay, Ian's asleep. The police aren't after us just yet. There's a flight to Florence at half eight tomorrow morning and I've booked us on it. And there's a cheap hotel just off the airport where we can stay tonight.'

'Why Italy?'

Jess hesitated. 'Because I like it. Because to look at it fills your eyes. But we can go somewhere else, if you'd rather.'

He shook his head. 'No. Italy's fine. Do we have an extra-dition agreement with the Italians? Isn't that what they say in films?'

'I don't know if it will come to that. Would you rather go back? It's not too late.' As Lizzie had pointed out. Rob looked up at her then, his sureness suddenly matching Jess's. They were not mother and son, she remembered.

'What about your daughter?'

'I spoke to her too.' Her face warned Rob not to press her any further. He thought for a second, the shortest time.

'What have I got to go home for?'

'Come on then. Let's find the hotel.'

It was a travellers' stopover of the most functional kind. Unwilling to go to bed and so commit themselves to ending the day, even though there were no more flights to anywhere until the early morning, they sat at a plastic table in the hotel coffee shop. Rob drank a beer and Jess absently dipped a spoon in the coffee that had spilled in her saucer. The balance between the two of them was changing again; they were aware of a kind of breathless wait for it to settle once more.

'You said you were going to tell me something.'

'Yes.'

'I want to hear it.'

She said again, 'Yes.' And at last she added, 'You should know. It's why Ian was so angry tonight.'

She could see how Rob flinched from and at the same time hardened his face against the memory. There was the demon, she thought. She couldn't make it go away but she could see it plain, at least.

She told him about Tonio, and the Italian summer of twenty years ago, and Danny's history. And about the photograph and Beth, and Ian's blind, wounded rage. That's it, she thought. Everyone knows everything now. No secrets. And Danny is

296

gone. Except for the chambers that he occupied in her mind and the parade of memories.

As she talked, Rob's eyes met hers, briefly at first, then locked with them. And at the end he put his hands out, gripping her forearms.

'I knew he was different for you. I knew he was particular, as if he was more cherished or more than just a son to you.' He was remembering Danny's cheerful cynicism, *I can wind my mum around my finger*. He had been jealous of Danny for having her devotion, for his abundant possession of what he had lacked himself.

Jess was sombre. 'He was. It was wrong, wasn't it? For him and for Beth.'

'I don't know if it was right or wrong. He knew you loved him. I'm sorry you lost him, Jess. I'm sorry it was me who caused his death.'

To her dismay and without warning, Jess found that she was crying. She dropped her spoon into the saucer and bent her head to try to hide it. Rob stood up and came around the table to her, holding her shoulders and drawing her against him. Looking down, Jess saw the fresh bruises on his knuckles through the refraction of tears.

Rob whispered, 'Now I know why Italy. It's looking for Danny, isn't it?'

Jess realised with amazement that she had not thought of it as that at all. She had wanted to be in Italy, with Rob, and to be free of the rituals of home. She pressed the heels of her hands into her eyes, conscious of the onlookers in the coffee shop. Rob and she were not the only travellers spending a night in limbo.

'No. It's looking for something else. Myself, I suppose.'

He stood still for a minute. Then he pulled her to her feet. 'Come on,' he said roughly. 'Come with me upstairs.'

Ian woke up, squinting through a red fog of pain that filled the front of his head. It was morning; daylight came in through a gap where the drawn curtains did not quite meet. He was safe in his own bed, but as soon as he recognised it the dreamy awareness was torn apart by recollection. This was Jess's bed, no longer his. The sense of deep familiarity was borrowed from another time. He sat up, wincingly covering his eyes with one hand. Beyond a further zigzag of pain, nothing happened. The boy hadn't done serious damage after all.

The boy. Jess and the boy. And trying to tell him that Danny wasn't his son.

He was lying back against the pillows, trying to sort through the morass of his feelings, when he heard the doorbell ring downstairs. Someone answered it quite quickly. There was a buzz of voices and footsteps climbing the stairs. Then a sharp rap at the door announced Lizzie. Her hair stood out in an unbrushed fuzz around her head. She peered appraisingly and not very warmly at him.

'What are you doing here?' Ian mumbled.

'Doing? Don't you remember what the doctor said? Christ, Ian, I've been coming in every two hours all night long to make sure you hadn't sunk into a coma. You look all right to me, so you'd better get up. The police are here about Jess's safe-breaking.'

Ian blinked, then put his hand carefully up to touch the focus of pain in his head. 'What did you say?'

'Jess has run away to Italy with Rob Ellis. After she left here last night she drove to the nursery and emptied the safe of the week's takings. She wants us to sell the house for her, to pay the money back. Her thinking is that it's less a theft than an unauthorised loan. The police and her boss take a different view, unfortunately.'

It seemed to Ian that Lizzie enjoyed telling him all this; her mouth was curled with contained amusement. He ran through the possible reactions that were open to him. Outrage and anger were the closest to hand, but he dismissed them. He didn't want to see Lizzie's mouth widen into derisive laughter, at him or Jess's doings.

'She's fucking crazy,' he snapped.

'I don't think so, actually.'

'Let me deal with this.'

Ian swung his legs out of bed. He remembered, in time, that he had insisted on undressing himself last night.

'I'll tell them you're coming down,' Lizzie murmured, as she tactfully withdrew.

Ian pulled on his clothes. Last night he had been raging and demanding the police, but Lizzie had eased him into bed with the promise that they would decide in the morning what was the best course of action. And now the police were waiting downstairs and he realised that events had manœuvred him into an entirely different position. By making serious trouble for herself Jess had wiped out the common boundaries of mere bitterness and resentment between the two of them. Of course he would defend Jess now, blaming her actions on grief, and he would make light of what had happened last night instead of seeing the boy charged with assault.

He shook his head, painfully, as he zipped his trousers. Either Jess was much cleverer than he thought or she had abandoned all calculation. He didn't know which, yet, but he would soon find out.

Later the same day, with an unaccustomed afternoon sun burning through the dust of carriage windows and making their eyes smart, Rob and Jess took a train westwards from Florence to the coast.

The little seaside town had expanded, having acquired a fuller skirt of brutal apartment blocks and new arterial roads, but the centre was not much changed. In the quiet square she remembered, Jess saw the *pensione* where she had stayed with Ian and Beth, and where Tonio had taught English to the daughter of the *signora*. Jess didn't point it out to Rob yet. She kept expecting a version of herself, a form of Tonio, to detach themselves from the shadows of the doorway and walk out with Beth's pushchair into the sunshine. Instead she steered Rob towards the cheaper hotels that stood a long way back from the curve of beach and the port. Tomorrow they would have to begin looking for an apartment to rent, and for work.

The narrow streets were busy with the evening's shoppers, and with laughing, animated groups of either girls or boys who met on the corners and in the narrow shadowy alleys, without quite coalescing yet. The day's warmth was held in the stone walls and the sky turned navy-blue behind the canopies of plane trees in the squares. Jess walked with her hand in Rob's, seeing how he took in the people and the buildings. She smiled because she was happy to be here.


Beth laid two places at the table in her kitchen corner. She folded one blue linen napkin, then the other, and moved a little glass vase of velvety red and blue anemones to the centre position. In the bathroom she could hear Sam whistling as he shaved. Sadie and the children were away, and Sam had spent the last two nights here with her.

When he came in, dressed in a crisp shirt that she had ironed and a neatly knotted tie, she looked across at him and felt a calm lift of satisfaction. He was here because he couldn't be otherwise. He needed her, she was certain of it, and she smiled as she thought of the night that they had just spent. Sexual confidence and self-assurance radiated through her. Her head lifted and her shoulders straightened because she knew that Sam was looking at her. She felt the warm weight of her hair at the nape of her neck, the play of the tiny muscles of well-being at the corners of her mouth.

'Coffee?' she asked carelessly, half turning away from him. Her arm and wrist made a smooth line as they reached for the pot. He came for her, reaching inside her loose cotton dressing-gown. His fingers, then the palms of his hands, found her breasts. Beth stretched, cat-like, with pleasure. For perhaps the first time in her life she was certain of her own beauty, sure of being in the right place in the right smooth skin. Sam's breath was toothpaste-scented on her cheek but then she saw the shadow of a frown as his fingers teased and stroked.

Beth slipped away, out of his grasp. She did not want her serenity destroyed. How odd it was, she thought, pouring coffee into French cups, that since Jess's departure she had felt so different. But some link had snapped: some chain of dependency was broken at last. Beth knew that she would shape her own life from now on because no one else could do it for her. Amazingly, her power seemed even to extend to Sam. For the first time, Beth felt his equal.

'Come and have your breakfast.' She smiled at him. She pulled her robe around her and fastened the belt.

'When's the family conference?' Sam asked, obediently sitting at the table. He knew the story.

'Tonight. I'll stay at my aunt's, and see my dad before he goes back to Australia. They want to talk about Mum, although I can't see what good talking will do.'

Beth's anger had faded, but she was still amazed by what had happened. The sight of a different, careless Jess within the fixed shell of her mother had opened new prospects for Beth, within herself as well as in the connections around her. Maybe there would not always be the same stale patterns to trace. It was possible, perhaps even easy, to draw flourishing new designs.

'When I come back,' she said, 'we can talk to Sadie. We can do it together, if you like.'

There was the shadow in Sam's face again. She thought he was going to say, *It isn't quite the right time now, perhaps after the summer*, and she was ready to contradict him. But what he did say was different.

'Beth, I felt something last night. And again, just now, when I touched you there.'

He leaned forward, moving aside the cup still half full of coffee and the glass vase of flowers. He undid the belt of her robe and gently moved the front of it aside. His fingers pressed and dimpled the skin of her exposed breast. Then, with his other hand, he lifted Beth's fingers to the same spot, a little below and to the side of her nipple. Beth felt it too. It was a lump, pea-sized, incongruously but definitely embedded in her private tissue.

'Did you know?' Sam asked. His eyes were close to hers, she could see the rays of colour spreading in the irises.

'No,' she said.

She wouldn't lose her equilibrium. Not now, when she had only just won it for herself. Beth deliberately smiled and squared her shoulders.

'I'm sure it's nothing. Lumps come and go, you know. But I'll get it checked out as soon as I get back from seeing Dad. Promise.'

He kissed her tenderly, glad to resign his temporary responsibility. 'Make sure you do.'

Lizzie lit a cigarette and breathed out exasperated smoke.

'Jesus. There must be something we can do.'

James said mildly, 'We have. I spent an hour with Mr Adair. A man can do no more.'

'It isn't funny.' Lizzie frowned.

'There are comical aspects.'

Ian and Beth sat opposite them across Lizzie's kitchen table. It was a mild evening, and beyond the open doors the garden was furred with the piquant green of early May. Beth had been looking at the guardsman-red tulips in a half-barrel on Lizzie's patio. The colour was so intense that it vibrated at the corner of her eye when she looked away. Automatically she put out her hand to cover her father's. Ian looked older; there were newly noticeable cords running up his thick neck to his jawline.

'We're her family,' Lizzie said.

'I just don't understand her,' Ian remarked, not for the first time. 'It's as if I never knew her. I know she lost Danny, but so did we all. We haven't turned safe-breakers and runaways, have we? Jess has responsibilities. And above all, I don't understand how she could involve herself with that boy.'

There was a little silence. Lizzie remembered the unexpected dart of envy of Jess that had pierced the smooth shell of her contentment. 'I think I can imagine,' she said slowly. 'We're shocked because we always expect Jess to be the good one. The pillar for the rest of us. Perhaps the pillar's foundations have been shaken. Why should Jess always do what she's supposed to? Have I? Have *you*, Ian?'

Beth's head lifted and her eyes met Lizzie's. There was the warmth of a sudden complicity between them.

'I sort of understand it too,' she said. Some aspects of her mother that had been mysterious before were now clearer.

Jess had seemed so balanced, but she had been living on the edge. Beth could appreciate the effort that must have cost her. Now, her withdrawal seemed to have given Beth an unexpected gift, the confidence in herself that she had always lacked. But she couldn't directly offer her mother understanding or gratitude or forgiveness. How complicated the relations between mothers and daughters are, Beth thought.

Impatiently Ian shook his hand free. He clenched his fists and thudded them on the table.

'Good Christ, what is this? You're not all hot for that kid, are you? What do you like, crawling rat's-tail hair and gym-bound muscles and that fuck-you sneer? Is that it?'

Embarrassed, James got up and went to the window. The redness of the tulips was receding into the dusk.

'No,' Lizzie said gently. 'It isn't that. What do his looks matter, anyway? Love's blind, as we all know.'

'What, then?' Ian's eyes bulged.

The women knew. It was that something terrible had happened, and out of the broken aftermath Jess had gathered up some pieces and made a bravely different woman of herself. It was not for them to judge whether or not the change was for the better. They each had their own smaller restorations to make.

Nobody spoke.

At length Ian made an angry grunt and tipped the contents of his whisky glass into his mouth.

'All right. Let's be practical. The money.'

'I told Graham Adair I will cover the full amount,' James said. 'He said he'll think about it, and talk to the police. I believe he'll agree in the end to whatever will cause him the least bother. He strikes me as a profoundly lazy individual. But the police may decide to proceed against Jess in any case, particularly given her association with Rob and his having skipped bail. We can't do much about that.'

'I'll put in half the money. I haven't got any more to spare,' Ian said.

James nodded. 'All right. That makes sense. What about the house?'

They looked at Beth. It had been her home more recently than Ian's.

'Sell it,' she said without hesitation. 'I've got my own flat, haven't I?' And soon she would have a home with Sam. She had no need of anything else.

'That's decided, then,' Lizzie said. The conference was concluded.

Ian stared round at them. It was not finished for him.

'Do you believe this about Danny? That I'm not his father?'

Lizzie said as gently as she could, 'How much does that history matter now?'

'It matters. Do you think it's true?'

'Jess would know. If she says it's the truth, then it must be.'

The cool air of the evening flowed into the room, and the garden was dark.

'I don't believe a word of it,' Ian said.

Nor did Ian believe in wasting time. Within a day of the family conference he was in Michael Blake's office, looking across the cluttered desk at a young man who seemed hardly older than Danny. Lizzie had told him, somewhat reluctantly, the name of Rob's solicitor.

'How can I help you, Mr Arrowsmith?' Michael asked.

If Danny had lived, Ian thought, would he have become anything like you? He could not imagine it, and knowing that he would never know Danny's future made an additional pleat of pain within him.

'My son,' he began, while Michael Blake waited. Ian read sympathy and a shadow of embarrassment in his face, and his manner grew more brusque in response. He told the solicitor what it was he wanted. The difficulty of uttering it made him sound ruder than he intended.

'I haven't received the prosecution evidence yet,' Michael answered slowly. 'And in any case I couldn't share details of any evidence with you. It would be breaching my client's confidence. The trial would have taken place in about a month's time. But now that Mr Ellis has broken his bail and left the country I can't tell you what will happen.'

'He's gone to Italy with Danny's mother. With my ex-wife.'

'I know,' Michael said. 'He missed a court hearing two days ago.'

'Well? Are they going to get him back again?'

'Yes, without a doubt. But it will take some time – months, maybe even longer than that. The police and the court are aware of what has happened, of course. If Robert does come home, he's likely to be arrested immediately.'

'I see.' The confirmation gave Ian less pleasure than he might have imagined.

'I'm sorry I can't help you,' Michael Blake said. 'But there are other avenues you could try. Have you contacted the hospital directly?'

'Not yet. And I have a wife and a job waiting for me in Sydney. I can't stay here for ever. But I'll find out the truth about my son if it's the last thing I do.' Ian gathered up his coat and the umbrella he had been forced to buy. Rain was needling the smeared windows of the solicitor's office.

Michael held out his hand and Ian perfunctorily shook it.

'Good luck,' Michael said to his retreating back.

Beth waited on the single hard chair in the closed cubicle of the outpatients' clinic. She listened to the nurses passing the door, showing other women to the boxes where they would sit and wait for their verdicts. Five minutes ago a nurse had looked in and told her that Mr Faraday would be with her in five minutes. He'd better be, she thought, aiming for detachment. She was taking far too much time off work.

When he did come in, she knew before he spoke that this verdict was against her. A strong reminder of the waiting room and the aching mundanity of the offices off Danny's ward filled her throat and mouth like nausea. She stretched her mouth into a smile for the surgeon as he set out her notes.

The pea-sized lump was stubbornly lodged in her breast. It had been prodded and pinched through the envelope of her flesh. Beth had come to the hospital for a mammogram, then for a needle biopsy. The tests had been performed with disturbing rapidity.

The surgeon met her eye. He looked wearily kind, as Danny's doctors had done.

'I'm afraid it isn't the best news. It is a malignancy, and unusual at your age. But it is a small one. I am certain that we can remove it completely.'

He took care to outline the possible treatment. He did not think it would be necessary to remove the breast.

'Thank you,' Beth said, as if he were making her a present of her own body. With another part of her mind she was calculating where and when she could telephone Sam, how soon she could speak to him. In this moment of crisis no one else entered her thoughts. Am I so isolated? she wondered. The doctor was still explaining what would be done to her. He was looking at her a little oddly now, as if her reaction was not quite what he was expecting.

Jess opened wide the metal shutters of the bedroom window and leaned on the window-sill to look out. From her vantage point she could look down on a glittering herringbone of railway tracks, and upwards to a net of overhead lines crosshatching the pearly sky. It was early in the morning and the sky carried only the faintest promise of heat to come.

The street below her was almost empty. Jess watched a street-cleaning truck trawl slowly along the gutter, swirling the night's litter into its innards as a workman in a blue overall plodded behind it, brushing up the residue. On the concrete wall opposite, between a garage and a small general store, a patchwork of out-of-date posters was scrawled over with graffiti. It was a tiny slice of urban scenery not so much different from the one she had left behind in England, but Jess felt as if she inhabited a parallel universe where the forces of gravity did not pull at her insides.

Ever since coming to Italy there had been an airiness beneath her diaphragm and under the bony plates of her skull that she had at first guiltily identified as happiness, and more recently had redefined for herself not as happiness, because that was bred out of rightness, but as a kind of rapture. In their situation rapture was perverse, even incredible, but she knew that was what it was. It transcended even her concern at being separated from Beth. Jess thought of her constantly, but without the sense of guilty deficiency that had clung about her for so long. She felt free to remember the details of happiness, and she translated the memories into long letters to her daughter. She interleaved these memories with little descriptions of the seaside town and its people, and drawings of plants and buildings. Writing to Beth had become one of Jess's pleasures. There had even been one or two replies, a little stiff in tone and containing only superficial news, but letters just the same.

Jess rested her chin on her fists, still gazing at the low-rent view. She knew every detail of it by now, at each hour of the day. There was a blue-painted upright chair and a metal table beside the door of the general store. Later, when the shop opened and the sun warmed the street, an old man would shuffle out to sit in his chair and watch the day go by. And only a few hundred metres ahead of her, invisible beyond the railway lines and the featureless apartment blocks, lay the sea. She could just catch the Mediterranean salt-and-pinewood scent of it. At this time of day it would be oyster pale and iridescent; later it would darken to postcard blue and in the late afternoon change again to opaque turquoise.

Smiling, Jess turned from the window. Her bare feet were cold on the clammy floor and she shivered a little. Rob was still asleep, turned inwards on his side to the space where she had been lying. His profile made a perfectly balanced set of lines and curves against the creased background of the pillow and she felt greedy tenderness stir and take a new shape.

Nothing would stay the same, however she might wish to catch this minute or any of the minutes in the weeks that had just gone by. She couldn't hope to hold Rob and herself together as they were, as they had been. He was very young, and he was alive. How could there not be change?

Rob opened his eyes. He reached out from under the covers and took her hand, drawing her down beside him.

'You're cold,' he murmured, wrapping her in his arms and hooking his leg over her thigh. He kissed her, his breath tainted with sleep and the reddish soft stubble around his lips scraping her skin as his hand found her breast. Jess's back arched as his fingers teased, pleasure stretching her joints. They were practised now. They were used to each other. Nothing stayed the same.

Later they lay still, locked together. Jess saw the square of bright light at the window filtered through the screen of his hair. She thought back, counting the days since they had left England.

It was more than three weeks now.

'Let's go to Lucca today,' she said. They had been promising themselves this trip. Rob had some casual work as a kitchen porter in one of the big hotels and today was his first full day off. Jess had not yet found anything, although she had tried every approach she could think of. She was conscious of Graham Adair's money inexorably dwindling.

Brutally she cut off the thoughts, for now. She moved her mouth against Rob's, smiling.

'We can go there on the bus. Walk on the walls and look at the churches. It's beautiful.'

His mouth curved in answer. 'Let's go to Lucca. Be a tourist couple having a day out together.'

The day was warm, but the broad walk on top of Lucca's city walls was opulently shaded by plane trees. In the dazzling brief intervals between the trees their shadows bit sharply into the dusty path. They bought a guidebook from a postcard kiosk, then walked arm-in-arm, in step, looking across at the tightly enclosed houses and rusty orange-speckled tile roofs. Jess read aloud from the guide, her pleasure in the city's intricate history heightened by Rob's appetite for it.

'Is it?' he kept saying. 'Is it that old? The *Romans* built that?'

They stopped in a niche of the wall to look at an ancient tower pierced by tiny arched windows. The tower was crowned by a tree sprouting defiantly over the parapet. Rob stood behind her as Jess leaned on the gritty wall, his hands lightly resting on her waist. Through her thin cotton skirt she felt the warmth of his thigh. There was a line of washing suspended across a narrow alley directly below them. Little baby dresses hung like rinsed flags in the heavy air. Rob shifted a little and his mouth touched the nape of her neck. They were entirely alone, even amongst the columns of Scandinavian tourists and the cyclists briskly circling the walls.

*Now*, Jess thought. *This is the moment I will keep. Or the one I would keep, if only I could.*

'You're right,' Rob said. 'It is beautiful. I've never realised it before, but I've never seen anywhere properly. Never even been anywhere very much. I never had enough energy to spare, or any curiosity for doing and seeing. It was all taken up inside myself with the effort of survival.' And after a moment he added, 'I don't feel so weary any more. I think I owe that to you.'

'I like the way you look at this,' Jess answered, keeping her eyes on the jumble of roofs and churches. From one of the towers a midday bell pealed, then another and another. In the stillness that followed she knew that this was indeed the moment. They loved each other like two bells pealing at the same instant. The peal would end and even the echoes would fade, yet the perfect note had still been struck.

*In our way we have been blessed*, Jess thought. And it is true that nothing stays the same. Every minute that passes is a kind of bereavement, but it is also a tiny progress.

'Let's walk on, shall we?' she said quietly.

After their circuit of the walls they found a restaurant with a handful of tables under wide canvas sunshades in a little courtyard. They had not eaten many meals out in Italy; to make their money go as far as possible Jess cooked pasta on the double burner of the kitchenette in their apartment. Today, however, they understood the need to celebrate. They read the menu eagerly and ordered antipasto as well as a local dish of rabbit *al forno*. Rob spoke to the waiter; Jess was surprised, as she had been almost every day since their arrival, by how voraciously he picked up Italian words and phrases.

They were absorbed in each other as they ate and did not see that the other diners glanced speculatively or enviously at them. One of the street cats insinuated itself between the table legs and rubbed its back lasciviously against Rob's shin, uttering thin cries of pleasure. Rob fed it a few scraps of rabbit and it licked them up ravenously, a triangle of pink tongue darting in and out until not even a smear of grease remained. Jess thought she would try a sketch of the hungry cat in her next letter to Beth.

When their plates had been taken away they ordered cups of electrifying strong espresso. Jess sat with the tiny thimbleful in front of her, looking across the square to a tier of shuttered windows. The city was subsiding into the stillness of mid-afternoon.

'Talk to me about Danny,' she said. She wanted him to be here, admitted to the day. To be admitted, so that she could begin to release him. She wanted it to be the real Danny, too, the boy Rob would have known and not her own idealisation of him. 'What was he really like?'

Rob shaded his eyes with his hand, thinking.

'You know what he was like,' he tempered.

'No. I never knew your Danny.'

He understood now what she wanted.

He began to tell her again about the last day, the morning they had spent at the gym and the afternoon playing snooker. Jess had heard the details before, but now that Rob did not have to obscure the truth he gave them a truer gloss. Danny had had his dark side. He always wanted to win and did not often care to count the cost. The evening with Cat and Zoe had been the indicator of that.

As he talked, telling Jess whatever came into his head about Danny, Rob also found the thought of Cat stealing into his mind. She came there more usually during the evening's *passeggiata*, when the young people crowded out into the streets and squares. He wondered what she was doing at this minute and knew that he missed her. A sense of another existence waiting for him, only pushed into abeyance for now, took shape in his mind.

At last Jess pushed her coffee cup away. It was finished. Rob saw that her face was composed beneath its sadness. He thought she looked beautiful.

'Shall we walk some more?' she asked.

They went arm-in-arm again past the top-heavy medieval houses and lamp-bracketed street corners of the Via Fillungo. They made a detour to look into the cool dimness of a pillared church and finally came out into the Roman amphitheatre. The perfect oval of tall buildings contained and concentrated the day's heat. A ramshackle open-air market was just unrolling itself for the evening's business, and they wandered between the stalls of glassware and vegetables and cheap shoes. Jess found a wide-brimmed straw hat and splurged a few thousand lire on it. Rob settled it on her head for her, seeing how her face was softened by the brim's shadow pierced with tiny flecks of gold.

They bought ice-creams and sat with their backs against a wall to eat them.

'I came here once before, with Tonio,' Jess said.

'Was it a day like this?'

'In some ways. In other ways, this is a happier day.'

He took her hand and kissed the damp cushion of her thumb. 'Thank you,' he said.

They sat for a while in silence, watching the market business.

'Where now?' Rob asked.

'Back home.'

Neither of them needed to confirm to the other that home was the little apartment overlooking the railway lines.

They waited for the coast bus where they had disembarked, in a parched and dusty square outside the city walls. Outside one of the scrubby cafés a group of boys in their early teens perched on bicycles and jostled on the kerb. They were calling taunts at each other. Jess watched the boy who seemed to be the target of most of the aggression. He was plump, dressed in oversized trainers and baggy shorts and an orange vest that clung to the cushiony swell of his belly.

Suddenly two of the boys on bicycles wheeled from opposite sides of the group and swooped towards the centre. The others scattered and the plump boy went to jump aside but gauged their direction wrongly at the last second and leapt into their path instead. One of the cyclists swerved and missed, but the other ploughed straight into him. The boy sagged backwards as if he had been punched and sat down hard on the edge of the kerb. The can of fizzy drink that he had been holding sprayed over his shoulder and arm and bounced into the gutter.

The cyclist recovered his balance and darted a glance to see how serious the damage was, then spun away behind the bus station. The other one melted after him and the victim was left in a sweaty heap where he had sunk down. The rest of the group stood at a safe distance.

Rob was already standing up. He made his way casually to the boy and stood a yard in front of him, hands in the pockets of his jeans. He said something Jess couldn't hear and the boy looked up. His broad, puffy face was taut with the effort of containing hurt and humiliation. When the others saw the size of Rob they moved even further off.

The boy answered with a shrug and Rob helped him to his feet. There was a dusty, reddening mark down his leg. He shook the droplets of spilled drink from his neck and arms, and Rob strolled the few steps to a street kiosk and bought him an identical can. The boy ripped it open and drank with a flourish. Then, as if they were old friends, Rob and he turned and walked slowly to the city gate. Rob waited in the shelter of it, watching until the plump boy was safely out of sight.

When he came back to Jess their bus was just drawing up.

'This is ours, isn't it?' he said.

The look he gave her disallowed any comment she might have been about to make, but Jess recognised the significance of the tiny incident.

'Goodbye, Bits,' she said coolly.

Rob seemed not to hear her. They boarded the bus and found two seats. Jess settled herself with her head resting on his shoulder. She watched the flat landscape unfold as they headed back to the coast.

# Sixteen

There was an unreality about the day that made Beth look at the familiar London landscapes as if she had never seen them before. Red buses clogged a road junction. A skinny tattooed man darted between the idling cars with his windscreen washer, bowing to the rejections of motorists. Posters advertising some concert at Wembley bled illegibly into the mess of colours and blocky shapes pressing against her eyes.

I have got cancer, Beth repeated, testing the enormity of it yet again in her mind. There is no certainty that I will not die.

The possiblity of her own death emerging from the vague thickets of decades into time measurable in single years made Danny seem close, as if he walked beside her. He was separated from her by a much thinner membrane than she had understood. As she made her way along the unreal street she found herself absorbed in a conversation with him.

You didn't have time to think about this, did you? Or did you know, when you were lying in that bed all caught up with the tubes and machines, what was coming? Were you afraid?

She heard his voice, amused and cocky, exactly as he had sounded when he condescended to her about music or sex or any of the things he did better or earlier than she did: *It's no big deal. It happens to everyone, doesn't it?*

*Only you got there first, Dan*, she thought. *I'm older, but you're quicker.*

He taunted her gleefully, *You're jealous. Always were, always will be.*

Beth stopped walking, then, so abruptly that a man hurrying behind collided with her and almost stumbled. He peeled away, recovering his step.

*No. I'm not jealous any longer. Didn't you know that, Danny? I can see the old pattern, hear the old resentment rising even when it's death we're talking about. But I can choose it to be other, can't I? I wish you hadn't died when you did. I would have liked us to be equals. We could be, now.*

Beth was surprised to find that she was smiling. The street readjusted itself somewhat. She could read the posters and the buses looked ordinary, not like extra-terrestrial machinery. She started walking again, then noticed that the man who had bumped into her was hovering a yard or two ahead.

'Hi,' he said.

'I'm sorry?'

'It *is* Beth, isn't it?'

He was in his late twenties, arty or hippyish, vaguely familiar, now she came to look at him. But from where?

'Yes . . .'

'We met at Lizzie's birthday party. We had quite a long talk, actually.' He rocked his head, miming a campy, amused petulance at her forgetting.

She remembered now. He was an actor, of course. He had been in Lizzie's serial, playing the rookie policeman.

'Nick,' she said, dredging the name up from her subconscious.

He looked pleased. 'Right. Look, fancy bumping into you.'

'I work not far from here.'

'Yeah? Listen, where are you off to? Do you want to have a quick drink or something?'

Beth was on her way to meet Sam at a bar they often went to when they didn't have time to go home to her flat. She had not seen him since her test, five days ago. He had been away at a sales conference. His absence meant that she hadn't told any of her friends or colleagues about the test result, or

315

even her family. Least of all her family. She wanted to see Sam first, to ask him face to face to see this through with her.

'I can't, Nick. I'm just on my way to meet someone. I'm a bit late, actually.' She looked automatically at her watch, not registering the time.

'That's a pity. Can we do it some other night? I've been thinking I might call Liz and ask for your number.'

'Yes. Let's meet, um, some time.'

Nick took out his wallet and produced a card.

'Here. Give me a ring.'

Beth took the little rectangle and tucked it in her pocket. Good. Now she wouldn't have to deal with him calling her.

'I will,' she said. 'Bye.'

'Bet you don't ring,' he called after her. 'But if you don't, you'll regret it.' She turned on her heel for a second, responding to the challenge in spite of herself.

'Don't be so sure,' she said ambiguously.

Immediately she forgot about him. Sam was waiting, sitting in their usual corner. He stood up as soon as he saw her, kissed her tenderly and led her to a chair. When he had bought her a drink and placed it in front of her he asked the question. His expression was kind, gravely concerned, longing for the best whilst prepared for the worst.

'It's breast cancer,' Beth said brutally.

And her unsettlingly clear vision of the day made her see that it was not at all the answer Sam had expected. He had intended her to say, *Oh no, nothing to worry about at all. Just one of those things.* The response that swam up through the layers of bone and flesh to settle over his face was plain dismay. He hesitated and she could hear his preformed words as clearly as if he shouted them. *Well, thank God for that. I knew it wouldn't be, but, darling, I'm so relieved. Give me a kiss. I'm going to take you out for the best dinner to celebrate.*

The little speech silently echoed in the space between them. She knew with equal certainty that he was swiftly reckoning,

*What does this mean? How much more will I have to do, commit, supply for her? When my resources are already spread so thin between Sadie, and the children, and work, and her?*

'Oh, God. I'm so sorry,' Sam whispered.

Beth took a mouthful of her wine. The robust flavour of it cheered her.

'What does it mean?' he ventured.

Briskly, she told him. The operation. Lumpectomy, ugly word. To be performed as soon as possible, next Tuesday as it happened. And after that, depending upon exactly what they discovered, radiotherapy or chemotherapy, maybe both.

'I'm sorry. Poor darling,' he said again. He was collecting himself now, warily. Beth studied his face. His neat, almost-handsome features seemed to be changing before her eyes. Shrivelling into an altogether less benign composition. For the first time since the beginning of the affair she could imagine herself not loving him. He pressed her cold hands between his.

'What shall we do for you?' he asked gently.

Not to love him was unthinkable, of course. What else was there?

Beth's resolve faltered for an instant, but then she fixed it again. She knew what she wanted and needed, and now she must tell him.

'I want you to leave Sadie,' she said in a low, clear voice. 'I don't want to wait any longer for us to belong to each other. I want you to tell her about us, tonight. I need it now, Sam. I need you to be with me to see this through. I can do it with you. Without you, I'm not sure that I can.'

He stopped stroking her hands.

'Beth. My Beth, that sounds a bit like blackmail. That isn't what you mean, is it?'

He was trying out his crumpled, rueful face on her, and as if the rosy, softening lenses of love suddenly popped out of her eyes she realised that it made him look like nothing more than a scolded puppy.

'It isn't blackmail. I'm just telling you what I want.'

He sighed. 'It isn't a very good time now.'

'Why not? Alice's ballet exams? Sadie having a tough time at work? Nanny thinking of leaving?'

The whip of her angry sarcasm stunned them both. Held in a tiny bubble of shock, they faced each other across the polished, accusing eye of the bar table.

'You're upset,' Sam said at last.

'Yes,' Beth agreed.

'I meant that this isn't the best time to make a major decision. After the operation, when you're well again . . .'

'No.'

'Beth, you have to listen to me.'

His eyes slid fractionally sideways, to the clock at the end of the bar. Sam had a business dinner to attend and he was calculating how much time there was left to soothe Beth and make her see sense before he would have to leave.

She knew what he was thinking because it was what he always thought, and she was tired of making allowances for the long list of his other commitments. The whole morass of their affair suddenly wearied her. She interrupted, 'I don't want to listen. You promised me that when the time was right you would leave your wife for me. In case you have forgotten, you said that you love and need me. I believed you, and now *I* need *you.*'

'I'm here.'

Slowly, she shook her head. 'No you aren't. You slide in when it suits you and slither out again. I'm an item on your agenda. Oh look, six thirty p.m. Time to fuck Beth and fly out to dinner with Sadie. Beth will understand. Beth will be *grateful.*'

There was a hard, bright pellet of anger lodged in her chest. The diamond hardness of it pleased her.

'It isn't like that.'

She knew it was exactly like that, but for a moment her anger dimmed and she wavered. What would she do without the consolation of his love, and the anchor of her passion? The glory of it all was diminished and she would be left a fool. But then she thought, it wasn't my love that was illusory, only the belief that Sam was worthy of it. Her assurance came back. She was right. She was right to feel powerful.

'Are you going to leave Sadie?'

His face had grown pouchy, as if the watery liquid of his self-interest had welled up from the inner reservoirs and bled into the empty spaces beneath the skin. If she pricked him harder, she thought, he would weep glassy tears of reproach at her for hurting him.

'I can't do it, darling. Not right now. It's the kids. It's their life too, and I can't . . .'

'Then you should have been thinking of little Tamsin and Justin and Alice instead of slipping into bed with me.'

'I know,' he agreed, much too eagerly, scenting that he was off the hook. 'I know I should have been.'

Beth stood up. Looking around the bar she saw that one or two people were already glancing at them.

She said loudly, 'You're a creep, Sam. You're a coward and a liar and a dirty rat. I wouldn't have you if yours was the last diminutive dick in the known world.' Sam was sensitive about the size of his penis.

She turned her back on him and marched out. Outside, on the pavement, she burst out laughing. Christ, she told herself. That felt so good it was almost worth the whole business.

Before the pain reaction could kick in she started walking, fast. She walked purposefully for a long way, with her head up and her arms swinging a rhythm. At ten to nine she was turning the corner into Sam and Sadie's street. There was no sign of his Saab. Of course there would not be. The dinner was with an important author and her agent and the sales and marketing people. There was no question that Sam would consider tonight's encounter with his long-time mistress important or threatening enough to bring him hurrying home, just in case.

Beth marched down the street and up the three steps to

Sam's front door. The window-boxes behind the iron-lace balconies were trimly planted with white flowers and trailing silvery green foliage. She put her finger to the shiny brass bell-push and heard the bell ringing deep in the house.

Sadie came to the door. She had changed out of her red office suit into jeans and a chambray shirt. She wasn't even wearing lipstick.

'I'm Beth Arrowsmith. We have met, but you probably won't remember. I used to work for Sam.'

Sadie poured New Zealand Semillon Blanc into two glasses and pushed one across the table to Beth. The kitchen was in the basement. It was exactly as Beth had imagined it. Dragged paintwork on the cupboard doors, children's art pinned to the walls above the worktops, blue-and-yellow French print curtains.

Sadie lit a cigarette and exhaled smoke. 'Did you think you were the first?'

'No. I thought I was the last.'

Sadie laughed, not unkindly. 'Jesus, I mean, you worked for him. Don't you know his reputation?'

'I believed I was different. He told me I was. Can I ask you something?'

'Go ahead.'

'Did you know about Sam and me all along?'

'Not you specifically. But as soon as I saw you on the doorstep upstairs I knew what it was all about. How old are you? Twenty-three?'

'Yes.'

'Yeah. Listen, Beth. I'll tell you the truth, which he certainly won't. Sam isn't going to leave me for you. Sam's aim is always to have both. Me and his home and his children, plus a nice, slightly awed and therefore compliant girl on the side.'

'My mother told me more or less exactly the same thing.'

'Of course she did. It's one of the reasons why he goes for the young. They're less dangerous than women his own age. Although I have to say he made a mistake with you, didn't he?

It must have taken some balls to come over here and tell me you're having an affair with my husband.'

'I didn't want him to get away with it,' Beth muttered, hoping she wasn't going to cry. She felt a thick pelt of embarrassment heating her neck and shoulders. Having expected to unpeel the hidden truth and for it to be greeted with due shock and outrage, Sadie's cool cynicism entirely disconcerted her. *I'd prepared for one answer and got an entirely different one*, she thought. *Making the same stupid mistake as Sam.*

'He won't, don't worry,' Sadie said. She poured them both more wine and offered Beth a cigarette. Beth shook her head. 'Why did you choose tonight, by the way?'

She felt suddenly spongy with fearful tears, as ready to liquefy into self-pity as Sam himself. 'Because I've just found out I've got breast cancer. I'm having a lumpectomy on Tuesday.'

Sadie's face changed. 'My God. Where?'

'My *breast.*'

'Which hospital, you fool.'

'Oh. St Mary's.'

'Right. Where's your mother? Is she somewhere near enough to look after you?'

'My mother robbed a safe and ran off to Italy with her lover almost a month ago. He's my age.'

Sadie glared at her until she realised that Beth wasn't attempting a joke. There was another second while they rocked together on the cusp between dislike and reluctant admiration, then Sadie began to laugh. She had an attractive laugh, deep and bawdy.

'Your mother sounds like quite a woman.'

'Oh, she is. She really is.'

Sadie insisted that Beth tell her the whole story. By the time it was finished the bottle of wine was empty and Beth suspected that she might have found a new friend. The shock of it jolted her. She was sitting with Sam's wife in Sam's kitchen, woozy with wine and disconcerted by liking. She put her glass aside.

'I must go,' she said.

'Well, thank you for coming. No, don't make that face. I mean it. I'd rather know what Sam gets up to, it makes it all less mystifying.' She stood up and came round the table, put her hand on Beth's shoulder. 'Don't let it upset you too much. You're better off without him. Believe me.'

There was regret and sadness in Sadie's voice, only partially veiled by the lightness of her tone. Beth nodded, and sniffed hard to keep in the wretched tears.

'I hope the operation's a success. I'm sure you've been told this over and over but recovery rates from breast cancer, if it's detected early enough, are great and they're improving. We did a big series of features in the paper a month or so ago and I read up all the figures. I can send them to you, if you want. You're young. You'll be okay.'

'I'm sure I will,' Beth whispered.

As she went down the steps to the road, Sadie called after her from the doorway, 'Keep in touch.'

In the end, Beth was surprised and warmed by how supportive her friends and colleagues proved to be. One friend from college drove her to the hospital and lent her a Frette bathrobe, and two more friends and a woman from the office came to visit her on the evening after the operation. Their flowers crowded on her tray table. She wasn't isolated, it was only that in her obsession with Sam she had imagined she was.

'My surgeon says it's all gone,' Beth reassured her visitors. 'They'll just give me some radiotherapy follow-up, to make sure.'

But the next day found her weepy with post-anaesthesia and filled with foreboding. How did they know the marauding cells weren't lurking in the interstices of her body? Where was Sam?

She lay curled on her side, her back to the door of the ward, awash with misery. She heard high heels clicking assertively down the centre aisle but paid no attention. Then the click-clack stopped beside her bed.

'Are you asleep?'

In a bleached linen suit and bearing armfuls of white lilies and glossy magazines, it was Sadie.

'Sister says it's no problem,' Sadie smiled at her when she saw that Beth was awake. 'I made her give me the full story. You're out of here in a couple of days, and you're never to darken their doors again.'

Beth tried to sit up. But Sadie and her kindness were more than she could bear. She flopped back against the pillows and tears boiled up and ran out of her eyes like flood-water.

It was a little time before Sadie could make any sense of the words hiccuped and swallowed between rending sobs. But at last she understood what Beth was saying.

'I want my mother,' she wept. 'I wish my mother were here.'

'Haven't you got a number?'

Beth had brought the small stack of letters, full of love and memories, into the hospital with her. There was a telephone number on the first page of the first one.

'She told me one I could use for emergencies.'

'Then ring her. Don't you think she'd want to be with you?'

*'Telefono.'*

The call came up the stairs to Jess. She went out on to the landing and leaned over the banister. She could see her land-lady's door standing open and her solid black-clad shoulders wedged in the dim hallway as she peered upwards.

*'Sì, signora. Telefono.'*

*'Vengo, grazie.'*

Jess ran down the stairs. She had found some part-time work as a gardener to the owners of a grand villa outside the town; perhaps this was a message from them. Let it not be that they didn't want her any more, she prayed.

She squeezed into the landlady's room, breathlessly smiling her gratitude.

'Mum? Is that you?' The sound of her voice was enough to set a pulse of foreboding ticking in Jess's throat.

'Beth, what's wrong? Tell me, quick.'

And while she listened to her Jess saw all over again the faces of the young policewoman who had come to her door in the night, and the nurses and doctors in Danny's ward. They were printed on her mind with shocking, lurid clarity and they crowded gravely around her again as if they were the witnesses to this new catastrophe.

'Why didn't you tell me straight away? Why, Beth?'

Jess's entire body shivered and twitched with the fierceness of her determination to fight for and see this child saved, who was all that was left to her.

Beth could hardly speak. Her voice was choked with tears.

'I was angry with you. But I want you to come home. Please, Mum, will you come home?'

'As soon as I can,' Jess promised. 'Sooner.'

'Can you?'

'Beth, it isn't *can*. It's *how quickly can I get to you*? Try to stop me.'

'I'll be here,' Beth said. 'I'm waiting. I want to see you so much.'


That evening Jess and Rob slowly walked in the thickening twilight towards the port. It was June, and they had been in Italy for two months. Swifts dipped and banked under the trees in a square where the owners of tourist cafés had put out the summer chairs and tables in competitive lines. Soon the season would fill the pizzerias and bars with holiday-makers.

'You must go,' Rob said. It was the opposite of everything he felt. Jess's abandonment of him took him back to child-hood, and the wallpaper islands and the smell of fear. The scale of what he had done blotted out the light: if he went home he would be arrested and if he stayed here he would be alone.

'I'm sorry,' Jess said despairingly. 'I have done a wrong thing bringing you here.' There was no doubt in her mind. Beth came first. She was struggling even now to contain her impatience to be gone, to reach her. It was the lack of a contest within herself that seemed almost the hardest to bear.

'No. You've given me a lot.' It was the truth as he saw it; how would he have navigated the past months without Jess? She had given him love, and it was only now that he saw it was conditional.

Maybe it was only a mother's love that owned the blindness and the tenacity to be unconditional.

'And I came here, you didn't bring me.'

'What do you want to do?'

Rob pretended to give a considered answer. 'I'll stay here, I think. I've got some work, and if I come home, what'll happen? I'll be arrested and put inside, we always knew that. At least here I've got some time to think and a place to live. After that, if they come for me, if they do extradite me . . .' He shrugged. 'I'll handle it when it comes.'

'Maybe I'll come back when Beth is better.'

'Maybe,' he agreed.

They reached the harbour and an undecorated bar used by the fishermen. They ordered two beers and sat without talking at an outside table, watching the swifts stitch their invisible patterns into the dusk. A space had opened between them and they both knew for certain that time and separation would amplify it.

Jess would need to catch the earliest bus in order to reach the airport in time for her flight. When their glasses were empty they retraced their steps, hand in hand, denying the windy distance between them. But when they reached the apartment overlooking the railway lines the atmosphere between them shifted again. Rob closed the metal shutters and the room became a sanctuary. The sound of the landlady's overloud television drifted up to them and they smiled. They had acknowledged in the past that her deafness was to their advantage.

Jess hesitated in the cramped space between the bed and the table. She had taken off her shoes and the cold tiles under her feet snagged a memory of the early morning before they visited Lucca, and the airy sensation within her skull that she had identified as rapture. *We had that*, she thought. *We had that much.* On that morning she had crossed to the bed and looked down at the planes and curves of Rob's sleeping face, and he had opened his eyes and reached for her.

The memory of it caused a contraction of her inner muscles that was almost an ache. Her mouth opened a little, and the high overhead light caught a glint of wetness on her lower lip. Rob was standing a yard away from her. The air between them thickened and seemed suddenly to roar like the blood in their ears. For a moment they looked, without moving. Jess was wearing a faded blue cotton shirt she had found in a second-hand shop. They had arrived with nothing and had bought very few clothes, washing and wearing what they did own over and over. Now Rob put his fingers to the top button of the blue shirt and slowly undid it.

Jess's long hours of gardening had laid a red-brown vee at her neck over the paler skin inside the shirt. When Rob undid the remaining buttons and took off the shirt her tanned forearms were also revealed in odd conjunction with the milky uppers. He had seen this new piebald skin of hers often enough before, but tonight she folded her arms and spread her fingers in an attempt to conceal it. That she should want him not to see this evidence of her hard work seemed infinitely touching to Rob, and at the same time struck a fierce chord of desire in him.

Although he wanted to tear off the rest of her clothes he made his hands work slowly. He unbuttoned her jeans and slid them down over her hips. She stepped neatly out of them, but he saw that her eyes were dazed and she was breathing faster and harder.

When she was naked he ran his hands over her shoulders and down to her hips. Then he turned her to the bed and made her sit on the edge of it. She sat obediently, her weight slightly creasing the covers that she had straightened this morning. Rob went to the door and took her straw hat off the hook. He put it on her head and the shadow of the brim fell over her face. At once she looked remote and mysterious, like a woman in a painting.

He knelt on the floor in front of her. He lifted one foot and put his mouth to the blue veins that faintly netted the instep. He kissed her ankle bones and the sharp blade of her shins, and parted her knees with his insistent hand. He sat back then on his heels and met her eyes under the brim of the hat. She became simply Jess for him once more, for tonight at least, neither a mother nor a stranger. Jess languorously smiled and leaned back, propping herself on her elbows, inviting him. Her head tipped and the hat fell off, unregarded. Rob moved forward, his hand finding her loosely curled fingers and folding his own around them. He buried his face between her thighs.

The landlady's television boomed forgivingly through the floor.

They had moved from the bed to a chair, and from the chair to the floor, clammy tile alternating against their skin with close air as they rolled over, locked and rolled again. They didn't speak. It was as if they had travelled in a circle, back to the beginning, to their first night together when the language of sex was the only expression they could give to the fury of grief and guilt. Tonight, as they had done on that earlier night, they found a balm in it.

Afterwards they lay under a twisted sheet. It was very late and the house was filled with silence that amplified their breathing and the sweaty kiss of their skin when they shifted against each other.

'I'll leave you the money,' Jess said, with her mouth against his throat. They had been careful, and there was plenty left.

327

Enough for whatever needs Rob might have for now.

'I don't need it.'

'I'm still going to leave it. I don't want to take it back with me.'

'All right,' he said.

Jess nodded to herself in the dark. She could feel herself beginning to dip helplessly into the shallows of sleep. He could travel on with the money, if he wished to. He could go further than she had ever been, slipping away until he was out of reach. She imagined him reaching South America. He could live free in Brazil. She imagined how he might recreate himself in a new world. He was good at languages and he was young and more attractive even than she had properly understood until she saw the Italian girls covertly staring at him on the beach. She knew how he might be. He would fall in love with a thin, dark girl and be happy, free of his miserable past and the mean grey strait-jacket of England. The loss of him to this placeless future twisted at Jess, so that she frowned in her first seconds of sleep and tightened her arms sadly around him.

Beth was already at home when Jess arrived from Italy. She opened the door of her flat and saw her mother. Jess was thin and sun-tanned, and her eyes seemed much larger in her face than was normal; for a second she was hardly recognisable. She was wearing odd, shapeless clothes and carrying a single small suitcase. She looked like a fugitive, even though Graham Adair's money had been refunded and he had reluctantly agreed not to press charges against her.

They didn't speak. Jess put down her bag and took hold of her daughter's hands. The journey had seemed endless, and the parting that had begun it had been painful. She saw that Beth was pale, but otherwise looked as she always did. On the train and the bus from the airport Jess's head had been full of different images, of Danny in his hospital bed and Beth's features superimposed on his, and lent the same terrible waxen beauty.

Then they stepped together and held each other tightly. As if for the first time they noticed that their heights were the same, their faces touched as if reflecting one another, their mouths made the same attempt to smile. The layers of mistrust and misunderstanding that had built up and thickened between them were still palpable but they changed their quality, becoming brittle, as if they might easily be broken and swept away.

'I'm okay,' Beth promised awkwardly as Jess held her. 'I will be, now.'

'I know you will be,' Jess echoed. 'Let me look at you properly.'

She drew her into the kitchen where the light was strongest and stood her in front of the uncurtained window. There were purplish shadows under her eyes but there were no lines bracketing Beth's eyebrows or hooking her nose to her mouth. She was so young. Jess took her in her arms again and rested her forehead against Beth's. She felt the miraculous and reassuring springing of her separate life, and the intricate and lovely connections of bone and muscle, as vividly as she had done on the day when she was born and the new package of her child was placed in her arms. Beth had always been herself and Danny had always been different, because of his history. That was the truth and the sadness of it. Jess stood motionless, overtaken with the sudden rush of love for her daughter that for now, just for now, washed away her grief for Danny.

'Where's Rob?' Beth asked with a touch of stiffness. The question had been sounding in her head.

'He stayed in Italy.'

'Did he? Was that difficult?'

'Yes,' Jess answered, not wanting to lie.

'Thank you for coming,' Beth said softly. The understatement was enough for both of them.

'I want to hear about the hospital. What happens now?'

'I have to have a course of radiotherapy. It means going in to the hospital every day. It will be quite tiring.'

'I'll stay here and look after you.' The rented flat was small, with only one bedroom. Jess looked around her with different eyes. 'I'll have to get a camp bed.' Lizzie had done as she had been asked, and put the old house on the market. There was an interested buyer; Jess knew that soon she would not have her own home any longer. The notion did not alarm her in the least. It gave her instead an odd feeling of elation and excitement, like being slightly drunk. If Beth could be well, and if Rob and Lizzie and Sock and James were safe, she had every-thing she needed.

'I've got one. It's a sort of folding khaki army thing on wooden legs. Hugely uncomfortable I should think.'

'Doesn't matter. I can sleep anywhere.' It was the truth. Slowly the ability to sleep and to find respite in sleep were coming back to her.

Beth was shaking her head and laughing at the same time. 'I'm so happy you're here. Don't go away so far ever again.'

'I won't. We both know I won't do that.'


'A theoretical date has been set for the trial,' Michael Blake told Jess when he tracked her down by telephone to Beth's flat. It was to be a week at the beginning of July. 'You know where Rob is. Will you tell him that if he were to come back to England voluntarily, in good time for the trial to take place, it might go a way towards making up for his having skipped bail? If he doesn't come back, on the other hand, they'll bring him out sooner or later.'

Jess listened to what he had to say.

'I'll tell him,' she said at the end, as non-committally as she could. She did not have the right to try to influence Rob's deci-sions. But that evening, when she knew he would be back from his hotel job, she did telephone the apartment house in Italy. After a lengthy interval the landlady answered. Jess struggled with the obstacles of her minimal Italian and the woman's deaf-ness. At last she made herself understood.

'Ah, sì. Ma il signor e partito.'

'*Partito? Quando?*'

'*Questo mattino, signora. Di buon'ora.*'

'I see. Thank you. *Grazie.*'

Rob had already gone, early that morning. She imagined him springing away, out of reach of the courts and the police, of Michael Blake, of herself. Out of his bad past, into a different place. Her sadness that he was gone was counterweighted by her happiness for him.

Rob was following a herd of disembarking passengers through an airless labyrinth of airport corridors. Like Jess, he carried only one bag, containing the few possessions he had accumulated in Italy. The sticky texture of acres of carpet snagged his feet and prickles of static accumulated in his clothes but he kept walking, his eyes fixed on the head of the passenger striding in front of him. In the no-man's land between the arrivals gate and immigration control there was nowhere to move but forward.

The momentum was broken as they reached the immigration hall and the passengers fanned into queues at the line of desks. Rob joined the nearest line and shuffled impassively towards the official at his booth. He tried to keep his mind empty but a tic of fear snagged at it like a riptide beneath a smooth expanse of water. He could feel currents of adrenalin shivering under his skin but he told himself that there was no fighting or running to be done. He would wait, and take whatever would come.

It was his turn at the desk.

He handed over his passport and waited while the immigration officer checked his name and his photograph. Rob had had his hair cut off; it stood up now over his head in a rough, reddish prickle. But even without the bronze coils hanging around it his face was unmistakable. The man snapped the passport closed and kept it under his hand.

'Stand there, please,' he said curtly. He spoke briefly into the telephone at his side and immediately two uniformed officers

331

came out from behind a mirror screen. They darted to Rob and took hold of his arms. Rob let himself be led away, past the curious stares of the arriving passengers at Heathrow.

The police cell contained four bunks, arranged in pairs, one above the other. The bottom left-hand one was empty, the top one was occupied by a motionless figure huddled under a blanket. On the bottom right-hand bunk sat two Asian men in jeans and bomber jackets. They were unshaven and their skins under the neon strip-light looked bruised with exhaustion. The officer undid Rob's handcuffs and nodded to the empty bunk. Obediently Rob crossed to it and sat down, rubbing his wrists. There was an overpowering smell of sweat and old food and excrement. After staring briefly at him, the Asian men resumed an urgent low-voiced conversation.

It was ten p.m. Rob lay down on his back and turned his face towards the wall. It was green-painted, blank, faintly clammy with moisture. There were no imaginary islands or continents to be distinguished here. After a while he closed his eyes. There was no rush of terror as he had feared there might be. He was in a police cell near Heathrow. Michael Blake had explained to him on the telephone that he would request further bail, but it would almost certainly be refused.

The man in the upper bunk began to snore, quietly at first, then more loudly so the snores seemed to break into the open through clotted webs of lung and larynx. It was as Rob had imagined prison would be. No worse. No worse yet, although probably that was to come. But now he was here, he thought he would be able to endure it. He had waited in Italy for almost a week but he had known from the beginning that there was no reason to be there without Jess. Nor did he have any wish to go further away from home and be lonelier than he was now. The past months had taught him how not to be lonely. He had come back to England because whatever sentence might be waiting for him was preferable to the interminable sentence of isolation.

Rob listened patiently to the snoring and the low, unintelligible murmur of talk. He thought about Jess and Beth and Danny, and Zoe and Cat. In the end, still lying patiently on his back with his head turned to the wall, he fell asleep.

# Seventeen

On remand, waiting for his trial to come up, Rob was allowed daily visitors. Jess came to see him at the first opportunity. They held hands across the table that separated them.

Jess asked, 'Why *did* you come back? I imagined you'd go away somewhere and start again.'

Rob laughed, surprising her. She was struck by the way that his fears seemed to have evaporated.

'I thought about it. I counted up the money and tried to work out where to go but it all seemed to be about someone else, like in a film. In the end I realised you can't start properly all over. You can only go on with what you've got, from where you already are.' He shrugged and his hands curled around hers. 'I came back because I wanted to.'

Jess knew that he hadn't come back for her. That had changed between them; it had begun to change even before she had left Italy. *Nothing stays the same.* Neither of them had ever suggested that there was anything as black and white as a choice to be made between Beth or Rob. But Jess had done what she could not help doing and so the connection between them had altered irrevocably. It was as if she held Danny's hands in hers now. They were precious and familiar. No less than that, but no more either.

'You did the right thing. I'm sorry I persuaded you to skip bail. I'm sorry it led you to this.'

He laughed again. 'You didn't persuade me. I came with you as fast as I could. I was the one who smashed your ex-husband

334

in the face, wasn't I? And listen, I was happy out there with you. Those weeks we had, they were absolutely different from anything I've ever known. I've got them inside me now, in my head, and I can keep them. I wouldn't not have lived them, even if it means being in here for now.'

Jess nodded, unable to speak for a moment. Rapture, that was how she had defined it for herself. A lightness beneath the plates of her skull and inside the cage of her ribs, and Rob had known it too. *We had that much*, she thought. *I knew it then and I still have it within me, just as he does. We did more than help each other*.

And then there was no daylight in the prison visiting room and the air smelled of cigarettes and stale sweat, and in this oppressive atmosphere Jess could only acknowledge that for all that they had shared they were still separated by more than twenty years, and by the knotted responsibilities and fierce, ingrained love that Jess felt for her children.

Sadly they released each other's hands.

'Is there anything else you need?' Jess asked. She had brought him food and books, and tapes for his cassette player.

He shook his head. 'No. Nothing at all.'

Jess was not his only visitor. At the end of the second week Rob was told that there was someone else to see him. He waited in the visiting room, expecting Michael Blake or his barrister. Instead, the door opened and Cat was shown in. Her eyes flicked around the room before they fixed on him. She was covering her unease with sulky bravado; she stalked to the chair opposite him and sat down sideways with her thin legs crossed and her head tipped away from him. It was one of her plain days. Her hair looked greasy and her face was a pallid, shadowless moon.

'Are you surprised to see me?' she demanded.

'I'm pleased,' Rob said gently. It was the truth. The warder who had shown Cat in shrugged and went out. The door closed behind him but the observation window remained open.

'You came back, then.'

He nodded, letting the obviousness of the statement pass. 'What about her?'

'If you mean Jess, she came back first. To look after her daughter, who has got cancer.'

Cat's gaze flickered for an instant. 'Did you come back to be with her? Once you get out of here, of course. Is she waiting for you?'

Rob said quietly, 'No.' The sneer in Cat's voice was masking something, some need or fear that he couldn't quite interpret. 'Not that it's any of your business,' he added.

Cat leaned back in her chair, crossing her legs more aggressively. A triangle of pvc miniskirt rode higher up her thigh and Rob gazed at the point where the corner of the table hid his view.

'So, are you wondering why I'm visiting you in jail? I haven't got a cake with a file in it.'

Her eyes flicked around the bare room again. Rob thought back to the evenings and nights they had spent together before Italy intervened. He remembered the way they had seemed to link him back to his life before the accident.

'Tell me why you are,' he said.

'I'm pregnant,' Cat announced flatly. 'It's yours.'

Rob moistened his lips. He leaned forward across the grey chipped Formica table top.

'Are you sure?'

'Am I sure I've fallen, or sure it was you?'

'Both, I suppose.'

A storm of reactions began to beat inside him, drumming against his chest and his skull. A *baby*, a weight, a being. Another new life. He found that he couldn't look at her.

'Yeah, I am. And it's nearly three months.'

'What do you want to do?' He didn't know if he should offer to help her.

Cat sniffed sharply, turning down the corners of her mouth at the same time. 'I'm not getting rid of it, if that's what you're going to tell me to do. I couldn't. I don't believe in it. And it's my baby. I'll keep it and look after it.'

'You just said it's mine as well.'

Their eyes did meet now. He saw that she acted defiant to shield her vulnerability and he found himself wanting to reach out and hold her. He remembered the blob, the baby belonging to Jess's sister, and a thread twisted inside him. It wound tighter, until he could hardly breathe. *Man*, the baby had said. It had sprawled ripely on his chest, a bundle of snot and pee. Cat was still looking at him, measuring his reactions.

'Yeah, it's yours, like I said. As far as that goes.'

There was a silence. Rob ventured, 'Can I . . . do you want me to help you? Is that why you've come?' When she didn't answer, only went on measuring him up, he added, 'I'd like to help.'

Now she gave her sharp sniff again. 'You're not much use in here, are you? And I've been told you could be inside for five years.'

'Or much less. It's an offer, that's all. You can think about it.'

Cat nodded at that. She uncrossed her legs and stood up, shouldering a shapeless bag.

'Yeah, all right. I'll come back and see you.'

She didn't look round on her way out. The screw came and took Rob back to his cell.

'How do you plead, Mr Ellis?'

'Not guilty,' Rob said.

From where he stood in the dock he could see Jess at the front of the public gallery. She sat on her own, calm-faced, gazing at him in her direct way. And a little further back in the gallery was Cat, also alone. He wanted to make some sign or gesture of reassurance to her but he could only wait until she looked up, then meet her eyes with the suggestion of a smile.

The court shuffled and collected itself. At the beginning of the day the room still seemed cool and airy, but it contained the threat of the day's heat slowly gathering under the discoloured ceiling. The case had come up for trial at last at the beginning of September, when the hot summer was fading into cooler mornings, and earlier sunsets were lent vivid colours by the polluted air.

Rob glanced at the jury. They were ordinary people in spectacles, humdrum clothes, most of them leaning forward with a sense of alert relief to hear the prosecution counsel's preliminary outlining of the case. They were lucky, the trial would be a short one. No months of listening to complicated fraud evidence for them.

A witness was called to the stand. It was one of the police officers from the panda car that had pursued Rob's van along the bypass. He took the oath and the prosecution's cross-examination began.

Rob listened, but on another level, deep inside himself where he kept it interred, he thought about his father and that other trial. Being in prison himself had not brought his father closer to him. The fatal similarity that he had dreaded all his adult life had failed to materialise. Rob felt farther from the man now than he had ever done, and so to find himself in the same place in almost the same position was less of an ordeal than he had feared. There was, even, a kind of relief in it. The worst had come.

It was also true that some aspects of prison life – the lack of privacy, the absence of small comforts – reminded him of life in the children's home and with the Purses, so he was well enough equipped to survive it. There had been plenty of time to think.

He had thought about Jess, with gratitude, and about Cat's visits. She had come and gone three or four more times. They had sat with their heads close together, urgently murmuring across the table's divide. Cat's determination to be independent with her baby had softened into an agreement that they might try to look after it together when he got out. Just to try, with no promises on either side. He had agreed to that.

Finally Rob had been driven within himself. He had allowed memories that he had shrunk from all through his outside life and at last he had found only reasons for a detached kind of pity, not disgust or shame. The taint of inherited violence seemed to have faded. He even discerned the hazy outlines of a kind of forgiveness.

Perhaps his father had not been truly violent either; only in drink or desperation.

In the witness box the officer stolidly recounted the details of the accident.

'The vehicle driven by the defendant approached the Pond Road bridge. There was another vehicle approaching from the opposite direction.'

In Rob's mind's eye the pictures ran and reran, always with the brownish spot of oblivion at the centre. He could remember the van's shuddering as he jabbed the accelerator down and the blue light flashing in his mirror, Danny shouting *Go*, and the blinding dazzle of oncoming lights. Then only the telescopically folded front of the van and Danny lying outside on the grass as if he were asleep.

'What happened as the defendant's vehicle approached the bridge?'

The policeman answered, 'I saw the vehicle waver, then swerve violently to the left. The brake lights came on and I heard his brakes squeal just before the vehicle hit the left-hand pillar of the bridge.'

Jess plaited her fingers in her lap. She knew that in the evidence still to be heard she would have to listen to much worse than this, and she had prepared herself for it. There was no question of her not being here. She looked from the witness back to Rob. He was pale and thinner, and his shorn head made him look vulnerable, but he appeared quite calm.

*

339

During the first afternoon of the trial the other policemen who had witnessed the accident and its aftermath were called, then the police vehicle reconstruction expert. The expert's evidence was detailed and technical, concerned with measurements of braking distances and tyre patterns and speed of impact. The van had been travelling at between fifty-five and sixty miles per hour, before it had suddenly veered from a straight line of travel towards the bridge pillar. The van's nearside rear tyre had deflated just before the skid began, as indicated by the shredded pattern of the marks left on the road.

The prosecution asked if the blown tyre might not have caused the skid, but resulted from it.

'The sequence of events as I have stated it is as plain,' the expert said, 'as a set of fingerprints.' But he agreed with the Crown that a sober and careful driver should have been able to control the vehicle and bring it safely to a halt.

Jess still gazed straight ahead of her, impassively listening.

The speed at impact had been nearly forty miles an hour. It seemed that Rob had been almost miraculously lucky to escape with minor injuries. Danny had not been lucky. The absence of him was the vacuum at the heart of all this trial, the reason for the police uniforms and the sheaves of evidence, the barristers in their wigs and the court recorder's fingers blindly pattering over the keys of the transcript machine. Nothing would bring him back. No oceans of grief and no weight of vindication.

She blinked to contain the pressure of her tears.

Rob's barrister re-established the sequence of blow-out, skid and swerve, then thanked the expert warmly for the clarity of his evidence. The witness for the defence was a road traffic engineer. He stated that in his opinion, given the nature of the blow-out, the speed and the weather and road conditions, even the most expert and sober driver would have had difficulty in avoiding the collision.

The last of the police witnesses was the inspector who had been in charge of the investigation. The room had fulfilled its promise of becoming hot, the motionless air grown tainted.

*Goodbye, Bits*, Jess had said to him in the bus from Lucca. And the memory of Bits and the pig boy and all the tight-packed stifling concerns around them did indeed seem to have faded. Rob looked across to the gallery where Cat was sitting. He longed to go to her.

The inspector was describing the day, the last day Danny had known. The gym, the pub and the restaurant, then the club. At one thirty in the morning a complaint had been tele-phoned to the police by a young woman resident of a bedsit house. There was a disturbance in the room of one of the other occupants, the noise of a violent struggle. When the police arrived at the address the accused and Daniel Arrowsmith had already left.

At the end of the inspector's evidence the judge took off his spectacles and massaged the bridge of his nose. He announced that they would resume at ten the next morning. Everyone stood as he left the court.

Rob was taken away. Jess watched him go, then edged out of the cramped row of seats. Her limbs were stiff with sitting and a pulse of tension beat at the corner of her eye. She went out into the bright afternoon and hesitated on the gritty pave-ment, wondering where to go. Cat was standing a few feet away, hesitating also. Their eyes met and it was Cat who sidled forward. She shrugged her narrow shoulders.

'I'm Cat Watson. I . . . We've never met. There's no reason why we should have done, is there? I don't know why I'm even saying this. I'm sorry, that's all. About Danny and everything.'

'Thank you,' Jess said simply. She accepted that the bare words contained more than conventional sympathy.

'It's just, you know, you looked so sad, sitting there.'

Jess had not considered how she looked. She was startled by this child's view of her.

'What really happened that night?' She blurted out the unconsidered words.

'Didn't Rob tell you?'

'In a way.'

'You don't know whether to believe him, is that it? I'll tell you, if it's what you want. Are you sure you do?'

'Yes.'

'Danny came on to me. I tried to push him off, he wouldn't have it. He hurt me and I was scared. I knew he was going to rape me. Rob pulled him off and they ran out together. I'm sorry,' Cat repeated.

There were the two versions of Danny between them, the dark and the light. Somewhere between the two extremes was the real one, the truth. Without considering why, except that she was suddenly certain of it, Jess lifted her head and said, 'Everything will be all right.'

'Rob will be,' Cat flashed back, as if Jess had challenged her. 'I know he will.'

Jess nodded, disconcerted. 'Yes. I believe that too.'

Discarded shreds of detail suddenly fitted together in her mind. She knew that Cat was the woman who had left her lipsticked tissues and mascara marks in Rob's room. She nodded again, finding a smile.

Cat hitched her rucksack over her shoulder, already looking away. 'Okay. Here's my bus. See you there tomorrow, I suppose.'

Crossing the road she looked physically small, and fragile. Another girl was waiting for her at the bus-stop and they stood earnestly talking. At first Jess only noted how alike they looked in their short skirts, heavy-footed in clumpy shoes that made their legs look even longer and thinner. They both rested their weight on one leg, pushing one hip forward so their skirts rose even higher.

Then, breaking the symmetry, Cat changed her position.

Feet apart, she briefly balanced her weight and hollowed her back. And at the same moment she rested the flat of her hand over her diaphragm. Her stomach was just perceptibly rounded.

As soon as she saw that she was pregnant Jess knew that it was Rob's baby.

From across the street Cat felt Jess's gaze and for a second their eyes met through the thundering traffic. Cat's stare contained a challenge still, and also a gleam of triumph.

*It's all right,* Jess wanted to tell her. *I'm not a threat to you and Rob. Everything changes, doesn't it?*

A tall lorry rumbled in front of Jess, blocking her view. When she could see again the two girls were climbing on to a bus, insouciantly alike once more.

Jess's house already seemed abandoned. The sale was going through as planned and she had begun to dismantle the formidable breakwaters of family possessions. As she dropped her keys on the hall table she noticed the unfaded rectangles of wallpaper where pictures had once hung. The patterns of tiny green flowers seemed unnervingly bright against the bleached surroundings. Had she once chosen that very shade of green?

Beth called out to her, 'Mum? I'm in here.'

She was in the living-room, sitting on the sofa.

'How was it? What happened? I wish you had let me come.'

Beth had finished her course of radiotherapy. Now she was staying with Jess, having a rest before returning to work. She was tired and listless, but the prospects were good. Her surgeon believed that the treatment had been undertaken in time and had been completely successful. Jess still repeated his words to herself, with dazed gratitude. She took Beth's face between her hands and bent to kiss her forehead. It was easy, now, to show Beth how much she loved her.

'It wasn't so bad. I just wanted to make sure, first. It's a small courtroom. Everything is formal, but peculiarly cosy as well. People yawn and sigh and scratch. It's gripping and boring, both at the same time.'

'And Rob?'

Jess thought of Cat. 'Rob will be all right.'

Beth said decisively, 'I'm coming with you tomorrow.'

Jess would be glad to have her there but she warned, 'They'll probably begin on the medical evidence tomorrow.'

'I was there when he died. I can bear to listen to the details of what happened. Lizzie wants to come too. Will you call her?'

'I want to go out and breathe some air first. Let's go and have a glass of wine in the garden.'

They took out a bottle and some glasses and sat on an old wooden bench. The air tasted thick and honeyed. Ambitious filaments of spiders' web stretched and swam between the mildewed shoots of shrubs, and the fat tortoiseshell spiders rested motionless in the web hearts. Jess tilted her head and looked up at the house. Beth was absently humming as she snapped off the heads of long-dead roses. Jess saw that the paint was peeling from the sun-baked window frames, and above the bathroom window the guttering hung at a drunken angle. Her purchaser had briskly pointed out this and other evidence of neglect, and had taken account of it in a reduced offer that Jess was still relieved to accept.

She closed her eyes, letting the sun warm her eyelids.

When she looked again she saw three just discernible vertical lines on an outhouse door. Danny had painted them one summer, as a wicket. She remembered him standing in front of the door, intently squaring his bat. A dark wing of sadness touched her and she quietly accepted the shadow of it, as she had learned to do. Then she turned her face towards the house again, and relief surged in her. It had become a weight, an empty responsibility, and she was happy to surrender it. She would be free, as she had felt in Italy.


The next day Jess sat in the public gallery with Lizzie and Beth on either side of her.

The divisional police surgeon's report was read to the court. Robert Ellis's blood alcohol level on the night of the accident was 120 micrograms per 100 millilitres. Rob had certainly been drunk. The question remained whether he might have been able to control the van's violent skidding when the tyre blew out if he had been sober.

After the surgeon's report came the pathologist's.

The exact nature and extent of Danny's massive head

injuries were minutely catalogued. The injuries were exactly consistent with his having been thrown from the van on impact, and his head having struck the kerb of the road. He had not been wearing a seat-belt.

All of this Jess knew. But out of the pathologist's dry recital that was somehow the more dreadful for its dispassion, one small detail sprang out at her. She heard the words without warning and they took root in her mind, and began to echo in her head, swelling in volume until the sound rang in her ears. She shifted in her seat and Lizzie glanced sharply at her, then reassuringly took her hand and squeezed it.

Beth looked at her too and whispered, 'Mum, are you all right?'

Jess managed to nod, dry-throated. There was no question that she had misheard: the pathologist had simply been stating the medical facts, describing what emergency measures had been taken by the casualty team when Danny was admitted to the hospital.

The defence contested the medical evidence. If Danny had been wearing his seat-belt he would not have been flung out of the van on impact.

Jess managed to sit still through the cross-questioning even though her inner scenery was shifting so fast that she shivered with waves of nausea. A new landscape gathered definition around her, developing before her eyes like a Polaroid snapshot of some crucial piece of evidence.

*Oh God. Why didn't I ever see it before? Why did I never so much as ask?*

At last the court stood for lunch.

Jess groped her way out into the foyer with Lizzie and Beth in her wake. Lizzie fumbled in her bag for cigarettes as soon as they were outside, and lit one with relief.

'Give me one,' Jess said.

'What's the matter? Did it upset you?'

'Mum, you've gone white as a sheet. Come on, sit down here.'

They found a bench and Jess drew on the cigarette that Lizzie put into her hand. She coughed, and the smoke made her eyes smart as she stared down at the grimy floor and the feet and legs of the oblivious passers-by.

'Jess?' Lizzie said sharply.

Obligingly, surprisingly, Jess's mouth formed words. 'His blood group,' she said.

'What are you talking about?'

'Danny's blood group. That man said the doctors ordered a cross-match as soon as he was brought into casualty.'

'They would do, wouldn't they? In case of internal bleeding?'

Jess interrupted, 'It's not that. It's *which* blood group he was. I never knew it. I never asked when he was in there, why would I? Danny was never ill before, never even went near a hospital, until . . . He said B positive, didn't he?'

The question was superfluous. The syllables beat in her ears. 'So?'

'I'm O,' Jess said.

'And me,' Beth added. She had submitted to enough tests lately.

'Ian is B.'

There was a small silence. In the tiny interval before she spoke again Jess saw Beth's chin lift, her head turn.

'Do you remember, he used to be a blood donor? He had a little booklet, kept his certificates in it. After so many donations he got a gilt and enamel badge, two inter locking hearts . . .' Jess's voice faltered. She knew that she was babbling. She went on more slowly, 'He always used to say B was the least common of the ordinary blood groups. Four per cent of the population. He was rather proud of it, for some stupid reason. Sometimes he would be asked to donate for a particular operation, a hole-in-the-heart or something . . .'

Lizzie stubbed out her cigarette.

'What are you implying?'

It was Beth who answered, all in a rush. 'Christ, don't you

know? She's saying Dad is Danny's father. Aren't you? *Aren't you?*'

'I'm only saying he could be,' Jess said. 'I don't know. I was always so certain he wasn't. Couldn't have been.'

There was another silence. Each of them thought of the shoe box in Jess's wardrobe, and the snapshot hidden at the bottom of it, the good-looking boy who looked like Danny.

Jess thought wildly, *Is it possible I willed my child to look like something, like someone, because I needed to believe what was more than the truth?*

Then she saw Beth's face. It was shining. Hope lit her up like a lamp being switched on beneath the skin. Seeing it, Jess understood the importance of discovering the truth, for Beth's sake.

'I'll find out for sure,' she promised, although reluctance froze her and the last cowardly refuge of uncertainty beckoned. 'Somehow. I owe everyone that much, don't I?'

Lizzie gave a sigh of irritation. But then she moved aggressively to Jess and wrapped her arms roughly round her. Jess caught the old, mingled scent of perfume and cigarettes and willingly submitted to a hug that was half a rebuke.

'Jesus. Whatever bloody next? You sort it out, Jess, d'you hear? Before any more ghosts can gather.'

'I will,' she promised.

When they reached home she looked up the number of Danny's consultant. Mr Copthorne's secretary informed her that he was with a patient, but if she would leave her number she would ask him to call back.

An hour later, when Jess and Beth were sitting out in the garden again, the telephone rang.

'Mrs Arrowsmith? How can I help you?'

Jess had blanked out the memory of the man's voice, but at the sound of it the ward and the hours of waiting and diminishing hope came flooding back to her.

'I have a question to ask. Not an easy question.'

He waited tactfully while she formulated the words.

'I want to find, to try to find out, if Danny was my husband's son. I . . . I had reason to believe that he was not. But now I am not so sure.'

As she explained she remembered Ian's bruised and baffled anger the last time she had seen him, and was glad that Beth had not been there. 'I don't know if my ex-husband will co-operate.'

'Mrs Arrowsmith, would it help you to know that your ex-husband came to see me some weeks ago?'

'I had no idea.'

'I could not perform a DNA test. But on the basis of tissue type and blood tests I was able to confirm beyond most reasonable doubt that Daniel was his son.'

Jess exhaled a long breath. 'I see,' she said. 'Thank you.'

Beth was still sitting on the garden bench. There was no need for Jess to speak; as soon as Beth saw her expression her face broke into a brilliant smile.

'He knew? It *is* true, then? Dad will be so happy.'

Beth's delight was almost unbearably touching. The sharp edges of Jess's self-reproach softened in the warmth of it.

'Dad already knows,' she said. 'He went to see the doctor weeks ago and asked for the tests. Did you know? Did he tell you any of this?'

Beth shook her head, puzzlement momentarily eclipsing her happiness. 'No. Nothing at all. We've only talked about me, and the lump.'

'What time is it in Sydney?'

Beth patiently reminded her, 'Very early tomorrow morning.'

Once again, with the memory of the morning when she called Ian to break the news of the accident vividly sharp in her mind, Jess picked up the telephone. Relief surged in her when she heard Ian's voice answering, fuzzed with sleep and distance.

'Did I wake you?'

Immediately his voice sharpened. 'Is Beth all right?'

'Yes. Yes, it's nothing like that. Ian . . .'

'I know what you're going to say. He's my son.' *Is*, not was. 'I knew it all along, but I was glad to have it confirmed.'

Even in her confusion, in the midst of all the tides of loss and change that swirled around her, Jess found herself smiling at Ian's bull-headed satisfaction in having proved himself right. Everything changes, she thought, and yet nothing does.

'Why didn't you say anything about this to me, Ian? Or to Beth?'

'Listen. Isn't it the truth that you can only know what you want to know? You made a version of reality, for God knows what reason, and you clung to it. You didn't want to know anything different. And now I suppose you have let the truth become plain, or haven't been able to close your eyes to it any longer. Am I right?'

'In a way.'

'And when you acknowledged it I wanted you to tell Beth. I didn't want her to be confronted with two versions of the story and have to ask herself, which shall I choose?'

In that moment Jess knew how much she had under-estimated Ian.

'I understand,' she said softly.

'And what about you? Are you home for good now?'

'I don't know about for good, Ian. The sale of the house is going through. I can pay you back your money soon.'

'Ah, the money's not that important. Is Beth there?'

'She is. I'll put her on in a minute. Can I ask you one more thing?'

'Sure.'

'Are you happy in Australia with Michelle?'

Jess did not ask because she wished or hoped for anything other, but because she needed to know this too.

'I am,' Ian told her truthfully. 'Look after my Beth for me, will you?'

'I'll do that,' she promised him, 'at least.'

\*

The civilian witnesses were called in turn, first the motorists who had witnessed the crash. Next came Zoe. She took the oath in a barely audible whisper.

'Miss Hicks, will you please tell the court in your own words what happened that night?'

Zoe began to tell the story. Here it was, Jess thought. The face of her son that she had never been allowed to encounter. The bitterness of the piece of missing knowledge, the partiality of her understanding of her child, were as painful as all the other mosaic fragments of her loss.

Greedy, golden Danny who always got what he wanted because she had never denied him anything.

From his place across the courtroom Rob was looking at her. It seemed finally ironic to Jess that Rob had envied his friend.

Cat was not called as a witness. Jess knew that it was because she was pregnant with Rob's baby. Nor was she in her place in the gallery.

At the end of the day the judge announced before he rose that he would begin his summing-up in the morning. It would be the fourth and probably the final day of the trial. Rob was led away for the last time.

The jury was out. They had retired at the end of the morning. Jess tried to read Rob's counsel's face as he stood gossiping in the anterooms with lawyers from another court, but she couldn't detect anything but professional optimism. Lizzie and Beth tried to persuade her to leave the building for some food and drink, but the atmosphere of tension and expectation held her fast. Every time a door swung open or a voice called out Jess's head jerked up in response. She laced her fingers around a plastic cup of machine coffee and assured them that she didn't want anything more.

'Nothing's going to happen for ages,' Lizzie said.

'I know. But I'll stay just the same.'

When they had gone, promising to bring her a sandwich, Jess found a seat to one side of the waiting room. An excitable group of supporters from another court clustered in front of her and she sat half-hidden, watching the hands of the clock on the opposite wall. Her stomach churned with anticipation. In an attempt to distract herself she watched the people hurrying through the doors and tried to guess what their business might be. She saw Cat and Zoe as soon as they came in. Neither of the girls had been in the gallery that morning. Now they hesitated inside the doorway, then Cat slipped through the crowd to ask a question of one of the ushers. She returned to Zoe and they looked across at Jess as they whispered together.

Cat must feel the tension even more than she did, Jess thought. She wanted to go across and talk to her, to share the ache of waiting. Waiting was the worst.

But Lizzie and Beth came back and intercepted her.

'What's been going on?' Lizzie demanded.

'Nothing,' Jess said. 'I've just been sitting here watching the world go by.'

Lizzie eyed the mingled lawyers and officials and criminal classes. 'Some world,' she sniffed.


The jury had reached a verdict. They filed back into the court and took their places.

There was a pause in which Jess felt the fine hairs prickle at the nape of her neck. Rob waited in the dock, his hands hanging loose.

The foreman of the jury stood up.

In answer to the first charge he said loudly, 'Not guilty.'

Not guilty of causing death by dangerous driving.

Cat leaned forward in her seat, her fingers splayed stiff against her lips.

'And how do you find in response to the second charge, that of causing death by careless driving while under the influence of alcohol?'

'Guilty.'

It was Cat Rob looked to first. His fingers made a small, involuntary gesture of affection and reassurance that was as explicit as a kiss. And seeing it, Jess felt a beat of pride and admiration for him, as strong as if he were her own.

The judge cleared his throat. He told Rob that before he passed sentence there would be a four-week interval. The time would allow for a probation officer's examination and reports.

Until then, Rob would be remanded in custody.

# Eighteen

The last few packing cases stood in the hallway of Jess's house, and only the ghosts of furniture and pictures lingered in dusty outlines on the walls and floors.

Jess said to Beth, indicating one of the boxes, 'Are you quite sure you don't want this?'

Beth grinned. Her face was rounder, with some of the lines of strain smoothed away. 'I don't know where I'm going to put half the stuff you've already given me. I don't need a bone china tea service, even if Aunty May did give it to you as a wedding present.'

'We'll take it to Joyce, then.'

They carried a cardboard box apiece out to the Citroën. The estate agent's sign nailed to the front gate had a **SOLD** bar tacked across it; the strip of garden had already taken on the neglected look belonging to a vacant house. Jess told herself that she must cut back the parched grass and leggy roses, then remembered that it was no longer her responsibility to do so. In three days the new owners would move in. She was smiling as she settled behind the wheel of the car.

Seeing it, Beth said, 'You look happy, Mum. I thought you never would again.'

Jess drove down the street. It was so over-familiar she couldn't see how it must look to fresh eyes, to the young family who were about to call it home. She would have no reason to come here any longer; the road and the suburban trees and the stolid houses would continue as before. It was only a place, not even a beautiful or remarkable one. It wasn't life.

'Don't you feel anxious about selling up, giving so many of your things away, not having a home any longer?'

Jess would have a little money, not much. And for the first time in her adult life she felt she had no duties, owed no obligations. She was going to buy a van and travel in it; to see where her inclinations led her.

She answered, 'At your age I would have been afraid. But now – it's just an adventure. You'd think it would be the other way round, wouldn't you? My life hasn't been very adventurous up to now. Do you feel anxious about me?'

Beth thought about it, then shook her head. 'No. I think you're old enough to look after yourself.' They laughed at this apparent reversing of their roles, and knew at the same time that the bond between them was the same old contentious tie between mother and daughter, only righter and stronger than it had ever been.

Joyce welcomed them in. The front door of her ground-floor flat in a Sixties council block led straight into a square living-room. Net curtains filtered the evening light, giving the crowded room a dim, subaqueous aspect. A huge television set chattered in one corner beneath a silent wall clock made to look like a flower-painted china plate.

'You look grand,' she repeated twice to Jess. 'You do. And Beth too. Like two sisters, you are.'

'Flatterer,' Jess protested.

'Mother? Mum, look who's here.'

The old lady sat in an armchair squarely placed in front of the television. There were thick polythene sleeves on the arms and cushions of the chair, and a mat of it under her feet, and she was draped in a white plastic apron from chin to knee. Her legs stuck out beneath the apron, mottled and dark, the skin folded and collapsed into leathery wrinkles over the brittle bones. Her watery eyes fixed on the visitors out of the sad depths of incomprehension.

'She won't put her stockings on,' Joyce said. 'But otherwise she's having a good day. You're just going to have your tea, Mother, aren't you? That's why you've got your pinny on, isn't it?'

There was no answer, only the moist, bewildered gaze.

'Don't let us interrupt her meal. We'll just put these down and go.'

'You'll do nothing of the kind. How many months since I've seen you, Jess? Mother can wait half an hour for her tea. Time doesn't mean much to her. I'll just put the kettle on and make us a cuppa.'

Jess indicated one of the boxes and the plump newspaper eggs nested inside it. 'Look at this first, then. It's the china I promised you.'

Joyce knelt and unwrapped the first parcel. It was a teacup. The china was so thin that the nacreous pink glaze of the outside shone through the translucent blue-white of the interior. The handle, foot and rim of the cup were scrolled with gold. Joyce's face reddened with pleasure as she cradled the cup in her hands. With one fingertip she rubbed a smudge of newsprint from the delicately curled handle.

'Will you look at this? Did you ever see anything so fine? You can't give this to me, girl. Beth should have it.'

'I've got nowhere to put it. And I make tea from a teabag straight in a mug. I'd never use a shell-pink tea service complete with slop bowl,' Beth said hastily.

Jess insisted, 'I want you to have it, Joyce. To remember all those days when we had our break together at the nursery.'

Joyce held up the cup so her mother could see it. 'Look, Mum. Now we can have the Queen to tea, can't we?'

The old woman's hands came up and plucked at her face. She pulled at the seamed skin as if she found its texture inexplicable and distressing.

'Is the vicar coming?' she demanded. Her voice was surprisingly loud and harsh.

Joyce shook her head. 'Not today. We've got enough visitors, haven't we? Let's make this tea.'

She filled the opulent teapot and laid out three of the new cups and saucers with a plastic drinking cup on a tin tray, while she chatted to Jess about the nursery.

'It gave me the best laugh I've had in twenty years when I found out you robbed Graham's safe. I tell you, the best.'

'I'm ashamed of it now.'

Joyce flicked her a shrewd look. 'Sorry unpicks no crooked seams, girl.' She put the beaker of milky tea into her mother's hand and turned the spout towards her mouth. But the old woman's eyes, suddenly focused, were glued to the pearly pink cups.

'I want that one.'

'You drink out of your own cup, Mother. We don't want any accidents.'

With a wordless howl of anger she flung the beaker aside. The lid flew off and tea thick with sugar splashed up the wall and over the carpet beyond the polythene mat. Wearily Joyce got up and fetched a cloth, but Jess took it from her and began to mop up the mess. Beth picked up an empty cup and put it in the old woman's hands. As if to reward Beth for allowing what her daughter had denied she gave her a radiantly sweet smile and held the cup with exaggerated care.

'Very nice,' she approved.

'Isn't it? It doesn't hold much tea, though. I prefer a half-pint mug.'

On the television screen behind Beth's shoulder the weatherman began to read the local forecast after the early news. Breaking off her conversation with Jess, Joyce was already out of her chair, but too late. The old woman saw and pointed accusingly at the weatherman, forgot she was holding the cup. It fell and smashed on the corner of the hearth.

Oblivious, she shouted, 'Joyce? Joyce? Be quiet, can't you? He's looking at us. He's looking, I tell you.'

Joyce snapped the television off. 'There, he's gone.' To the others she explained, 'She's got a thing about some of the men on the telly. She thinks they can see her.'

356

The mother subsided in her chair, the threat of the weatherman already fading into confusion. Exhausted tears spilled out of her eyes and shone on her cheeks until Joyce patted them away with a tissue.

'Let's not have tears, there's a good girl. There's nothing to cry about. I'll get you your dinner now. Don't worry about the cup, Beth. I'm never going to have six VIPs to tea all at once, am I?'

She came back with a bowl of puree and a chunk of wholemeal bread. While her mother crumbled her bread on the plastic dip of her lap, Joyce spooned the food into her mouth. She scooped up the dribbles as they escaped from the mumbling lips and fed them back again, and nodded her encouragement until the bowl was empty and the last spills wiped away.

Afterwards she led the old woman to the bathroom, then brought her back to her chair. She switched on the television for her again.

By the time Jess and Beth were preparing to leave, she had fallen asleep. Joyce left her for a moment and came out into the cool twilight with them. Techno music pounded from an open window along the block. She forestalled their concerned sympathy with a quick gesture.

'There's nothing to be done. I shouldn't wish her dead, but I do, sometimes. And that's enough of that. Where exactly are you off to on your travels, Jess?'

'To Scotland, maybe, or Ireland, first. I've never been to Ireland.'

'When?'

'A few more days yet. I have to go to court first, as a character witness for Rob Ellis.'

Joyce gave her another appraising look. But she only said, 'That's a decent thing to do. He'll be glad of it. Now, you make sure you send me a postcard from somewhere exciting. And keep in touch.'

'I'll do that, Joyce.'

'Thanks for the tea-set.'

'I wish it were . . . well, you know what I wish for you.'

Joyce stood at the door of her block to wave them off, framed by a warm rectangle of yellow light. Then the door closed behind her and the light was extinguished.

In the car they were silent for a long time. At last Beth breathed out a long sigh and let her head fall back.

'Christ,' she said. After another long interval she added, 'It's just like having Sock.'

'Except that every day Sock learns something new. Each is a small triumph of gained independence. Whereas she forgets something and loses another scrap of dignity. Would you do for me what Joyce does?'

Beth blew out her cheeks. 'Feed you? Change your knickers? Forget it. You're my mother. You're supposed to look after me.'

'Exactly. I did it for you.'

'I'll do it for your grandchildren.'

The suggestion caught Jess unawares. Sentimentally imagining the tiny arms fastening around her neck made her throat clench and her eyes sting, until she had to blink and tighten her grip on the wheel.

'Okay,' she said softly. 'It's a deal.' And she thought, *Did I believe I was going to be free and adrift for ever?* The question made the time ahead of her, the interval she did have, seem all the more precious and inviting.

'I want to call you as a character witness on Rob's behalf,' his barrister said. 'Will you do that for him?' And when she had agreed he warned her, 'It probably wouldn't be helpful to give the impression that your friendship with Rob was any more than just that, Mrs Arrowsmith. I think it's very unlikely that the judge will jump to the conclusion of his own accord.'

'I understand,' Jess said.

*

358

The courtroom looked exactly the same, only now the jury benches were empty. Jess stood in the witness box.

'Mrs Arrowsmith, how long have you known Robert Ellis?'

It was Rob's barrister who asked her the question but she looked straight at the judge, at the grey corrugations of his wig and the light reflected off one lens of his spectacles. She said, 'Since the night my son was killed. I saw him in the hospital waiting room, and later in the intensive care ward.'

'What was he doing in the ward?'

'He came to see Danny. Danny and he were close friends. My son . . . admired him.'

'Would you say that admiration was justified, Mrs Arrowsmith?'

'Yes. I would say so.'

'And how did Mr Ellis react to the death of his friend?'

'With shock, and grief, and great remorse.'

'And did you and Mr Ellis subsequently become friends?'

Jess's face was calm and her voice was cool. Only her hands might have betrayed her with their shaking, but they were at her sides and hidden by the folds of her skirt.

In the witness box the times they had spent together flashed before Jess's eyes. She remembered the grief-driven, bitter passion of their first night and the sad tenderness of their last, in Italy. She was touched with sudden regret for the loss of him. But she did not let her voice waver.

'We became friends, yes. The experience of grief was a bond, although it was a painful one.'

In the public gallery Lizzie and Beth were watching her. The firmness of their support seemed almost tangible to Jess. There was no sign of Cat.

'Robert and I were able to help each other,' she said.

'And so you could say that you forgave him for the loss of your son?'

Jess lifted her eyes. The judge's spectacles flashed blank discs of light. 'I do not believe there was anything to forgive. I believe now that my son's death was a tragic accident.'

'That is all, Mrs Arrowsmith. Thank you.'

It was time for the judge to pass sentence. Rob stood with his hands in front of him, the fingers of one circling the wrist of the other as he waited.

The judge intoned, 'Mr Ellis, you have been convicted by the jury of the offence of causing death by careless driving when under the influence of drink. I am satisfied that the principal reason for this accident was that you had drunk too much to allow you to control your vehicle adequately. However, I bear in mind that the initial cause of the incident was the blow-out in your rear wheel.

'I also bear in mind your age, the fact that you have no previous motoring convictions and that you have a good work record. I take into consideration the tragic circumstances of your family background and I am impressed by the evidence of Mrs Arrowsmith, who speaks of your positive qualities. I am taking into account the likelihood that you will have on your conscience for the rest of your life the death of a friend.'

Rob turned his head slowly to look at Jess. Their eyes met, and held.

'Therefore, with the consideration that you have already served a period of thirteen weeks in custody, I propose to make you the subject of a community service order of one hundred and eighty hours.'

*Oh, God,* Jess thought. *Thank you. And you, Judge, thank you.*

The judge gave a dry exposition of the community service obligations. 'Are you prepared to accept this, Mr Ellis?'

Rob moistened his lips, looked back to the judge. 'Yes sir.'

'You will be disqualified from driving for three years. You will also be required to pay part of the cost of the prosecution in the sum of five hundred pounds, payable within six months.'

Rob looked at Jess once more. He smiled at her and it was a weary, grateful, adult smile that she had never seen before.

The judge put aside his papers, looked to the clerk of the

court. It was time for the next case of the morning to be brought on for sentencing. This one was over.

Rob came out into the daylight. He had shaken hands with his barrister and with Michael Blake. It felt odd to walk out of the Crown Court building, to know that he could catch a bus and go wherever he wished. Jess was waiting for him. Her daughter and sister must be somewhere around, he had seen them in court, only they must be staying tactfully in the background. He stood still, suddenly disorientated. Jess's hand touched his and her arms came round him. Her cheek rested against his face and he realised that she was limp with relief. He brushed away her hair so he could look into her eyes.

'Thank you for speaking for me,' he said formally.

'I wish I could have done more.'

'You have done everything.'

There was a moment when neither of them heard the roar of traffic, or noticed the new wintry bite of the wind and the whirl of litter it whipped around their ankles. Rob nodded at last, touched her mouth with the tips of his fingers and released her.

'What now?' he asked. Their speculation about the future had always taken this point, Rob's release, as its farthest limit.

Jess hunched her shoulders with a moment's fear of being alone, with no goal or safe haven to head for. But she spoke quickly, covering up the hesitation. 'I'm going to take some time off. Travel a bit. What about you?'

But Rob was looking beyond her. His hands shaped blocks in the air before he answered and Jess could sense the smooth carpentered mass, the solid weight of his determination. 'I'm going to build some kitchens for money and make some furniture to sell. I'm going to make everything good.'

'I know you will,' she said, and turned to see who it might be that he was looking at, although in her heart she already knew.

Cat was wearing black leggings and an oversized checked

shirt. She was noticeably pregnant now and she was crying and laughing at the same time.

'I couldn't be there to listen,' she sobbed. 'I just couldn't bear it.'

'It's all right,' he reassured her. 'I'm here now. You don't have to worry any more.' Then he rested his hands on her shoulders and bent his head over hers.

Jess felt as if she was spying on them.

'I have to go, my sister's waiting for me.'

Cat's arm went round Rob's waist. The touch of him seemed to renew her strength. She rubbed the sleeve of her shirt across her face and stood up straighter. She eyed Jess briefly, then sniffed at Rob, 'Who said I was worried?'

Rob laughed and Jess caught a glimpse of what he must have looked like before Danny died. Or maybe the way he might have looked, if he had been allowed to grow up differently.

He would be a good father, Jess believed. A child would give him roots, and reasons for surviving that he had lacked before. She did not think that Rob and Cat would give each other an easy life, but – only briefly – she envied them their chances.

'Good luck,' she wished them both formally.

Cat grinned. 'We need it.'

Jess had walked only a few yards before Rob caught up with her and held on to her arm.

'Wait, Jess. I want to tell you something. I think about him, I think about him often. At different times and places he comes into my head, and I can see him and hear what he'd say if he were with me. I won't forget him.'

'I'm glad. I don't believe any of us will ever forget him.' She waited a second, then she asked, 'Are you going to be a father to this baby?'

'I'm going to try, if she'll let me. It was an accident, you know. Neither of us intended it. But maybe a happy accident. I won't let anything touch him, anyway. Nothing like what touched me.'

'I know you won't.'

They didn't say goodbye. Jess walked slowly on to the car-park, where Lizzie and Beth were waiting for her.

James lifted the bonnet of the camper van and peered into the engine depths. He left the bonnet propped open and walked around the van in a slow circle, examining the tyres and checking the bodywork for rust. Jess stood upright inside, under the extending roof canopy. There was just enough headroom. The extending seats and the brown Formica-fronted cupboards and the tiny cooking rings made her think of an unambitious doll's house. This small space, this mobile self-containment, was exactly what she wanted.

The elderly couple who owned it stood anxiously to one side.

'She gave us years of pleasure, and never a minute's trouble,' the husband offered. 'We call her Polly. Because of the number plate, PLY, you know.'

His wife shook her head at him. 'They don't want to know that, Ted, do they?'

'She's lovely,' Jess said.

James completed his examination and she drew him aside.

'Well? What do you think?'

'I'm no expert. It looks sound enough. Why don't you get the AA in?'

'I might lose it. It's such a bargain and I've got a good feeling about it. No one who calls their camper Polly can be a dodgy car dealer.' She beamed with the pleasure of the decision. 'I'm going to buy it. Polly and I will ride into the sunset together.'

The deal was struck. Jess shook hands with the owners and promised that she would come back tomorrow with the money, in cash. Afterwards James drove her home, to his home, where she was staying because the new owners had moved into the old house and Jess's worldly goods were reduced to a couple of suitcases and a few boxes stored in Lizzie's attic.

'I feel like I'm getting a big present,' Jess laughed. 'A camper van and a ticket of leave.'

Always a careful driver, James watched the road and the rush-hour traffic. He avoided the route that would have led them round the bypass and past the bridge.

'You're not running away again, Jess, are you? Taking flight?'

She thought about it, trying to examine her motives dispassionately as if they were baldly printed on a foolscap sheet.

'Only in the sense of having grown some wings at last, perhaps.'

She wasn't soaring into the blue; it was more like venturing newly fledged towards a destination she couldn't yet see because the light was in her eyes.

James lifted one hand briefly from the wheel and patted her knee avuncularly. 'Don't go too near the sun.'

'I don't think there's much risk of that. Not in a recent pedestrian like me.'

Sock was dressed in his pyjamas, and his ringlets of uncut hair were damp from the bath. He bustled to his bookshelf and brought Jess a book of nursery rhymes, then clambered on to her lap. He smelled of soap and baby skin.

'Read Jack now,' he commanded.

Jess turned the pages obediently and found the picture he liked. 'Handy spandy, Jack-a-dandy,' she recited.

'Hop, hop, *hop*,' Sock yelled, unable to wait for the punchline.

'That's right. See him hopping?'

Once the highlight of Jack was done with, Sock's thumb found its way into his mouth as he listened to the other rhymes. Jess stroked his hair and listened to his breathing as it settled into a rhythm. By the end of the book he was almost asleep.

'Shall Beth come and kiss you good-night?' she whispered as she lifted him into his bed. He nodded seraphically.

'And Mummy.'

Lizzie was downstairs with her feet up on the sofa, drinking gin and reading a magazine, while Beth watched television.

'You're both summoned to bestow the kiss.'

'Jess, you angel. You don't know what bliss it is to have someone else put him to bed once in a while.'

Jess laughed at Lizzie reluctantly putting her drink aside and heaving herself to her feet. 'Why do we always want what we haven't got? He was so lovely this evening I nearly ate him.'

Lizzie gaped in fake dismay. 'Gawd. Not feeling broody are we, darling, by any chance?'

'Nope. I'm just waiting for the grandchildren.'

'Ah. My guess is you won't have to wait long, then.' She winked exaggeratedly at the back of Beth's head. 'Nick phoned her *again* this evening.'

Beth snapped, 'I'm not about to have his babies. He helped me with buying the flat and now he's going to help me move, okay? That's all.' But she still turned faintly pink as she kept her eyes fixed to the screen.

She had telephoned Nick the actor. He was no substitute for Sam; but then, as Sadie would no doubt have briskly advised her, she wasn't looking to substitute one set of unhappy inadequacies for another.


When James came home from work he opened the good wine and they sat down to dinner. None of them chose to say so, but they each knew that this was the last meal they would share for some unspecified time. Jess would soon be leaving; Beth was returning to London in the morning and going back to full-time work the next day. Jess had given her money from the house proceeds to put down a deposit on a flat of her own, instead of the old rented one. The new flat was a good-sized place, big enough for two.

'I might even get a lodger. To help with the mortgage, you know,' Beth had said non-committally to Jess.

And Jess had answered, equally non-committally, 'Good idea.' Young actors tended to be impoverished and itinerant. She thought that Nick would probably value a secure base.

James held up his glass. 'Here's to us,' he said. 'And Jess's journey.'

They drank and Jess looked at each of them around the table as she said softly, 'Here's to Danny.' She thought, as she did every day and still in almost every hour of every day, that the space he had left would never lose its hard and massive definition. It was complete, and final. Nor would the pain of his loss ever entirely leave her and she supposed that it was a stage of the healing that now she no longer wished for it to be gone. She lived with it and took it as part of herself.

'To Danny,' they echoed her. If it was Jess's fear that her golden boy might be forgotten, their tenderness assured her that he would not be.

After dinner, at Beth's suggestion, they brought out the box of family photographs that had not yet been consigned to its new storage place.

Beth lifted the lid and saw the old snapshot of Tonio tucked in amongst the rest. She left it there and took out a double handful of the others. And as they had done on the night of Danny's funeral they looked back and remembered the Cornish summer holidays, the birthday and Christmas parties, the barbecues and sports days and successive unheroic events of family life. As in all photographs, the blue skies and seas and groups of camera smiles laid a gloss over the discord or disappointment of the true history. But then, Jess thought, there was no harm in choosing to recall happiness in place of pain.

The most recent pictures were of Sock's second birthday. Seeing these amongst all the others and understanding that new fragments of history continued to be pasted over the collage of years, even though Danny was not there to witness them, became a comfort as well as a sadness.

Jess looked up from the pictures and met her sister's eyes. Lizzie sniffed and smiled, rubbing a smear of teary mascara across her cheek. Beth knelt beside her in the scatter of photographs, making a sequence of herself and Danny year by year on the beach at Polzeath. Jess was thinking how learning the truth about Danny's father had cut down her ferocious belief that he was hers alone. Danny had been given back to the whole family; he belonged to each of them.

'I don't think I could have lived through this time without you,' she told them. Her mouth went crooked, sliding out of the control of her cheek muscles so that she didn't know whether to expect a smile or a sob from it. 'I don't know how to say this without sounding sickly. I'll just say it. I love you all.'

'We're family,' James said with finality, as if that took account of all the credit of happiness and the debits of secrecy and resentment that needed to be totalled up.

Beth completed the arrangement of her photographs. The sunny squares lay face up and innocent on the scuffed carpet.

'You know what? I think these are the family silver.'

Jess patted her shoulder. She could make her mouth obey her again and she directed it into a smile. 'I think there are a couple of teaspoons and a salt dish, somewhere, as well.'

'Then we are rich beyond measure, aren't we?' Beth said calmly.

Jess drove north-westwards in the camper van that had once been called Polly. North Wales was an intermittent spectacle of purple hillsides and rain-polished black rock faces that drifted in and out of curtains of rain. It was the middle of October; already it was cold in the mornings and evenings, and condensation ran down inside the windows of the van, to gather in sinister pools on the brown Formica. She realised that, with her unsuspected talent for miscalculation, she had chosen the wrong end of the year to set out on her odyssey. It would soon be too wintry to sleep in the van. She began to speculate about warmer climates; even as she reached Holyhead and nervously steered the van across the ramp and on to the Dublin ferry, she was considering southern Spain and the imagined dunes and oases of north Africa. On the crossing of the grey and choppy Irish sea she sat in the bar and listened to the rollicking banter of homebound Irishmen.

In Dublin, she parked the van and stayed the night in a bed and breakfast. In the single room with its green candlewick bedcover and wooden crucifix pinned to the wallpaper over the bed, she took out the one postcard that Tonio had sent her so long ago. She knew the picture of the village overlooking the sea and the brief written message as well as she knew her own hand. Now she opened a road map and studied the route. Dublin to Port Laoise, Limerick and Tralee, and westwards to a vanishing point overlooking the Atlantic.

Jess closed the map and stood up, staring into the spotted trinity of mirrors over the brown-varnished dressing-table. Her reflection was greenish, wide-eyed, apprehensive.

'If ever there was a wild-goose chase,' she said aloud, 'this is it.'

The acknowledgement didn't alter her intentions. Danny's death had begun to unpick a knot that she had believed would stay fast for ever. In the months that followed the ends had worked loose, until the recognition that Danny was Ian's child freed them entirely. She did not any longer carry the secret of a child who belonged to Tonio as well as to her. There was no longer any sense of obligation to gnaw at her, or any guilt to suppress. She had not deprived Tonio of a son, nor had she lost for him a child he had never even known. Tonio had become in her heart no more and no less than a man she had been deeply in love with long ago.

There was no impediment left to finding him, except that she had no way of knowing, then or now, whether the postcard was an invitation or a clue or a postscript.

*This is a beautiful place to live*, he had written. And signed it with his full name, Tonio Fornasi, as if she might otherwise have failed to identify him from the dozens of Tonios who populated her world.

She could only use the card as a starting point for her belated search.

\*

By the morning, the rain had stopped. The sky was blue with flat-bottomed clouds briskly wheeling across it. Jess drove slowly, savouring the undramatic twists of the scenery and the fertile space that widened ahead of her. She stayed that night in Limerick, in a pub with rooms above. She drank a pint of thick Guinness in a dark wooden bar and talked briefly to a merry-faced builder who had recently come home after twenty years in London. When she went upstairs she lay between chilly sheets listening to the talk and music drifting up from below. She closed her eyes and slept, dreamlessly.

The next day was cloudier, with a sharp wind that whipped moisture into her face and caused her to duck as she lifted her overnight bag into the van. She eased herself into the driving seat, her back and thighs already familiar with its contours and her feet with the play and resistance of the worn pedals. She could imagine how it would be to drive on and on, with only the refrain of her thoughts and memories for company.

In the afternoon she reached the sea. It was the colour of slate, broken with caps of pewter and silver as it ran towards the rocks. From the crest of a low hill she saw the village where Tonio had once lived. There seemed hardly more than a dozen low white houses, turned away into the fold of the land against the gales that would sweep in from the west. In the single street there was a tiny general store with dusty shelves and a deserted bar-room to one side. She stood at the shop counter and looked at the packets of biscuits and cereals arranged on blue oilcloth, until the shopkeeper came out of his back room, wiping his mouth. Jess was suddenly overcome with awkwardness. She bought a packet of cornflakes and a half-pound of local butter that the man carved off a big block and silently wrapped for her in thick greaseproof paper. She paid for her purchases, slowly counting out the change and wondering when Tonio had last come in here to buy groceries or to sit on the oak settle and drink a pint of stout.

Without a second's warning, from having been so real to her for so long, Tonio suddenly became evanescent, her memories of him thinning and breaking up like mist under the heat of her presumption. Jess's heart knocked uncomfortably behind her ribs.

'Visiting, are you?' the shopkeeper asked, without real curiosity. Jess was only a tourist; there must be plenty of holidaymakers here in the summer, although they would be thinner on the ground for the next six months.

'That's right.'

She went to the low door with her shopping in her arms. The man was already going back to his tea when she hastily gabbled her question, 'Do you know Tonio Fornasi by any chance? Does he still live here?'

The shopkeeper was silent, dispassionately contemplating her as if she were some unthreatening but entirely alien being.

'He is Irish,' Jess added, as if the outlandish name needed a modifier.

The man raised one eyebrow. 'Irish, is he? Then he'll be standing out of the crowd here.'

In spite of herself, she laughed. She leaned against the door with the butter and the box of cornflakes slipping in her arms and laughed at her own idiocy. She had come here, to almost the westernmost point before America, in response to a few words on a fifteen-year-old postcard. After a moment, the shop man laughed too.

'It's Tony you'll be after,' he chortled. 'The last house down the street there, on the left. Facing the sea.'

Jess's laughter died as her throat tightened and she stared at him.

'The last house,' she whispered. 'Facing the sea. Thank you.'

She melted into the street. The end of it was only fifty yards away and there was a house, with a blank whitewashed rear wall, seemingly hunching its shoulders against the threat of the wind. She walked towards it.

There was a square of garden separating the house from an

unmade track that ran along the sea-front. On either side of the short straight path the garden had been laid out with smooth boulders and pebbles and planted with low, hummocky bushes and grass. The effect was tranquil, Japanese. Jess opened the gate into the garden and went up the path to the green door. She knocked, uncertainly. She waited, and knocked again, but there was no one at home.

She retraced her steps and closed the gate behind her, then crossed the track and sat at the edge of the rough grass to look at the sea. A white rock a few yards into the water was crowded with black-backed gulls, all staring seawards as if in greedy anticipation of some sign or signal. She heard the sound of light wheels on the grit of the path and turned her head. A man was coming, pushing a bicycle. He had thick, greying hair and a lined face, a body growing heavy with middle age. It was Tonio, just. Jess stood up to face him. In her mind she was piecing together the misty shreds of her memory, stitching them into this new version of him. She would look as different to him. His eyes were the same blue.

'Michael in the shop told me I had a visitor. It is Jess, isn't it?' His voice was the same, too.

'It is.'

He leaned the bicycle against the stone wall of the garden and put his hands on her arms. He shook his head, smiling in the way he always had done.

'Jess, after all this time. Come on inside with you.'

He opened the door and ushered her in. As she stepped over the threshold Jess realised that she had never allowed herself to imagine this moment. It was extraordinary but it was the truth; she had never pictured it, how it would be when she looked around his place and saw the details of it. The details that would tell her in a language more eloquent than any words what his history and his present were.

The ceilings were low, dark-beamed. There was a stone grate with a wide hearth and cut logs in a basket to one side. The alcoves were lined with paperback books, the white walls decorated with paintings, most of them sea views. There was a polished oak dresser with framed photographs set out on it. The nearest was of a girl, perhaps eleven years old, long-haired, in a tie and white school blouse. There were houseplants, Begonia rex and *Ficus*, well watered, a television set and squared magazines and a dusted grandmother clock. It was a family room. Meals would be eaten and homework written at the table against the wall.

'What do you do now?' Jess asked, still looking around her. The details swam up with such vividness that they seemed already familiar, even inevitable. A workbox with knitting, a cat with malevolent eyes disturbed in its afternoon sleep.

Tonio stood in front of the hearth. He was uncertain how to welcome her; she could see it plainly.

'I'm a painter. Self-taught, mostly. These are all mine. I can sell a good few in the summer. Megan, my wife, is a chemistry teacher in the secondary school. She's Welsh. From Swansea.'

There was a wedding photograph on the dresser. White veiling, flower buttonholes.

'From Swansea?' Jess repeated mechanically. 'From Swansea.'

'Brigid, that's our daughter, goes to the same school. She's our only one. She's thirteen now. And you?'

'Beth. You remember.'

He glanced down, away from her. It would have been the same, Jess thought with a beat of sympathy that shivered beneath her skin, if Tonio had arrived one empty afternoon at her house before Ian came home.

'I do,' he said.

'I had a boy, Danny. He was killed in a car accident almost eleven months ago.'

'Ah. Ah, dear God, that's terrible. I'm so sorry.' And now it was Tonio who spoke to her straight out of the years, not the thickset man who had replaced him. Jess took a step and found the cushioned sofa and sat down in a heap. He came next to her and took her hands and rubbed them, gently, as if to chafe the wayward blood back into her fingers.

Jess looked sideways, out of the window that faced the sea. Raindrops were splitting on the glass. She began to feel an immense calmness descending on her, as if her heartbeat slowed to the tick of the grandmother clock. She had been right to come. Soon, time would jerk itself back into a rhythm that she had lost, and begin to run on again.

'You must be wondering why I've come here, after so long.'

'I am. Although I'm happy to see you.'

'I sold my house and bought a camper van. Ian and I are divorced. Beth is grown up, Danny is gone. I'm just driving, Tonio. Heading wherever my inclination takes me.' *Here*, the silent words added. *Here, my inclination is, or was.* 'Do you think I'm mad?'

He shook his head. Now she saw his face close up, it was not so much changed. 'No, I think it's a fine thing to do. If you can find what you are looking for, that is.'

A gust of wind drove the rain harder against the windows.

'I will,' Jess said, knowing that she would, where only a moment before she had had no idea.

Tonio sat straighter. 'I'm not looking after you. Let me make some tea. Or would you rather a drink? A drop of something?'

'No. I don't want anything. Just let's sit here for now.'

'Right you are. Megan and Biddy will be back before too long. They'll like to see you.'

'I want to meet them, too.' Tonio would introduce her as an old friend, from way back, lost touch with for how long?

'How long have you been married?' she asked.

'Fourteen years.'

The postcard had come before it. An invitation, a warning and a postscript. Slowly, understanding, Jess inclined her head.

'You never came,' Tonio said, his voice husky.

'It wouldn't have been right,' she said simply.

The truth then, if not now. And now, there was still some travelling to be done. Jess did not mind that. The details of this room that was bounded by the open sea crowded in on her, seeming the more confining by their juxtaposition with the moving water.

After all, she thought, what was the point of growing wings if she was not to take flight?

# If My Father Loved Me

## Rosie Thomas

*Is it ever too late to forgive?*

Sadie's life is calm and complete. She is a mother, a good friend, and the robust survivor of a marriage she deliberately left behind. She has come to believe that she has everything she wants, or deserves.

But now her father is dying: the vital, elusive man who spent his life creating perfumes for other women is slipping away from her. When she realises that she can never make her peace with him, Sadie begins to look back over her childhood. In pursuing his separate life, Sadie's father ignored her, subjecting her to a succession of 'aunties', leaving her loveless and alone.

As Sadie confronts the truth about her father, her relationship with her son Jack appears to be breaking down and she is intent on saving it. Then the arrival of one of those fleeting women from her father's past starts a train of events that even Sadie cannot control . . .

# All My Sins Remembered

## Rosie Thomas

*'A master storyteller'* Cosmopolitan

Jake, Clio and Julius Hirsh and their cousin Lady Grace Stretton formed a charmed circle in those lost innocent days before the Great War – united against the world.

Old now, Clio recounts their story for her biographer: Jake's wartime experiences, which moved him to work as a doctor in the London slums; Clio and Grace, flappers flitting through bohemian Fitzrovia to emerge as literary lion and pioneering Member of Parliament respectively; the music that drowned for Julius the crash of jackboots in thirties Berlin.

But for herself, Clio remembers a different story. Desperate lies and bitter secrets, hopeless love and careless betrayal, jealous loyalties more like fetters. And above all, the truth about Grace, beautiful, destructive siren at the centre of the circle.